Readers everywhere are loving the Danf[orth]
Praise for book one, *Ashton ...*

"The first installment of Pura's The Danforths [intro]-duces the inhabitants of Ashton Park, a centuries-old manor near the shores of northwest England. Tensions of the early twentieth century, including WWI and unrest in Ireland and Palestine, create a backdrop for a tale rife with suspense and emotional twists as the large extended Danforth family encounters its share of romance, human tragedy, and skullduggery. Sir William and Lady Elizabeth and their brood of inde-pendent-minded daughters and gallant sons have their honor tested, the bonds of family strained, and the goodness of God questioned. Amid trials and treachery, Pura draws poignant exhibitions of integrity, staunch lessons in forgiveness, and tender pictures of love and devotion…a most enjoyable introduction to an intriguing family saga."

Publisher's Weekly

"Your best writing ever! I like the way you tie in history in a clear way…Is there another one after *Downton*, I mean *Ashton*?"

Karen Anna Vogel
author of The Amish Knitting Circle series

"Just finished reading *Ashton Park*…LOVED IT! Can't wait for the next installment of the series."

Carolea from Nova Scotia, Canada

"The book drew me in from the first page (from the first wild, carefree gal-lop). Really appreciate a good history lesson along with the plot. If I could just get my other work done, I could curl up and get lost in the Danforth lives yet once again!"

Debbie from Mitton, Canada

"This was an amazing book…It had well-developed characters, interest-ing story lines, and a host of well-described landscapes. The relationships between characters was complex and real, not namby-pamby. I wanted to "see" the castle and the ash trees. I could feel the breeze through them. This author is on the order of Jane Austen but for our time…I would highly recommend this book and hope to see it in a mini-series or movie."

"If you love Downton Abbey you will love this book!…Set in the early 1900s in England during World War I, this book will take you on a grand adventure…You will laugh, cry, and find yourself cheering for your favorite characters."

And for book two, *Beneath the Dover Sky*…

"Murray Pura could write technical manuals, and I'd read them. He pours his heart into his writing. Depth comes to mind."

"In this second installment of The Danforths of Lancashire, the compelling story of a loving family is continued as they overcome obstacles none of them thought they would ever face. They will make you wish you were part of their family, even with all the problems they have to solve despite the odds! My favorite element in the story (besides the well-rounded characters that are absolutely memorable) is that the women are strong in their beliefs and determined to achieve their goals in life. Pura does not make his female characters swoon at the sight of every handsome man, and that is to be commended—especially with the seamless tie-in of historical facts and events."

"I very much enjoyed reading this book. There were several unexpected twists and turns that literally made me gasp and of course kept me turning the pages. As always Pura's writing touches something deep inside me."

THE DANFORTHS OF LANCASHIRE

LONDON DAWN

THE DANFORTHS OF LANCASHIRE

LONDON DAWN

MURRAY PURA

HARVEST HOUSE PUBLISHERS
EUGENE, OREGON

Cover by Garborg Design Works, Savage, Minnesota

Cover photos © Chris Garborg; Paul Wish, Alvin Gacusan, Marlene DeGrood, johnbraid / Bigstock

LONDON DAWN

Copyright © 2014 by Murray Pura
Published by Harvest House Publishers
Eugene, Oregon 97402
www.harvesthousepublishers.com

Library of Congress Cataloging-in-Publication Data
    Pura, Murray
    London dawn / Murray Pura.
        pages cm.—(The Danforths of Lancashire ; book 3)
    ISBN 978-0-7369-5887-5 (pbk.)
    ISBN 978-0-7369-5888-2 (eBook)
    1. Aristocracy (social class)—England—History—20th century—Fiction. 2. Social classes—England—History—20th century—Fiction. 3. World War, 1914-1918—England—Fiction. 4. Baptists—England—Fiction. 5. Lancashire (England)—Fiction 6. Domestic fiction. I. Title.
    PR9199.4.P87L66 2014
    813'.6—dc23

                                                              2013028685

Printed in the United States of America

         13 14 15 16 17 18 19 20 21 22 / LB-JH / 10 9 8 7 6 5 4 3 2 1

Acknowledgments

London Dawn marks the seventh book I have worked on with Nick Harrison. The longer we work together the smoother it goes and the stronger the novel that results. Thanks for everything, Nick. Thanks also to the team at Harvest House—Barb Gordon, Kim Moore, Gene Skinner, Shane White, Katie Lane, Laura Knudson, and many others.

Cheers to my family and also to my cat Kokomo—she sits by my side day after day and watches every story come into being on my Mac.

And special thanks to the many veterans, living and dead, whose words I took to heart as I researched this novel, delving into book after book and watching interview after interview on YouTube. Men like Robert Stanford Tuck, whose tale is found in Larry Forrester's *Fly for Your Life*; Douglas Bader, immortalized in Paul Brickhill's *Reach for the Sky*; Geoffrey Wellum, who wrote his memoir in *First Light*; Brian Lane, who penned his personal account in *Spitfire!* before being killed in action; and many others whose stories are included in histories of the Battle of Britain, such as *Fighter Boys* by Patrick Bishop and Stephen Bungay's *The Most Dangerous Enemy*. Never in the field of human conflict was so much owed by so many to so few.

THE CHARACTERS

Lord Preston (William Danforth)—husband to Lady Preston, father, and Member of Parliament (MP); head of Ashton Park, the family estate in Lancashire, as well as Dover Sky, the summer home in the south of England, and Kensington Gate, their house in London

Lady Preston (Elizabeth Danforth)—Lord Preston's wife and mother to their seven children

Sir Arthur—Lady Preston's father
Lady Grace—Lord Preston's mother

Edward Danforth—the eldest son, a Member of Parliament, and a former Royal Navy officer
Charlotte Danforth—Edward Danforth's wife
Owen—their eldest son
Colm—their youngest son

Kipp Danforth—an RAF pilot and the middle son of Lord and Lady Preston
Caroline Scarborough Danforth—his wife
Matthew—their son from Kipp's first marriage
Charles—their son from Caroline's relationship with Tanner Buchanan
Cecilia Printemp—their daughter

Robbie Danforth—the youngest son, who serves in the British army in Palestine
Shannon Danforth—his wife, from Dublin
Patricia Claire—their daughter

Jeremy Sweet—Anglican clergyman
Emma Sweet—his wife and the eldest of the Danforth daughters
Peter and James—their twins
Billy—their youngest son

Albrecht Hartmann—German professor and theologian

Catherine Moore Hartmann—his wife, widow of Albert Moore, and second Danforth daughter

Sean—their son from Catherine's first marriage

Angelika—their daughter

Terrence Fordyce—officer in the Royal Navy who serves on HMS *Hood*

Libby Fordyce—his wife, widow of Michael Woodhaven, and third Danforth daughter

Jane—their adopted daughter

Ben Whitecross—an RAF pilot and Victoria Cross winner

Victoria Whitecross—his wife and the youngest of the Danforth daughters

Ramsay—their eldest son

Tim—their youngest son

Harrison—groundskeeper at Ashton Park

Holly—his wife, the Ashton Park manager, and the youngest sister of Lord Preston

Skitt—butler to the Fordyce family

Montgomery—his American wife and a maid to the Fordyce family

Paul Terrence William—their son

Tavy—butler to Lord and Lady Preston at Kensington Gate in London

Norah Cole—maid to Lord and Lady Preston at Kensington Gate

Mrs. Longstaff—cook at Kensington Gate

Baron Gerard von Isenburg—German acquaintance of the family and also a high-ranking member of the Nazi Party and the SS

Eva—his daughter

Tanner Buchanan—Member of Parliament and nemesis of the Danforth family

Lady Kate—his consort

Wolfgang von Zeltner—German pilot and lifelong opponent of Kipp Danforth and Ben Whitecross

1

April, 1934
Ashton Park

"There you go! There you go!"

Lord Preston threw the ball as far as he could. The three Belgian shepherds raced after it, yipping with excitement, and vanished among the tall ash trees. The leaves were fully open after two days of rain followed by two days of sunshine.

"Top of the morning, m'lord." Harrison lifted the fedora off his head. "Those three are hard at it."

"Good day, Harrison. They need a strong run. I've been absent for weeks and I'm not sure old Todd Turpin ever gets the fire out of them. Too many parliamentary sessions tie me down in London. Well, if they catch scent of a hare I shall not see them again in a fortnight." He put his hands behind his back. "I have renamed them, you know."

Harrison shifted his staff from one hand to the other. "I'd heard that."

"Wynken, Blynken, and Nod. From the American poem."

"Very good. How are they responding?"

"Badly. If at all. But I shall keep it up. Something had to be done to address the baron's treachery."

"Yes, m'lord."

"The dogs and I needed a fresh start."

"I expect you did."

"I saw him, you know, Harrison. On a newsreel from Berlin. Hopping and stomping in a black SS uniform with Herr Hitler and his stooges. Ghastly. I thought I knew the man."

"A chance at power changes many a good soul."

"Is that what he considers power? I suppose it is power after a fashion. The way a freak windstorm knocks off chimney pots and tears brick walls to pieces and hurls trash bins down an alley—raw force, out of control, of no benefit to man or beast."

"Have you heard from Lady Catherine or her husband, the theologian? Are they well?"

Lord Preston listened a moment to the distant barking of the dogs. "I believe they have caught the scent of something. No ball ever rolled that far." He began to stride into the ash forest. "No, Harrison. Not a word. You might pray about that, please."

Across the English Channel in Germany, Catherine was well aware she was behind in her letter writing. She had finally finished one to her sister Victoria, who was living in Africa with her husband Ben and their two sons. Now she felt guilty she hadn't sent so much as a note to her mother and father in more than a month. She pulled a fresh sheet of paper toward her and lifted her fountain pen.

> Dear Mama and Papa,
>
> You will wonder at my long silence, and you have, I suppose, fretted a good deal over it. I apologize. Life has been a mad rush here in Tubingen. But let me set your minds at rest about your grandchildren—Sean is doing very well indeed at school, and baby Angelika has never been better.

A soft knocking sounded at the front door.

Catherine was seated at the dining room table on the ground floor. Albrecht was upstairs chatting with Sean and Angelika while he worked on his university lectures for the next day. She knew she should be the one answering the door, but she hesitated. It was past nine o'clock and dark, and she was not expecting anyone. Clutching her pen, she waited.

The knocking sounded a second time.

"Are you going to get that?" Her husband's voice came down the staircase. "Please?"

"*Ja, ja*, Albrecht," she replied. "I was just working on a letter to my parents."

She got up and went to the door, continuing to hope the knocking would stop and whoever it was would walk away. Risking Albrecht's annoyance, she stood facing the door but did not open it. The knocking came a third time—soft but rapid. Certain her husband would call from his office again, she took hold of the door handle.

"I have it, Albrecht. You needn't worry."

A smell of rain on pavement rushed in as she swung the door back, surprising her. She hadn't noticed any drops against the windowpanes.

"*Ja?*" she asked the figure on the sidewalk.

The man slipped into the house and shut the door behind him.

"*Was?*" exclaimed Catherine. "What are you doing? Get out of here!"

The man took off his hat.

"Baron!" She didn't know what to say next. "Of all people I did not expect to see you!"

"Where is Albrecht?"

"Upstairs."

"The children?"

"They're with him. He's working at his morning lectures."

"There will be no morning lectures. The Gestapo will arrive here at two in the morning. You must be well gone by then."

Cold air seemed to fill the room, pouring off his trench coat.

"The Gestapo! Gone where? Where can we go?"

"My plan is to get you to France or Switzerland. But first we must get you into a hiding place outside of Tubingen. If they don't find you here they will go to all of your friends' homes. They will go to the university professors. Comb the city from one end to another. I have a car around back. You have half an hour, and then you must be in it and we must be gone."

"We can't be ready in half an hour. Angelika is only four. There is so much we must prepare."

"Half an hour. We cannot take the risk they may come earlier."

"This is mad. You can't come raging in here and demand we load our children into a car with you. Why should we trust you? You betrayed us once."

"I saved Albrecht's life. He would have died in that house with the others."

"You're SS."

"It's just as well I am. Otherwise I would have no idea of the movements of the police. If you don't trust me, you will die here just as Albrecht would have died in that house with the Brotherhood of the Oak. Last time I used a gun on Albrecht to work my will. If you force my hand I will do so again." He patted the pocket of his trench coat. "Get your husband. Get your children. Get what you need and get in the car."

Catherine started up the staircase, her face whitening. She turned her head. "You can say what you want about the Gestapo. It's you I don't trust."

"I'm fine with that so long as we drive away from here at ten o'clock."

"You could have been followed."

"I wasn't followed."

"They could be watching you."

"Then we'll all die together. Will you trust me if that happens?"

Albrecht stood at the head of the staircase. "What are you doing here?"

"He says the Gestapo are going to arrest us," said Catherine.

"Arrest us? Because of my lectures?"

The baron looked up at him. "Your lectures. Your protests against the firing of Jewish professors. Your refusal to join the Nazi Party. Most of all, your books. Oh, yes—they know you are the author of those anonymous books and pamphlets popping up all over Germany."

"How do they know that?"

"The SS found the men who do your printing last night. Smashed the presses. Shot them in the street."

Albrecht started to say something and stopped.

"Get what you need, Albrecht." The baron's voice was quiet and flat. "Leave what is superfluous. We have twenty-five minutes left."

Two days later
Ashton Park

Tavy received a telegram at the door and took it to Lord and Lady Preston, who were having tea in the library.

"Where is it from, William?" Lady Preston asked her husband. "Africa?"

"No, it's not from Africa. It's from Germany."

"What is it? Is it Catherine? Is everything all right?"

"The telegram is not from Catherine. It's from the baron."

"The baron! Why on earth would he write us? He knows how we feel about him!"

LORD PRESTON

YOUR DAUGHTER CATHERINE IS SAFE. SO ARE HER CHILDREN. SO IS HER HUSBAND ALBRECHT. YOU WILL NOT HEAR FROM THEM IN A VERY LONG TIME. BUT THEY ARE NOT PRISONERS AND THEY HAVE NOT BEEN HARMED.

THE BARON

As Lord Preston was reading the telegram to his wife in England, small pieces of chocolate were being handed to Sean and Angelika in a cold, dark cellar in Germany.

"Happy birthday, my son," whispered Albrecht. "I had this in my briefcase. You are eleven today. Blessings."

Sean took the chocolate but didn't eat it. "Thank you, Father."

Mimicking the mood and actions of her big brother, Angelika clutched her square of chocolate but didn't smile or put it in her mouth.

"Go ahead," urged Albrecht. "It's Swiss."

"You said we were going there." Sean spoke without emotion. "How long will it take?"

"We will stay at this house today. Tonight we will move again. And the night after that. Never longer than a day in each house. But each house brings us closer to the Swiss border."

"So we are going to the chalet in Pura?"

"*Ja.*"

"And both of you are staying with us?"

Albrecht put his arm around Catherine. "Your mother and I will be with you. Wherever we go, we go as a family."

"Are you sure?"

"I am."

"What if the police find us?"

"The baron has very good friends. They will not betray us."

"It's because of your writing, isn't it, Papa?" Again, no tone of accusation, just a question that was a statement of fact.

"Sean, it is because the Nazis are what they are."

Sean put the chocolate in a pocket in his shirt. "I will eat it once we've crossed the border."

"Very well."

"Me too." Angelika placed hers in a small red leather purse she carried with her everywhere.

"Make sure it doesn't melt," said Catherine. "You wouldn't want it to melt in a shirt pocket or purse, would you? Such a waste. And such a mess."

Sean finally smiled a very small smile. "I'll be careful."

"We'll all be careful." Albrecht put a hand on Sean's shoulder. "Now each of us must take a nap. We didn't get a great deal of sleep last night, and tonight will be no different."

"How many nights will it be, Father?" asked Sean. "Ten or twelve?"

"I don't know. That sounds right, but we're still a good ways from the border."

"But Switzerland is not that far."

Albrecht nodded. "No, not so far from Tubingen. But we must move slowly and carefully because the SS and Gestapo will be hunting us. They're aware we have a home in Switzerland. The border crossings will be closely watched."

"What if we can't get into Switzerland?"

"We're just as near to France as we are to Switzerland. If we cannot get to the chalet safely we will cross over into Alsace-Lorraine and make our way to the English Channel."

Catherine smiled. "Then you will see all your cousins, Sean. And Grandmother and Grandfather Danforth too."

"I would like that." Sean's eyes were large in the darkness of the cellar. "But I will miss Grandfather Hartmann. And Grandmother Hartmann as well."

"Of course you will." Catherine smoothed back her son's hair from his forehead. "But the Nazis will not be in power forever. The German people will come to their senses and reject them. That will be the time to see Grandmother and Grandfather Hartmann again."

"How soon?" asked Angelika.

"A year. Or two. No more."

"I'll be a big girl then."

"*Ja.* But not so big Grandfather and Grandmother Hartmann can't fuss over you and give you dolls and baskets of sweets."

A smile, bright in the gloom, darted onto Angelika's face.

"Now we need to nap." Albrecht handed each of them a woolen blanket. "Night is not far off."

"I'm hungry," Angelika said.

"There will be food when you wake up," promised Catherine, wrapping the blanket around the little girl's shoulders. "Or you can eat your chocolate now."

"I'm saving it for a special day."

"All right, you save it for a special day. Meanwhile, after you have had your nap, there will be a bowl of noodle soup for you."

"Are you sure?"

"Very sure. The lady of the house told me so herself."

June 5, 1934
The Parliament buildings, Westminster, London

"What's bothering you? We must do our part to get things ready for the rally."

"I'm well aware of that, Buchanan." Edward glanced at the traffic moving up and down in front of the Parliament buildings. "I'll be ready."

"The rally at Olympia is in two days, Danforth. We intend to set London on its ear. Fill the Grand Hall. The British Union of Fascists is at its peak."

"I said I'd be ready."

Buchanan tapped the silver head of his cane against his leg. "It's the matter of your sister, isn't it? Lady Catherine? I thought the embassy was sorting that out."

"The embassy has no idea where Catherine and her family are. They simply vanished without a trace."

"Mightn't they have fled? Sir Oswald asked you to write that Hartmann fellow and get him to stop penning those anti-Nazi books and pamphlets. They were infuriating fascists in Spain and Italy and England as well as Germany and Austria."

"I wrote him. He never responded." Edward looked up at the sky as drops of rain fell on the sidewalk. "They could have been abducted and shot."

"Yes, well, there's that." Buchanan opened a black umbrella. "You're not getting cold feet about the rally, are you? Sir Oswald counts on you creating quite a stir with your appearance. And your announcement."

"I don't have cold feet, Buchanan. But it will be a shock to my father and mother when their son stands on a platform with the leader of the British fascists. Not to mention I'll be drummed out of the Conservative Party. I'd like to spare them all that with Catherine missing."

"They'll bear up. Especially once you're a success. You have everything to gain by going public with your fascist beliefs. Yes, you'll have to sit as an independent. But in the next election we'll take a majority of the seats. The *Daily Mirror* and *Daily Mail* are on our side, and we have well over 50,000 supporters now. Remember how easily Herr Hitler got in and took over."

"He was appointed chancellor. He never got in by popular vote. I wish we could appoint Sir Oswald like that, but that's not the way a British democracy runs."

"Well, we'll change all that, won't we? You always chafed at the slow and awkward movements of democracy, didn't you? Look at Hitler. See what a strong man in power can get done and done swiftly? Why, Berlin has the Olympics in thirty-six, doesn't it? All sorts of buildings are being erected at an absolutely feverish pace. You really must pop over to Berlin with the lot of us next time and see for yourself. That's what we want for the British Empire."

Edward nodded. "I believe a strong man at the top would be for the best." He continued to look out over the traffic, avoiding eye contact with Buchanan. "But look here, what about the danger of a riot? What are we prepared to do about those hecklers who follow Sir Oswald about from speech to speech? All the Jews and Communists? It's enough I have to drive penny nails into my mother and father's coffins while they're grieving over Catherine and the grandchildren. Can't we put on a class affair? At least give my parents something to take comfort in?"

"You're worrying far too much for your own good, Danforth. Get home to your wife and have a glass of port. Have two. This will be a major rally, comparable to the finest rally in Berlin. Music, flags, marching, chants—it will be a spectacle. A lot of Jews and Reds are not going to spoil that for us, believe me. We've recruited hundreds more Blackshirts. They'll be stationed strategically throughout the Grand Hall and outside on the grounds as well. One look at them and our enemies will shrink away. Your parents will open up the morning paper and read about a well-run show. A nationalist show with a good deal of pride in Britain and Britain's future."

Buchanan lifted his umbrella sharply, and a black cab pulled over in front of them. "There you are, Danforth. Enough chitchat. We don't want too many to take notice of us. Home to your beautiful wife and that glass of port. We'll see you at Olympia on Thursday."

"Right." Edward entered the back of the cab after the driver came out and opened the door. "Thank you for dropping by Parliament to have a word with me, Buchanan. I hope everything will come off according to plan."

"It will. Remain calm."

"I stand to lose a great deal," said Edward.

Buchanan didn't respond until after the cab had sped away. "Indeed you do, Danforth."

"Good evening, my dear." Edward came up behind his wife as she was brushing her long black hair and kissed her on the cheek. "Where are Owen and Colm?"

She smiled and turned around, slipping her arms about his neck. "At Jeremy and Emma's with their cousins. The rectory has quite the biggest yard this part of London."

Edward kissed her again, this time on the mouth. "Better than the postage stamp of a yard we have here, in other words."

"Don't be upset. Kipp and Caroline's townhouse has a smaller yard than ours, and your father's new townhouse is certainly not Ashton Park, is it?"

Edward tossed his top hat on a sofa and lit a cigarette. "I'm not upset. Just sorry they don't have the property to run around in I had when I was a child."

"Summer is just around the corner. Then they can play at Dover Sky all they like."

Edward sank down on the sofa next to his hat. "Dad's planning on renovations this summer, Char. I don't think the house can be occupied."

She sat on the sofa with him, moving his hat onto a small table. "Well,

Ashton Park is splendid enough, don't you think? They'll have even more room to run about."

"So long as they stay away from the sea cliff."

"Oh, heavens, Edward, what's gotten into you today? You're fretting like a mother hen. That's my job, isn't it?" She moved so that she was able to get in behind him and began to rub his shoulders and neck. "You're tight as a drum."

He blew out a lungful of smoke and said nothing.

"Is there a big speech coming up? Some piece of legislation you need to introduce? A bill to vote on? Is that what has you wound up like a grandfather clock?"

"I expect."

"When is this coming to pass?"

"Thursday."

"Well, then, Friday evening we should take the boys for a boat ride on the Thames. You know how Owen loves anything to do with ships. Gets it from you, I imagine, his naval officer father."

"The war was a long time ago."

"It doesn't matter how long ago it was. You served king and country, and he's very proud of you. So is Colm. We all are."

"King and country, eh?" He drew in on his cigarette. "My patriotism hasn't done much for me, has it?"

"What do you mean?" She stopped rubbing his neck a moment and rested her chin on his shoulder. "You're an MP and you're on the ladder of success in the Conservative Party."

"Am I? If I were ignored any more than I am by the Party I'd be as much a pariah as Churchill."

"Oh, my goodness, you're quite a long ways off from anything like that." She took his jaw in her fingers. "I thought you liked Winston. You got along famously when your father had him up to Ashton Park at Christmas."

"I admire his fight. And his national pride. But I don't wish to be banished to the wilderness anytime soon and join him in solitary confinement."

"You're Lord Preston's son. No one's going to do that."

"Not yet."

"What do you mean, not yet? Not ever." She kissed him lightly on the lips. "You really have got yourself tied up in knots. I shall have to unravel them."

He stubbed out his cigarette in an ashtray. "How will Charlotte Squire do that, I wonder?"

"Oh, I have a tried and true Lancashire method."

"Which is?"

"Me. Just me."

She kissed him with a strength and passion that pushed him back farther and farther into the sofa. Her blue eyes glittering, she paused and looked down at his face.

"How's that?" she asked.

"It'll do for a start."

"Will it?"

She placed both hands on his shoulders and kissed him much longer and with even more vigor. A tear slipped from the corner of his eye, and she drew back.

"Whatever's the matter? Have I hurt you somehow?"

"I want you to be proud of me. I want you and the boys to be proud of me."

"My goodness, Edward, we are proud of you, I've told you that. You're a fine husband and a brilliant father. No one could ask for more."

"I dread the day you're disappointed with me. I dread it like the grave."

"Edward. Stop it. That's never going to happen. I adore you. Owen and Colm adore you." She put her arms tightly around his back and hugged him to herself. "What's gone wrong, love? What's put a knife in your heart? You could never do anything that would turn the boys or me against you. It's impossible."

June 7, 1934
The Grand Hall at Olympia

Edward sat with his head down, two Blackshirts guarding his room from intruders. Sir Oswald Mosley had looked in on him just minutes before. The hall was crammed and the grounds were bustling. The rally would be a smashing success, and Edward would be the centerpiece of the event. Mosley's delight had been obvious.

"Lord Preston's son. An MP of the grand old Conservative Party kicking off the traces and joining the British Union of Fascists to better serve his country. A true patriot. Why, you'll sway thousands, Lord Edward. Mind you, stay right here until I announce you. We don't want anyone to spot you and spoil the surprise. Especially the press. They'll have full access to you once you've declared your allegiance to the BUF and have stepped down from the stage."

Edward finished one cigarette and lit another off it before dropping it in the ashtray. A band was playing. He imagined the red, white, and blue lightning flag of the British Union of Fascists being unfurled. He heard some singing but couldn't make out the words. Sir Oswald's voice rang out over the Marconi public address system. Edward had heard a hundred similar speeches in public and whenever Sir Oswald sat across the table from him. But now he did not listen. Instead, he went over his own words in his head.

It sometimes becomes necessary in the long march of human progress for a man to break formation and head in another direction, keeping his steps in time with another band and another marching tune. That is what I am doing today. Not because I don't love my country but because I do love my country. Not because I don't honor truth and justice but because I honor them enough to change allegiances in order to better serve them. Not because I don't care for the British public or its values but because I care for the British public above all others. God, country, the good of the British people—they are why I am declaring my break with the Conservative Party and announcing my membership in the British Union of Fascists. I follow an enlightened and blessed leadership straight ahead into Great Britain's marvelous future. I invite you to join me. One country under one flag, one God, and one leader—Sir Oswald Mosley!

A Blackshirt ran up and caught his breath at the open door to Edward's room. "We need your help!"

"What's the matter?" demanded one of Edward's guards.

"There are too many hecklers and they're disrupting the rally. We'll need everyone to clear them out of the hall."

"Commies and Jews!" spat Edward's guard. He glanced at Edward. "Wait here, sir. Don't leave the room under any circumstances. We'll sort this out."

As soon as the Blackshirts left, Edward stood up and stepped into the hallway. He could hear the shouting and yelling and Sir Oswald making use of the public address system to speak above all the noise. There were the sounds of things being smashed and broken. And then screaming. He crept through the corridor to a spot near the stage that permitted a view of most of the Grand Hall. Blackshirts were punching and kicking people and using choke holds as they dragged men and women outside. Many of the persons they wrestled with were fighting back. Sir Oswald kept trying to finish his speech, but the brawling got worse, breaking out all over the hall as Blackshirts beat heckler after heckler. Edward saw blood spring onto hands and faces. Sir Oswald stopped and stood back from the microphone.

Get out.

The voice in his head was so strong Edward thought a man was behind him. He made his way quickly to a stage door that should have been guarded by Blackshirts. It was locked from the inside. He slipped the bolt and pushed it open. Blackshirts were fighting with people on the grass and in the parking lot. He tugged the brim of his top hat down to cover as much of his face as possible and made his way off the grounds and down the street. Bobbies ran past him. He continued to walk as swiftly as he could, finally taking an alley and emerging on another street, where he hailed a cab.

"How are you then tonight, guv'nor?" asked the driver as he edged into traffic.

Edward stared at the trucks and cars and wagons that streamed back and forth and watched men and women mingling on the sidewalks and in front of the shops.

"Never better," he replied.

The end of June, 1934

The Hartmanns were still in hiding when the baron arrived at midnight, his Luger in his fist as he hurried up the ladder into the attic where the family was waiting. Seeing the gun, Albrecht immediately stood up in the cramped space.

"So you've finally come to do what you planned all along?"

The baron's face was hard and sharp. "I had to shoot my driver."

"What? Why?"

"Before he shot me. I also had to shoot the man and woman who have been keeping you here."

Albrecht's face tightened. "I never heard the shots."

"I had the Luger under a pillow."

"What on earth are you doing, Baron?" asked Catherine, her arms around Sean and Angelika. "Why are you on this killing spree?"

"We are betrayed. Herr Hitler has begun a purge of the Brownshirts and the Communists and everyone else he perceives as a threat to his grip on power. My driver said he had been ordered to execute me because I was hiding Jews. But his shot hit the car door. Mine hit him in the throat. When I left the car I saw the man of the house peering through the window. He aimed a rifle at me but I ducked out of sight. I thought he had mistaken me for Gestapo. But I heard him shout to his wife to get the other gun and go to the back door and shoot von Isenburg. I entered through the outside cellar door and came up into the hall behind the woman. I snatched a pillow and placed it over the Luger and shot her as she turned. You heard nothing but the man did. He rushed into the hall and I shot him as well."

Catherine shook her head. "Why have they turned against you? Aren't you still SS?"

"Someone has suggested I'm harboring Jews and spiriting them out of the country. It did not come from Hitler or the *Reichstag*. It was one or two individuals spreading the word to others. But whoever they are, they know what I'm doing and where our safe houses are. If they were able to persuade my driver, they have a great deal of influence indeed. I trusted him with my life."

The baron was white. He put the Luger in his trench coat pocket and sat down on a trunk.

"People are being murdered all over Germany tonight. I'm no threat to Hitler's power, nor is he killing SS. Someone is using all the bloodshed and mayhem to cover up my own death. I don't believe this has anything to do with Hitler's purge. It has to do with stopping what I'm doing. Someone doesn't want me getting you out of the country. Someone doesn't want you to live, Albrecht, or continue to write your books against the Third Reich."

"But we're not Jews," protested Catherine.

"They used that to stir up the people they informed. To get them good and angry at me."

"Wouldn't using Albrecht's name get them angry enough?"

"No. Not if they're unaware of his books or that they were burned.

As for the anonymous books and pamphlets that have been distributed across the country, no one knows he's the author of those except the SS. It was better for those hunting us to say I was protecting Jews who had been charged with crimes against Germany. That's something the simplest people understand. That's something they feel duty-bound to bring to a halt."

"Who have all these people with their attics and cellars thought they were protecting?"

"Refugees from Communist persecution. They understood they were keeping you from harm at the hands of left-wing death squads."

Albrecht stared at the baron a long time.

"Catherine and I have talked about you. Gerard, you make no sense. Every day we're expecting a trap. Why should you rescue us? Why should you help me survive and write more books against Adolf Hitler? You are SS. You think he is the savior of Germany. Yet here we are, less than fifteen miles from the Swiss border, and it is you who have brought us here."

The baron looked at his hands. "It was necessary to fool everyone. To make everyone believe. Even you. I am where I wish to be. Deep inside the Nazi organization, trusted by my fellow SS, I have been close enough to Herr Hitler on several occasions to pull out my Luger and shoot him through the head. But the time is not yet. Brutal as he is, Hitler is still the only one capable of bringing our nation out of the bones and ashes of the war. In two years our athletes will be winning gold medals in Berlin. He will give us back an army and air force and navy. So long as this trend continues I am his bodyguard. Yet I remain his executioner. If he crosses the line and is bad for Germany, I kill him. In a few years it will be even easier for me to do than it is now."

"But you are discovered."

"I told you. None of this is the doing of Berlin. Berlin is not hunting the SS. It is only a few. These few who turned my driver and the household here against me are using the purge as a smokescreen."

Albrecht sat back down. "Who is it? Who has done this to you?"

The baron continued to study the veins and creases on the backs of his hands. "I am tempted to take you across the border tonight. On my authority. But who knows how far this person's reach extends? The border guards may have been alerted. A person will come to this house in the morning. Probably a carload. The perpetrator of all this will be in the car or will have told those who arrive what to expect and what to look for. In either case, I will find out who is the source of all my trouble—by direct confrontation with the individual or by questioning those who drive up. I will get a name one way or the other."

He lifted his head. Seeing the pinched faces of Sean and Angelika he smiled. "I am sorry for all your weeks of running and hiding, my dears. I'm sorry I've frightened you with my gun and my stories. I am your friend and your uncle even though for some time it hasn't seemed that way to you or to your mother and father. But trust me, I will get you across the border, and you will soon be in your chalet in Pura. First, however, you must catch up on your sleep. I'm going to guard the house while you rest. No one will get past me. In the morning we will have a good breakfast and be on our way. All right?"

Neither Sean nor Angelika responded.

The baron got to his feet. "I will be downstairs. A car will come in the morning. It will come very early. They would have expected a phone call from the driver or from the husband and wife. Now they must find out for themselves what has happened."

He reached into his pocket, brought out the Luger, looked it over, and tossed it to Albrecht.

"You may need it. Who knows? I will do my best."

The baron climbed down out of the attic, closing the trapdoor behind him.

Albrecht leaned back, closing his eyes, the Luger in his right hand.

"Do you believe what he says?" asked Catherine.

"I don't know."

"What do you think is going to happen in the morning? Do you think these people he spoke about will come?"

"I don't know that either."

They are praying for us. I know my mother and father are praying for us. Perhaps even my brother Edward is praying for us. Lord, please open a way. Please take us safely over the border.

Catherine looked up as Albrecht returned to his blanket. "How are the children?" she whispered.

"Sleeping," he whispered back. "Thank God."

"I've been praying. And I've been thinking about all the others who must be praying for us even though they don't know where we are or what's happening to us. Surely it will make a difference. Surely the prayers will save us."

Albrecht didn't reply.

She put a hand on his shoulder. "Sometimes it seems prayer hardly does a thing. Is that what you believe?"

"I believe prayer moves heaven and earth. But I confess I have no idea how it works. One time God will intervene quickly in response to prayer. Another time nothing happens for years. Other times people who don't even pray or have faith are rescued." He put his arm around her. "But I am grateful others are thinking of us and praying for us. It can't hurt. And really it is our only hope. Heaven alone knows who is behind this betrayal. But whoever they are they must be very close to the baron to be aware of all the details of our escape route. And to be able to turn a trusted friend such as his driver? No, they are good friends and colleagues. What a shock to him."

Catherine put her head on his chest. "Do you trust him?"

"I don't. On the other hand, if he'd wanted to kill us he could have done it in Tübingen. Why bring us all the way to the Swiss border to put a bullet in you or me? As strange as it seems, I think he really does care about the children and us. It's almost as if he's forming his own underground movement, a sort of resistance to the Nazi regime, something to use if the Third Reich doesn't do what he believes is right. One day he probably will be hiding Jews if it gets worse for them."

"I'm afraid, Albrecht. I'm frightened about the morning. I'm afraid of who is going to come here and what will happen to the children."

"Shh. Don't let your fears get the best of you. The baron is a tough old bird. He can more than handle himself. I suspect it will be unpleasant for him once he discovers who the traitor is. But he will have steeled himself for that. He is one of the old guard, a kind of Otto von Bismarck. *Blut und Eisen*—blood and iron. He will be more than ready to face whatever comes his way over the next few hours."

She gathered up the front of his shirt in her fingers. "I feel like ice."

He kissed the top of her head. "We are going to make it. Be strong."

"What if a dozen men come here? The baron can't fight them all. They'll overwhelm him and kill all of us."

"They won't. I won't let them."

"You won't let them? You abhor violence—you always speak against it."

"I do abhor it. But when men of violence come to do violence to my wife and children, and there are none to stand in their way—no police, no soldiers—then I must stand up to them, mustn't I? I'm obliged to see myself in the position of a soldier or police officer bound to preserve civic order. God has raised me up to do what others have been ordained to do but who are unable or unwilling to do it. I am your police, Catherine. The baron and I are your army."

"How strange it is to see you holding a pistol. I don't know whether I feel better or worse about matters with your finger on a trigger."

"We'll get through this to the other side, Catherine."

"I'd like to believe you."

"Try to rest now." He kissed her briefly on the lips. "Let me hold you. That's my job right now. Yours is to dream."

"I don't think I'll be able to dream."

And when Catherine did wake up she couldn't recall a dream, just colors of gray and white.

She propped herself on one elbow. Albrecht wasn't at her side. She got to her feet in the dark attic and moved as quickly as she could toward Sean and Angelika. They were still asleep. She sat by them a moment. Then she went to the trapdoor, opened it, found the ladder had already been swung open, and climbed down. She went through every room in the house but couldn't find her husband or the baron.

Through one of the kitchen windows she saw the baron's tall blonde daughter, Eva, emerge from a black car and run to him as he came around the side of the house. She was in a white blouse and black skirt and wore a red swastika armband high up near her right shoulder. Carefully Catherine opened the window wider.

"Papa! Papa! Thank God you're safe!"

"What made you think I was in trouble?" asked the baron.

He didn't put his arms around her as she kissed him on the cheek.

"Why—I knew you were trying to get the Hartmanns out of the country of course. All this killing is going on, this purge. So I feared the worse."

"The killing is still going on?"

"Yes, yes. I was afraid the Communists or Jews had retaliated against you."

"Why, my dear? Why should they care about me? Why are they concerned about my trying to get the Hartmann family to Switzerland? Why should they wish to stop it?"

Eva drew back and looked at him. Her hair hung down in two large pigtails.

"Papa, are you cross with me? I had to make sure you were all right. I knew you would be at this safe house last night. I called and called but no one answered."

"I heard the phone ring. Who is in the car with you?"

She looked behind her. "Oh, a few men, just to make sure I would be safe and to assist me if you were in some sort of difficulty." She turned back to him with her brightest smile. "Thank God you are alive and well. Where are the Hartmanns?"

"Inside."

"And Ernest Schultz? And his wife?"

"You remember their names? They were only one house in a long string of houses."

"But I keep a list."

"I never told you their first names."

"Well, I found out on my own." Her tone sharpened. "I don't understand why you're interrogating me. I came here because I was worried to death. I'm your daughter."

"My daughter, yes. And the Reich's daughter."

"Of course the Reich's daughter." She stepped back from him. "Where are Ernest and Rosa Schultz?"

"I had to kill them."

"What?"

"I had to kill Walter as well."

"What are you talking about? He's been your driver—and your friend! I don't believe you—what's wrong with you?"

She kept moving back toward the car.

The doors swung open and men began to climb out.

The baron had both hands in the pockets of his trench coat. "Walter told me you had recruited him. That you told him I was a traitor to Adolf

Hitler and to Germany. A man who defended Germany's enemies and gave them every encouragement possible."

Catherine watched Eva's face change instantly into a snarl of lines and ridges.

"What else could I have told him?" Eva screamed. "Albrecht Hartmann writes poison! He writes hate! And you help him! Our Führer is beautiful, he's a gift from heaven, a blessing from God, and you permit Hartmann to malign him and skewer him and spread lies about him! Shame! You're as much a traitor as he is! How can I call myself your daughter anymore? How can I cherish you as my father! Traitor, traitor, monstrous traitor!"

She threw herself flat on the ground.

"Kill him!" she shrieked. "Kill him!"

The men yanked guns out from under their long coats.

The baron didn't take his hands from his pockets. Both erupted in flame and smoke, and bullets struck the car and its men again and again.

Another car suddenly raced around the side of the house and skidded to a stop behind the baron. He turned in surprise as gun barrels poked out of its windows. Catherine had one hand to her mouth and the other clutched her stomach. But before the guns were fired, the windows of the car shattered, and bullet holes perforated the side of the vehicle. The noise of a machine gun banged through the kitchen, coming from somewhere beyond the baron and aimed squarely at the second car.

My Lord, what is this? What is happening?

Stunned, unable to move or look away, Catherine watched. Moments later her husband crawled out from behind a cart of manure. The gun in his hands was much smaller than a rifle, and its barrel was dotted with holes. It was still pointed at the car. She was unsure if any were still alive in the vehicle, and she realized that Albrecht was unsure as well. But no one got out or fired back. Her husband edged up to the car, gun still trained on it, and glanced through its windows. Only then did he appear to take his finger off the trigger. He looked at Catherine, still watching from the open window.

"They are all dead," he told her, raising his voice. Then he walked toward the baron, his face as white as bone. The two men stood and looked at each other.

"A Bergmann MP Thirty-Four," she finally heard the baron say. "Where did you get that?"

"It was in a closet with several shotguns."

"I only found the pistols—in the pockets of the husband and wife." The baron stared at him. "I did not expect you to fight."

"'These are the times that try men's souls...Tyranny, like hell, is not easily conquered.' I have to do my part. Such are the times we live in."

They both looked at Eva, who remained lying in the dust. Tears cut across her face.

"You swine," she hissed. "You ugly, stinking swine. I hope God strikes both of you dead."

"*Nein.* He struck your friends dead first," replied the baron. "Gestapo?"

"Yes, Gestapo. True Germans, and they will be missed. Their comrades will hunt you down and kill you."

"They won't. The Communists will be faulted for this. Fighting back against Hitler's purge."

Eva shrieked and jumped up, clawing at her father's eyes.

He slapped her across the face with an open hand. She stopped, a look of shock on her face. He slapped her again with a pistol. She fell and he caught her in his arms. Catherine saw a tear moving out of one of his eyes.

"We must get you to the border now, Albrecht. We must risk it. I don't know if the Gestapo contacted the closest border crossing. In any case we will go to one farther away. I have papers authenticated by the SS. You must get your family up and into my car."

"What about the dead?"

"I will leave them as they are and phone in a Communist attack."

Catherine left the house and walked out to Albrecht and the baron. They watched her come. She hesitated a moment, looking into their eyes. Then she put her arms around her husband's neck.

"I'm sorry," she said. "I'm sorry we had to come to this place of choosing in our lives. I'm sorry you had to do this."

"Yes, you're right, it was a choice. If I had not made it you and the children would be at the mercy of men who have no mercy."

Catherine looked at the baron as he held his daughter in his arms. "What are you going to do about Eva?"

He gently wiped a drop of blood from Eva's cheek with his fingers. "I thought I would have to kill her. She knows everything. But I cannot do it. God help me, I cannot do it."

July, 1934
Ashton Park

Lord Preston was pacing the library with an open letter in his hand.

"It's always a godsend to hear from Victoria and Ben in Africa. Victoria is very regular in her correspondence. And here we have this letter from Robbie and Shannon in Jerusalem, long overdue, and twice the blessing for that. All is well. At least as well as can be expected when your children are living so far from English civilization. Even Libby's and Terrence's letters from Portsmouth and HMS *Hood*, as infrequent as they are, never fail to keep us abreast of their comings and goings. But Catherine! What can have happened to Catherine and Albrecht and the children? Edward and I get nowhere with the German embassy. All they do is throw up their hands and say there is no knowledge of their whereabouts. '*Ich weiss nicht!*' That's all the fool ambassador can say! '*Ich weiss nicht!*' Jeremy has made inquiries through the Lutherans and the Catholics but nothing has come of that either."

Lady Preston, her wrinkled hands clasped in her lap, watched her husband stride back and forth. "I know, dear, I know."

"And what of von Isenburg, that Nazi ogre? One telegram, weeks and weeks ago, and nothing since. Does he do that to torture us? I should like to go over there and wrap my hands around his neck and choke the truth out of him."

"Please don't come up with any outlandish schemes to race across the Channel to Berlin, William. It's quite like you and I won't hear of it. You're seventy now, not twenty or thirty, and well past the age of jumping aboard ships and swinging your sword about your head to battle evil. Edward is going over there soon and he has promised to leave no stone unturned. He will get to the bottom of this."

"We pray and we pray and no good comes of it."

"Hush, William, you're overwrought. Your faith is all you have right now. Without that to hang on to you'll be washed away by family dramas and the politics of Europe." She got to her feet and took his hand. "Enough of this. Let's go to the chapel and pray. We haven't done it for days. It will do us a world of good."

"I don't want it to do us a world of good. I want it to do Catherine and her family a world of good. I want to hear that they are alive."

"Will you come with me to the chapel or not?"

Lord Preston bowed his head. "I'll come. I'll pray. But God help us."

That evening, as summer shadows slipped over the grass and trees of Hyde Park, Buchanan waited impatiently for Edward Danforth, tapping the silver head of his cane against his palm. Finally a cab dropped Edward off nearby, and Buchanan stepped out from behind a tall tree a moment so he could be clearly seen. Then he drew back into its shadow.

"Sir Oswald wonders where you've been," Buchanan said as soon as Edward joined him.

"I was a bit put off by the June seventh performance at Olympia," Edward replied.

"You can't blame that on the BUF. The Jews and Reds started the brawl."

"It doesn't matter who started it. What matters is how it finished. Blackshirts beating up men and women."

"All of them were fighting back."

"Of course they were fighting back. You'd be the first person to give someone a taste of your cane if they were raining blows on your head."

"We'll recover, Danforth. There will be more rallies, more marches."

"We've lost support. We've lost the newspapers."

"We'll gain them back. Look how popular Hitler is in Germany after his purge. Look how the Italians adore Mussolini despite all his Blackshirts. And keep your eye on Spain. Much good will happen there yet."

Edward lifted his eyebrows. "Fascism has been forced out of Spain."

"Don't believe those precious newspapers you think we need on our side. There will be a revolt. The fascists will return and the Catholic Church will help them return. We'll get the same support from the Church of England one day."

"Do you really think that, Buchanan?"

"I really think that, Lord Edward." He glanced across the field at a police officer walking slowly along a walkway. "So you're still with us? You're still willing to announce your allegiance to the British Union of Fascists?"

Edward's eyes followed the same police officer. "I have my trip to Berlin with other members of the Conservative Party. I'll let Sir Oswald know what I intend to do after that."

"Don't get cold feet now, Danforth."

"You said I would be overwhelmed by the progress in Berlin. Especially as they make preparations for the Olympics. Right then. Let's see how impressive it all is. Let's see if fascism really is rebuilding Europe. If it is, I'll sit down and make new plans with Sir Oswald about telling the world I belong to the fascist renaissance."

"Fair enough." Buchanan tapped his palm with the head of his cane. "You won't be disappointed."

July 14, 1934
Berlin

My dear Char,

I will see you in less than a week but I thought I'd write and let you and the boys know what I've been experiencing here. It really is quite the show. Best hotels, best food and restaurants, whizzed about in a smashing Mercedes Benz, clean streets, smiling people…none of this rubbish about Jews being beaten on the streets. I haven't seen one Jewish shop or synagogue that's been vandalized. And no Brownshirts either, at least not many of them. Herr Hitler cleaned up that lot in June. Altogether the atmosphere is refreshing.

All this to say nothing of the construction tied in with the Olympics. I confess I thought my colleagues in England, the ones who'd already been, were exaggerating. But I see for myself how astonishing it is—boulevards laid out, scores of trees planted, a massive stadium going up. It's beyond words. I shall have to bring the three of you here on another trip, that's all there is to it. And we must buy tickets for the Olympics. I'm told I can get them rather cheaply as a member of the British government. Owen will be fourteen and Colm seven. We'll have a splendid time.

I'll drop this off so it gets to you quickly. Tell the boys I have seen plenty of bands and plenty of marches and I shall be bringing them back some flags for souvenirs.

All my love,

Edward

PS—I have been unable to find out anything of Albrecht and Catherine's whereabouts. I cannot even locate Baron von Isenburg. No one seems to know where he has been assigned with the SS. It's a very strange business. I shall keep trying, of course. I know Mum and Dad must be absolutely frantic.

August, 1934
Ashton Park

"My lord."

"Hm? What is it, Tavy?"

"There is a courier at the door."

Lord Preston looked up from the morning newspaper he was reading in his large chair in the library. "He won't just give you the note?"

"He won't, my lord."

Lord Preston pushed himself out of his chair. "I see. Well, Tavy, let's get this sorted out."

The courier was in a neat suit and tie and bowler hat. Lord Preston spotted a shiny black car parked in front of the house as he approached the open doorway.

The courier bowed slightly. "Good morning, my lord."

"Good morning. What's all this secrecy?"

The courier had a leather briefcase under one arm. He opened it and brought out a letter.

"This came by diplomatic pouch, Lord Preston, to Westminster. It was imperative I hand it directly to you and no one else."

Lord Preston took the envelope and turned it over in his hand. "From what embassy?"

"Our embassy in Switzerland."

Lord Preston opened the envelope. There was a smaller envelope inside, writing scrawled across it in blue fountain pen ink. He suddenly grasped Tavy's arm.

"Fetch Lady Preston!"

"My lord?"

"Fetch her, I say! This is Catherine's handwriting!"

Pura, Switzerland

Catherine bent and splashed lake water over her her face as the sun topped the mountains to the east.

Mother and father will certainly have the letter by now. I'm so glad. All their worrying will come to an end. Most of it, at any rate.

She sat down on a flat rock and let the sun work its way over her face. Closing her eyes, she tilted her head toward it.

But how will we ever know how the baron is doing? He will not send telegrams to us, he says, and he will certainly not use the regular post or a diplomatic pouch again. How are he and his daughter faring? He talked about imprisoning her and saying her allegations were the ravings of a Communist agent trying to cast blame elsewhere. Will we ever know?

"How are you feeling?" Albrecht sat down next to her, smiling.

"Well enough, I suppose," she answered, opening her eyes and returning the smile. "Each day is better than the day before. Each day Germany and our weeks of hiding slip further and further into the past."

He tossed a stone into the lake. "I've let Sean go with old man Salzgeber and his horses. Angelika is with the nanny."

"All right."

He showed her a book he was holding in his hand.

"*Bearing the Cross.* Frederick von Pauls. Is he the American theologian you mentioned?"

"Yes. The book came in the post this morning."

"When did you order it?"

"That's the thing. I didn't. It came from the American embassy here in Switzerland. A note with the book explains it was forwarded to them by the American embassy in Berlin."

"What? Why?"

"Well, besides the fact it is a very good book that has not yet been translated into German, this was tucked inside its pages." He brought out an envelope. "A letter from the baron."

"No!"

"Read it for yourself."

She took the envelope. "But what does he say? Don't make me read a long letter to find out how he is doing and what has happened with Eva."

"The gist of it is that my family's castle has been appropriated by the SS and that the baron has been appointed the commanding officer. They are using it for a training center and a high-security prison. Eva is kept there under guard. Apparently the SS believe the baron's story that she was a double agent and on the payroll of the Communists and Moscow."

"But she will hate him for this."

"She already hates him."

"But she will spout information about the safe houses. The SS will check on what she says and realize she's not making things up."

"The SS have checked on everything she's told them and have come to the belief that's exactly what she's doing—making things up. Long before the SS interrogated Eva, the safe houses had been shut down and the families that owned them moved far away to other locations in Germany and Austria. The whole situation has changed, and Eva knows nothing about the changes. The SS do not question her anymore. Everything she tells them leads to a dead end."

"She will try to escape. I can't imagine her putting up with the situation as you describe it."

Albrecht nodded. "She did get away once. Right out of the castle and out onto the grounds. But the property is vast, and all of it patrolled by armed sentries and dogs. Eva was shot."

"Albrecht!"

"The bullets struck her in the leg. She was given medical treatment of course. But she will be on crutches for half a year. I don't think she will try that again."

Catherine opened the envelope and pulled out the baron's letter. It was handwritten in German.

"I do not see what good will come of this in the end," she said. "You cannot imprison your own daughter and expect to have any sort of future with her."

"He couldn't very well let her run free, denouncing him and spying on all his activities, could he? These things will have to work themselves out over the course of time. Perhaps the day will come when Eva experiences a change of heart."

"Or pretends she does. She's very good at that sort of thing. How could you believe her even if she told you she had decided to fight against the Nazis? How could you trust her?"

Albrecht picked up a few stones and threw them into the lake. "I don't know."

October, 1934
Edward and Charlotte's residence, Camden Lock, London

"Ah, there you are, my dear," Edward said, coming through the door. "Where are the boys?"

"At the vicarage as always. Kipp and Caroline's boys are with them too."

"Are they? So we're home alone again, are we?"

"Apparently."

Edward looked more closely at his wife. "What's wrong?"

"Nothing's wrong. Your supper's ready."

"Hang my supper. What's going on with you? Tell me."

Charlotte gazed out the window behind him. "Do you lie to me much, Edward?"

He removed his top hat and unwound his white scarf. "Lie to you? I've never lied to you in my life."

"You're lying now."

"What are you talking about? Why are you acting this way?"

She folded her arms over her chest, still looking out the window. "A telegram came for you," she finally said. "I don't know why it came here instead of to your office. You know I don't open your correspondence, so I set it aside to give you when you returned from Parliament. Somehow Colm got ahold of it and opened it. I scolded him and took it away but it was impossible for me not to read the message, it was so brief."

"I see. Who is it from?"

She took the telegram from a pocket in her skirt and handed it to him, never taking her eyes off the window.

> DANFORTH
>
> EVERYTHING IS SET. SIR OSWALD WOULD LIKE YOU TO ANNOUNCE YOUR ALLEGIANCE TO THE BRITISH UNION OF FASCISTS AT THE NEW YEAR'S CELEBRATION. WE EXPECT BIG THINGS IN 1935.
>
> BUCHANAN

"I'm sorry," Edward said, holding the telegram in his hand.

"You're sorry?" Charlotte turned away from the window, tears making her blue eyes shine. "You're betraying your father, your family, and your country. You're betraying me and you're betraying your sons. Your *sons*! They worship you! Are you going to teach them the Nazi salute now, Edward? Are you going to put swastika armbands on their school uniforms? Will you take them with you on your next trip to Berlin so they can shout '*Heil* Hitler' along with all the other fascist youth?"

"Char, Char, it's not like that…it's not like that at all." He made a move to comfort her, but she pulled away, her face as pale as the gray sky outside the window.

November, 1934
Plymouth and Devonport

"I so dread this time of year, Terry." Libby put her arms around her husband from behind. "So does Jane."

Terrence Fordyce, out of uniform and wearing a sweater and pants and tennis shoes, put one of his hands over his wife's. "We still have Christmas to look forward to. And New Year's. It's always a splendid time at Ashton Park with your family."

"It's never that splendid. Your departure looms over the festivities like a great dark cloud."

"You make it sound so grim."

"It is grim. You're off to the sunny Mediterranean and we're here alone with a lot of rain and drizzle."

"The butler and the maid keep things lively."

Libby leaned her head on his back and laughed despite herself. "Skitt and Monty are cards, I admit. Their young love is so refreshing to watch. But even their antics and the way they take care of us here doesn't make up for the winter absence of Terrence Fordyce, RN."

"Well, pray about it then."

"I do pray about it, believe me."

"Pray vigorously."

She laughed again and squeezed him. "Oh, Terry, I'm not one of your sailors aboard HMS *Hood*. D'you think if I holystone the deck and put my back into it, everything will come out all right with God?"

"I don't know about God. But it would go over favorably with the admiral if you rubbed stones into the planking and made the wood white." He lifted one of her hands to his mouth and kissed it. "As for the prayers, keep at it and you never know what will pop up. The Royal Navy might berth all their ships here for the winter."

"Wouldn't that be something? 'Every ship needs new propellers!'"

"Where is Jane, by the way?"

"Didn't you hear her chattering away at breakfast? She's off to London with Montgomery for Christmas shopping. Skitt's driving them. They'll meet up with Caroline and Emma and Char and have a grand old time. Even mum is coming down by train from Liverpool. It's a two- or three-day affair, you know."

Terrence turned around, taking both of her hands in his. "Two or three days! No butler or chambermaid for two or three days!"

"It is rather shocking, isn't it?"

"And Jane's all right with being away from the old man and the old lady for that long?"

"More than all right. Her aunts and grandmother will spoil her rotten and all her boy cousins will tease her without mercy. She'll have the time of her life."

Terrence pulled her in closer. "Will she? I rather think that oft-used expression should apply to us."

"Do you?"

"All alone. No one snooping or prying. No admiral to whistle aboard. No butler to walk in unannounced. Just two old lovers."

"I wish you'd stop using the adjective *old*. I haven't felt this young in years."

"Let's put that youthful energy to good use then."

"Doing what? Holystoning decks?"

"Holystoning me." He winked at her.

"Really? And how do I go about holystoning you?"

He put his lips to the side of her neck. "Use your imagination, Chief Petty Officer."

"I never liked that rank. I don't think anyone should be considered petty."

"I can call you Chief for short."

"Chief I like."

She began to return his kisses, slowly at first and then with increasing strength and ardor. "Do you like my holystoning, Commander?" she murmured, kissing his lips again before he could answer.

"I do," he finally managed to get out.

"Will I receive a medal or a promotion?"

"Indeed you will. Promotion to our private chambers." He scooped her up in his arms and she began to giggle, burying her face in his chest. "Effective immediately."

"I like Christmas shopping," she said as he carried her up the staircase.

"So do I. You never know what sort of gifts you'll find that'll catch your eye. A few bob and they're yours for life."

"A few bob?"

"A figure of speech, Lady Libby."

She put a finger on his lips. "Shh. No more talk and no more joking."

Their eyes came together and the mirth died in his throat. "As you wish," he said in a quiet voice.

Christmas Eve, 1934
Ashton Park

"Right!" cried Kipp, a glass of eggnog in his hand. "One more carol and then I have an announcement to make! Jane, you start! Oh, here we come a-wassailing…"

> Here we come a-wassailing among the leaves so green;
> Here we come a-wand'ring so fair to be seen.
>
> Bring us out a table and spread it with a cloth;
> Bring us out a moldy cheese and some of your Christmas loaf.
>
> God bless the master of this house likewise the mistress too,
> And all the little children that round the table go.
>
> Love and joy come to you, and to you your wassail too;
> And God bless you and send you a Happy New Year,
> And God send you a Happy New Year.

"What's the announcement?" asked Terry in a loud voice. "Are you finally joining the navy?"

Kipp pointed his eggnog at Terry. "Closer to heaven. I'm back with the RAF."

"You're not."

"I am. The Air Ministry has a number of new planes on the drawing board and I've been asked to join the crews that test the prototypes."

"What happens to the airline?" asked Edward. "You're not giving it up?"

"We are. Dad and Mum know about all this so it's no surprise to them. I've been doing more and more paperwork and less and less flying. It's time to get my boots up off the ground again."

"That doesn't sound very safe. Put a good ship under your feet and you'll be as solid as the Rock of Gibraltar."

Kipp laughed. "Don't want to be solid, Terry. Want to be footloose and fancy-free and up with the angels." He struck the dramatic pose of an orator, his eggnog behind his back.

> I know that I shall meet my fate
> Somewhere among the clouds above;
> Those that I fight I do not hate
> Those that I guard I do not love;
> My country is Kiltartan Cross,
> My countrymen Kiltartan's poor,
> No likely end could bring them loss
> Or leave them happier than before.
> Nor law, nor duty bade me fight,
> Nor public man, nor cheering crowds,
> A lonely impulse of delight
> Drove to this tumult in the clouds;
> I balanced all, brought all to mind,
> The years to come seemed waste of breath,
> A waste of breath the years behind
> In balance with this life, this death.

"Bravo!" Terry clapped along with the rest of the family in the library. "But you and Yeats could have chosen a cheerier theme than your 'lonely impulse of delight' and 'waste of breath' and 'balance with this life, this death.' What a dreary set of lyrics you've planted in your beautiful wife's head."

Caroline smiled and nodded. "Thank you, Terry. I do wish we could do some sort of roundabout and head back to the carols and more rousing lyrics."

"Rousing lyrics? You want rousing lyrics?"

"Now you've done it." Libby shook her head. "You've brought out the sailor in him."

Terry was on his feet. "I have a Royal Navy song that will shake the woolies out of you all and warm Caroline Danforth's heart as well. Where is Owen?"

Twelve-year-old Owen, half a foot taller than he had been in the summer, jumped up from his spot on the floor. "Here, Uncle Terry."

"Come, join me, lad. You're a proper tar, ain't ye?" growled Terry, imitating an old sea dog.

"I am, Commander, I am." Owen hurried to his uncle's side. "What song is it?"

"You'll see, you'll see. *Ahem*. Let me clear my throat."

"For heaven's sake, Papa, what's in the eggnog?" asked Emma.

"Eggs," replied Lord Preston. "Eggs and a bit."

"Here we go, Owen, weigh anchor!" cried Terry.

"Aye, aye, sir."

> Come, cheer up, my lads, 'tis to glory we steer,
> To add something more to this wonderful year;
> To honor we call you, as freemen not slaves,
> For who are so free as the sons of the waves?

"Do you have the hang of it?" Terry asked Owen.

"Yes, sir, I know the song. Da taught me the words and Grandpa sings it when we sail in the Channel."

> They say they'll invade us these terrible foe,
> They frighten our women, our children, our beaus,
> But if should their flat bottoms, in darkness set oar,
> Still Britons they'll find to receive them on shore.

"Right!" called Terry to the others in the room. "You all must know the chorus!"

Libby was laughing and tugging on his arm. "Horatio Nelson, we're supposed to be singing Christmas carols."

"In a minute, in a minute, my love. Please, all of you, join in."

> Heart of oak are our ships, jolly tars are our men,
> We always are ready; steady, boys, steady!
> We'll fight and we'll conquer again and again.

"Not bad, not bad. Another verse and then the chorus again, if you please, Master Owen."

"I'm with you, sir."

> Britannia triumphant, her ships rule the seas,
> Her watch word is justice, her password is free,
> So come cheer up my lad, with one heart let us sing,
> Our soldiers, our sailors, our statesmen, our king.
>
> Heart of oak are our ships, jolly tars are our men,
> We always are ready; steady, boys, steady!
> We'll fight and we'll conquer again and again.

Lord Preston stood and clapped. "Hurrah! Now we must do our best to find our way back to Christmas again after having been boarded by Nelson's best. Capital singing, young Owen. And capital singing deserves a capital ship. Come, mother, where's the gift?"

Lady Preston looked up from her chair. "What gift is that, William?"

He moved toward the large pine tree hung with colored balls and bright with electric lights. "The one for Owen, of course. Whom have we been talking about?" He waded through boxes wrapped in red and green tissue paper. "Confound it, we have enough here to sink a ship. Where is it?"

Tavy stepped up to the tree. "The one in blue, my lord. Blue for the navy, y'see."

"Ah. Very good, Tavy." Lord Preston fished the box out of the heap of gifts and presented it to Owen. "Here you are. Merry Christmas, my boy."

"It's not Christmas, William," mumbled Lady Preston.

"One present on Christmas Eve. Just the one. Family tradition, my dear."

Owen hesitated, looking from his grandmother to his grandfather.

Lord Preston thrust the box into Owen's hands. "Come, come, young man, never spurn a gift at Christmas."

"Thank you, Grandfather. Thank you, Grandmother."

"Well, open it, boy, open it." Lord Preston waved his hand at Owen. "Let us share in your joy."

"Yes, sir."

Owen peeled back the paper and opened the box while everyone watched and the children crowded around.

"It's a ship!"

Owen laughed and held it high.

"A ship! A wooden battleship! Does it float?"

Terry came over quickly. "That's the *Hood*! Why, I stand here all the time." He pointed to a part of the deck near one of the gun turrets. "In fair weather or foul."

Lord Preston pressed his way in to Owen and Terry. "Teak and mahogany. The fellow would go down to Portsmouth and make sketches and photographs and then do the carving and gluing and painting in his studio in Brighton, you see."

"It's brilliant, absolutely brilliant. Look at the detail. Here, Jane. You've stood on this spot two or three times while we were on parade."

Jane, taller than any of the boys as well as many of the adults, and looking at least five years older than her seventeen years, remained seated by Caroline and Charlotte. "I can see from here, Dad."

"No, you can't. How can you? Can you see over all these heads?"

"I can, actually."

Terry went back to his huddle with Lord Preston and Owen and the younger boys. "Can we put it in a tub of water?"

"You cannot." Lord Preston was horrified. "It's meant for dry land display. If you want to go to sea, set foot on the real thing."

"I shall do. But can we put this somewhere grand with a light on it and just give it a good gaze?"

"Well, it's Master Owen's, isn't it? But while it's here at Ashton Park perhaps he'll let us set it up on the great shelf under the oil of the *Victory*."

"Is there anything for me?" Colm suddenly asked. "Do I get a Christmas Eve present too?"

"Hm? What's that?" Lord Preston looked at five-year-old Colm, Owen's brother, as if he had just woken up from a dream and was seeing him for the first time. "Of course, of course." He mussed Colm's black hair. "Everyone receives a Christmas Eve present. We just need to find one with your name on it."

"I'll take care of that, Grandpa." Peter, one of Jeremy's and Emma's twins, jumped up from his seat. "I like playing Santa Claus."

His ginger hair and bright green eyes made his face vivid as he grinned and held up a box wrapped in red paper. "Who's Colm Alexander the Fifth?"

Colm looked up at Lord Preston.

"Come, come, no one wrote that." Lord Preston pointed his finger at the present and waggled it. "Read precisely what it says."

"Half a minute." Peter turned to his twin brother, James, with his brown eyes and dark hair. "D'you have a pen on you?"

James was wearing a navy blue blazer with an Eton public school crest. "Hang on."

Jane smiled and poked James. "Faster."

He plucked one out of the inside pocket of his blazer and handed it up to his brother. "Here we are."

"Cheers." Peter winked at Jane. "Santa could use an elf."

Jane laughed. "Elves are short."

"So you'll count as three of them."

She got up. "All right. You have such a clever way of putting things."

"As clever as he is, I'm even more clever," said James.

She flashed a smile at him as Peter was writing on the tag on the present.

"Ignore him," said Peter without looking up.

"I have no intention of ignoring either of you. You're much too much fun."

"Even if we're not bashing you over the head with a sword anymore?"

"Pardon? Who bashed who?"

"We let you do that because you were the only girl."

"Indeed? I think it's because I was older and stronger and smarter, don't you?"

Peter held up his hand and wiggles a few fingers. "You're only older by a few months."

"Come, come." Lord Preston clapped his hands together. "We could have had the real chap down from the North Pole by now. You can squabble later over cake and hot cider."

Peter lifted the present. "It says Colm Alexander the Fifth right on it. Do you want it or not?"

Everyone in the room laughed but Lord Preston.

Colm looked up at his grandfather a second time. "Is it mine?"

"Yes, it's yours, my dear. You'd better run and get it before they write King George the Fifth on it and give it to him."

Colm seized the box and tore the paper off. "It's a ship! It's a ship! It has guns too! And it's almost as big as Owen's!"

Lord Preston laughed. "In real life I believe it's bigger. HMS *Rodney*, Colm, my boy. But no bathtubs, all right? And no floating it on the pond."

"No, sir, it will be a carpet ship."

"Very good, a carpet ship, ha ha."

Jane, wearing a red gown and bracelets, gave people their presents while Peter, in a white shirt and Eton school tie, handed them up to her as he rummaged through the boxes under the tree, often scribbling something on their tags. Soon Cecilia, at five, the daughter of Kipp and Caroline, had a dollhouse. Matthew, at twelve, and his brother Charles, at thirteen, Cecilia's brothers, both had large models of airplanes. And Billy, younger brother to the twins at fourteen, had a brass microscope. The adults wound up with socks and shoes and ties, and Jane was given a necklace by James and a bracelet by Peter.

"How on earth can you two afford gifts?" asked Jane, immediately putting the necklace about her throat. "I thought you were both pinching pennies for Christ Church at Oxford."

"So we are," responded James. "But faint heart never won fair lady."

"'Faint heart never won fair lady.' Oh, James, don't talk such rubbish."

"I'm serious. That's my class stone, y'know. It's real garnet."

"And the necklace is garnet too." Peter punched his brother in the shoulder. "Not to be outdone."

James pushed him. "You're always outdone and outgunned. Give up the ship while you still have breath in your lungs."

Jane slapped them both playfully on the tops of their heads. "No one gives up ships in my family. Remember, my father is commander on the *Mighty Hood*." She slipped the bracelet on her right hand. "Ohhh, it's rather large."

"Eat more cake," teased James. "Eat till you puff up properly."

"Thanks very much, Sir Galahad, I won't. Perhaps I should stick with Peter from now on so I don't think of myself as the fatted calf."

"Hear, hear." Peter clapped his hands. "I concur completely. Throw the scoundrel out on his ear."

James tossed a wad of wrapping paper at him. "I'd like to see you try, Hercules."

Libby laughed, watching them from across the room. "Aren't the three of them sweet together, Mum?"

Lady Preston nodded and sipped at her tea. "I enjoy their antics. But the twins are practically men now. They can't both pop the question."

"Oh, Mother, surely it's just a bit of fun and games, isn't it? No one's thinking of marriage."

"Why, your father was at seventeen. Oh, yes. I put him off for three years but he never took the hint." She smiled. "No matter. It's turned out for the best." Peter and James were chattering away, one on either side of Jane. "I shouldn't mind at all if one of them did pop the question."

"Surely they're more family than anything else, Mum."

"Family they are. But to my mind it's a second- or third-cousin relationship. James and Peter are eminently suitable to wed Jane Fordyce. Especially since we are nobility." Her gray eyebrows came together sharply as she smiled again. "Just not both of them at the same time."

The Nelson Room

The men drifted upstairs to the Nelson Room, the ladies to the Rose Room. The younger boys and Cecilia stayed in the library with Harrison and Holly, and Peter and James and Jane decided to go for a walk in the rain. Kipp lit the fire in the Nelson Room while Edward glanced over the large wooden model of the *Victory*, Horatio Nelson's flagship at the Battle of Trafalgar in 1805.

Jeremy took a seat. "Fancy being back on the high seas, Edward?"

Edward immediately turned away from the model. "Hm? No, no." He poured himself some hot cider from a teapot. "Just admiring the handiwork." He took a chair next to Lord Preston. "That ship you gave Owen is extraordinary. Well, they both are, Dad, Owen's and Colm's. Thank you."

Lord Preston tapped his hand on his armrest. "You're most welcome, my boy, most welcome." Abruptly he turned to face his son. "Have you ever thought of returning to sea?"

Edward was startled, pausing as he lifted the cup of cider to his mouth. "You're joking."

Lord Preston kept tapping his hand on the armrest. "Germany is rearming. They've broken the Treaty of Versailles. Heaven knows what Hitler intends to do in the long run."

"Dad, he's just restoring pride in the German people. You said yourself the terms of the Treaty were too harsh. A few planes, a few ships…what's the harm?"

"This *Graf Spee* they launched in June, this *Panzerschiff*, it's a powerful warship."

"It's within the ten thousand long tons limit—"

"I'm afraid not." Lord Preston struck the armrest several sharp blows. "Her full load displacement is over sixteen thousand tons. She carries six eleven-inch guns in two triple turrets. It takes less than the fingers I have on one hand to count the number of French or British ships that could catch her and sink her."

"Who's talking about catching and sinking her? She won't be finished for another year. And even when she is—"

"She'll be capable of more than twenty-nine knots—fifty-five kilometers an hour."

"Dad, honestly. They're getting ready for the Olympics, not another war." He looked around the room for support. "We know what it means to have national pride, don't we? I mean, we're sitting here in the Nelson Room, for heaven's sake."

"They're laying down two more battleships in the spring."

"You don't know that."

"I do know that, Edward. I even know the names that will likely be used—*Scharnhorst* and *Gneisenau*."

"There's been all kinds of talk."

Terry stood with his back to the fire. "Of course, the *Graf Spee* is out there for all to see, so no question as far as that goes. But we've heard the rumors about the new battleships, Edward."

"Rumors."

"They put up the Dornier 17 on the twenty-third of November." Kipp was pouring himself a cup of cider and picking up a few chocolate biscuits from a plate. "It was a successful flight."

"A twin-engine mail plane," protested Edward.

"A twin-engine bomber. And there's the Heinkel. The single-engine version broke speed records. They'll be putting up the twin-engine version in February or March. What will we have then? The fastest passenger plane in the world?"

"I don't know. Why not? What's wrong with that?"

Kipp sat down and sipped his cider. "They're building another single-engine plane. Fast. Sleek. All the fliers have heard about it. The Germans will test it in the spring. A man named Willy Messerschmitt designed it. It's no secret. What do you think it's for? It doesn't take passengers, and there's no storage area for mail."

"Look." Edward held up both his hands. "I'm not the family apologist for the Third Reich. I just think they've come a long way and that they deserve credit. For the most part, it's my understanding they've kept within the strictures of the Treaty—a Treaty that Dad's condemned for fifteen years—and if they step over the line here and there, is it really such a crime? Look at what the Japanese Army has done in Manchuria, look at the blood and slaughter they've perpetrated in Shanghai, and what have any of us done about that? What has the League of Nations done? It's sheer hypocrisy to go after Germany over a few well-made ships and planes that haven't caused anyone any harm."

"But neither Germany nor Japan are part of the League of Nations anymore," Jeremy spoke up, dressed in his black clerical suit jacket and shirt and pants. "They both withdrew last year. You can't expect the League to be able to exert pressure on them successfully. And America's not a member either. So we've lost a good deal of clout there."

"Oh, Britain will find the clout it needs if the Japanese go after Hong Kong. Count on it." Edward raised his thick eyebrows. "For now it's only Manchurians and Chinese who are dying, so it's no great cause for concern. But Germany...ah, Germany, our nemesis in the last war, it's found its sea legs again, so that has the lot of you shaking in your boots. Hitler's harmed no one, mind you, hasn't lifted a finger to France or Holland or England, but he's the one to be chastised."

"Except the Jews," his father said.

"Excuse me, Dad?"

"Herr Hitler's harmed no one except the Jews. And the Communists."

"Jews and Communists, Father. Honestly, does that matter a great deal?"

"There's your sister Catherine. And Albrecht. And their children. They had to flee Germany."

"He was writing scurrilous comments about Hitler and the government. He's a traitor. Isn't that it basically? Albrecht turned against his country. We'd treat him the same here for going against the king or prime minister."

Kipp drained his cup of cider. "People criticize the king and prime minister all the time, brother. Politicians do it every day. No one considers them traitors or thinks they should be tossed in prison. How does speaking up against Hitler's policies constitute treason to the German nation? Isn't it quite the opposite, in fact? The sign of a man willing to stand for what he loves about his country even in the face of those who have the power to harm or silence him?"

Edward shook his head, laughed, and pushed himself out of his chair. "This has turned into something of an inquisition. Pardon me while I step out for some fresh air. You can chat about the concentration camps we put the Boers into while I'm gone."

"Edward."

Edward stopped as he opened the door. "Yes, Dad?"

"Think over what I said. Kipp is taking to the air. You can take to the sea. A commission is available. You would serve on the battleship *Rodney*, a distinguished ship. Britain needs you."

Edward shook his head again. "I don't understand anything that's going on in this room. You act like it's nineteen fourteen all over again." He patted the pocket of his suit jacket. "I have my tickets to the Berlin Olympics. I picked them up at the German embassy before we left London to come here. That's what Germany means to me. Gold and silver medals, a pint of lager, and civilization."

The Emerald Room

Edward rubbed his hand over his face.

Taking a small carton from his pants, he fished out a cigarette, put it in his mouth, and lit it. Both the cigarettes and the lighter were American. He leaned his back against the wall and took smoke into his lungs.

Papa, look! It's the Mighty Hood! *Isn't it fantastic?*

He stared at the wallpaper swirls on the other side of the hall.

Could I see the real ship someday, Da? The real Rodney? *Will it look like this?*

He wandered along the hall. If the women hadn't gone to the Rose Room, he would have sought out his wife and drawn her aside. Someone had been talking to his father, and it could only have been her. A cold anger put ice in his blood. How dare she be so deceptive?

The door to one of the rooms in the hallway stood ajar. A candle was lit inside. He blew out a stream of smoke and poked his head in, wondering if some of the boys had made their way upstairs.

"Hullo?"

Charlotte brought her head up sharply. "What do you want?"

Edward stared. "I had no idea you were in here. I thought it might have been...well, it doesn't matter." He remained in the doorway. "I expected you'd be with the ladies in the Rose Room."

"I was for a while. But I wasn't in the mood for making merry."

"Why are you in here? We used to call this the Emerald Room because of the green wallpaper."

She was standing at a desk and suddenly put her hand over an open book. "All the other doors were locked."

He stepped inside. "Now that we've run in each other this wonderful Christmas Eve, I should thank you for going behind my back to my father. You've got him nicely tucked in your pocket, haven't you?"

"I've not the slightest idea what you're talking about, Edward."

"I can tell he knows everything. Who else would have told him?"

"I haven't mentioned the matter between you and me to anyone."

"That's odd. How do you suppose he found out? A little birdie that flew down the chimney?"

"I haven't the foggiest."

Edward dropped into a chair. "Offered me a commission in the Royal Navy." He snapped his fingers. "Just like that. He wants me out of England. Out of England and out of politics and out at sea. He knows about my fascist connections all right."

Charlotte faced him. "I don't agree with anything you're doing or plan to do with the British Union of Fascists. But I didn't tell your father. I didn't tell a soul."

"There's no other explanation."

Even in the candlelight her blue eyes were vivid. "Look at me. I am not lying to you."

"Charlotte—"

"I am not lying to you."

Edward let his cigarette burn into the fingers of his right hand before stubbing it out on the wooden arm of the chair. "All right. I believe you."

"Thank you."

"I can't think." He looked around the room at the wallpaper. "I remember hiding in here with Kipp. The girls were after us for making a mess of their dolls. Kipp and the RAF. Germany builds a few boats and planes and now Britain starts rearming too." He glanced at the desk. "What's the book?"

"Never mind."

"Are you still planning to head up to Scotland with the boys?"

"I am."

"I've not been back since our wedding."

"Neither have I."

"You'll stay there for New Year's? They'll miss their cousins."

"It can't be helped. I won't be here when you stand next to that horrid Sir Oswald Mosley and tell the world you're on the same side as Hitler and Mussolini."

"It's not about sides, Char."

"Of course it's about sides. All of life is about what side you're on. You used to be an Englishman."

"I am still an Englishman."

"No, you're not. You're a Blackshirt."

"They're not mutually exclusive."

"They are, Edward. In my eyes they certainly are. And in the eyes of a lot of other Englishmen and women."

"I can't help that. That's the narrow way they think."

"In the eyes of a lot of English boys. *Your* boys, Edward. Your sons."

He looked at her but didn't respond.

"Do you want to know what's in this book?" She lifted it up. "It's nothing special. It's a diary I've kept since I was twelve. I came to this room to read some of it. I talk about you. The first time we kissed in that hut under the ash trees. The hut's still there. They've never pulled it down."

"I know it's still there."

"The pages are filled with you. How we were split apart but came together again. Our wedding at the hunting lodge. The years in Canada where Owen was born. The magic of the snow and the mountains and the cold. Your first election win. How proud I was of you. Your first speech in Parliament. Colm's birth. It's been a beautiful life. I've been praying to God in this room, Edward. Praying you won't throw it all away."

He glanced down at the floor. "Listen, Char—"

"There's something else you should know. It's in the book too. But I've never told you."

He looked up.

She extended the book to him. "I'm Jewish, Edward. My grandmother is Levy on Mum's side. I have Jewish blood. And so do your sons."

Christmas Morning, 1934
Lord Tanner's residence, London

Lord Tanner Buchanan came to the door in his dressing gown, anger and annoyance scribbled across his face. "For heaven's sake, man, it's two in the morning. What do you mean by coming here? Are you mad?"

Edward wasn't wearing a hat, and the rain made his hair fall over his forehead. His eyes burned with a deep darkness.

"You went to my father," he said in a low voice. "You told him. Showed him notes and telegrams to prove it."

"I don't know what you're talking about. Is that what the old fool told you? I—"

Edward hit him and knocked him back into the hallway. Before Buchanan could recover Edward hit him again, and he flew into a wall, blood on his mouth. He shook his head, spat out the blood, and came at Edward with a roar. They gripped each other and tumbled out onto the London street, falling and rolling in rainwater and mud and car oil as they choked and pummeled and kicked. Edward got on top and punched Buchanan again and again until Buchanan lay limp. Edward staggered to his feet.

"You tell Mosley no. Not New Year's. Not anytime in 1935. Not ever. Do you hear me? Not in a thousand years."

Buchanan opened his eyes. "We'll crush you, Danforth. You and your whole family. You'll lose the next election and we'll sweep you out of Parliament and out of the country. You'll be a refugee in Poland and Ukraine and Romania. You'll be adrift for the rest of your life and die in a gutter while the Nazis rule the world. The German Nazis and the Italian Blackshirts and the British Union of Fascists. You'll be nothing."

"Take a message to Herr Hitler for me. Tell him to stay away, far away, or I'll be the one doing the crushing. I swear it. Warn him to keep his ships away from our shores or I'll sink every last one of them. I don't care how big or fast they are or how powerful their guns. I'll sink them."

"A brave man on a street in London."

"An angry man on a battleship in the Channel." Edward dug into a pocket, brought out a handful of tickets, and threw them in Buchanan's face. "Enjoy the Olympics on my coin."

Buchanan spat. "I don't need your coin."

Edward pointed his finger at Buchanan as he lay in the street. "You stay away too. You and your ilk. All you goose-stepping clowns. Don't come within ten miles of my family at Camden Lock, Lord Tanner, or I'll put a bullet through your black shirt and your black heart. All your black shirts and black hearts."

Edward began to stride away.

Buchanan got up, the rain slashing his face and body. "Why the change in weather, Danforth? Why the cold heart? Why the ice in the veins? What happened to your faith? How did you lose it?"

"I didn't lose it. I found it, Buchanan."

The black morning swallowed him up.

Christmas Day, 1934
Ashton Park

"Are you quite all right, Lady Charlotte?"

Charlotte turned away from the rain-streaked window with a start. "Oh, Tavy. Good morning. I'm just waiting for someone."

"Who is that, my lady?"

"Lord Edward. He had to make a run down to London last night."

"At Christmas? That's at least four hours each way."

"It was urgent."

"Political affairs?"

"Yes, yes, that's right."

"No one will be stirring for another hour. Can I get you some tea?"

"Tea? Tea would be lovely, Tavy. Thank you very much."

He bent and peered through the dark of the window. "One of the Liverpool cabs. Lord Edward managed to catch all the right connections, I expect. He must be exhausted. I'll brew some tea for him as well, shall I?"

Charlotte hurled open the front doors and walked out. "Yes, perfect, Tavy, a pot, please, a whole pot for both of us."

"Very good, my lady."

She stood in the rain and watched him pay the cabdriver. The car pulled away, and he was facing her.

"You're wet," she said.

"Very wet," he replied.

"I'll fetch a towel."

"Don't. Don't go anywhere."

The downpour flattened her hair and ran into her eyes and mouth. "Are you quite settled in your mind?" she asked.

"I am."

"Did you—did you kill him?"

"No. I warned him to stay far away."

"Fancy. This is Christmas morning."

"It is."

"I remember being with you in another rainstorm a long time ago."

"Not so long." He opened his arms. "For love of you, Charlotte. I throw it all away and count it rubbish for love of you."

She held back. All the time her eyes were fixed on his. All the time his arms were open for her. The rain drove against her dress and against his cloak. Finally she came toward him, slowly at first, then walking faster and faster until she threw herself into the open arms and they closed tightly around her.

"Edward…Edward."

She was crying and running her hands over his face as the storm intensified and the wind began to blow so that the raindrops hit them with the sting of lead pellets.

"Shh, shh, my love," he whispered.

"Are you back? Are you honestly back? My Edward? My man? Is it you?"

"I was like a person in the grips of a fever. Now it's broken. I want you. You and my sons and my God. That's enough." He put his lips to the wet skin of her face. "I am going to take the commission."

"But what about becoming prime minister?"

"I'll become an admiral instead."

"We'll have to move."

"No, no. You and the boys stay in London where there is family. You and Libby can keep each other company when Terry's in the Mediterranean and I'm heaven knows where."

"Are you sure?"

"I've been on the trains all night. I'm sure. Stay in London. Wait for me here." His lips were on her wet hair. "Dark shapes will move toward our shores in the years ahead. Just like they have before—the Normans, the Armada, the ships of Napoleon. I need to be there when they do." He kissed her. "Will you pray for me, Charlotte Squire?"

"Oh, how can you ask that? As bad as it's been between us I've never stopped doing that."

"So you're with me?"

"I am."

"You still love me?"

"I never stopped."

She tugged his head down and began to kiss him with all her heart and strength as the rain beat on their shoulders and backs.

Inside the house Emma and Libby looked on as Tavy stood nearby with a tray of tea, cream, sugar, and rolls.

"I thought something was wrong," said Emma. "Things seemed so strained between them."

"Clearly that's been smoothed out, whatever it was." Libby smiled and crossed her arms over the front of her dressing gown. "Now the only thing we need to worry about is whether they'll catch their death."

Emma raised an eyebrow. "I doubt that will happen, sister, dear. They're generating enough heat to run the *Hood* and *Rodney* both with plenty to spare for the lesser ships of the fleet."

Libby laughed. "How cheeky of you."

Emma glanced at Tavy. "Hot tea for the lovers, Tavy?"

He cleared his throat. "Lady Charlotte requested it."

"I think it will just get cold the way matters are developing out of doors. Would you mind serving it to Libby and me in the parlor?"

"Not at all. Once I've set the tray down I'll get a fire started first thing."

"Thank you so much, Tavy. Merry Christmas, by the way."

"Merry Christmas, Lady Emma. And to you, my lady." He inclined his head toward Libby.

"A smashing start to the day, I'm sure. Merry Christmas, Tavy. The Savior is born."

Christmas Day, 1934
The library

"A capital breakfast." Lord Preston rubbed his hands together. "My compliments to Mrs. Longstaff and her staff. Praise the Lord for such a feast." He lifted a sheaf of papers. "We've had our morning prayers, emptied our socks, opened our presents. Time to bring you greetings from the far-flung members of the family."

He put on reading glasses. "First, Catherine and Albrecht in Switzerland, where we thank God they have safely landed along with Sean, who is eleven this Christmas, and Angelika, who is four, the youngest among us. All is well. Albrecht is writing a new book to form a trilogy along with *My Spirit* and *My War*. It's to be called *My Fatherland*, Catherine writes, and is an appeal to the German people to remember their rich Christian past and bring it to the fore once again. He is receiving any number of invitations to speak at Swiss churches and universities, even to do a lecture series on von Pauls's book *Bearing the Cross* and tie it into gospel teachings on Christ. Praise the Lord. The children are once more enchanted by their white horses, the Lipizzan stallions of Herr Salzgeber."

He put several sheets of paper down. "You may read the whole letter for yourselves, I shall leave it on the side table." He adjusted his glasses. "Now we have Shannon's missive from Jerusalem. Robbie has been promoted to colonel."

"Hear, hear!" cried Edward.

Lord Preston glanced at his eldest son over the top of his glasses. "He outranks you, Edward."

"Only on land."

"And not in the air," quipped Kipp.

Lord Preston smiled. "Indeed."

Edward got to his feet. "Still we must give credit where credit is due. Ladies and gentlemen, charge your glasses, there is plenty of orange squash about. Charge your glasses, I say. A toast to Colonel Robert Danforth. All the best to our brother in arms. God bless him."

Kipp was up. "Amen."

The others rose, juice glasses half filled, the boys and little Cecilia as well.

"Heah, heah," she said.

They laughed and drained their glasses in one swallow.

"Very good." Lord Preston returned to the letter. "I thank God, Shannon tells us things continue quiet since the riots several years back. And Patricia Claire is six and thriving. Her favorite foods are dates, figs, falafel, and, unsurprisingly, chocolate ice cream."

People laughed and clapped.

Lord Preston set the letter aside.

"Finally, here is news from British East Africa, from Kenya. Victoria Anne wishes everyone a very Merry Christmas. Their mission is going well. Ben is flying to remote areas where they've planted all sorts of small churches. He's been preaching and teaching and bringing in medical supplies—they have two nurses and a physician with them as well, you see. Praise God. She writes that Ramsay and Timothy will spend Christmas Day learning to ride elephants for the first time."

All the boys in the room groaned in jealousy, including James and Peter, and Jane joined in.

Lord Preston peered at them over his glasses. "Why, they are quite old enough. Ramsay is all of twelve and Timothy will be ten in the spring. High time they rode elephants if they are in Africa."

"And what can we ride?" Peter called out.

"The wind." Kipp smiled. "I haven't sold all my planes to Hicks and Winthrop yet. I have a nice one at the airstrip here I intend to keep. Who wants to go up this afternoon? I can take two or three at a time."

Jane's hand shot up. "Oh, I want to do that, Uncle Kipp, please, take me, please!"

Peter's hand went up as soon as he saw Jane's. "I'm in for a penny."

James's hand was just behind his brother's. "And I'm in for a pound!"

Kipp laughed. "Right. There's our first flight."

"Oh, Kipp, dear." Lady Preston set down her teacup. "Surely the rain isn't cooperating. This is not decent flying weather."

"The meteorologist on the BBC forecasted the showers would end by noon and we might even see a bit of sunshine. Straightaway after lunch we'll fill *Gladys* with petrol and head up for our tumult in the clouds."

"Not a tumult, please, Kipp," his mother complained. "We had enough of those in the Great War."

"I won't do any dogfighting, Mum, I promise. Unless Wolfgang von Zeltner happens by. In which case we go on the attack." Kipp turned to Jane. "Fancy a few stunts?"

"Yes! Oh, yes! Let's fly like starlings or swallows, dipping and diving and swinging about all over the sky!"

Peter and James glanced at each other.

"Are you quite done?" Lord Preston lifted the letter in his hand. "I have a hike up Mount Kilimanjaro to commence."

Several hours later
The ash grove

"So you felt good about all that flying?" asked Caroline.

"I did," replied Kipp. "A splendid time was had by all."

"All? I saw a few green faces get off the plane."

"Well, that's to be expected. Some were up for the first time."

They were walking far back into the ash trees on the Ashton Park estate, hand in hand.

"Tell me how Jane the daredevil did."

"Jane? She must be a bird, I swear. Nothing fazed her. Not loops or spins or barrel rolls."

"What about her boyfriends?"

"You mean James and Peter? Nothing like her, though they'd never admit it. They hung on, I will give them that. Neither of them disgraced himself. She wanted barrel rolls and they wanted straight and level—that's the size of it. They never said as much of course. 'Faint heart never won fair lady.' You know."

"Yes, I know." She leaned her head on his shoulder. "What about our boys?"

"Perfect. Born fliers. I gave each of them a go at the stick. Calm as could be. No nerves whatsoever."

"Lovely. But don't put any ideas about RAF careers in their heads. One in the family is quite enough for me."

"Oh, well, it's too soon for any of that."

"What's up for Boxing Day then?"

"Dad's heading down to Dover Sky with anyone who wants to go out on *Pluck*. So Edward's taking Colm and Owen. Char's going with them, her three men. Terry and Libby are off with the lot as well, but Jane's staying here. So we'll take her up again. Her and Peter and James and Matt and Charles. And we'll need to keep an eye on her. Terry and Lib will be at Dover Sky for the week."

"I'm sure we don't need to keep an eye on her, Kipp. She'll soon be eighteen. What about Billy. What's he fancy?"

Kipp laughed. "He had them poking their fingers and putting drops of blood under the microscope. Swore they'd be able to tell one another's blood apart. They couldn't, of course. I'm surprised there's enough blood left in any of them to keep them running and jumping and chattering. In any case, he's staying here with his microscope and his books. So with all their boys remaining at Ashton Park, the good Reverend Jeremiah Sweet and his charming wife, Emma, will be planting themselves here in Lancashire as well."

"Sounds jolly. And you sound awfully jolly yourself. Are you sure you won't miss the airline? No regrets at selling it off, love?"

"None at all. It's in good hands, and I get to fly fighter planes for a living. What could be better than that?"

She rolled her eyes, her head still on his shoulder. "Oh, not much. You always must have your adventure, mustn't you? I hope chasing girls like their cousins Peter and James will be excitement enough for our sons."

"Well, don't hold your breath, Caroline."

"I never hold my breath in this family."

Boxing Day and the Feast of Stephen, December 26, 1934

"Dad?"

"Hm?" Lord Preston was putting an expensive pair of binoculars in his suitcase, wrapping them around with thick woolen socks. "What is it, my boy?"

Edward stepped into his father's bedroom. "Can we talk a bit?"

"Are you packed for Dover Sky?"

"Char's got us squared away. I'm thinking of taking her on the *Rodney* with me." He chuckled. "I'd be so shipshape they'd promote me to admiral in a fortnight."

Lord Preston laughed as he fitted his binoculars carefully among his sweaters and pants. "We like the cut of your jib, Commander Danforth."

"Something like that. Listen, Dad, I wanted to thank you for arranging for me to return to the Royal Navy at my old rank."

"Well, you earned it in the last war, didn't you? A spot of training, a bit of a refit as the navy says, and you'll be up to snuff in no time."

"Dad." He hesitated. "I know Lord Tanner approached you about my connections with Sir Oswald Mosley and the British Union of Fascists. I'm not sure what seeds of discord he hoped to sow. I don't deny I was caught up in all of it—wanting a strong man at the top, wanting less democracy and more action, admiring Rome and Berlin. I understand you felt you needed to get me out to sea and away from the whole thing. I don't blame you. My siding publicly with the fascists would have hurt the Conservative Party and it would have hurt you. Indeed it would have hurt my whole family, Char and the boys no less than anyone else. I want you to know you did the right thing by offering me the commission and giving me a chance to put it all behind me. I'm grateful, and I'm glad to be going aboard the *Rodney*." He took a breath. "You're a great statesman. But you're even a greater father. You'll be proud of me again, and you'll forget all this mess with the fascists. I swear it."

Lord Preston had stopped packing. "My boy, I am proud of you. A great talent resides within you, and you are young yet. I hope to see you back in the House before many years pass."

"To tell you the truth, that thought is farthest from my mind. I enjoyed the speeches and debates. I liked getting my point across. But I'd like a break."

Lord Preston smiled a soft smile. "A break before you become prime minister?"

Edward smiled too. "That's right. Get my sea legs back. Fill my head with the cry of gulls and my lungs with the bite of the salt air. A few years of that and I'll be holystoned through and through and ready to be the first man in the nation."

"That's the spirit." Lord Preston thrust out his hand and his son took it. Then he drew Edward in and clapped him on the back.

"God bless you, my boy. God bless you."

"Thank you, Father."

"Are you ready to head down to Dover? Ready to shove off and put *Pluck* through her paces in the Channel?"

Edward nodded, still gripping his father's hand. "Aye, aye, sir. Let's weigh anchor."

January, 1935
Plymouth and Devonport

Libby and Jane stood in the fog and damp and watched the *Hood* move away from land toward the Atlantic just as they had watched it leave England so many times before. As the great gray ship vanished among mists and waves with the vessels that always accompanied her, the two walked back to the car, where Skitt stood ready to drive them to the house.

"Another dreary winter for us, Skitt," moaned Libby, "and another sunny one for Commander Fordyce in the Mediterranean."

"Yes, my lady, but we'll soon be in London with the others. You always look forward to that."

"I do. So does Jane. She has her boyfriends after all."

"Mum!" protested Jane as she slid into the backseat.

"But I would dearly love to have the *Hood* stay here for a winter and get refitted and whatnot so Terry could spend the season with his family for once."

"I understand." Skitt closed the doors and got in behind the wheel. "Montgomery will have tea and crumpets ready. And some of that excellent marmalade from the London shops."

Libby laughed. "Well, that's something. We'll substitute crumpets and marmalade for my husband for the time being. What a proper English woman our American girl Montgomery has turned out to be."

Skitt smiled and started the engine. "Aye. It's a gift, isn't it? A rare gift."

Libby looked out the window at the gray water that lapped against the docks. "That it is."

January, 1935
Gibraltar

MY DEAR LIBBY

YOUR PRAYERS ALONE SHOULD ASSURE YOUR
APPOINTMENT AS ARCHBISHOP OF CANTER-
BURY. WE WERE RAMMED ON THE PORT SIDE
BY HMS RENOWN. AN ACCIDENT OF COURSE
BUT HEADS WILL ROLL. THEY'VE PATCHED US
UP HERE IN GIBRALTAR BUT WE MUST RETURN
TO PLYMOUTH FOR MORE EXTENSIVE REPAIRS.
SO AT LONG LAST YOU SHALL HAVE YOUR
WISH. WE WILL BE IN ENGLAND FOR THE WIN-
TER. HURRAH. SUCH TIMES IN PLYMOUTH
AND LONDON AND ASHTON PARK WE SHALL
HAVE. BLESS THE LORD O MY SOUL AND FOR-
GET NOT ALL HIS BENEFITS. WE SHALL SEE YOU
VERY SOON. LOVE TO JANE.

YOUR SAILOR HOME FROM THE SEA

TERRY

February, 1935
Plymouth and Devonport

"Oh, this is splendid! I'm so pleased!"

Libby had her arms around Terry's neck as he disembarked from the
Hood. He hugged her and kissed her on the cheek.

"You look wonderful," he said. "And you smell wonderful."

"Oh, any man would say that after being at sea with a thousand sailors
and no woman within a hundred nautical miles."

"A hundred? Try ten hundred. Well, my three-day leave starts now. Let's
not waste it on the dock. Where's Jane?"

"She has examinations. Her tutor is hovering over her like a hawk. I
wouldn't have brought her anyway, Terry."

"You wouldn't? Why not?"

She hugged his arm as drops of rain began to fall. "I can't give you the

Mediterranean climate. But I can give you myself. We're going to a little seaside hideaway for a day and a night. Just the two of us, the Royal Navy commander and his bride. No telephones, no telegraphs, no mail. All you'll have is Libby Danforth Fordyce."

"That sounds a bit dangerous."

"You're quite right." She pulled him toward the car. "I'm driving. No Skitt either."

"Now you do have me worried."

She opened the passenger door for him and saluted. "Heart of oak are our ships, jolly tars are our men. We always are ready; steady, boys, steady."

The drive to the hideaway was about fifteen miles. A half dozen stone cottages were strewn about a shoreline like shells. She took him to the one farthest from the others. It sat under a high cliff, and high tide stopped about twelve feet from its door. Terry eyed the ragged sprawl of seaweed.

"Suppose there's a storm surge?" he asked her.

Libby smiled and opened the cottage door. "I'll cling to you."

The rain did fall more heavily that afternoon, and the wind picked up, hurling waves onto the stony brown sands. Terry stood at the window with a cup of tea as white exploded over the beach.

"It looks like the royal fireworks," he said.

Libby knotted a dressing gown and slipped her arms around him from behind. "That's a dramatic way of putting it."

Terry continued gazing out the window.

> Break, break, break,
>   On thy cold gray stones, O sea!
> And I would that my tongue could utter
>   The thoughts that arise in me.
>
> O, well for the fishermen's boy,
>   That he shouts with his sister at play!
> O, well for the sailor lad,
>   That he sings in his boat on the bay!
>
> And the stately ships go on
>   To their haven under the hill;
> But O, for the touch of a vanished hand,
>   And the sound of a voice that is still!

Break, break, break
    At the foot of thy crags, O sea!
But the tender grace of a day that is dead
    Will never come back to me.

"Well, aren't you cheery?"

"I don't think of it as cheery or not cheery, the sea. I just find its rhythms take me to eternal thoughts. On board ship I scarcely ever get to drift away like that. You know, as if I were a bit of wood or flotsam being carried about by the whitecaps."

"My poet sailor."

Terry put down his tea, turned around, and took her in his arms, kissing her ginger blond hair, her eyes, her cheeks, and finally her lips. Her grip tightened and tightened as his kisses grew longer and stronger.

"Oh, Terry." She kept up her whispering. "I'm so glad that battleship knocked you about. I'm so glad I've got you to myself this winter."

He picked her up and carried her away from the window. The rain was coming against it now, harsh and full, as if pails of water were being thrown at the glass. She heard the gulls shrieking and saw them dipping and wheeling and fighting through a pane blurred by the storm. She caught the high burst of a comber as it struck a large rock and split in half. Iron wave after iron wave marched into shore behind it.

February 1, 1935
Grenada, HMS Rodney

Dearest Char,

We've just dropped anchor here. The weather, as you might expect, is marvelous. *Rodney* had full-scale gunnery exercises in the Channel just two weeks ago, complete with star shells and searchlights, and now we're in the tropics. What a change.

Rodney is a great ship, lots of wood and brass, teak decks, enough room forward to chalk out a football pitch. The return to the navy really has done me good. It's quite the cliché to say it, but I feel like a new man. Especially here with palm trees all around. We'll be paying a visit to Trinidad,

St. Lucia, Dominica, and St. Kitts as well. Back across the Atlantic to Gibraltar in March.

I didn't drop you a line to rattle on about my adventures, though I know the boys will be keen to hear about my ports of call. I wanted to tell you we will certainly be back in England for the king's Silver Jubilee and the Fleet Review in July. Terry and the *Hood* will be there as well. The captain assures me there will be a brief stay at Devonport, so please be ready to come down with Owen and Colm, and we'll rent a cottage. After that, who knows? But at least we can have a few days together, so plan for that, my sweet.

The sea may be just what I needed, but I miss you very much. It is impossible to gaze at the clear blue of the skies here without thinking of your eyes and your beauty. I love you.

Your Edward forever and ever

February—November, 1935

The *Hood* was repaired at Plymouth during the winter and spring. As predicted by Lord Preston, the Germans laid down the battleship *Gneisenau* in Kiel and began construction in May, just as *Hood* was anticipating her return to sea, while the battleship *Scharnhorst* was laid down in Wilhelmshaven in June. Work on the battleship *Graf Spee* continued at a steady pace in the same city where the *Scharnhorst* was being built.

In the air, the Heinkel 111, a twin-engine aircraft, had its first flight in February, while an improved version of the Dornier 17, with two engines and two tails, took to the air for the first time in May. The single-engine plane Kipp swore was a fighter, the Messerschmitt, also had its maiden flight in May. As the Germans tested and retested their aircraft, the British tried to catch up with a fighter designed by Hawker Aircraft Ltd. taking off in early November, and a fighter put together by R.J. Mitchell of Supermarine Aviation Works that would not find its way into the air for another four months. Kipp, champing at the bit, would have opportunities to help test both aircraft in 1936.

Meanwhile the family gathered in London at Easter; saw Edward off to Portsmouth and HMS *Rodney* while Terry enjoyed a fortnight's leave at Ashton Park; received a copy of Albrecht's latest book, *Mein Vaterland*, which was being smuggled into Berlin, Munich, Tubingen, and other German cities; received good reports from Ben and Victoria and the Methodist mission in Kenya; and was relieved when letters from Shannon and Robbie arrived declaring all was well and that Jerusalem, though restless as always, remained at peace.

The *Hood* did not leave English waters through the spring and summer, and Libby was ecstatic. She and Terry and Jane had never had so much time together as a family—hiking, sailing *Pluck* off Dover, going on long drives in the country, and enjoying family meals at Ashton Park and Dover Sky. Twice they had Peter and James over to HMS Picadilly, as Jane insisted they call their house near Plymouth, and once in July they enjoyed the company of Edward, Charlotte, Colm, and Owen, who visited and dined with them.

"I feel so full of summer," declared Libby in August. "Attending King George's Silver Jubilee Fleet Review and getting Jane ready for Oxford have quite put me over the top in the most wonderful way."

"The house will be very quiet without our girl," said Terry.

"I shall keep you here to make up for it. I've written the king, the First Sea Lord, and the Archbishop of Canterbury. Something's bound to break my way."

"There is a strong possibility of war between Italy and Abyssinia, the Ethiopian Empire."

"Oh, Father's been going on about that all year."

"I know you've been expecting us to stay in English waters until after Christmas as we usually do. But the threat of conflict in northern Africa may change all that. We've spent years training in the Mediterranean. It's only natural for them to put us in there early if they have to."

They were sitting in the garden behind HMS Picadilly, and Libby had her head back and her eyes closed.

"Really, I'm listening to bees hum and flowers open. I'm very lazy today. I don't want to hear about wars and rumors of wars. Tell me I'm pretty and that you'll love me forever and that the admiral has assigned you to shore command."

"You are pretty and I will love you forever, but the admiral told me today we could ship out as soon as next Wednesday."

Libby opened an eye. "You're joking."

"I'm not."

"A fine time you picked to tell me."

"I don't think there is a fine time. I'm as disappointed as you are. I was sure I'd have Christmas here. And I wanted to see Jane settled in at Lady Margaret Hall."

"Oh, hang the navy." Libby sat up. "What business is it of ours what happens between Mussolini and Ethiopia?"

"Britain wants Italy on our side in case we come to blows with Herr Hitler. Ethiopia certainly can't help us politically. So we're letting Il Duce have a free hand in Abyssinia. The Mediterranean Fleet is already helping move supplies for him and the Italian Army."

Libby poured herself ice water from a pitcher. "That's absurd. We're not going to fight for Mussolini as well as carry cargo for him, are we?"

"No. Just run errands with the Union Jack proudly flying."

"I see. What does Edward think?"

"Well, the old Edward who marched with the fascists is long gone. The new Edward, like most people who turn away from something they fervently embraced, takes every opportunity to rant and rave against what he left behind. Our government's support of Mussolini is nothing short of treason in his mind. He believes the Italians will certainly side with Germany against us should war come. He's been reprimanded quite a few times for speaking out. He fancies he's still in Parliament with the freedom to debate in whatever manner he sees fit. But he's on a ship of war flying the Royal Ensign, and there's a difference."

"Why can't the League of Nations sort this out? What are they good for?"

"The short answer to that is, not much. They haven't done anything for China even though Japan's still invading their country and attacking Shanghai. They won't lift a finger to help Ethiopia either. Well, how can they? Britain's already made its loyalties clear, France is looking the other way too, and the United States won't even join the League." He watched a robin drop from branch to branch of a nearby tree. "I can't help thinking we'll all regret the actions we're taking now."

"No gloom. The possibility of your weighing anchor next week is enough of a raincloud for now."

"Or sooner, love. It could be sooner."

"I don't want to hear that either, Terrence Fordyce. Can we talk about something that has absolutely nothing to do with the navy or Mussolini or your traveling thousands of miles away from me?"

"Right. Golf. Fancy a game of golf? Loser buys fish and chips at Cuttlefish Mary's."

Libby perked up. "Golf? Fish and chips? With malt vinegar?"

"Of course malt vinegar. D'you think I would ruin your chips with ketchup like the Yanks do?"

She was on her feet. "There's nothing better. Golf and chips. You're a tonic. I'll get my clubs and may the best man win."

"That's the spirit, my girl."

The navy rang Terry up at four the next morning. Less than forty-eight hours later the *Hood* was on its way to the Mediterranean and Gibraltar.

A little over a month after it sailed, the Italian Army invaded Ethiopia on October third. The fighting raged on through the fall.

Kenya was on the southern border of Ethiopia. By the end of November all mail from Ben and Victoria had ceased.

March, 1936
RAF Martlesham Heath, Suffolk

"Right. You have a go, Danforth."

"What did you think of it, Captain Harrington?"

"I don't know what I think of it. You take her up and tell me what I should think of it after you've landed."

Kipp grinned. "Very good, sir." He jumped up onto the wing and slid into the cockpit of the aircraft. "What does Sammy say?"

"'The aircraft is simple and easy to fly and has no apparent vices.' He claims it responds very well. So now we'll let the old man give her the once over."

"Not that old, sir. Still in my thirties, and my eyes are like a hawk's."

"I've read your medical report, laddie. I still think you'd love to be climbing into a Sopwith Camel rather than this Hurricane."

"Is that what they call it?"

"That's what Hawker Aviation calls it. The Air Ministry hasn't approved the name or the plane yet." He patted the fabric-covered wing with his hand. "Tell us what you think."

"Will do, sir."

"What're your thoughts on the new king?"

"The Prince of Wales?" asked Kipp.

"Edward the Eighth now, laddie," replied Harrington.

"He's capable enough, isn't he?"

"He doesn't act much like a king, if you ask me. No respect for the way things have been done for centuries. But our dear King George has passed on, and there's nothing for it but Edward the Eighth now."

"He flies a plane, sir, that's something."

"Yes, he flies a plane. But a king needs to do more than sit in a cockpit." Harrington put his hands in the pants pockets of his RAF uniform. "Did you hear the news this morning? The Germans have reoccupied the Rhineland."

"What? But that violates the Treaty of Versailles, doesn't it?"

"Herr Hitler doesn't give a fig for the Treaty of Versailles or the Treaty of Locarno. The old war is long in the past. Time for a new Germany and a new Europe. Oh, he claims it's a move against being trapped by the French and the Soviet Union. They made a pact together last year, you see."

"What does the prime minister have to say, sir?"

"Not much, Danforth, not much. But what with the new planes and the new ships coming out of the Third Reich, it's easy enough to see the writing on the wall now that we have German soldiers on the French border again." Harrington ran his hand over the wing of the Hurricane. "Whatever happened to that brother-in-law of yours, the chap who won the Victoria Cross? Went into missionary work, didn't he? Africa?"

"That's right."

"How's he getting on? Marvelous that he got himself up flying again after that crash that took both his legs."

"He's…well, he's…" Kipp stopped putting his leather flying helmet over his head. "We've not heard from him or his family in four months, sir. Not since the start of the war in Ethiopia."

"What? British officials in the region don't know anything?"

"The family's far back in the bush. Officials claim they can't get any clear information on their whereabouts."

"Your father must have some leverage as an MP. He's always backed Stanley Baldwin, hasn't he? Now that Baldwin's in as prime minister, surely there's a way through the jungle?"

"Dad's certainly on top of it, Captain. A bit exasperated, but he'll give Westminster no rest until he has some answers."

"Good show. Let me know, will you? I have no doubt but we'll be needing men with his fighting spirit a few years from now."

Kipp buckled his leather helmet. "Will they let him in without legs?"

"If he can still fly rings around the moon and he's fit from the knees up."

"Are you sure?"

"My plan," Harrington almost whispered, "is to get him in here testing planes alongside you and the other blokes. Supermarine Aviation Works will have a fighter for us in a few months and I'd like him in on that. If he proves himself capable as test pilot, the RAF will clear him for combat flights with the stroke of a pen."

"Combat flights? Aren't we getting ahead of ourselves?"

"Ahead of ourselves? Do you honestly think so, lad?" He slapped the fuselage of the plane twice. "Away you go."

The engine roared, and the Hurricane made its way down the runway and lifted smoothly into the gray sky. Kipp immediately put it into a steep climb and was happy with its response to the stick. He barrel rolled it a few times, brought it out straight and level, and pushed its speed as far as he dared. Next he flung it into a dive, buzzing the huts and hangars and tower, and promptly put it into another climb, another dive, and three spins. He opened up the throttle once more and screamed over the airfield and village. He stayed up half an hour.

"You think my hair's not regulation length, is that it, Danforth?" snapped Harrington once Kipp had brought the Hurricane down and slid back the canopy. "You felt the need to trim it back with the prop when you did your little flypast?"

"Speaking of the prop, sir, this is a brilliant plane—I'll take it over the Sopwith Camel any day—but we must do something about the prop and blades."

"What's wrong with them?"

Kipp jumped to the ground and went to the front of the plane, putting his hand on the wooden propeller. "Watts, isn't that what I read? Fixed-pitch."

"What of it?"

"It's fine in the air, superb at attack speeds, but it doesn't do the job at takeoff. Takes too long to get the plane airborne. You saw that yourself, didn't you?"

"Put it in your report," grumbled Harrington.

"She's really a beauty, sir, stable as a good biplane and fast as a comet.

But I'm sure we could get better dive speeds in a dogfight if we got rid of the fabric-covered wings and used all-metal wings instead."

"Is that what you think? Well, no one else has mentioned it."

"The added strength would make all the difference. Especially if we have to go up against something like the Messerschmitt."

"The Messerschmitt! Now who's getting ahead of himself?"

"They're not building them to fly mail, sir. They're rearming."

"I know they're rearming, Danforth!" snapped Harrington. "The whole world knows they're rearming! That's why you and I are standing out here in the middle of this runway in March weather!"

"Will we do anything about it, sir, besides try to play catch-up with our own fighter planes?"

"Of course we'll do something about it, Danforth. We'll all go to the Olympics in Berlin this August and cheer like mad for the British runners and swimmers."

"There is something else, sir."

"You were only up the once. I don't want an encyclopedia."

They began to walk toward the huts. "No, sir, and I'll want to take it up several more times, but it doesn't recover from a spin well. I'm really not sure why. The rudder's gone, you see. It's just not there when you call on it. I did three spins, and it was difficult to pull out of all three of them."

"Hmm. Type it up. I'll ask Sammy what he thinks the next time he takes her up." Harrington abruptly stopped walking. "Who the devil is that?"

A car had pulled up in front of one of the huts, and a woman driver had emerged.

"Why, that's—" Kipp began.

"She's stunning, absolutely stunning." Harrington smoothed down both sides of his moustache. "Do you think she's here to see me?"

Kipp smiled. "I'm sure she is, sir. Most likely to get a full report on your test pilot's activities. She's my wife, Caroline."

"Your wife! Why didn't you say so, man? I thought she was up in London!"

"She is. Or rather, she was. I honestly have no idea what she's doing here, sir. But I can't say I'm sorry."

Harrington barked out a harsh laugh. "I don't imagine you can. Neither can I."

"Caroline!" Kipp put his arms around her. "Why'd you drive all the way down here? I'll be up in London this weekend."

She kissed him on the cheek. "I couldn't wait, could I?"

"And they let you through the gate?"

"I did collect an RAF pass in London."

"This is Captain Harrington," he said, taking her by the hand.

"How do you do, Captain? Kipp tells me how much he enjoys working with you."

"Does he? Does he indeed? I'm glad to hear it." Harrington clapped Kipp on the shoulder. "Crack of dawn tomorrow. All the best."

"Thank you, sir." Kipp saluted and smiled at his wife. "What's going on?"

"I'm in love with you and I'm a messenger boy."

"I don't understand."

"Hop in and I'll explain."

Kipp climbed into the passenger seat of the small car, and Caroline drove back through the front gate with a wave at the sentries and continued along the road to the village.

"Do you know where that track off to the left goes?" she asked.

"Bushes and pastureland eventually."

She turned onto the track and drove until they couldn't be seen from the road and parked behind a tall hedge of gray winter leaves. Then she took Kipp in her arms and gave him a long kiss.

"I've missed you," she whispered.

"I feel the same way, love. But it would only have been another day or two."

"Well, I'm down for the weekend. Our brood is with their cousins, so I have you all to myself in beautiful Suffolk. I hope you have room in your flat for me."

"I'll sleep on the floor."

"No, you won't. If you're on the floor, I'm on the floor with you."

He laughed and tilted her chin up with his fingers. "You look younger and more beautiful every day. How do you do that?"

"Charmer. Good genes, I suppose."

"So are we supposed to be like a couple who've snuck off to the bushes so they can be alone?"

"Yes. Why not? But first." She produced an envelope from her coat.

"What's this?"

"It's from your father."

"Must I read it now?"

"I'd rather we get it out of the way, yes."

"My mind's on other things now." Kipp began to kiss her on the cheek and neck.

She closed her eyes. "Is it?"

"It was on aviation an hour ago, but now I can't even recall what I was flying. Do you?"

"A plane of some sort, wasn't it?"

"I'm not sure." He ran his hand through her thick blond hair and pulled her closer. "There. I had the name for a moment but it's gone."

"Oh, Kipp." She tried to squirm loose. "We must talk first."

"You started it."

"I started it?"

"You showed up looking so inviting."

"In this ratty old coat? With my hair all windblown?"

He kissed her ear and her hair. "You look perfect."

"I do not look perfect. I was in such a rush to get here. There was barely time to pack a few things."

"What was the rush? Was I the rush?"

"Oh, yes, you were the rush." She pushed him back with both hands. "They've found Ben and Victoria."

"What?" Kipp pulled back. "When? Are they all right?"

"Physically they're fine. Ben was forced down by an Italian fighter before Christmas. He was ferrying some medical supplies near the border with Ethiopia and took a burst of machine-gun fire. Crashed in the jungle. He had a hard time with no legs making it to a town where he could contact Vic. Some bigwigs from Westminster got involved and told him not to say anything. That Britain's official policy is not to offend Rome. Oh, it's all a big mess. They just started letting their mail go through a few weeks ago. Your father is furious. But no one in the family is allowed to go public about what happened to Ben. All hush-hush. So the mission is without a plane and there Ben sits with Victoria and the boys at his side."

Kipp hesitated, taking it all in. "He's not hurt."

"Banged up from the crash. Nothing serious."

"I can write him then."

"Yes, of course. But they'll jail you if you speak publicly about the incident with the Italian fighter."

"Dad wanted you to come down here and tell me this?"

"In person. No telegrams. No phone calls. No letters."

Kipp lifted up the envelope she'd given him. "What's this then?"

She shrugged. "There were a lot of things on his mind. Once I said I'd drive down here with the news about Ben he dashed it off."

"I should read it."

"Go ahead."

> My dear boy,
>
> With Caroline running to Martlesham Heath to give you the news about Ben and Victoria I thought it best to jot down some of my thoughts. First, let me say I pray for you daily and I thank God you are where you are. German rearmament is surging ahead at a frenetic pace, and no one is in a position to put a halt to it, so you must help rebuild our air force. Our government is playing a fool's game by favoring Italy in the Ethiopian War, believing Rome will side with us against any aggression from Herr Hitler. Nonsense. Fascists will flock with fascists. Which brings me to the trouble in Spain.
>
> You must keep this very close to your chest. I only put it in writing because Caroline is bringing this letter to you. We anticipate an uprising of Spanish fascist elements against the Socialist government of that country. My sources are fairly certain Britain will side with the fascists. We want untroubled access to Spanish ports and Gibraltar and feel we will get them from the fascists more so than the Socialists or Communists. As you know, Terry is down there with the *Hood* and the Mediterranean Fleet right now, keeping an eye out for Italy's interests, though the fight is very one-sided and Ethiopia must surrender shortly. The *Hood* will most certainly not be recalled to English waters if the threat remains of conflict in Madrid and Barcelona. Your brother Edward is down there as well, you remember, HMS *Rodney* and the Home Fleet was dispatched to Gibraltar weeks ago.

I am not at all happy with the decision to continue siding with fascist elements. I have reliable information the Germans are going to begin construction on two more battleships this year. Terry and Edward have heard about this too, and Edward swears the ships will be mammoths. Although my sense is the German nation is more concerned with those they consider their natural enemies, like the French, I'm convinced they won't hesitate to turn the guns of their ships on us just as they did in the last war. Ah, but so many in our government want to play at being clams and have buried themselves deep in the sand of illusion. Germany will go away if we just dig deep enough and keep the other European fascists in the sand with us. It will not work. Churchill warns us about all of this in Parliament every opportunity he gets and is ridiculed for his pains.

My jottings have turned into a speech. I will close. All this to say please pray for Britain in her folly and keep your hand at the task God has appointed you to. Your work is so very much needed and appreciated, my son.

Much love,

Your father

Kipp leaned back against the car seat and closed his eyes.

"May I read it?" asked Caroline.

He handed her the letter, eyes still shut. "By all means. It's very political."

When she was done, she said, "How do you feel about all that? Do you think he's exaggerating?"

"Not at all. The feeling in the RAF is that Churchill is right and war will come if we don't trim Herr Hitler's moustache. The trouble is no one has the razor to do it. Certainly not us. We're still testing planes and the Nazis are building them. If it came to a fight this year we'd throw up Tiger Moths and other biplanes and they'd throw up modern fighters and twin-engine bombers and shoot us out of the sky."

"You frighten me with that sort of talk, Kipp. I don't want another war. The first was jolly well bad enough. The boys talk about being pilots like their father. I don't want them being pilots like their father. Not with shadows falling over Europe again. I want them to be bank clerks or Cambridge professors or bakers of bread."

"Bakers of bread?"

"I don't care. Anything but pilots for the Germans or Italians or Spanish to shoot down."

He opened his eyes and smiled over at her. "Just boys' games, love."

"They won't be boys much longer."

"The whole world is going to Berlin to have a party. For all you know that will defuse everything. Germany will be on her best behavior and might just decide to stay that way."

"Now you sound like one of the clams."

He reached for her but she drew away.

"Caroline, what—?"

"There's something else you need to hear."

"And what is that? The sky is falling?"

"Lord Tanner came by twice this week."

Kipp sat upright. "Tanner?"

"He had that Lady Kate with him each time. Insisted on seeing the boys. Chatted with them both and gave them each ten pounds on his last visit."

Anger moved across Kipp's face in dark lines and edges. "What else?"

"He drew me aside when Matthew and Charles were outside saying goodbye to Kate. Said he'd have Charles back. You or I wouldn't stand in his way."

"We'll stand in his way all right."

"Worst of all he invited the boys to the Olympics. Told them he had excellent seats for the equestrian events and the sprints. That he personally knew the stunt flier who would be performing at the games and might be able to get them in the cockpit."

Kipp smacked the dashboard with his fist. "He's filth. He's always been filth."

"The boys are very keen on going, Kipp. They talk about nothing else. We even had a row when I told them it was out of the question."

"They'll have to get used to the idea. No one in our family sets foot in Nazi Germany."

Caroline took a handkerchief out of her coat and dabbed at her eyes several times. "Your father and mother are going. They invited Charles and Matthew without knowing a thing about Lord Tanner's offer. So it's just made things worse."

"Father and Mother? Why?"

"A British Olympic team is going, naturally. Prime Minister Baldwin asked a number of MPs to attend the Berlin Games as a goodwill gesture. And to show the government's support for our athletes."

"Just what we need. Next thing you know little Cecilia will be squawking about going with her brothers."

"Little Cecilia will be all of seven this October and thinks she's the Queen of the Nile. She's already asked her grandparents to take her and they've said yes."

"For heaven's sake."

"I really don't need you to work yourself up, Kipp. I'm worked up enough as it is. I need my cool, calm, test pilot, my handsome RAF flier, my sweet and kind golden boy. Can you be that for me?"

"Caroline, Lord Tanner Buchanan is an absolute villain."

"And you're an absolute hero. I need my hero right now. I need him to hold me and kiss me and tell me everything is going to sort itself out. I need him to pray with me. All right, Kipp?"

Kipp wrestled with his thoughts, the darkness in his eyes coming and going and then coming again. Finally he let out a lungful of air, his eyes cleared completely, and a full smile broke over his face.

"All right, love. We'll put it in God's hands. That's where it needs to go. Somehow all the pieces will fall into place."

Her eyes glimmered. "Thank you, Kipp. I've been feeling absolutely wretched since Tanner showed up at our door."

Kipp gathered her into his arms. "Shh. Shh. Let me pray. Then let me kiss you. Then let me take to you my flat. How does that sound? Does that sound like I've got everything lined up in a good and proper row?"

She leaned her head into his chest as tears darted down her cheeks. "Yes."

Dear Ben,

I just got the news, so I'm writing you a note to say how grateful to God I am you're all right and how sorry I am the whole thing happened at all. I'm not sure what your plans are now. I imagine you'll keep preaching and organizing the mission where you are, but it's tough you can't fly to the other churches you've started until the Methodists are able to get you another plane.

So I expect you're praying about what God's will is for your family as you sort out this mess. Let me throw something else into the pot. I know I shouldn't, but what are brothers-in-law good for if they're not a source of constant challenge and irritation? Here it is—might God not want you back in England, even for a while? I say this because the situation is getting a bit rough. The Germans have rearmed at a fast pace. We've let them do it, and now we're trying to rearm in order to defend ourselves. We need test pilots and flight instructors in the RAF, and they've made it pretty clear they wouldn't mind seeing you at Martlesham Heath. Your family could rest and regroup in London while you test aircraft that go well over three hundred miles per hour. What do you say, Ben Whitecross, VC? Give it a prayer and see what our Commanding Officer at seventy thousand feet plus has to say about it. Christian civilization needs you as much here as it does there in British East Africa.

Kipp

May, 1936
RAF Martlesham Heath, Suffolk

Harrington snapped the newspaper open. "Right, so with the war in Ethiopia well over, there weren't any obstacles to the return of Ben White-cross, VC, to his mother country, hm?"

"I expect him this morning, sir. He arrived in London two days ago with his wife and his two sons."

"Have you spoken with him?"

"No, sir. My wife rang me once they made it in."

"I expect he's having the physical assessment done by the RAF I requested. Filling out all the paperwork they want for a raw recruit. Though I'd hardly consider Ben Whitecross, VC, a raw recruit."

"No, sir."

"Well, we can't wait forever. Humphrey's typing up his report for the

Air Ministry. It's favorable. He wants an undercarriage position indicator, but other than that it's a thumbs up. I'd still like to hear from you and Whitecross though."

Kipp looked out the window at the aircraft crouched on the ground as if it were about to leap into the air on its own. "Yes, sir."

Harrington glanced up from his reading. "You fancy the plane, Danforth. I don't see why you can't just hop in and give it a go."

"I promised Ben he'd get first crack at it. He's had a disappointing year. This is something he's been looking forward to. Almost three hundred and fifty miles per hour."

"He might push it past that—you never know." Harrington slapped the newspaper with the back of his hand. "What do you think of this Mussolini? They reckon he had close to six hundred aircraft and almost eight hundred tanks while the Ethiopians had…what, two or three planes and two or three tanks? Yet it took Il Duce over half a year to subdue those tribesmen. Incredible, eh? I think we backed the wrong horse."

"I think we're backing all the wrong horses, sir."

"Hm? What do you mean by that, Danforth?"

"I believe that's him, sir." Kipp practically ran out the door. "Just pulling up. He's brought the whole brood."

Ben came out from behind the wheel of his car in a blue RAF uniform. Kipp laughed and shook his hand and slapped him on the back.

"You're dark as Birmingham coal, Ben."

"That's Africa for you. You're looking well."

"Of course I'm looking well. I'm flying fighter planes again." Kipp wrapped his arms around his sister. "Vic! No woman ever looked so stunning in short hair!"

She hugged him back. "Thank you, dear gallant brother who never ages. We had a wonderful visit with your wife and children before dashing down here."

"Ramsay! Darker than his father."

Ramsay shook Kipp's hand and grinned. "Hullo, uncle. How are you getting on?"

"Taller than his father too. I'm excellent, Ramsay. Sorry to pull you out of Kenya."

"I hope to go back once I've got my pilot's license and some Bible training."

"Do you like it there, Ram?"

"I do, Uncle Kipp."

"The mountains, the jungles, the lions?"

"Yes, sir."

"So what are you now? Fifteen? Sixteen?"

"Fourteen."

"Fourteen! What are you feeding them, Vic?"

She smiled. "Bananas and wildebeest milk."

Kipp thrust his hand at Timothy. "Hullo, Tim. Are you on your way back to Africa as well?"

Tim's black hair and blue eyes flashed along with his smile. "I don't mind being here, Uncle Kipp. I like seeing the castles and beaches. We hardly ever get to swim in Kenya."

"Sure we do," argued Ramsay.

"We never swim in the sea."

"It's too far away. We went to the ocean once."

"Once."

"It was beautiful. White sand. You don't remember. You were too young. Practically a baby."

Tim's eyes sparked. "I wasn't a baby."

"You're only eleven now. How old could you have been?"

"I wasn't a baby!"

"Timothy!" snapped Victoria. "Ramsay! Stop it, both of you! Remember where you are and who you are!"

"Vic," Kipp spoke up, "Ben, Captain Harrington is just here."

Harrington had stepped out of the hut. Ben came to attention and saluted. Harrington returned the salute.

"You look smart in your uniform, Whitecross," said Harrington. "How was your trip home?"

"Very good, sir."

"I understand you had a bit of a disagreement with an Italian fighter pilot."

"That's right, sir. Still looking for him, sir."

"Hm. Well, you won't find him here." Harrington turned to Victoria. "How do you do, Lady Victoria? I trust I find you well?"

"Thank you, sir, quite well."

"No trouble at the gate?"

"No, sir. They seemed to be expecting that my husband would be accompanied by his wife and children."

"I told the guards there was a good chance of that. They were instructed to treat you with kid gloves."

"Oh, they certainly did that, Captain."

"Good show." Harrington turned to Ben. "They rang me up and asked me to evaluate your flying skills. Are you ready to take Reginald Mitchell's latest design for a hop?"

"The fellow who built the fast flying boats? I am, sir."

They all looked at the aircraft on the runway.

"What do you think, lads?" It was the first time Harrington had acknowledged the two boys' presence. "Fancy a go with it?"

"Oh, yes, sir," piped Tim.

"I would love that, sir," responded Ramsay.

"Stay keen. Stay sharp. Watch out for one another. The day will come sooner than you think." Harrington continued to stare at the plane. "They were going to call it the Shrew. Then a chap hit on the idea of naming it after one of his children. A wild one, I expect." He glanced at Ramsay and Tim. "Spitfire."

Kipp peeled off his fleece-lined leather flight jacket. "Here you go, Ben. You didn't need an Irvin in Africa but you will here."

"Thanks."

"There's a scarf in the pocket."

Ben tugged on the heavy jacket. "White silk?"

"Navy with polka dots."

"What?"

"The latest thing. You've been in the jungle too long."

Ben pulled out the scarf. "Maybe I should go back to the jungle."

"Nothing wrong with it. Sturdy English manufacture. It'll save your neck all right."

"Maybe I should risk the skin rash."

"Oh, nonsense." Victoria took the long scarf and wound it about Ben's throat. "You look smashing."

Harrington flicked his chin at the Spitfire. "Get her up."

Ben made his way in the stiff-legged gait his artificial legs forced on him. He got up on the wing and swung first one leg and then the other into the cockpit. After a few minutes he began to move the plane along the airstrip. Then he opened up the throttle, the engine howled, the fighter raced over the ground, and Ben was in the air.

"Dad tells me you're going to Berlin with him and Mum," Victoria said as she stood by her brother and watched the Spitfire climb.

Kipp's face tightened. "That's right."

"Why the long face?"

"Our old friend Buchanan is going to meet up with us there."

"Lord Tanner? He isn't!"

"Oh, he is. He's dropped by with his lady friend a number of times. Offered the boys tickets to the sprints. Then Dad up and wanted the lot of us to accompany him and Mum to the Olympics. We said no, but Charles and Matt gave us no peace until we relented."

"Didn't you tell Dad about Tanner?"

"Of course I did. He quoted the Sermon on the Mount and said it was time to forgive Buchanan and move on."

"I see. So you're stuck. Dad's asked our family along as well, you know, so at least you'll have Ben. You won't have to take Tanner on alone."

Kipp's eyes hardened. "I've taken him on alone before and I'll do it again if I have to. But Ben's welcome to whatever's left."

The Spitfire roared in so low and so loud that even Kipp ducked his head a bit and clapped a hand over one of his ears.

"You both must drink from the same pot of tea!" roared Harrington.

"Have you told Charles who his father is?" asked Victoria, putting her mouth close to her brother's ear as the scream of the Spitfire engine obliterated all other sounds.

"Caroline did years ago when she and Buchanan talked about getting married. Charles hasn't forgotten. He brought it up during one of the fights about going to Berlin. 'He's my father…you're not my father…I have a right to go wherever my real father goes.' Stalks around the house and brags about meeting up with his dad in Berlin and being introduced to Hitler and the Nazi stunt pilot at the Games. That sort of rubbish."

"Oh, Kipp, I'm so sorry. How miserable that must be. One can only hope Charles will see Lord Tanner for who he truly is and be repulsed."

"I do hope that. But Buchanan will be on his best behavior with such a large audience."

They watched Ben put the Spitfire into a spin.

"Who is the Nazi stunt pilot?" asked Victoria.

"Didn't I tell you? The trip to Berlin gets better all the time, dear sister. The pilot's our nemesis from the Great War, Wolfgang von Zeltner."

"You're joking."

"No, I'm not. It's shaping up to be quite the show at the Eleventh Olympiad, on the track and off. I just don't know who's going to win all the medals, us or them."

The Spitfire went into a steep dive, finally leveled out, and blasted over their heads again.

August, 1936
XI Olympiad, Berlin Olympic Stadium

"Well done!" cried Ben Whitecross as the American runner Jesse Owens ascended to the top of the podium. "That makes three gold medals. Herr Hitler will have to tear down all his swastikas now."

Kipp stood and applauded beside him. "He won't tear down anything. He'll just refuse to shake the hand of a black man."

"He isn't shaking anyone's hand anymore. Your father was telling me the Olympic Committee warned Hitler he had to shake the hands of all the medalists, not just German ones. He refused, and now he doesn't shake anyone's hand. After all, you never know which athlete is going to be a Jew."

Kipp looked down the row to see Lord Tanner and Charles still in their seats. Matthew was up and clapping along with his cousins Ramsay and Tim and Owen and Colm. He saw his father frown at Lord Tanner and Charles, but the pair ignored everyone.

Caroline glanced at Charles, closed her eyes, and then made up her mind to clap even louder and even waved a handkerchief as blue as her eyes.

"I wish God would take that man out of my life forever," she said to Kipp in a low voice. "He is an absolute pestilence. I'm certain he will convince Charles to move in with him."

"He can't force the issue without going to the courts," replied Kipp. "And a son born out of wedlock would be a scandal laid against his name."

"And ours."

"I'm sure if he could devise a plan of laying it all at our door he would do it, but he can't. So nothing will happen."

"He can turn Charles against us."

"I'm sure that's his intention."

"How will we be able to stop that?"

"Arguing with Charles won't help the matter. He'll just continue to dig in his heels. We shall have to take the route the Good Book advises. 'If thine enemy be hungry, give him bread to eat; and if he be thirsty, give him water to drink: for thou shalt heap coals of fire upon his head, and the LORD shall reward thee.'"

Caroline pouted. "I am not in the mood to be loving toward Tanner Buchanan. Or toward Charles Danforth right now for that matter."

"'A soft answer turneth away wrath: but grievous words stir up anger.'"

"Listen to you," snapped Caroline, sitting down as the applause and cheering came to an end. "Are you to rival Jeremy as the family vicar?"

"Somebody has to say it. Otherwise it will be pistols at dawn in a day or two, love."

Caroline's face was set in sharp, dark lines. "I wish it *would* be pistols at dawn and that you'd put a silver bullet right through his wicked heart."

Hotel suite, Berlin

"William!" Lady Preston paused before sipping from her cup of tea. "You must stop this pacing. It's driving me to distraction. Robbie has written to say he and Shannon and Patricia are perfectly all right."

Lord Preston held up a folded newspaper and covered his left eye with his hand. "I don't like what I'm reading here, Elizabeth. Another uprising in Jerusalem, the brutality of the civil war in Spain…"

"William, do calm yourself. I wish you'd never put your hands on an English language paper. What is wrong with your eye?"

"There's nothing wrong with my eye. I got a bit of dust in it at the stadium. Our navy is evacuating British tourists from Madrid and coastal resorts in Spain. Not just tourists of course but British citizens working in Spain as well. That's something, at least. The rest of the time I feel the navy is aiding and abetting Franco and the fascists in Spain, Elizabeth. I do wish our government would stop appeasing the fascist element every time they meet up with it."

"Keep on that line and soon enough they will have you lumped in with poor Winston. If that happens you might as well both take up residence on some desert island for all the good you'll do in Parliament. No one listens to Winston and soon no one will listen to you."

"They jolly well should start listening to Winston. The Nazis will be up to all sorts of mischief once the Olympics are over. They're already filling the skies with their planes and the sea with their ships."

Lady Preston poured fresh tea into her cup. "If your line of reasoning is correct, we'll curry favor with Hitler just as we have with Mussolini and Franco. So what's the point of wagging your finger at Prime Minister Baldwin? He'll simply turn his back on you."

"My heavens, we already are currying favor with Herr Hitler. Why, we even let some of their *Luftwaffe* chaps poke around our aircraft factories back home. And I'm certain the *Reichstag* is not backing the Jews when it comes to Palestine, yet we say nothing to them about it."

She leaned back in her seat. "You're getting much too excited, William. The grandchildren are having a marvelous time here. Don't spoil it for them."

Lord Preston continued to read the newspaper, his hand still over his eye. "Hm? Spoil it for them? Charles doesn't look too badly off. The next thing you know he'll be trying to grow some hair on his upper lip."

Lady Preston made a face. "Don't talk rot. It's not as bad as all of that. Our family is having a splendid visit to Berlin. It's not like it was five or six years ago. Herr Hitler got rid of those nasty Brownshirts, didn't he? So I say bravo for him and his Third Reich."

Just down the hall in another set of rooms, Charles was laughing and telling Kipp and Caroline and Matthew about meeting Hermann Goering, Wolfgang von Zeltner, and other Nazi celebrities.

"Herr Goering was an ace during the war and he introduced me to von Zeltner, who was also an ace, and Ernst Udet, who shot down almost as many planes as Richthofen." Charles tugged an empty pack of cigarettes out of his pocket. "They autographed this for me."

"Kipp was also an ace in the war," Caroline said quietly. "For the British side."

"They didn't know him, but they knew Uncle Benjamin. And sides don't matter. They said that."

Kipp looked up at him from his chair. "So did you go up with one of them?"

"I went up with von Zeltner in his stunt plane and then I flew with Herr Udet in his. Both were absolutely brilliant."

"They both took you up?" asked Kipp, raising his eyebrows.

"Oh, they treat Dad like a prince or something. 'Lord Tanner' this and 'Lord Tanner' that. I'm going to meet Herr Hitler this evening."

"The family is dining together this evening," Caroline reminded him. "Your grandmother and grandfather are taking everyone to a fine restaurant on the river."

Charles shook his head. "I'll have to bow out, I'm afraid. There will be plenty of opportunities to dine with the family in the future but few to dine with Adolf Hitler. Unless I attend school here in the fall."

"Attend school here?" Caroline's eyes flared. "What on earth are you talking about?"

"My father—he has so many connections."

"Your *father* is my husband, Kipp Danforth. He has been the only father you've known. And no one has discussed you taking a year's schooling in Berlin."

"I could even finish here. And then enroll at a German university."

"It's out of the question, Charles."

"If I want to, mother, you must let me. It's true I love you very much. But there comes a time when a man is called upon to be a man."

"Who has been filling your head with such nonsense? You're just fifteen."

"I'm old enough to know what I want."

"You don't have the language skills to attend school in Berlin."

"Father would get me a tutor."

Caroline's face darkened. "What have you two been doing? Hatching schemes behind my back?"

"We only began to discuss this today and yesterday."

"I won't permit it."

Charles's eyes began to burn. "I'll do as I wish. I'm not a child."

Caroline turned on Kipp. "Don't you have anything to say? He's your son as well as mine."

Kipp gazed at Charles until the young man glanced away.

"Apparently not." Kipp nodded with his chin. "What's that sticking out of your pocket, Charles?"

"What?" Charles looked down. "It's nothing. A gift from Herr Goering. You wouldn't understand."

"It looks like one of those armbands."

"Oh, Charles," groaned Caroline. "Not a Nazi armband."

His face flamed. "I knew you wouldn't understand. Don't worry. I won't wear it around the house. It's a keepsake. Nothing more." He stuffed it farther into his pocket.

"The Hitler Youth are marching tonight," said Kipp. "Do you plan to join them?"

Charles glared but did not reply.

That evening Lord Preston kept an appointment with Baron von Isenburg at a sidewalk table in front of the hotel. The baron was wearing his black SS uniform.

"Are you sure you want to meet out in the open like this?" asked Lord Preston, taking a chair.

"It's the best way, believe me," responded the baron. "They expect to see us together. The intention is I recruit you as a good friend of the Third Reich, one who will look to our interests in the British Parliament. If we were to meet in secret, the Gestapo would be suspicious."

"So what game are you playing now?"

"The same game I was playing before. Pretending to be a Nazi. Pretending to be SS. All the while looking for an opportunity to overthrow this regime."

"You had me fooled. You had all of us fooled."

"I'm sorry to have stung so many with my actions. But everyone had to be convinced or it wouldn't have worked."

"What you're doing is high treason."

"As high as it gets."

A waiter came to their table.

"Coffee," said the baron. "William?"

"Yes, that would be fine. And a sweet roll, please."

The baron folded his hands on the tabletop. "When next you write to Albrecht, you must advise him to speak with less venom about the Third

Reich. He can be critical but not inflammatory. If he does not tone it down you can be sure Berlin will begin to pressure Swiss authorities."

"To do what?"

"Who knows? Throw him in jail. Deport him."

"Switzerland has always prided itself on its democracy and neutrality."

"Of course. But they see what is developing on their doorstep even if the rest of the world ignores it—a war machine. Who knows? Despite the estimate of a million casualties, Herr Hitler may decide an invasion of Swiss territory is worth the risk. Certainly some officials in Bern will be thinking along those lines. So if Berlin complains about Hartmann's books and public speaking and rattles its saber a bit, Albrecht will be asked and then ordered to cancel all speaking engagements and book publications. They will muzzle him."

Lord Preston frowned. "If he disobeys—"

"As I said, if he disobeys they'll throw him in prison. Or out of the country."

"Out of the country isn't so bad, is it? He can bring his family to England."

"So long as war hasn't broken out in Europe. If it has, the journey to England will be hazardous. Once German troops are out in force, the SS will be with them. Should Albrecht be spotted he will be arrested and returned to Germany for trial."

"In which case they will hang him."

"If he is lucky."

The coffee arrived and a sweet roll for Lord Preston.

"I will certainly write him." Lord Preston poured cream into his coffee. "I shall let him know what's afoot. Whether I'll have any success in persuading him to quiet down, well, it's doubtful." He leaned back and drank from his cup as traffic whizzed past. "Speaking of quieting things down, what has become of your daughter?"

The baron shrugged. "Eva is a daughter in name only. She despises me for locking her up in that castle and discrediting everything she tells others about my activities. She screams that I have put the Jews ahead of her, that vermin matter more to me than my own child." He looked at his cup of coffee but didn't drink it. "Of course she is partly right. We still get Jews out of the country who are at risk. We still have safe houses. But she matters as much to me as they do. It's just that I know how to help them. But her....I don't know how to help."

Blaring trumpets and loud drums momentarily halted their conversation. A column of young men, four abreast, in white shirts and shorts, swastika armbands on their sleeves, were marching along a street beside the hotel. The baron turned in his seat to watch, and Lord Preston craned his neck. There was no singing or chanting. They marched with a force and a strength, it seemed to Lord Preston, that needed no other voice than the harsh stamping of their feet.

"William." The baron pointed. "It's strange. That tall fellow there looks like one of your grandsons."

At one in the morning the table was still there, as well as the chairs. Nothing had been stacked, and waiters continued to serve the men and women who drank and smoked by candlelight on the sidewalk in front of the hotel. Cars moved past, headlights slicing at the night.

Kipp came through the front doors and sat at the table. Five minutes later a man with a walking stick made his way along the sidewalk and joined him.

"Another gold medal for Owens today," the man said by way of opening the conversation. "Astonishing."

"Do you mean astonishing, Buchanan, or do you mean astonishing for a black man?"

Buchanan laughed. "Well, he wouldn't have pulled it off but for our Nazi athlete Luz Long giving him advice about the long jump, would he?"

"Our athlete?"

A waiter came and lit the candle at their table. Both ordered coffee. Buchanan opened a silver cigarette case and offered it to Kipp, who shook his head. Buchanan took a cigarette, placed it between his lips, and lit it with a silver lighter with an eagle engraved on its side.

"The British Union of Fascists failed to put anyone in Parliament in last year's election," Buchanan said. "Sir Oswald has big plans for thirty-six and thirty-seven. Good things are happening even across the sea in Canada and America. But I don't think much will come of any of it if Germany doesn't remain strong. Should Germany continue to go from strength to strength, other nations will adopt fascist ways in due course.

Especially with the good things happening under Mussolini's leadership in Italy and Franco's in Spain. All this to say I have decided to relocate. I've been offered a post with Goebbels, the Minister of Propaganda. I shall be making radio broadcasts starting in October."

"You're going to live in Berlin?"

"That's right."

"And that Lady Kate of yours?"

Buchanan drew in on his cigarette. "She likes Berlin."

"She didn't accompany you here."

"She is visiting family in America."

The waiter set down their coffees as well as a bowl of sugar and a small pitcher of cream. Buchanan put three teaspoons of sugar into his cup and stirred, the spoon making a clicking sound. Kipp brought his coffee toward him but did nothing with it.

"Look here, Lord Tanner," Kipp blurted. "You can live on the moon with your marching bands and swastikas for all I care. But I want my son back in England where he belongs."

Buchanan drank, set down his coffee, and drew in on his cigarette till the tip was bright red. "Your son? I'm his father, Danforth. You've been no more than a wet nurse all these years. I'm grateful, of course, but now he and I have a lot of catching up to do. He will be enrolled in a fine school in Berlin this fall and go on to Humboldt University a few years after that."

"Don't do this."

"Don't do what? Be Charles's father? I've been denied that role long enough. You can take it up with the courts here in Berlin if you wish. But I don't think you will get far. They're Nazi courts, after all, and I am an aide to Joseph Goebbels while you…well, you are no more than an Englishman with decidedly anti-fascist tendencies."

"The British courts—"

"Come, Danforth, do you seriously think Britain will have a row with Germany over a custody case? Even if it is Lord Preston's grandson? And do you really want the scandal between your wife and myself to run the length and breadth of Britain?"

"I didn't meet with you to mix it up and come to blows. I'm here to ask you to stop what you're doing and consider Caroline's feelings—and Charles's future."

"It's time I consider my own feelings, Danforth. And really, it's up to Charles, isn't it? Ask him yourself. 'Charles, do you want to be in England with your mother or in Berlin with your father?' After tonight's march along the boulevard and the opportunity to meet Adolf Hitler, I believe I can predict what his response will be."

With that, Buchanan stood and tossed a few Deutschmarks on the table. "That should cover it."

"Remember that I met you here, Lord Tanner," said Kipp. "Remember that I tried to reason with you."

"What are you going to do, Danforth? Shoot me in the back as I walk away? Not very sporting of you."

"There won't be any shooting in the back. I'll leave that up to your Gestapo and SS. But this doesn't end here at a sidewalk café in Berlin, Lord Tanner. Bear that in mind."

Buchanan leaned on his silver-headed cane. "There has always been enmity between my house and yours. But one by one I shall overcome you all. Gaining my son back is a sweet victory. Putting a swastika on his arm and rubbing your nose in it is sweeter still. But drawing Caroline back to my side will be the sweetest triumph of all."

"Caroline! She'll never return to you!"

"Oh, she will, Danforth, she will. You don't know how weak Caroline Scarborough is, but I do. If I tell her she can be with her son again, and never be separated from him, she'll do anything I ask. Live with me, eat with me, attend Nazi galas as my escort. That will indeed be the sweetest revenge of all."

He took a drag on his cigarette, flicked it on the ground at Kipp's feet, and walked away.

October, 1936
Terry and Libby's house, HMS Picadilly, Plymouth and Devonport

"Look, we have another seven days before the *Hood* heads back to the Mediterranean, love—"

"Shh." Libby put her fingers to Terry's lips as they lay together on their bed in the dark. "Don't use that word 'Mediterranean' again. I've come to loathe it."

"The water is beautiful. Often enough it's the color of your eyes."

"Then I shall change the color of my eyes. All that horrid sea does is take you away from me. The winter exercises were bad enough. But now it's war after war. First the Italians going after those poor Ethiopians. Then Franco and his fascists going after the Spanish people who don't think like him. And whose side are we always on, Terry? The side of the bullies."

"We never fired our guns in support of the Italians, and we won't fire them in support of Franco and the Nationalists either. All we want is Gibraltar left unmolested and to have access to the ports on the Spanish coast. We believe the Nationalists can guarantee that and the Republicans can't. It's no more mysterious than that."

"Oh, our sympathies aren't mysterious at all, Terry. How the world must wonder. Whose feet shall we kiss next? Herr Hitler's? The emperor of Japan's?"

"You are wrought up, aren't you?"

"I have every right to be. You and your 'heart of oak' and 'jolly tars' rot. I wish you were a carpenter in Ipswich."

"No, you don't."

"Yes, I do. Imagine seeing one another all year round. But what do we have instead? No Christmas together again. And Jane growing up so fast, her second year at Oxford—"

"The three of us had a splendid summer."

"We always have splendid summers. And like all English summers they are soon spent."

Terry leaned his head back against his pillow and groaned. "I don't know how to please you, love."

"Well, I do. When I'm cross like this I need to be held much more tightly. You must also accept the fact that the more arguments you muster, the more I shall muster until you are awash in them, so it's best to leave off early. And I don't want to talk, I don't want to kiss, I don't want to do anything except lie in your arms and listen to your heart beating."

"Right. I can do that."

"Then do it. And you can make silly promises too. Even if I'm well aware that it's not in your power to keep them. Daft, I know, but it works."

"I guess I'm not sure what sort of promises you mean."

"Well, is there any chance you might make First Sea Lord one day and be permanently based in England?"

"First Sea Lord! Libby, that is as far beyond me as the heavens are above the earth."

"But it's feasible, isn't it? It's remotely possible?"

"I suppose it is."

"Promise you'll try to make First Sea Lord."

"Libby," Terry protested.

She pinched him. "Promise me."

"Right. I promise you."

"You always say the *Hood* is badly in need of a touch-up."

"Touch-up? She needs a rebuild! All these new German warships are quite beyond her in speed and armor plating. Worst of all, their guns can point faster and hit far more accurately. Naval gunnery is developing at a rapid pace and—"

"Excellent. So promise me you'll come back for a rebuild. A long rebuild."

"Certainly we need it."

"Come on. Don't be so slow to catch on. Tell me what I want to hear."

"*Hood*'s coming in for a rebuild. The sooner the better. It'll take a year. Perhaps more."

"Wonderful." She placed her head on his chest and closed her eyes. "More tightly, please."

Terry tightened his arm around her back and shoulders.

"Very good, Commander. Now make more silly promises. Someday you'll take me down to that horrid spot with you and we'll be together all winter."

"I will do."

"Someday there won't be any more running about with the Mediterranean Fleet, and you'll be permanently stationed at a more suitable port like Portsmouth or Scapa Flow."

"This is likely to happen any day now, love."

"You'll be home for Christmas. Your ship will turn around like it did last year and come right back home again with a propeller problem."

"We do need an overhaul of the propulsion system."

"Now we're playing cricket. You'll not only be home for Christmas, but after the propeller is fixed up and you're off to that horrible puddle in the south, quick as a wink the war will be over, Franco will have lost, Spain will be a republic once again, and you'll be back in Portsmouth in April or May. Am I right?"

"Spot on as usual."

She smiled, her eyes still shut. "Now, you see? I'm content, very content." She kissed his chest. "And I love the steady, strong beating of your heart."

January–March, 1937

The winter rains swept over Britain and Europe.

King George V had died in January of 1936 and been succeeded by the Prince of Wales. But Edward VIII had not even lasted a year as the reigning monarch. Instead he chose marriage to an American woman named Wallis Simpson, twice divorced, over the English throne. His brother Albert, who became George VI immediately after the abdication by Edward VIII in early December, was the new king.

With Terry gone, Libby packed up what she needed and took Skitt and Montgomery along with her to their townhouse in London. This made it easier for Jane to get back and forth from Lady Margaret Hall at Oxford and have a visit. It also placed Libby in the same neighborhood as the rest of the family—Caroline, who kept house while Kipp tested improved models of the Hurricane and Spitfire in Suffolk; Victoria, who did as Caroline did with Ben testing fighter planes alongside Kipp; Charlotte, a sea widow like Libby, her husband Edward serving on HMS *Rodney* with the Home Fleet, which was once again at Gibraltar just like Terry and the *Hood*; and Emma, keeping an open door at the vicarage of St. Andrew's Cross, welcoming all with tea and biscuits on the table and with her husband, the Reverend Jeremy Sweet, at her side. And something new—Lord and Lady Preston purchased Kensington Gate as their London residence. It was on Kensington High Street, near Hyde Park, Buckingham Palace, and Westminster. It replaced a smaller townhouse that had been adequate only for Lord Preston.

The stately home, with a vast lawn surrounded by high stone walls, four floors, round turrets, and tall windows, allowed Lord Preston to be at home every night after Parliamentary sessions and permitted him and his wife to see a good deal more of their grandchildren than they did sequestered far away in Ashton Park. They brought Tavy along with them, and Mrs. Longstaff, and a half dozen other chambermaids and footmen, as well as the dogs. The Belgian shepherds were still called Wynken, Blynken, and Nod, though Lord Preston had considered changing their names back to Flanders, Charlemagne, and Poppy. Sir Arthur and Lady Grace, each well into their nineties, could not be budged from Ashton Park, and a number of servants remained behind to see to their needs. To Harrison and Lady Holly fell the rule of the Lancashire estate in Lord and Lady Preston's absence.

So, well before the gray rains of winter became the brighter rains of spring, the greater part of the Danforth family was situated in London at Camden Lock and at Kensington Gate.

April, 1936
The vicarage, St. Andrew's Cross

"Come in, Caroline, come in." Emma held open the door. "You look absolutely sodden."

"I thought I could make the short walk between our houses without an umbrella." Caroline half laughed. "Then came the deluge."

Emma helped her off with her coat. "I'll hang it up by the fire. It will be dry in no time."

"Thank you."

"Jeremy has tea for you in the parlor. I'll be along in a minute."

Jeremy rose as Caroline entered the room, smiling and taking one of her hands in both of his, his one hand the healthy hand, the other the wooden one. "Hullo, my dear, so good to see you."

"Cheers, Jeremy."

"Tea?"

"Yes, please."

He poured as she took a seat in an armchair. A peat fire flickered nearby and lent a smoky aroma to the parlor. Jeremy handed Caroline a cup and saucer and sat down with his own mug of tea. He was wearing a cardigan sweater over his black shirt, but his clerical collar was still visible.

"How are Matt and Cecilia?" he asked.

Caroline was stirring cream into her tea. "Oh, very good. They always look forward to the fortnightly family gatherings at Kensington Gate. We missed the last one because we drove over to Suffolk when Kipp couldn't get up to see us. But we're sure to be there this coming Sunday."

"Tell me, how are the two of them doing without Charles in the house?"

Caroline sipped at her tea, stopped, put it down suddenly, and clenched her hands in her lap. "It's not going well, Jeremy. That's why I asked to speak with you and Emma alone. I miss Charles terribly. But the worst of it is his letters to Matthew and Cecilia. They're always full of splendid stories about Germany, and now the pair of them are clamoring to go to school in Berlin. It's out of the question, of course. Losing Charles to that blackguard Buchanan is bad enough. But it brings me a lot of heartache, especially with Kipp away during the week. On top of that, I'm not coping well with my boy being in the Nazi Youth and learning German and marching in those horrid parades. I want him home but he doesn't want to come home." Tears started. "Don't mind me, I cry from one end of the week to the other. When Kipp's home on Saturday I cry even harder. And that's the greatest worry of all."

"Why?"

"I can see how much my pain bothers him. It was a long and rocky road to our marriage, but now Kipp loves me very deeply. I believe he would do just about anything for my sake." She hesitated and then said, "Including murder."

"Murder? What do you mean?"

"Kipp is always the one to take action, isn't he? I honestly wouldn't put it past him to make up some excuse to fly down to Berlin, pull a gun on Lord Tanner, and take Charles from him by force."

"Surely not. It would create a scandal. He must know Charles wouldn't come with him willingly."

"He'd bind and gag Charles if he had to. And do the same to Lord Tanner if he didn't put a hole in his heart first."

Emma entered the parlor and sat down, folding her hands in the lap of her dress.

Jeremy was no longer drinking his tea. "He has not told you he'd do all this, has he?"

"Not in so many words." Caroline dabbed at her eyes with her fingers. "But I can tell what's going on in his head. I've always known what Kipp was about to do. Even when we weren't together."

"Have you tried to reason with him?" asked Emma.

"He says it's not as bad as all that. 'I have no intention of committing a crime,' he tells me. But I see his eyes at certain times and I know he's hatching a plan."

"I see." Jeremy looked at his mug of tea but did not pick it up.

"Prayer is our best course of action right now," said Emma. "There's really little that can be done but that, humanly speaking."

"If I could only control my emotions," moaned Caroline. "None of this would be happening if I didn't grieve over Charles so much. Kipp can't stand seeing me hurt, so he'll take whatever steps he feels are necessary. If I could just manage this stiff upper lip we English are supposed to be good at…"

"Nonsense." Jeremy reached over and patted her arm. "You can't blame yourself for loving your own son. Of course you're going to shed tears. Lord Tanner has engineered the whole affair. It wouldn't surprise me at all that part of his plan was to provoke Kipp to the very deed you are describing to us here. That way he can take his revenge on as many members of the Danforth family as possible. He'd probably have the police ready to pounce and place Kipp under arrest."

"Or he might shoot Kipp himself." The tears covered Caroline's cheeks.

"Let's not get ahead of ourselves." Jeremy picked up a Bible. "I'll read from the Psalms. Then Emma and I shall pray with you. This is a matter we need clear guidance on and we are going to pray until we get it."

Caroline had her hand over her eyes. "Thank you. I hope we can see our way out of this. I hope God will open a door for us. I'm afraid of what will happen if He doesn't. And I must tell you that Lord Tanner has asked me to leave Kipp and become his wife."

"What?"

"I couldn't keep the letter from Kipp. I didn't want him to find it and think I was scheming. He was furious, of course. I told him I wouldn't go back to Lord Tanner, not for Charles, not for anyone, not in a thousand years would I go back. But his eyes only turned that hard green they get sometimes, dark and deep and haunting as jade. When that happens, anything is possible. You cannot begin to imagine what he might turn his hands to."

Four days later Emma opened the door to her sons Peter and James.

"Why, hullo." She looked at their faces. Both had bruises and swollen eyes. "What happened to the two of you?"

"Rugby," answered Peter.

"And cricket," added James.

"My heavens, you don't get knocked about like that playing cricket." She turned James's head to one side. "I thought you two weren't home until May first."

"Well, we're early," said Peter.

"Not by much," said James.

She kissed them both on the cheek. "What's the real story?"

Peter shrugged and unloosened his tie. "We've been suspended."

"Suspended! Whatever for?"

James smiled. "Fighting."

"You've been suspended for fighting? And you're smiling?"

"It was for a good cause," replied James.

"What good cause?"

"Jane."

"Jane?"

"A couple of rotters called her names. In reference to her Chinese ancestry. So we dealt with it."

Peter nodded. "We were raised to deal with it."

"You weren't raised to fight," protested Emma.

"'Course we were," said Peter.

"The whole family fights," James added.

"Dad too."

"Army, navy, air force."

"I see. And how bad were the names?"

"Bad." Peter glared. "We won't repeat them."

"Were the other boys suspended?"

"All but one," rumbled Peter. "Lord Cheswick's son got off."

"What? Why?"

"Because he's Lord Cheswick's son."

"Did he call Jane names?"

"He was the worst of the lot. He even shoved her."

"And how is she?"

"Fine enough. We escorted her home."

"So does Aunt Libby know about this?"

"I expect she does by now."

"Well, come in, you two. I shall have to ring up your father. He's at the church office." Emma shut the door firmly behind them. "How long does the suspension last?"

"I dunno, really," responded Peter.

"January," replied James.

"You miss out on a whole term?" Emma was aghast. "Your father will be writing letters to the university, you can be sure of that." She put her hands on her hips. "Did you have to fight?"

"Yes!" Peter and James declared at the same time.

"And what do my knights-errant intend to do with themselves until nineteen thirty-eight?"

"The RAF," said Peter.

"The Auxiliary," added James.

"We've already signed up at Oxford," Peter boasted.

"We had every intention of telling you and Dad," James said.

"Eventually," Peter added.

"A tad sooner than eventually."

"Especially after what happened on Monday." Peter's face was dark.

"The Germans bombing that Spanish town. Using their Heinkels and Dorniers and Junkers, calling them mail planes and passenger planes." James's face mirrored his brother's.

"Incendiaries, Mum. They burned women and children to death."

"You didn't raise us to stand by and do nothing. Not when it comes to Jane. Not when it comes to Nazi Germany blowing civilians to pieces."

Emma's face was sharp. "Your father and I know about Guernica. We read the newspapers. We listen to the BBC." She kept her eyes on her sons. "We'll discuss all this once your father is home. I'll call him. Meanwhile fix yourselves something to eat. The new maid, Suzanne, has just baked fresh bread. The butter is on the sideboard."

"Thanks, Mum," Peter said.

"Thanks awfully, Mum," James added.

They raced each other to the kitchen.

Emma watched them go. She smiled, frowned, and then smiled again. She was still smiling when she picked up the phone to call Jeremy.

A month later, in late May, Emma ushered Jane into the parlor, where Jeremy was reading the *Times*. The day was warm, so there was no peat fire and all the windows were open, lace curtains fluttering. Jeremy glanced up and got quickly to his feet.

"Jane." He extended his healthy hand. "This is a surprise. How are you?"

She smiled tightly. "I'm not badly off, Uncle Jeremy. I'm sorry to pop in unexpectedly, but I really needed someone to talk to and I wondered if you and Aunt Emma—"

"Of course, of course. Take a seat here. I was just reading about Stanley Baldwin's resignation. Fancy having Neville Chamberlain running the country now."

"I'll just ask Suzanne to brew some tea," Emma said and left.

Jeremy smiled as he sank back down in his armchair. "The boys will be sorry to have missed you. They're out training with the Auxiliary, you know."

"Yes, that's why I came today. I knew they'd be gone."

"I see."

Emma returned and took a chair. "The tea will be along directly."

Jane half smiled. "I…I feel terribly. Peter and James are such princes… such princes."

"Why, what's troubling you?" asked Jeremy.

"I…I…" She looked helplessly from Jeremy to Emma. "It's quite ridiculous. But ever since the incident with Lord Cheswick's son and the others, I can't…well, I can't…"

"It's quite all right, my dear," soothed Emma. "Whatever you tell my husband and me remains with us. No one will hear anything at all about it. Certainly not the twins."

"The twins! I wish I could tell them. I wish somebody would tell them for me!"

"Why…" Emma stared at Jane. "Whatever do you mean?"

"I love them. I love both of them. It's awful, it's wretched, but there you are."

"Jane…" Emma began and stopped, not knowing what else to say.

"I've tried to talk myself out of it. I've tried to pray myself out of it. It's no use. I don't love one more than the other. I love them both the same... I mean, I love them both terribly. But I can't marry one and not the other, can I? So I'm wretched, absolutely wretched. I shall have to marry someone else who I don't love as much as either of them. I'm doomed to a life without love and without a shred of passion."

"Steady, there," said Jeremy. "You're still young—"

"I'm almost twenty!"

"Yes, yes you are, but waiting until twenty-one or twenty-two is perfectly fine. Even twenty-three is not unheard of."

"Twenty-three! I'd be an old maid!"

"Perhaps," suggested Emma in a quiet voice, "another year or two would straighten matters out in your mind."

"Oh, Aunt Emma, I can't possibly wait that long. I would like...well, I would like to be held, you know...to be held by one of them. I want that very much. I'm tired of dreaming about it. I should like to go to the flicks with them, or to a pub, or take a walk along the Thames, but not with both at the same time, just one, just one of them with his arm around me. But if I choose one over the other, if I choose Peter over James, I'll break James's heart, and if I choose James over Peter, I'll break Peter's heart. I can't do that—I could never do that. So I must date another man I don't give a fig for. It's dreadful. This whole dilemma has flattened my world completely."

"Calm yourself, my dear." Emma pulled her chair over to Jane and sat next to her, rubbing her arm. "It's not as bad as all that. Surely a little bit more time—"

"Aunt Em, I've kept it bottled up long enough. I'm going to burst, I am."

"Listen." Jeremy leaned forward. "What you've just suggested may yet save the day, Jane."

"I haven't mentioned anything, Uncle Jeremy, except that I'm going mad."

"No, no. You ask Peter to walk with you along the Thames on the Friday. You ask James to take you to the pub on the Saturday. The next weekend Peter takes you to a movie on one night and James takes you to an art gallery on another night."

"They won't agree to that."

"Oh, I think they will."

"But what if…what if…" She began to blush, the dark red spreading out from her neck over her face.

Emma patted her arm. "I know my boys. Peter will not begrudge James a little goodnight kiss from you so long as there is a goodnight kiss in store for him."

"I can't play one off the other."

"You aren't playing one off the other. You're just enjoying the company of both of them. Fairly. Equally. Without any desire whatsoever to provoke jealousy in either of their hearts."

"I don't want them fighting over me."

Jeremy and Emma both laughed. "They already fight over you." Jeremy was smiling. "This will just make it more interesting for both of them."

"I wish I could believe that. I adore Peter and I adore James. I don't want either of them getting hurt."

Emma patted Jane's arm again. "If you give them the news that you are going to go out with both of them, you will make their day, believe me. Why, you will make their week, make their year. You know what they will say the instant you tell them, don't you?"

Jane looked at Emma. Then a smile worked its way over her lips.

"Faint heart never won fair lady!" cried Jane as she laughed, tossing her hair back.

Jane's sudden happiness, it seemed to Emma, brightened the room more than the sunlight that came and went as clouds moved back and forth over the face of the sky.

The second week of June found Jeremy in his study at the church finishing a letter to Albrecht Hartmann while simultaneously working on his sermon for the coming Sunday.

"Now the Lord is that Spirit: and where the Spirit of the Lord is, there is liberty," he murmured, reading from an open Bible in front of him. He took off his round-rimmed glasses and pinched the bridge of his nose tightly between his thumb and forefinger. "Liberty to do what? Liberty to be who you are in Christ? But what does that look like exactly?"

He returned his glasses to his eyes and began to scribble on a sheet of paper with a fountain pen.

"People worry there will be another war," he said out loud as he wrote.

"They worry their sons will be sent to trenches in France and Belgium. What kind of freedom is God able to give their spirits in anxious times like these? And how do they acquire this freedom? Prayer? Faith? Is it already in them? Or do they need to pull it down from heaven and tuck it into their hearts?"

He turned from the Bible and his sermon and wrote a PS at the bottom of his letter to Albrecht.

> Listen. I am doing a series on the Corinthian correspondence. I'm not sure how fast our notes are going to make their way back and forth between England and Switzerland, but I wonder what you think of 1 and 2 Corinthians. You will not be able to respond in time to offer advice on 2 Corinthians 3:17, "Where the Spirit of the Lord is, there is liberty," for I am preaching on that this Sunday. Still, I would like to know your thoughts on it for I may revisit it later in my series, perhaps in August or September. *Danke*.

He turned back to his sermon, read what he had written, scratched it out with long, smooth strokes of his pen, and started writing a new paragraph underneath.

"Liberty to be free from fear. Liberty to be free from hate. Liberty to liberate others."

There was a knock on the door.

"Yes?" He kept his eyes on the open Bible and the notes he was scribbling. "How can I help you?"

"Reverend Sweet?" A man's tentative voice.

Jeremy glanced at the door. "Come in, please."

Skitt and his wife, Montgomery, entered the study.

Jeremy pushed back his chair and rose to his feet. "Libby's maid and butler, isn't it? How do you do?"

He came around the desk and extended his hand.

"We're sorry to interrupt, Reverend, but we've come on a matter of some urgency." Skitt shook Jeremy's hand. "Is this an inconvenient time? We should have rung you up first but—"

"Not at all, not at all. Pray take a seat, both of you." Jeremy nodded and smiled at Montgomery and returned to his chair behind the desk. "I trust you are both well?"

Skitt looked white and narrow as he sat facing Jeremy, and so did Montgomery.

"Well, Reverend, here's the thing. My wife is with child—we only found out a few days ago—and it presents us with something of a dilemma."

"Why, that's wonderful news, wonderful! Congratulations!"

"Thank you, sir, thank you. But we don't know what to do about it all."

"What?" Jeremy raised his eyebrows. "This is a wanted child, isn't it?"

"Oh, very much, Reverend, very much—don't take my meaning wrong. It's just that…well, Lady Libby told us a few years back it would be difficult to keep us on if we ever decided to start a family of our own, you know. She said she wouldn't be keen on Monty fussing over a baby and trying to tend to household chores at the same time."

"How busy are you?"

"Lady Libby's on her own a fair bit, so she goes out to visit her sisters and the house is easy enough to keep tidy then. But she often has the others over and that keeps us running. And when Commander Fordyce is in town he likes to have some of the officers up to the London house here and stay over, and that's a lot of work for two pairs of hands, sir."

"Quite."

"But we feel we could keep up even with a baby in our lives. Montgomery would have him in our room and no one would hear a thing. We need the work, Reverend, and there's a good understanding between ourselves and Lady Libby. I shouldn't like to see that come to an end."

"No, neither would I." Jeremy leaned forward in his chair. "Let me pray with you and encourage you by way of the angel's words to Mary: 'Nothing is impossible with God.' It does seem to be a delicate situation. Libby will want to know how you'll manage with a baby to tend to if you already find it hard enough on your busy days. But let us see if God will not find for us a way."

"Thank you, sir."

Montgomery smiled a small smile for the first time. "Thank you, Reverend. I have high hopes."

Jeremy smiled in return. "Talk to her today. After you have left St. Andrew's. Tell her you are with child. Then ring me up with the news. I have high hopes as well."

Skitt and Montgomery spoke with Libby after they had served her high tea at four that afternoon. She immediately set down her cup and laughed.

"Why, that's marvelous news!" she exclaimed. "Don't you find this house is much too quiet without Commander Fordyce or Jane?"

"We thought your ladyship might find a baby in the house overwhelming."

"Overwhelming? It will be a godsend. I'm dreadfully lonely and I should like nothing better than to help care for the infant. When is all this happening, Monty?"

"In January, my lady."

"That shall give us ample time to get a room prepared for the infant. Of course there's the problem of what colors to use. But blues work with boys and girls, don't you think? So long as the blues are not too dark." She lifted her teacup to her lips but set it down again without drinking. "I'm so pleased. It is something of an answer to prayer. A baby I can fuss over at last." She caught the look on both their faces. "Whatever's the matter?"

"We thought…well, we thought," Skitt stumbled, "you might want us on our way with a child coming."

"What? However did you two get that idea? How could I possibly manage either the home here in Camden Lock or at HMS Picadilly in Plymouth without the pair of you? Especially when all the captains and admirals and whatnot descend upon us? No, no, we shall see this through together. If you cannot be with the child, Monty, I shall, and we shall spell each other. Jane will be ecstatic, you know, absolutely ecstatic. I expect her to come down from Oxford more often once we tell her the news."

Montgomery beamed. "I'm so glad to hear the enthusiasm in your voice. Will Jane be home for supper? May I tell her about the baby?"

"Jane home for supper? Not if the twins have their way. No, she is out watching the pair of them fly. Then there is some sort of RAF Auxiliary ball. Lady Emma will be her chaperone. Nevertheless, sometime after midnight, I expect our Cinderella to return. I'm sure what you have to say will be the perfect cap to her evening."

Around two in the morning, Emma Sweet slipped under the covers at the St. Andrew's Cross vicarage. She did not do it quietly. Jeremy mumbled in his sleep.

"Are you awake?" asked Emma.

"I'm not," he said into his pillow.

"The ball was quite a success. At least in terms of how matters went as far as James and Peter are concerned."

"Mmm."

"Jane danced exactly as many times with one as she did with the other. She danced with some of the other Auxiliary pilots as well, which I think was a good thing. And I'm given to understand they each had their first kiss. So they are flying without airplanes."

"Do they tell you everything?"

"Probably not."

"So they could have had more than one kiss each." Jeremy was still speaking into his pillow.

"They could."

"No pistols at dawn between them?"

"Oh, never. It's the grandest sport, you see. The loser has to stand for the winner as the best man. And if one of them dies the other has to make sure he marries her on behalf of both of them."

Jeremy snorted. "What nonsense."

"Not to young men who have their blood up."

"We'll need to pray some extra prayers. The Catholic priest may have to help us as well. And the Baptists and Methodists."

"My heavens. All the heavy artillery."

"There's Billy to worry about next."

"I don't think he's at all interested in girls. It's rugby and football and cricket that take up his waking thoughts, dear."

Jeremy put his pillow over his head. "Don't you believe it for a minute."

July, 1936
Kensington Gate, London

"Good night, Winston. Our butler will show you to your room."

"Very good, Lord Preston. What time is breakfast?"

Lord Preston smiled, his hands in his pockets. "There is a first breakfast at eight. A second breakfast, specially designed for the more leisurely pace of summertime, is at eleven."

"Ah. The very thing. Shall I see you and Lady Preston at the second breakfast or will I be on my own?"

"You shall certainly see us there, Winston."

"I will look forward to that. Can the butler bring the newspapers up to my room in the morning?"

"Certainly. Any particular time?"

"As soon as they arrive. He can just place them at my door. I'll keep an eye out. Though a light tap or two wouldn't be out of place."

"I think the butler can manage a light tap or two, can't you, Tavy?" asked Lord Preston.

"I can, my lord. The papers will be at your door first thing, Mr. Churchill."

Churchill nodded. "Thank you very much indeed."

Tavy led the way down the hall to Churchill's room. Lord Preston watched them go and reflected on how the butler and the politician had the same gait and build and height. Then he knocked gently on a nearby door and opened it.

Lady Preston was sitting up in bed reading Agatha Christie's *Murder on the Orient Express*, glasses halfway down her nose.

"Winston's abed," said Lord Preston, shutting the door behind him.

"Have his feelings improved since we dined together?"

Lord Preston took a chair by his wife's bed. "Not really. He is stoic one moment and the tears are in his eyes the next."

Lady Preston put down her book and removed her glasses. "Do you truly believe he is finished politically?"

"Very near it."

"Just because he warns Parliament about the German military?"

Lord Preston shook his head. "It's more than that. He's been backing the wrong horses all along. Supporting Mussolini till just this year. Supporting Franco in the war in Spain—when Guernica was firebombed he was accused along with the fascists. Fighting against India's independence, fighting against granting her Dominion status in the face of strong support in the House. For heaven's sake, he supported the Japanese in their invasion of Manchuria. And what's freshest in everyone's minds is his support of Edward VIII even when the king made it clear he would throw over the throne to marry that American divorcee—the whole House howled against him the day he made that speech, howled and raged like a North Sea tempest. I've rarely seen such viciousness. No, he's done, my dear. The Conservative Party does not trust him, the House of Commons does not trust him. He is left with his dogs, his wife, his estate, his oil painting, and his writing. I expect that will have to be enough."

"But you trust him, William."

"I suppose I do."

"Why? When he has made so many errors in judgment?"

Lord Preston half smiled. "I don't know, unless God Almighty is directing my thoughts and inclinations. I like Winston. I know he won't always be in the right, but there's a dogged determination and love of England I find refreshing. And often enough he is spot on in his judgments. The rest of us hope Nazism and Communism will simply fall apart and disappear from the earth. He knows better, and he forces us to look reality in the eyes by means of his insight and his eloquence. So I am for him despite his faults. But alas, my being for him will help him not at all in the political arena."

"Surely you have some influence, William. You were able to make the university come around, weren't you? James and Peter will be back at classes this fall and their suspensions stricken from the record."

"The university is one thing, Elizabeth. The British government is an entirely different matter. Peter and James were in the right in defending Jane's honor. Winston has been in the wrong time and time again. So now even if he is in the right about the threat of Nazi Germany, and I believe he is, no one will listen to him, and no one will listen to his supporters. Moreover, I am not close to Prime Minister Chamberlain, you know that. I do not have his ear. There is nothing I can do, my dear, except pray."

She reached over and grasped his hand. "Then I wish you would do that, William. I read Agatha Christie to force my thoughts elsewhere, but I'm terrified at the violence Robbie and Shannon are facing in Palestine, I'm distraught over young Charles being raised and molded by that brute Lord Tanner, and I'm in a panic the war in Spain will precipitate a war in Europe. I have nightmares about those horrid German planes dropping their incendiaries on London and Liverpool just as they did on Guernica."

Lord Preston patted her hand. "Now, now, calm yourself, my dear, no bombs are going to drop on London."

"They bombed us in Folkestone in the last war, didn't they? And zeppelins bombed London more than once. And those Gotha aircraft killed eighteen schoolchildren in East London."

"Yes, of course, it was dreadful, but there is no war between England

and Germany now, nor does there ever need to be. My sources tell me Herr Hitler is concerned about being equipped to resist France and Russia. He does not consider England an enemy. We fought beside Blücher at Waterloo, remember?"

"Do you recall the last war? The Somme? Vimy Ridge? Verdun? Who fought against England then?"

"I know."

"And if you respect Winston, aren't you concerned about his warnings against the war machine of the Third Reich?"

"Of course."

"Then I wish you would pray. For Robbie and Shannon and Patricia. For Charles. For our country. Pray and do my poor soul some good. Agatha Christie can only do so much, bless her heart."

"Indeed." He held her hand in both of his.

> God is our refuge and strength, a very present help in trouble. Therefore we will not fear, though the earth be removed, and though the mountains be carried into the midst of the sea; though the waters thereof roar and be troubled, though the mountains shake with the swelling thereof. There is a river, the streams whereof shall make glad the city of God, the holy place of the tabernacles of the most High. God is in the midst of her; she shall not be moved: God shall help her, and that right early.

October 12, 1937
Jerusalem

DAD AND MUM

A QUICK CABLE TO LET YOU KNOW ALL IS WELL. THANKS FOR THE PACKAGE AND CADBURY CHOCOLATE. IT REACHED US ON PATRICIA'S NINTH BIRTHDAY. SHE IS GROWING LIKE A WEED AND LOVES SWEETS. THINGS ARE TENSE SO YOUR PRAYERS ARE MUCH APPRECIATED. YOU WILL HAVE HEARD THE ACTING

DISTRICT COMMISSIONER IN THE GALILEE, A
CHAP NAMED LEWIS ANDREWS, WAS KILLED BY
ARAB GUNMEN TWO WEEKS AGO. WE TAKE ALL
THE PRECAUTIONS WE CAN AND FEEL QUITE
SAFE IN JERUSALEM SO PLEASE DON'T WORRY.
SHANNON WILL WRITE YOU A LONGER LET-
TER IN A FEW DAYS. GOD BLESS.

MUCH LOVE,

ROBBIE, SHANNON, PATRICIA CLAIRE

November 15, 1937
Jerusalem

Patricia pointed from the terrace of their house. "That palm. That is
my favorite one."

"Ah, is it?" asked Shannon. "And why is that?"

"I like the way the fronds fall away from the top. Very prettily."

"Very prettily?" Shannon smiled. "Well, I guess now that I look at it
closely, you're quite right."

Robbie walked out onto the terrace with a tall glass of orange juice in
his hand. "Why, that's been my favorite palm tree for years."

Patricia whirled to look at him. "No, it hasn't."

"It has. Ever since you were a baby."

"No."

"Doesn't it dominate the skyline so nicely? Of course it's much taller
now than it was nine years ago when you were born."

Patricia smiled. "You never noticed it before today. You can see beautiful palm trees in all directions. You're just teasing me."

"I'd never do that over something so serious. The Patricia Palm, I have
always called it."

"Always?" Patricia laughed.

"Are you packed for the road trip?"

"Not quite yet, Papa. I wanted to add a few things."

"*Yella, yella*—hurry up! Pretty soon the driver will be honking his horn."

"No sergeant would honk his horn at a colonel." But Patricia raced off
into the house.

Robbie offered Shannon the orange juice, and she took a long drink.

"Bless you, it's chilled. How did you manage that? I thought the electricity was on again, off again."

"It is. So the sergeant fetched us a block of ice, and I turned the refrigerator back into a proper ice box."

"Bravo." She put her arms around his neck, glass of juice still in one of her hands. "Are you really taking us to the seashore, Colonel?"

"The Mediterranean one, yes. Not the one in Galilee."

"It's safe and sound?"

"There's nothing there but an army camp. The ocean will do us all good. You know, like taking a dip at Brighton."

"I trust the water is warmer than at Brighton."

"One can only hope."

"And we'll have your bodyguards along?"

"They'll be riding in vehicles ahead of us and behind us." He took his orange juice from her and sipped it. "It kills two birds with one stone. I need to have a sit-down with the commanding officer at the camp, and you and Pat have been cooped up in the city long enough. It's a quiet area. There's nothing at all worth attacking."

"That's grand. The fighting makes you forget how beautiful the land is."

He kissed her on the lips. "But not how beautiful the women are."

"You taste like orange juice."

"So do you."

She kissed him back. "Why are you so playful today?"

"It's such a relief to get away, isn't it? Even for a day. And to think of building Pat's first sand castle, splashing her…it's quite something to contemplate simply doing normal things in Palestine, normal British things."

"They're normal Irish things and normal human things too."

Patricia suddenly appeared on the terrace, knapsack over her shoulder and a floppy cotton hat on her head. "Ready."

"Right." Shannon took the glass from Robbie again and drained it. "Let's head down there, Tricia." She glanced at Robbie. "You coming, love?"

"I just need my briefcase," he said. "I'll be right along."

Robbie went to his study. His revolver was lying on the desk, and he slipped it into the holster on his hip and snapped the flap shut. He checked the documents inside his briefcase and snapped it shut as well.

"I forgot the bucket and shovel Papa got me!"

Robbie glanced out a window. Patricia was running back into the house. Shannon threw up her hands and stepped into the car as the driver held open the door. Soldiers had parked armored vehicles in front of the car and behind it. Robbie turned away as he heard his daughter running up the staircase.

"Have you forgotten the beach things?" he asked as he stepped into the hall.

She ran past him. "They're under my bed."

There was a rumble from somewhere, and then the house shook, sending plaster raining onto Robbie's head and shoulders. He heard Patricia cry out, and then a roar and a blast of heat swept through the windows and rooms. Despite a sharp pain in his leg, he pushed himself to his feet and staggered back up the stairs. Patricia was sitting on the floor holding her head in her hands.

"Are you hurt?" He picked her up in his arms. "Are you cut?"

"I don't know, I don't know! What's happened?"

"Let's get out of the house."

"Where's Mum?"

"She'll be outside."

He went down the stairs with his daughter, but not to the front street. He went out the back door to the garden. Patricia had buried her head in his shoulder and her arms were around his neck, so she didn't see what he saw when he craned his neck to look over the wall to the street. Dust hung white in the air. The car was gone. Both armored vehicles were gone. Rolls of dark smoke rose from a large crater, mingling with the dust. Whistles blew. He heard the loud sound of many men in boots running. There were shouts.

"What is it, Papa?" asked Patricia. "What is it?" Tears cut through the grime on her face. "Where's Mum? Where is she?"

"Shh. Shh." Robbie walked away from the wall and farther into the palm trees and plants of the garden. "It will be all right. Don't be afraid. Everything will turn out all right."

November 19, 1937
Kensington Gate, London

Lord Preston stood gazing down into the fire in the front parlor.

"He'll be home in a fortnight, the prime minster assured me. Transfer of duties. They'll plant him at a desk here in London. Best thing for him, really. And for little Patricia." He glanced back at his wife. "She'll need us, Elizabeth. How she will need us."

Lady Preston was in a chair, her eyes dark and swollen, a handkerchief crumpled in her fist. "We prayed. What good did our prayers do? Our family has had more than its share of suffering, William."

"All the prayers in the world won't make this life heaven. It's a broken place, a shattered house. Think of how Jesus suffered. Think of how the apostles suffered. It's a pitched battle, isn't it?"

"I don't want a pitched battle. I want peace."

"What makes you think Robbie or Patricia would have survived if we hadn't prayed? What if our granddaughter hadn't rushed back into the house? What if all three of them had climbed into the car together?"

Lady Preston closed her eyes. "Wasn't the pain of Ireland enough? Why did she have to experience the same sort of hate and fighting in Palestine that she did in Ireland? Why twice in her lifetime, William?"

"I don't know. Except to say there are many places on this earth where the same sort of tragedies are played out again and again. It's common to the human race. Many go through the same trials and tribulations. At least you and I can walk through them with God, walk through them to the other side. I do not believe Shannon is dead. She is alive, Elizabeth, more alive than we are. She is like an angel. No more sorrow. No more heartache. If she can see us, she knows that her husband and daughter are coming to us, coming to England, and that they will be greatly loved and cared for. She will have an overwhelming peace."

"I'm glad someone has it because I don't. I suppose if I didn't believe in God I might be better off, for I would have expected nothing more than the back of the hand from this world. But I prayed to God and expected something better, and now I'm bitterly disappointed. First Albert. Then Christelle. And Michael. Now Shannon. It makes me wonder if there will be any of us left in two or three years."

"Come, my dear, don't talk that way. God is with us. Our children survived the war. Our grandchildren are hale and hearty. Robbie and Patricia are coming home to us. Thank God for that. Grasp ahold of your faith. It must be your anchor in such a time as this. It must or you will be swept away."

"Shall I sing a stanza of 'It Is Well with My Soul'? Would that please you? Is that what you're looking for?"

"What I'm looking for is your Cornwall blood. What I'm looking for is the faith that stands with God and light and hope in the face of all fires and floods and pestilence. Your forefathers had it, and they dealt with far greater horrors than we have had to bear up under. Where is yours, Elizabeth? Where is yours now that our family needs it the most?"

She sank her head into her hand. "I don't know, William. I honestly don't. It's lost at sea. It's vanished into thin air. It's in the grave along with Albert and Christelle and Michael and Shannon. It's gone."

December 11, 1937
St. Andrew's Cross, London

"Hullo, Jeremy."

Jeremy came out from behind his desk. "Robbie. I'm so glad you've made it here for our meeting. When I saw you the other night I wasn't sure if you meant it or were just saying something you knew would make your mother happy."

"What? Getting together with you and talking it out? I meant it all right." Robbie shook Jeremy's hand. "I really must do something or I'll go mad."

"I understand. How's Patricia?"

"She's with Cecilia. She's just turned eight, you see, so they get along famously. It's a gift. I thank God, it's a gift. Patricia needs so much more than I do. She's so young."

"I'm glad to hear it. Please, take a seat."

Jeremy took an armchair next to Robbie, the one man in black with his white collar, the other in full uniform.

"I can brew some tea," offered Jeremy.

Robbie waved his hand. "Perhaps later."

Jeremy nodded. "Right."

"I honestly don't know what to say or what help you can offer, Jeremy. I feel my mother ought to be here instead of me. She's experiencing a towering rage against God. All I feel is a bleakness. I've seen combat. I've watched comrades die. I've killed. But this is different. I've lost my wife. I could protect the Jews of Jerusalem but not her. Why didn't I order that the car be inspected? Why didn't I tell them to lift the bonnet or open the boot? Why did I let her go down first with Patricia? Shouldn't I have been there ahead of her, ahead of both of them, making sure everything was in order? After all, there was a war going on, wasn't there, the Arabs against the British and the Jews? Why was I taking things so casually? Why did I feel my family and I were immune? You see, Jeremy, for me it's not a matter of where was God. I keeping asking myself over and over again, where was I?"

Jeremy peeled off his black suit jacket as he came into the vicarage that evening, tossed it on a chair instead of hanging it up as usual, walked to a window, and looked out at the street he'd just walked down for half a block. He watched the cars and trucks and people move past and did not turn away even when Emma leaned her head against his back.

"Ha'penny for your thoughts, Reverend," she said.

"They're not even worth that much, really. There's nothing profound going on. I'm pretty empty-headed. I didn't have anything to give to Robbie to settle his soul. It strikes me I didn't have much to give Kipp when Christelle died or Libby when Michael was killed in that plane crash either."

"I'm sure that's not true."

"It is true. I can't bring people back to life, can I? Or tell them the moment they cry a hundred thousand tears their bad fortunes will be reversed and everything will be as lovely as it was two or three weeks or a month before. That's what folks who are grieving want, Em. Miracles. Words of comfort aren't miracles."

"Of course they are."

"Oh, they might change a person's mind, but they don't change what's real. Shannon's gone, Em, and I can't bring her back with my prayers or my faith. Hatred took her…love couldn't keep her. God has her, but Robbie and his daughter are left all alone."

"They're not alone. They're with us."

"It's not the same."

"No, it isn't. But it's much better than nothing. Don't sell yourself short. You've been blessing people for years, our family included. The words matter, the prayers matter, your messages matter. The mind and heart are real places too, Jeremy, not just what happens all around us."

"I wish I could be as sanguine as you are."

She put her arms around him. "I have enough of that for both of us. And equal measures of faith and hope besides."

January, 1938
Kipp and Caroline's townhouse, Camden Lock, London

"So Montgomery's had a little man." Caroline laughed as she hung up the telephone. "Libby's so excited you'd think the baby was her own."

She came into the kitchen, where Kipp was finishing his breakfast and enjoying a cup of coffee. He lifted the coffee cup in salute.

"Capital. What's the lad's name?"

"Well, it isn't Skitt, thank goodness. Paul Terrence William."

"You're joking."

"William for your father. Terrence for Terry, of course. And Paul for Skitt's dad. Did you know he flew in the war?"

"No, I didn't."

"Shot down twice. They awarded him the Distinguished Flying Cross in September, nineteen eighteen."

Kipp set down his cup. "What? Skitt never said anything about it when he was working at Ashton Park during the war."

"I gather his father and him were at odds with one another at the time. Later on they sorted everything out. He's gone now. Do you know he was almost forty when they gave him the DFC? But they thought he was thirty."

"Good for him. I'll have to remember that trick."

"Oh, no, you don't. No flying for you in another war. No flying for anyone in this family. If it comes to a head with the Italians and the Germans, we can let the other young men of Britain sort things out."

Kipp cleared his throat. "Speaking of the Germans, I've been tapped to go to Berlin for a couple of weeks. Sort of a liaison position, you know—keep the RAF in good relations with the *Luftwaffe*, that sort of thing. I head over in March."

"In March? You?" Caroline sat down across the kitchen table from him. "Did you ask for this posting?"

"No. Actually I thought they'd send Ben. But I got the nod."

"Refuse."

"I can't refuse, love. This is the RAF, not the airline Michael and Ben and I ran. I'm no longer my own master in case you hadn't noticed."

"You'll see Charles, won't you?"

"I will. If he'll see me."

"You can't go, Kipp. You mustn't go. I know what will happen. You'll get into all sorts of trouble on my account. You'll demand Charles return to England with you. Get into a fistfight with Lord Tanner and have yourself thrown into some horrid Nazi jail."

"A fistfight is the least of Lord Tanner's worries."

"You see? You're spoiling for a battle with that monster."

"You want Charles back, don't you?"

"Of course I want him back. But not at the expense of losing you. And as much as I love my son and miss him, I don't want him back at gunpoint. He comes willingly back to England or he doesn't come at all."

"Suppose he wants to come but Lord Tanner won't let him? What then?"

Caroline stared at her husband. "I don't know."

"I couldn't very well leave him behind in Nazi Germany, could I? Not if he pleaded with me to bring him home. Tanner or no Tanner. Hitler or no Hitler."

"For heaven's sake, Kipp Danforth, don't use this whole affair as an excuse to start another war."

"I don't want to start another war. I just want to make you happy."

"I am happy. I'm ecstatic. I love being here with you and Matt and Cecilia."

"I've let you down plenty enough in my lifetime. I need to make everything right."

"Oh, everything *is* right." She got up and sat on his lap, running her hands through his hair. "My golden boy. How I love you. How I've always loved you. There's nothing more you need to do. I know how much you care for me. I don't want you getting yourself killed to prove it." She gave him a long kiss on the lips. "Promise me."

He put his arms around her. "Promise you what?"

"No Kipp Danforth heroics. No taking on Herr Hitler and the Third Reich. No tossing Lord Tanner Buchanan in the River Spree in Berlin."

Kipp responded to her kisses with kisses of his own. "I won't toss him in the River Spree."

"Or any river?"

"Or any river."

"No pistols at dawn? No rapiers?"

He put his lips to her throat. "None of that, my love. And no jousting from horseback either."

"Well, that's a relief." She wrapped her arms around him and squeezed as tightly as she could. "I'm glad Matt and Cecilia are with their cousins this morning."

"So am I."

March, 1938

Nazi troops crossed the border into Austria on March 12 as Hitler once again defied the Treaty of Versailles by annexing the Austrian nation to Germany. Lord Tanner defended the action in his first broadcasts to Britain as the English-speaking announcer in the Ministry of Propaganda. He claimed the *Anschluss* had the support of the vast majority of the Austrian people and that Germany existed once more in its historic entirety.

Hitler himself visited Braunau, his Austrian birthplace, that afternoon. On the fifteenth he was at the center of a huge rally in Vienna. Lord Tanner reported on this event as well for his British listeners. He repeated Hitler's announcement at the *Heldenplatz*: "*Als Führer und Kanzler der deutschen Nation und des Reiches melde ich vor der deutschen Geschichte nunmehr den Eintritt meiner Heimat in das Deutsche Reich*—As leader and chancellor of the German nation and Reich, I announce to German history now the entry of my homeland into the German Reich."

"There is much love for Herr Hitler in Austria," broadcast Tanner. "It's overwhelming. Compare it to the absence of affection for your current prime minister in Britain, Mr. Neville Chamberlain. It's like night and day, isn't it? Have you watched the newsreels? Have you seen the cheering crowds? The Germans come as liberators to the Austrian people, not conquerors. Shouldn't Britain benefit from the same sort of liberation? Wouldn't her economy improve as rapidly as that of the Third Reich? Aren't Germany and Britain the staunch allies of Waterloo? The day must come when London is festooned with Nazi flags as Vienna is today. The day must come when crowds swarm Hyde Park with cheers and Nazi salutes as Herr Hitler proclaims the inclusion of Britain into the Greater Germanic Empire. Pray that day may come speedily, Great Britain, aye, as speedily as possible, for on that day you truly will be great again."

Two days later, on St. Patrick's Day, Thursday, March 17, the aircraft carrying Flying Officer Kipp Danforth and a number of other RAF officials touched down in Berlin. On March 19, Baron von Isenburg met with Kipp at the café in front of the hotel where the Danforth family had stayed during the Berlin Olympics. They both ordered coffee and chatted a few moments. Immaculate in his black SS uniform, the baron eventually leaned forward across the table.

"Himmler and the SS are making thousands of arrests in Austria—Jews, Communists, Austrian nationalists," he said in a low voice. "It's only the beginning. Between now and this plebiscite they want to hold on the reunification of Austria with Germany, there will be many thousands more. Some are being sent to concentration camps to wither and die. Others are of special interest and will be interrogated thoroughly. My castle is being chosen as the place to imprison some of the most important—hundreds of them. So the prisoners we have now are going to be executed or sent to camps where they will be worked to death." He paused. "I must get Eva out of the castle and out of Germany. Is there any way you can help me?"

"Baron. I understand. But I can't possibly—"

"I beg of you. I have treated Eva harshly enough. I must give her an opportunity to choose liberty over the Third Reich and its growing list of monstrosities. How long are you here? Can you not smuggle her aboard your aircraft? I would have her drugged."

"The RAF would never permit that, Baron."

"Is there some other means?" His eyes were dark with pain. "I beg of you," he repeated.

Kipp drummed his fingers on the tabletop. "There may be something I can do." Kipp looked at the afternoon traffic. "I'm here about four weeks. Till just after Easter. There may be something I can arrange. But not with aircraft."

"Please. It would mean the world to me."

"I will do what I can. How can I reach you?"

"I will be in touch with you on a regular basis." The baron leaned back and sipped at his coffee. "In return I will do something for you and your charming wife."

"Baron, there is no need—"

"I will arrange for Lord Tanner to release Charles to your care, and I will personally clear any possible obstructions to his return to England."

Kipp stared. "How can you do all that?"

"My connections within the SS extend to Himmler himself."

"But there is bound to be trouble. Lord Tanner will cause a disturbance."

"There will not be trouble. There will not be a disturbance." The baron continued to sip at his coffee. "Just keep your end of the bargain. To a special friend of your father."

Kipp finally brought his own coffee to his mouth. "I will do that, sir. Depend on it."

Two days later a note was hand delivered to Kipp at the hotel by an SS courier on a motorbike.

> Kipp,
>
> Eva has been transferred to a concentration camp in Germany. There was nothing I could do to halt it other than order her to be shot on the spot. This will cause some delay, but I will get her out and to the location you choose for a rendezvous. I shall contact you every other day and meet with you in person whenever I am in Berlin. Proceed with your plans. Make every possible effort. I will bring Eva to you if I have to tear Nazi Germany in half to do it.
>
> Baron von Isenburg

March 29, 1938
Ashton Park

"Harrison! Where are you? Confound that man! Harrison!" Holly scanned the landscape looking for her husband.

A head with a fedora on top popped up from behind a bush. "Did you have to make so much noise? I had the fox eating right out of my hand."

Holly narrowed her eyes. "Out of your hand? I thought you were going to do away with him once you'd caught him."

"He won't bother our sheep or chickens now that he knows he can eat here without any effort."

"What a peculiar groundskeeper you are."

"You married him, love."

"I did." Holly was in a tweed jacket, pants, tall black riding boots, and a pith helmet.

"You're dressed oddly."

"Thank you very much."

"Are you Dr. Livingstone today then?"

"I am not. I am Lady Holly on safari. Care to join me?"

"I should like that very much."

"Jolly good. But no getting lions to eat out of the palm of your hand, good sir."

"No fear of that. I only get Lady Holly to do that when I'm on an expedition."

"Ha." She handed him an envelope. "This came from a courier just now. The letter came in a diplomatic pouch from our embassy in Berlin."

"Diplomatic pouch?"

"I fear you're moving up in the world. Or perhaps the Harrison I've loved so many years isn't a humble groundskeeper at all. It may be you work for MI6. It may be you're a spy."

Harrison opened the envelope. "Anything is possible in these troubled times." He read the letter and his good nature was gone. "Oh dear. I'm afraid I must leave for Germany at once, Holly. A flight out of Liverpool has been arranged for this afternoon."

"What on earth is going on?"

He put the letter in her hand. "Read it for yourself."

She scanned it quickly. "My heavens. What is Kipp up to?" Her face had whitened. "You're too old for this sort of derring-do, love. Let the younger men ferret Eva and Charles out of Nazi Germany."

"He's asked for my help. When have I ever denied your family my service?"

"Harrison, you have been a good and faithful friend to the Danforth family from time immemorial. Lord Preston would never expect this of you. It's extremely dangerous. If the SS get ahold of any of you they'll shoot you dead and burn your bodies. There will never be any proof of what they did. And that includes Lord Kipp. As well as his faithful servant."

"You can't expect me to say no."

"Of course I can."

"And leave young Kipp in the lurch? To be shot and stabbed and tortured? Because I wasn't there? Because I kowtowed to a pack of goose-stepping bounders? That will not happen in my lifetime, Lady Holly, not if I had a million lifetimes."

Holly dropped her hands to her side and groaned. "No, I expect not."

April 5, 1938
Harrison's hotel room, Berlin

"They look at me as a bit of snob now, you see," Kipp said. "Must have my personal valet with me at all times. Must have my servant. After all, I'm Lord Kipp, RAF swank, upper crust, English nobility, all that rot. I hate to give them that impression but it's working in our favor."

"It is right enough."

Harrison and Kipp were bent over a map at one in the morning. Kipp tapped it with his finger.

"According to Baron von Isenburg, young Charles will be as docile as a lamb, and Lord Tanner himself will ensure the boy knows his place," said Kipp. "Whatever leverage the baron and the SS have on Tanner must be considerable. I've only met Tanner the once since I've been here, and he never caused any trouble, never even raised an eyebrow."

"Good-oh," responded Harrison. "So I continue to hang about with you and fetch your things and bow and curtsy and all. What happens Good Friday?"

"You collect Charles and stay with him here in this room. I have no official duties Easter Sunday. I'll come by then. The three of us will head out on a bit of a sightseeing trip. The camp is four hours from Berlin. The baron will be waiting for us with Eva. We'll be in SS uniforms. It's meant to look clandestine because the idea is we're collecting Eva to take her to her execution, you see. That's what the camp commandant understands. The drive to the camp actually brings us closer to our destination in France by two hours. We should be in Calais early Monday morning while it's still dark. We'll have shed our uniforms before we reach the French border. A ship will be waiting in Calais. I can't cross the Channel with you—I must return to England with the RAF group on Wednesday morning."

"Right." Harrison rubbed his jaw. "The boat knows what's up?"

"Not at all. Only the captain. To the crew we're just paying customers traveling cheap by taking a cargo ship." Kipp glanced up from the map. "Are you sure you're fine with all this skulduggery?"

"'Course I am. Don't take a few gray hairs as a sign I'm ready to be wheeled about and fed baby food with a spoon, Lord Kipp."

"The one loose bit in my mind is Buchanan. I still think he may try something. Perhaps on the road out of Berlin. I don't know if he might not follow us, him and a pack of his cronies, and do some mischief. After all, he has powerful friends in the Nazi hierarchy himself. He works for Goebbels and the Ministry of Propaganda. He might appear meek as a lamb now, but he's a proud man. I can't believe he won't try to strike out at us in some fashion."

"We can handle him. I owe Buchanan one for the beating he gave me with that walking stick of his. I'd love to have the chance to make a scarf out of that stick and wrap it snugly about his neck."

"Don't be too eager. God may grant you your wish."

"I hope so. I've given up ale and chips for Lent, and I trust the Lord has taken note of that."

On April 15, Good Friday, after more than a week of running about after Kipp and ferrying his briefcase and bowing and scraping to him and high-ranking RAF and *Luftwaffe* officers, Harrison held steady in his hotel room and waited for the knock. It came at noon. Lord Tanner was at the door, swastika armband on his suit jacket, his hands resting on Charles's shoulders. Charles was dressed in a new suit and wore a swastika armband as well. His face was a death mask as he glared at Harrison.

"I've done what I've been ordered to do," Lord Tanner said. "See that no harm comes to him."

"I'll get him safely to his mother," Harrison replied.

Lord Tanner glanced about the room. "Just you in here, Harrison?"

"That's right."

"No shotguns under the bed?"

"No, sir. None are needed. Though I see you still carry your silver walking stick about with you."

"Does that trouble you, Harrison?"

"Not at all. You'll never land a blow on my back with that thing again."

"You think not?"

"I am quite certain of it, Lord Tanner."

"I may disappoint you."

Harrison grinned. "It wouldn't disappoint me if you tried. Tying a knot at your throat with it would give me the greatest pleasure. Bring two or three canes with you when you call again. A triple knot in the tie is my specialty."

Harrison steered a stone-like Charles into the room and shut the door.

"Can I get you something to eat or drink, lad?" he asked.

"I don't need a thing."

"You needn't be afraid. We're getting you home to your mother, nothing more."

"I'm not at all afraid. I've been ordered to go to England and I shall obey and accompany you there. Then I shall join the British Union of Fascists. I shall help change that country from the inside out so that Nazi flags fly all the way from Edinburgh Castle to Buckingham Palace."

"'That country'? It's the land of your birth, Charles Danforth."

"It's not the land of my rebirth. I am Third Reich through and through. My father has dropped the name Buchanan and taken the name Mahler. As my father's son, I have done the same. That is how you may address me. I will not answer to the name Charles Danforth ever again."

"Right. Well, Charles Mahler—"

"Von Mahler."

"Von Mahler. Your room is in here. You can't leave the suite or the hotel for any reason whatsoever. Understood?"

"I'm not going anywhere, groundskeeper. Not because you can stop me, but because I gave my word. And because my father gave his word. On the day England is annexed to the Third Reich I will see him again. Until then, we have the permission of the SS to write one another."

"May I ask why the SS has such a hold on you and your father?"

Charles went into his room and shut the door.

For the next two nights and all through Saturday he emerged only to use the washroom. Each time he did, he drank a glass of water. Harrison would make a brief effort to engage him in conversation, but Charles would ignore him and return to his room. When it was time for bed, Harrison, not trusting Charles or his father, blockaded Charles's door and the door to the apartment with sofas from the suite and slept on the one that barred the front door. He was not disturbed on Friday night or Saturday night, sleeping with a cricket bat in his hand, often sitting up to listen and then going back to sleep again.

Kipp showed up before dawn on Easter Sunday with a package under his arms.

"How was he?" Kipp asked Harrison.

"No trouble at all. He kept to his room. Said he'd honor his word and go to England and that his father would not try to stop us. What have the SS got on the pair of them?"

"I'm not privy to that information. The baron won't speak a word about it." He opened the package, peeling back the paper. "SS summer uniforms. White tunics and pants. Red swastika armbands. Silver braid and death's heads on the caps. Charles will be a junior officer. That should make him happy. We each have a set of identification papers as well."

"And what's our story?"

"The official story we give to the commandant at the camp is that we're transferring Eva to a higher-security SS prison. The commandant expects to hear that. He knows the truth. Or thinks he knows it. That we are transferring Eva von Isenburg to a secret place of execution under her father's orders. This makes the baron out to be even more ice-blooded than the Nazis already think he is. *Der Mann aus Eisen*—the man of iron."

"And you know enough German to pull this off?"

"Don't forget, the baron will be there."

"They'll still expect you to talk."

"I have enough German to mutter a few things. But I'll be a very tight-lipped, unsmiling SS officer. So will Charles. And you'll be a very tight-lipped, unsmiling driver with a wedge cap and a noncommissioned officer's uniform."

"Fine with me. All I know is the salute and how to sing "Lili Marlene." But what are you going to do if Charles chooses that moment to bare his soul to the camp commandant and trap us all?"

"He dies. The commandant dies. Any guards with us in the commandant's office die. We drive away very quickly and get across the border into France."

"If we aren't quick enough…"

"We die too."

"Jolly good. I'm glad you have a plan."

Kipp smiled. "Let's get into our uniforms and wake up Charles."

"I doubt he sleeps. I think he sits in that room with his back ramrod straight and his eyes wide open all day and all night. Do I get a monocle?"

"No one gets a monocle."

"Pity that."

Charles didn't smile or flicker an eye when they opened his door in their uniforms. He used the washroom and put his on without a murmur. A staff car had been parked behind the hotel for them. They drove it out of Berlin and toward the concentration camp. They lost their way twice but still were able to reach the camp just after ten in the morning. The sentries were expecting them and opened the gate to the section of the camp where the German soldiers and officers had their quarters. Harrison parked in front of an office building draped with Nazi flags.

As soon as the car pulled up, Baron von Isenburg stepped out and saluted. He was still in his black winter uniform. "*Heil* Hitler!"

Harrison, Kipp, and Charles returned the salute, lifting their arms. "*Heil* Hitler!"

"*Kommen in, bitte.*"

Harrison remained at attention by the staff car. Kipp and Charles entered the office behind the baron. The commandant was standing by his desk. He gave them the stiff-armed salute, which Kipp and Charles returned.

"*Sie wird hier in einem Augenblick*—She will be here in a moment," said the commandant. He glanced out the window. "*Naturlich, war sie im Stammlager*—Of course, she was in the main camp."

"*Sind da nur Deutsch Gefangenen hier*—Are there only German prisoners here?" asked Kipp in a brisk tone.

"*Nein,*" responded the commandant. "*Wir haben die Juden auch*—No, we have Jews as well."

Kipp offered him the transfer papers. The commandant merely glanced at them and nodded, continuing to look out the window.

"*Ah.*" The commandant turned from the window to face the door. "*Hier ist sie.*"

The door opened. Eva came into the office first, followed by two female guards. She was dressed in simple prison camp clothing that consisted of a shirt and pants and round cap. Her hair was cut down to her skull, her cheekbones were sharp, her blue eyes were dark with dark smudges under them. Her lips were pale and thin. She was not the woman Kipp had studied in photographs, and he had to force himself not to react in anger or revulsion. He glanced at the baron quickly. The baron did not flinch, and his face was like rock.

It was Charles who spoke out loud. "*Was haben Sie getan mit diese Frau?*—What have you done to this woman?"

The commandant's eyes were blank. "*Sie ist ein Verräterin des Reichs*—She is a traitor to the Reich."

Charles looked at the baron. "*Aber ist das nicht Ihre Tochter?*—Isn't this your daughter?"

The baron showed no emotion. "*Setze sie Auto*—Put her in the car."

She sat between the baron and Charles. Kipp was up front next to Harrison. They drove through the gate and back down the road.

"We're not using a normal border crossing into France." The baron leaned forward and spoke to Harrison in English. "Follow my directions."

"Yes, sir."

Charles kept looking at Eva and trying to get her to speak, but she stared straight ahead. Harrison had taken on more fuel at the camp, and they drove to the border without stopping. The baron directed him down a dirt track, where field guns and soldiers were hidden under camouflage netting. Finally they pulled in by a group of officers and a small French sedan with French plates. The officers gave normal army salutes with their hands at their foreheads, and everyone in the staff car but Eva gave the stiff-armed Nazi salute.

"You are English tourists," said the baron, handing out sets of clothes to Harrison and Charles and Eva. "There is a picnic basket in your sedan. The car is a rental. There are French troops all around this area. Pretend you are lost if you get stopped."

Harrison and Charles changed quickly but Eva made no move to remove her camp clothing. The baron took her into the trees and undressed her, gently replacing the camp shirt and pants with a skirt and blouse and sweater.

"Go to the civilian docks in Calais, Harrison," said Kipp. "There is a British boat called *Pea Porridge Hot*, a small cargo ship. The captain knows who you are. He will get you safely into Dover."

"All right."

"Road maps and identification papers are in the sedan. Head straight for Calais. You are crossing over the Channel at night. All should go well. I'll return from Berlin with the RAF contingent in a couple of days and look you up at Kensington Gate."

"Right."

Kipp shook his hand. "God bless, Harrison, and best of luck."

"Thank you."

The baron gathered his daughter in his arms. "I love you. God go with you. Someday you will understand."

She stared at him after he released her. Then she spat in his face.

Charles took Eva by the hand, and they sat in the backseat of the French car. Harrison started the engine and nursed the sedan forward along the track. A high section of barbed wire had been rolled to the side, and he drove through the gap. German soldiers saluted, and Harrison, in a tweed jacket and cap and dark brown pants, nodded his head. The track twisted back and forth on the French side and often looked as if it had disappeared entirely. Harrison nursed the car through a large cluster of bushes and onto a wide dirt road.

"Which way to Calais?" he asked out loud.

Neither Charles nor Eva responded.

He turned right. It came to a dead end and three French tanks. The soldiers leaning against the tanks stared.

"Calais?" asked Harrison. "Calais?" He waved a map he had found under his seat.

Several of the soldiers wandered over to the car, speaking French rapidly. They took the map and turned it around. One of them marked a circle near the German border and said, "*Ici, ici,*" and then jabbed at the coastline where Calais was printed in bold, black letters. He drew a line along various roads from the border to the coast.

"*Merci.*" Harrison smiled and turned the car around.

One of the soldiers slapped the hood. "Get away from the frontier, eh? You should not be here."

"Yes, yes, thank you very much indeed."

"*Allez.*"

They did not see soldiers or tanks again, but Harrison noticed tread marks on the dirt road as they headed north and west. In half an hour he steered onto a paved road with no shoulders and saw signs with Reims, Paris, and Calais painted on them.

"The country to our right will soon be Belgium, not Germany," Harrison said.

Once again there was no response from the backseat, where Charles sat in his shirt and pants and sweater, Eva beside him in her skirt and blouse and headscarf.

Eventually they began to drive past farms and carts pulled by horses and oxen. Men and women were walking with their children to and from church. Some waved, and some ignored the car. Traffic was heavier as they approached Reims, and Harrison thanked God when he got through Reims to the other side.

"The French drive like madmen!" he practically shouted. "Did you see that? Even on a Sunday! And Easter Sunday at that!"

Soon after they had gone past the towns of Laon and Cambrai the road split, the right heading to Dunkerque, the left to Calais.

"It won't be long now." Harrison glanced at the backseat. "Are you two all right?"

"How do you expect two people who are being abducted to feel?" snapped Charles.

The sun had dropped into the fields, and shadows swarmed over the sky and land as Harrison steered into Calais. After taking a number of wrong turns and asking for directions to the docks half a dozen times, he guessed correctly and made his way to the waterfront. Stars were coming out when they left the sedan and walked from ship to ship, looking for *Pea Porridge Hot*. They took ten minutes to find it. The captain was on deck and read the letter Harrison presented him from Kipp, looked all three of them over, and jerked his thumb at the bow.

"Make yourself comfortable up there. There'll be a sea chill, so I've piled a few woolen blankets by the cargo we've got netted down on the deck. Mind your heads. We'll be shoving off soon enough. She's a slow boat but sturdy. It'll take us a little under three hours to cross to Dover."

"Are French authorities going to want to talk to us?" asked Harrison.

The captain grunted. "No French officials are going to come near this boat. Your friends in high places made sure of that, didn't they?"

Pea Porridge Hot was moored with its stern to the dock. Harrison and Charles and Eva walked forward to the bow. Charles gave two blankets to Eva and helped her wrap them around her body. He drew one over his own shoulders and left the last two for Harrison. Then he stood beside Harrison and looked out at the dark waters.

"I'm surprised you got us this far without killing us," said Charles.

"There won't be any killing. Just a homecoming."

"Neither of us is going home. What do you intend to do with Eva?"

"I expect she'll stay with Lord and Lady Preston. They're good friends of the baron."

"Why can't she stay with my mother and Lord Kipp?"

"That's not for me to say."

"Is it possible?"

"You'll see Lord Kipp in a few days. You can ask him. Or ask your mother tonight. We'll be going from Dover straight into London."

"Why don't you ask me instead?"

Harrison turned quickly at the voice. Even in the dark he knew Lord Tanner was standing behind him.

"What are you doing here?" demanded Harrison.

"You mentioned a homecoming a few moments ago. That is why I'm here. To take my son and Eva von Isenburg back to Berlin."

"But father…" Charles's face was white in the blackness. "We gave an oath."

"And I've kept it. But Harrison here met with an unfortunate accident at the Calais waterfront. He drowned. The captain refused to take two young people across the Channel. I was contacted by the French authorities since I'm your father. I had no recourse but to bring the pair of you back to Berlin. I will explain all this to the SS."

"Father, they won't believe you."

"Of course they'll believe me. The French will make sure they believe me because they'll produce the body and explain the situation on my behalf."

Two tall men appeared on either side of Lord Tanner.

"The captain'll not let you get away with this," protested Harrison.

"Of course he will. I've given him twenty quid. He'll stay below till Charles shouts man overboard. I'll wait until French officials have contacted German authorities and then drive up. I was in Calais on business, you see."

"Father—"

"Don't trouble yourself, Charles. The SS will be fine. Trust me." He pointed with the silver head of his walking stick. "Take the young lady around to the port side. No doubt Harrison will put up a fruitless struggle, and she doesn't need to see that."

"It won't be fruitless." Harrison squared his shoulders.

Lord Tanner laughed and turned his head to one of his men. "Kill him and pitch him over the side. A sharp blow to the head is what's needed. Use your clubs and—"

Harrison threw himself at the man on Lord Tanner's left, knocking him flat and seizing his head swiftly in his large hands and banging it twice against the steel deck so that he went limp. Then he struck out with his legs and took Tanner off his feet. The other man swung at Harrison with his club and hit his left arm a hard blow. Harrison winced but propelled himself at the man headfirst, hurling him over the side of the boat into the water.

"I don't need dockyard thugs." Tanner was back on his feet. "I'll kill you myself." He drew the sword from his cane. "Where's your shotgun, Harrison?"

Harrison tore off his jacket as Tanner lunged and snagged the sword with it. As Tanner struggled to pull his blade free, Harrison punched him twice in the face and slapped his arms around Tanner's neck from behind, squeezing as he kicked and squirmed until the brawny Scotsman collapsed. He expected Charles to do something, but the young man remained where he was, one arm around Eva.

Harrison turned to face Charles. "Are we all right? Or do you want to mix it up?"

"I gave an oath," was all Charles said in reply.

"I haven't killed him."

Harrison dragged Tanner off the boat and tossed him on the dock. Then he did the same with the man he had knocked unconscious. When he looked around for the one he'd thrown into the water he spotted a tall figure, water pouring off its back, half running and half limping along the waterfront. Harrison went below, grabbed the captain by the front of his shirt, snarled at him and his crew, and told him to get the ship to Dover before midnight.

"And I'll take the twenty quid for my troubles," he growled.

The captain was staring at Harrison in horror.

"What's the matter?" Harrison demanded.

"There's blood all over your face."

"Is there? Well, don't worry yourself. It's not mine."

Pea Porridge Hot docked at Dover just after eleven. Three RAF officers were waiting for the travelers, and they were whisked away in a car to London. Harrison was in the backseat with Eva and Charles, and he was conscious of Eva's eyes remaining fixed on him throughout the drive. Finally he looked at her.

"What is it?" he asked.

"I saw death and murder in that camp." Her voice was rough, and she could barely speak. "I saw the devil." She reached out with narrow boney fingers and clutched his arm. "You could have rescued me from that. You could have fought them all and set me free."

He put one of his hands over hers. "I just have."

Three days later
Ashton Park

"It's not the best that could be hoped for but it's not the worst either." Holly rubbed her hands as hard as she could into Harrison's bare back as he lay on his stomach.

"What's that supposed to mean?"

"It means that while you were out surveying your domain, Caroline rung me up and we had a little chat."

"How are those two kids getting along?"

"That's the thing. They aren't as talkative as Caroline could have wished, particularly in her wildest dreams, but neither are they as morose or sullen as she feared they'd be. Once she granted Eva permission to stay with them, instead of going to William and Elizabeth's, Charles thawed thirty to forty degrees. He spoke with Caroline then, even called her Mum, and wasn't averse to saying a few words to Kipp once he showed up. No torrent, mind you, but a few raindrops are better than nothing. Even Eva is opening her mouth. Not a lot, but she's talking."

"I thought she'd clam up tighter than a Nazi drum."

"We all did."

"Why the change, do you think?"

"Apparently it's you, my love."

Harrison rolled over on his side. "Me? Why, I was the one who abducted them."

"Eva doesn't speak about it that way. She hated what she saw at the concentration camp. You were the one who liberated her from that. What's more, you proved you could protect her when you laid low those blokes on the boat and sword-wielding Lord Tanner." She patted him on the shoulder. "Back on your stomach, Bravest of the Brave."

Harrison grunted as he lay flat again. "What was it about a few weeks in the camp that had such an effect on Eva?"

"She hasn't said a great deal about it. But she saw women and children executed. She saw them worked to death. Not just once. Every single day she was there. You freed her from that. Caroline says she hardly opens her mouth but your name doesn't come up. Evidently that goes for *Heil* Hitler Charles too. He told Kipp you'd be a worthy commander for the *Wehrmacht*."

"And what is that?"

"The German name for their armed forces—army, navy, air force, the lot."

Harrison snorted. "Not likely."

"In any case, they've both asked to see you."

"See me? You're joking."

"No, they really do wish to see you."

"I've nothing to say. They'll have to work things out as best they can. I've Ashton Park to look after."

"I told them you'd be by tomorrow and that you'd stay over a few nights."

Harrison rolled over on his side again. "You did what?"

"I can manage things here perfectly well, love." She slid her crimson fingernails over his chest. "Now don't disappoint me. You can do a great deal of good for those children."

"They're hardly children—"

"They *are* children and they're asking for you. For all you know, Charles feels liberated too." She put her scarlet lips to his chest, leaving a red smudge, and to his mouth. "I'm proud of you. And you're going to make me prouder."

"I'm too—"

Her kiss cut him off. She held it for a long time, her hands braced against his chest, before she pulled back.

"Now, what were you saying?" she asked.

Harrison was catching his breath. "It's slipped my mind."

"You do this for me and the children, and your reward will be great, Sir Calvert Harrison."

"Rubies?"

"Greater than rubies."

"Diamonds and gold?"

"Much greater than diamonds and gold."

"The Crown Jewels then?"

She kissed him gently on the lips again. "There will be more when you return."

"Ah, you know my weakness, my dear. Even without the kisses I'd do it. You only needed to make the request as you have done."

"That's the spirit of chivalry. Now don't you wish the noble deed was finished and you were marching back through those oaken doors to collect your bounty from your lady?"

"I do. I very much do."

He winked and began to sing softly.

> See, the conqu'ring hero comes!
> Sound the trumpets, beat the drums.
> Sports prepare, the laurel bring,
> Songs of triumph to him sing.
> See, the conqu'ring hero comes!
> Sound the trumpets, beat the drums.

Harrison stayed a fortnight at Kipp and Caroline's townhouse in Camden Lock, surprising himself and his wife. At first, while Eva and Charles were glad to see him, the talk was general and mostly about how he drove them through France and how he fought off the three men on the boat, including Lord Tanner. Charles stuck to his favorite topic of Germany annexing England until a week of meals and walks with Harrison had gone by. One afternoon, after listening to his father's broadcast on the superiority of the German air force, he found Harrison where he was trimming a hedge for Caroline.

"You say Mr. Danforth—Kipp—is testing aircraft?" he asked as Harrison snapped away with his garden shears.

"That's right."

"Where exactly?"

"Suffolk. Out east."

Charles watched Harrison work with the shears a few moments. "I suppose it's a restricted area."

"It is indeed."

"Are the planes any good? They can't be better than our Messerschmitt."

"It would depend a great deal on the pilot, wouldn't it?"

"I've flown with some of the best."

"Some, but not all."

Charles was silent again as Harrison worked his way along the hedge. "Is there another pair of shears, do you know?" Charles suddenly asked.

"The tool shed is just at the back of the house. You can take a look."

"Can I go down to see my—can I go out to Suffolk and watch Mr. Danforth fly?"

"Mr. Danforth?"

"Well, Kipp. You know, Kipp."

"Lord Kipp." Harrison paused with the shears open. "When were you thinking?"

"Could we...well, Friday?"

"Friday? Don't you have a date to meet up with some of the British Union of Fascists?"

Charles put his hands in the pockets of his shorts and glanced at a robin perched on the eaves trough of the townhouse. "I'd rather go to the airfield."

Harrison set down his shears. "What's all this about then?"

"What do you mean?"

"You were keen on marching with the Blackshirts a week ago and changing England from the inside out."

"I still want to do that. It's just that...well, talking with you, seeing my Mum, listening to Eva's stories..."

"What sort of stories?"

"About the camp. The tortures and the killings. She cries a lot, you know. When no one's around. When she thinks I'm not listening."

Harrison took the fedora off his head, smoothed down the hawk feather in the hatband, and turned it over in his hand, examining it. "You've always put across you're a hard-boiled Nazi. So does Eva."

"We're both committed to Germany. We're both committed to the Reich."

"So why the long faces?"

"Some things...some things are not as they should be."

"What things?"

Charles sat down on the paving stones and drew his legs up to his chest. He rested his arms on the tops of his bare knees. "Hitler and the Nazis have been very good for Germany," he said. "They certainly put a new soul in my body. Britain is just so soft and undedicated compared to the new Germany—it has no purpose, whereas the Third Reich has great purpose."

Harrison pulled off his gardening gloves and sat down next to Charles. It began to sprinkle, and raindrops beaded on their hands and boots.

"It is very exciting…all the energy, the ambition, the march into the future," Charles went on. "Eva feels the same way I do. But there are some who come into the movement and do things that are not good for Germany."

"It may be those things were in the movement right from the start and perhaps you just didn't notice…or care to notice."

"Oh, but I think I *would* have noticed. The question of the Jews, yes, that was always before us. But I did not expect such a large number of executions. Certainly not of children."

"You could write your father about it."

"What good would that do? He can't say anything about it on a broadcast, can he? And for all I know he wouldn't want to. Yes, deal with the Jews, we must deal with the Jews, but slaughter? That is not a way of German or Nazi honor."

"Maybe not German, Charles, but I'm not sure about Nazi."

The young man's face was grim. "You think we are all monsters."

"Who runs the concentration camps?"

Charles stared straight ahead and did not answer. "I just want to put something else in Eva's head, something else in her dreams. Can she come to that airfield where Mr. Danforth tests the aircraft?"

"I don't even know if you can. I'll have to talk to your mum and make a few calls. Are you sure you want to go down there?"

"I'm sure."

"Lord Tanner won't take too kindly to that once he finds out, will he?"

Charles didn't respond. Slowly he peeled up the side of his shirt that faced Harrison. There were three long jagged scars.

Harrison sucked in his breath between clenched teeth. "Those aren't very old."

"I don't wish to discuss it. I don't wish you to talk about it with anyone. My father felt it would make me stronger. There were other ways and means he employed. Some obvious, some not so obvious." He pulled the shirt back down. "I never thought about it until Eva spoke to me about the concentration camp. Until the weeks I've had here."

"I don't understand what you mean by that."

"You are strong. And you are tough. But you would never do that to make me just as strong or tough."

"No, I wouldn't," Harrison replied. "Neither would Lord Kipp."

"Eva has worse wounds. Let her come with us to the airfield."

"I have no idea what they'll say. I can't promise anything." The rain grew heavier, but neither of them moved. "What makes you think a trip like that would help Eva?"

"I don't know. But she can't just be a spectator. She has to go up."

"Go up? I doubt very much they'll let either of you do that even if you are granted permission to visit."

Rain poured over Charles's face. "She's very strong. But a flight would make her stronger. It would get her through. Otherwise I don't know if she'll make it."

"What would flying do?"

"The freedom…of the eagle, of the falcon. She was imprisoned for a long time. The concentration camp added another ten years in just four weeks. She needs the flying."

"And you need it too."

"*Ja*, I need it. But she needs it more than I do. So if only one can go up with Mr. Danforth…with Kipp, it should be her."

"How do you know she's not afraid to fly?"

"I don't know. But she is a good German. She has to overcome any fears and do what she must. If I sense it, she must sense it too. She has to fly. Everything that binds her to earth has to fall away."

Harrison wiped the rainwater from his eyes. "I'd never have taken you for a philosopher. You're like your Uncle Hartmann."

"Hartmann's a traitor. I'm not him and I'm not a philosopher. Unless perhaps you wish to compare me to a good Nazi philosopher like Nietzsche."

"Can't say as I know the chap."

"Nietzsche knew the importance of strength. And throwing off shackles."

"Right." Harrison blinked up at the rainclouds. "We'd best put the shears away and get indoors. I'll ring up some of those RAF folk you and this Nietzsche fellow are anxious I talk to."

"I'll sit out here a while."

"In the rain?"

"Yes, in the rain."

"Suit yourself." Harrison got to his feet. "Take your time."

Charles hugged his knees to his chest and closed his eyes.

Two hours later Harrison was handing the phone to Charles.

"Go ahead," Harrison said to Charles's white face and dark eyes. "He wants to speak with you."

"Who does?"

"Lord Kipp. I rang him about the trip to the airfield."

"Hello," said Charles.

"Good afternoon, Charles. How are you?"

"I'm all right."

"Harrison tells me you'd like to come out to Suffolk."

"Yes, sir."

"That you might even like to go up like you did with Udet and von Zeltner during the Olympics?"

"Is it possible?"

"I'll speak with my commanding officer. It's unlikely he'll let you go up, but I might catch him in an ebullient mood. He has one of those now and then."

"I don't know what that means."

"Cheerful. He might relent and let us both squeeze into the cockpit. *Might*. As a favor to me—and if he thinks you're a potential RAF recruit from the Danforth family."

"It's more important that Eva fly with you."

"Eva? I can't imagine being given the nod to take her up."

"She has to go in the plane."

"Why?"

"She has been trapped."

"I'm not sure I'll be able to get permission, Charles."

"Please try, sir."

"I'll do what I can if you think a flight in an airplane will make that much of a difference to her."

Later that evening, Caroline found Harrison in the library, where he was sipping a coffee and flipping through the pages of a newspaper.

"I've been with Eva," she said, taking a seat. "She even let me pray with her a bit."

Harrison put down the paper. "I'm glad to hear it."

"I rang up Kipp at his flat by the base. His commanding officer isn't keen on the idea of Charles or Eva coming down."

"No, I didn't think he would be."

"It's all rather silly, isn't it? A plane ride. For that matter we could find a flight instructor to take her and Charles up for a couple of pounds. One of the chaps from the airline Kipp and Ben sold off might do it for free."

"So they might. But apparently that's not the point."

"Why does it have to be Kipp?"

"I don't know. Eva doesn't even know him, and Charles hasn't had much use for him for the past couple of years, has he?"

Caroline looked at his cup. "Shall I fetch the pot?"

"Not at all. That's enough for me for the night."

"I wish you'd speak with her."

"Me?"

Caroline lifted one shoulder in a shrug. "You were her liberator."

"What do you want me to say?"

"That she'll live."

"Is that what's bothering her? I thought she missed the fatherland. I thought they both did."

"But you've spoken with Charles. You know it's more than that."

"The whole thing puzzles me, Lady Caroline. I really don't know what to make of their mix of Nazism and German pride and pain and desperation."

"I don't either. Still, she asked for you."

"Right. Nothing much in the paper in any case. A lot of nonsense about the Germans demanding a piece of Czechoslovakia for their empire."

He went down the hall with the cup of warm coffee in his hand and knocked at Eva's door. She responded in German. He entered her room.

"Hullo," he greeted her.

She was in a pale blue dress and sitting on the edge of her bed. Her arms and legs were still thin and her face sunken. Her eyes were like black holes.

"My father locked me away so I wouldn't tell anyone about the Jews he was hiding."

Harrison sat in a chair facing her.

"I hate the Jews. I hate him."

Harrison said nothing.

"You brought me out of all that. You unlocked my prisons."

"Not just me."

"I know. Mr. Danforth as well. He organized the entire affair."

"So did your father."

"No, he didn't."

"How do you think we got the SS uniforms? Why do you think the camp commandant released you so easily? Who made it possible for Charles to be with us? Your father arranged all of that."

"It doesn't matter. I'll never see him again." She clenched her hands together. "I'm frightened to death of flying. Did Charles tell you that?"

"No."

"But I believe it would be another key in another lock. Opening it. Do you see that?"

"The likelihood of your going up with Lord Kipp is slim, Miss von Isenburg."

"Please don't call me that."

"I don't think it can be done."

"They shot some of the children in the back of the head. Others were so young they wouldn't waste the bullet. So they crushed their little skulls with rifle stocks or the heels of their boots."

"I'm sorry."

"I never heard such shrieking and pleading in my life. The mothers. It didn't matter. The SS shot them too."

"You don't have to go back."

"I want to go back. But not while my father's alive. Not while there are SS. A Germany five or ten years from now."

"What sort of Germany will that be, do you think?"

"If the SS is gone, something stronger will have removed them. But not without a fight. So perhaps Germany will be like me. Broken to pieces yet still wanting a second life."

"I wish you would eat more."

Eva stared at him with her dark eyes. "All in good time."

Harrison lifted his cup. "I can get you some coffee."

"Will we keep talking?"

"Yes."

"I'll try some then."

Three days later
Ashton Park

"Come along, Eva. The plane's ready for you."

"I like the ash trees. There are so many of them." Eva looked at Holly. "Would you mind if I stayed here a few days?"

Holly smiled. "Stay as long as you like. It's a great empty old estate with so many of the family off in London. I'd love to have you."

Eva's eyes remained dark and empty. "I'd like to live in a forest."

"We can furnish you with a tent. But come along. Kipp only has loan of the plane for a few hours."

The two women began to walk out of the trees toward the airstrip by the Ashton Park manor.

"I still don't understand why the commanding officer wouldn't let us into the air base in Suffolk."

"I suppose things are more tense all around and he didn't want Germans or Nazis on the grounds. It's nothing about you, Eva. It's about Europe and its politics."

"I don't like to hear about it but you should tell me just the same."

"Herr Hitler wants the Sudetenland—regions of Czechoslovakia that have a large number of Germans residing in them. He feels Sudetenland should be part of the German nation. There's a lot of fuss and bother and Britain's heavily involved."

Kipp was standing with Harrison and Charles by a biplane. A huge green meadow stretched all around them.

"There you are." Kipp extended a hand toward the front cockpit. "You're in the front. I'll be flying the aircraft from right behind you in the rear cockpit."

"It looks like something from the war." Eva held back.

"Well, we use it to train young pilots. It's called a Tiger Moth. Steady as a rock." He grinned. "RAF gave me the loan. To make up for barring us from their base."

"Go on, Eva," Charles urged.

"I'd rather you went first," she responded.

"We've been through all that."

"Here." Harrison linked his arm through hers, and she let him walk her to the plane. "You said you wanted to open more doors."

Kipp handed her a leather jacket, a flying helmet, and a white silk scarf. "There were many great German fliers in nineteen eighteen. That's only twenty years ago. It will be just like you're one of them."

Harrison helped her on with the jacket and helmet and goggles. "There you are." He wound the scarf about her neck. "Now fly. Fly like a falcon."

In a matter of minutes the Tiger Moth lifted from the ground and was hurtling over the grass. Eva stared to her left and her right. Three swallows burst over the top wing and swung down through the air. The sky had turned from gray to blue with long trails of white clouds the plane swept through. They went higher and higher. Ashton Park seemed like a dollhouse, and the people watching the Tiger Moth were as toy figures. Then the plane wheeled right, and there was no longer any earth, only vast stretches of the blue and the white touched by lances of light as bright as fire.

Eva bit her knuckles. "*Oh, mein Gott, was haben Sie gemacht?—Oh, my God, what have You made?*"

As Kipp banked the Tiger Moth into the sun and a flock of blackbirds broke apart in response to the roar of the engine, gold filled Eva's eyes, and she could feel tears begin. She couldn't stop them. Her whole body heaved and her shoulders shook. She pulled off the goggles and put a hand to her face, struggling to control herself and fighting for the breaths she took, her chest cut with the pain and the beauty of everything she was feeling.

Kipp tapped her back from behind.

She turned her head and glanced back, the tears moving quickly down her face.

Kipp didn't appear to notice. "Take—the—stick!" He spoke the words loudly and slowly, forming each word with his lips. "Take—the—stick!"

She shook her head. "I can't."

He nodded his head in slow, strong movements. "Take as much time as you need. I need you to fly the plane."

"I don't understand you."

"I—need—you—to—fly—the—plane."

"No, no, I can't."

"I'm not able to fly the plane the way you need it to be flown. Only you can do that."

"Lord Kipp—"

He lifted his hands in the air, palms toward her.

The Tiger Moth dipped, and Eva seized the stick. As the plane began to dive, she pulled up on it with both hands. It began a steep climb, swaying from side to side. She closed her eyes and took one hand off the stick.

"*Als ob ich Sie fühlen Kann*—If I can feel You."

She banked the plane to the left. Eyes still shut, she leveled the aircraft out.

Harrison's face was clear in her mind. So was the face of Charles.

"*Fliegen. Fliegen wie ein Falke*—Fly like a falcon."

She opened her eyes and gazed at the blue and gold she was streaking through.

She took in deep breaths.

She pulled her goggles down again and could see the vast forest of ash trees ahead and below and white birds rising from them as she nudged the plane toward the sea. Suddenly they were over the waves. The spread of blue and emerald and sky and water seemed unlimited to her. She pushed the Tiger Moth farther and farther, light flashing off its wings. Gently she curved the plane north over the curve of the earth and the curve of the ocean.

"*Ich habe getraumt, so viele Traume*—I dreamed so many dreams."

Later Eva stood in the forest, and it was raining. She had eluded everyone and was completely on her own by one of the Ashton Park ponds. Her face was dark in the water of the pond. The rainfall kept disturbing the surface and distorting her image.

Eventually she made her way along a narrow track and emerged from the ash grove. She stood on a cliff looking at the sea that she had flown over two hours before. A wind had come up, the whitecaps were larger, and there were thousands more of them. On the cliff edge the raindrops stung like small stones. She wanted that. She spread her arms and let the wind and rain lash her body and scour her skin.

Into her mind came the image of a small boat and a sail, and she could hear the cry of gulls even though there were no gulls flying above the cliff.

"Is there a sailing boat?"

"Yes, but not here, Eva. My brother, Lord Preston, keeps it moored in Dover."

"May I go there, Lady Holly? May I sail on it?"

"Why, of course. Parliament will have its summer recess soon enough, and my brother and his wife intend to spend the summer months at the family estate at Dover Sky. We can go down with you for a few days."

"I would like to stay there a very long time…if it is possible."

"If that's what you would like, you certainly may do so, my dear. But I warn you, Lord Preston will try to turn you into a sailor. He is always keen to take on new members to crew his ship."

"And what is the name of his ship?"

"*Pluck.*"

"*Pluck*? What does that mean, Lady Holly?"

"Courage, Eva. It means great courage and spirit."

July, 1938
The English Channel, near the Port of Dover

"Have you nothing to recite for us, Owen?"

"Of course I do, Grandfather. I don't want to bore our guest, that's all."

Eva smiled as the *Pluck* smacked into another wave, white foam breaking over its bow. "You won't bore me."

"It's not a German poet."

"It doesn't have to be a German poet to please me, Owen."

She watched the young man with the curly dark red hair and striking blue eyes hold the pose of a pompous orator, and she laughed. He laughed too. Then his handsome young face grew serious, and he put his hands in his pockets.

> I care not for the land or its shores
> Its teeming cities or ravenous throngs
>
> I look instead to where there is no end
> Of sea or sky or air or light
>
> I look to where white birds sing
> And cry with a harshness that has a sweeter ring
>
> Than all the ballads and arias of man
> All the instruments played by our hands

I long to sail on waters so deep
It seemed I flew in skies spread under my feet

With fish of gold and scarlet for my birds
Reefs for mountains and coral for clouds

Jade and amethyst for what I must breathe
Pearls and sapphire for all I need see

And give me a storm that puts wind in my heart
Give me a thunder of breakers on rock

Let me open my wings like the Caspian tern
Let me burn, let me illumine, like the rays of the sun

I will have the sea and all that it gives
All that it promises and all that lives

Deep in its soul and I shall be free
To drink of its years and learn of its hours

To sail on its colors and all of its waters
With no end in sight
No ending to light

Eva's lips had parted in surprise as Owen recited the poem with a spirit and intensity she hadn't expected in a boy. She knew he was sixteen, but he grew older than that before her eyes until he was almost twenty like her, or even twenty-one or twenty-two or twenty-three.

She took a handful of her blond hair that had grown longer and softer, tucked it under the collar of her pea coat, and got to her feet, bracing her legs in the swell, and clapped as loudly as she could.

"Wonderful, *wunderbar*!" For all the care she had taken, the sea breeze caught her hair and tugged it loose, spreading it like a wave over her shoulders and back. She didn't see the light that came quickly into Owen's eyes when this happened. "That was a beautiful recitation. Now you must tell me the name of the poem and the poet."

Owen smiled, looked down, and shook his head.

"Oh, come, my bright English sailor, how can you be shy now when you were, yes, bold as brass while you spoke all those beautiful words?"

Owen looked to the bow. "Excuse me, I must tend to a line." He scrambled forward.

Eva hugged her arms around her chest and pouted. She appealed to Lord Preston, who was at the helm. "Grandfather, won't you tell me?"

"Why, my dear, I'm sure I don't know." He turned the wheel slightly to port. "Wordsworth? Tennyson?" He snapped his fingers. "John Masefield. It's John Masefield."

Owen came back from the bowsprit. Eva couldn't help but notice the water drops in his hair and the shining on his face. He laughed, and she felt as if the sea breeze had darted down her throat and swept through her veins and lungs right through to her stomach. Her fingers went to her lips.

Don't be mad. You're almost four years older than him.

"It isn't Masefield," he said.

"Then who is it?" demanded Lord Preston. "You can't crew on my ship and not declare the poet and the poem. It's just not done. I'll keelhaul ye."

"Oh, all right." Owen put his hands in his pockets again and looked out over the starboard side and past Eva where she stood, her hair swirling in the wind like wings. "I wrote it."

"What?" Eva stared at him. "*Das ist unmoglich*—That's impossible."

He tugged two crumpled pieces of paper out of a back pocket. They had been folded many times. He handed them to her.

"It has lines crossed out and other lines written on top, and there's ink spots and all that, but I think you can still read it."

Eva took the pieces of paper, astonishment remaining on her face, and unfolded them.

"I say, that's capital." Lord Preston smiled at Owen. "I can't blame our female crewmember for her skepticism; that's rather a lot of finesse for a young lad like yourself. But you and I have been reciting the great poems back and forth for years, so I can't say as I'm very much surprised. She's only been out with us half a dozen times, so she hasn't an inkling the sort of poetry that's lodged in our heads. What do you call what you've written?"

"I'd rather not say."

"Why, it's jotted down here." Eva looked up. "Crossed out twice and printed in large black letters one final time. I don't understand, Owen."

"What is it?" demanded Lord Preston.

She waited for Owen to speak. "'Eva,'" he finally said. "I named the poem 'Eva.'"

"You named the poem 'Eva'? That's brilliant. What a nice gesture. What do you think of that, my girl?"

Eva was still looking at Owen. "*Ich denke, es ist sehr schon*—I think it's very beautiful. I'm touched, Grandfather."

Owen finally met her gaze.

"So you are sixteen," she said in a low voice that the wind and waves snatched away from Lord Preston's ears.

"Almost seventeen." He offered her a smile but she didn't smile back.

"And I am almost twenty, Owen. With already a long history. And so many scars I feel I am forty or fifty. Why would you write such a poem and put my name to it? Surely you have a girl you like at school?"

"I wrote the poem first. It did not fit anyone. Except yourself."

"How can you say that?"

"I thought about it. I even prayed about it. The words do not work for any other person. That's all I can tell you."

Despite herself, Eva could not keep from smiling at the beauty of his youthfulness, at the sea blue of his eyes, the windburn on his cheeks, the dark red tangle of his boyish hair.

"So you may be sixteen, Owen, but in your soul you are far older than I am. What am I going to do? Am I getting to know the younger man or the older man?"

He shrugged and tried another smile. "Both, I suppose. Is that quite unpleasant for you?"

"It's not unpleasant at all." She returned his smile. "May I keep this?"

"Of course."

She looked at the waves that were curling near their bow. "I have a proposal for you. Let us stay friends. *Ja*, I know the eager young man with the soul of a thirty-year-old does not want to hear that. But I'm not finished. Read the poem to me again, from memory, like today. Read it to me after you have turned eighteen. Let us see what kind of man you are then. That's not too long to wait, is it? Recite the poem when we are in the Channel here and we will know. *Ja*? All right."

Owen looked down again, his face glum. "Whatever you say."

She leaned over quickly and placed a kiss on his cheek. And patted one side of his face. "Do not be sad, Owen. You are a very special young man. Thank you for being a healing for me."

She folded the poem and put it in the pocket of her pea coat.

"Let us see what happens in nineteen forty," she said. "That is not so very far away, is it?"

"Nonsense." Lord Preston noisily cleared his throat.

Eva and Owen were both startled, turning their heads quickly to look at him.

"The man does not always have to be older than the woman. Where is that written?" Lord Preston passed the spokes of the wheel through his hands. "Still, nineteen forty is a good idea. I will pray for the two of you, and we shall see where nineteen forty finds us. Eh?"

"Yes, sir," replied Owen.

Eva smiled. "Yes, Grandfather."

Two months later, Prime Minister Neville Chamberlain stood outside his offices at 10 Downing Street and spoke to the crowds gathered there. It was October 1. He had just returned from Germany the day before, where he had signed the Munich Agreement with Adolf Hitler. This had resolved the crisis over Czechoslovakia to his satisfaction—Hitler would get the Sudetenland, and the rest of Czechoslovakia would never be touched. Chamberlain was also happy about a peace treaty with Germany he had signed.

"My good friends," he said, "for the second time in our history, a British prime minister has returned from Germany bringing peace with honor. I believe it is peace for our time. We thank you from the bottom of our hearts. Go home and get a nice quiet sleep."

"Good man," American president Franklin Delano Roosevelt cabled from Washington.

As Chamberlain spoke, Nazi troops were marching over the border into Czechoslovakia and claiming the Sudetenland for Germany, a right Chamberlain had granted with his signing of the Munich Agreement. Lord Preston's friend Winston Churchill spared no words when he attacked Chamberlain in the House of Commons for giving in to Hitler's demands over the Sudetenland. "You were given the choice between war and dishonor. You chose dishonor and you will have war."

He glanced at Lord Preston at his seat, nodded, and fixed his harsh gaze on Chamberlain once more. "And do not suppose that this is the end. This is only the beginning of the reckoning. This is only the first sip, the first foretaste of a bitter cup which will be proffered to us year by year unless by a supreme recovery of moral health and martial vigor, we arise again and take our stand for freedom as in the olden time."

Charles was ecstatic about Hitler's occupation of large sections of Czechoslovakia. But when Jewish shops and synagogues and houses were burned and looted in Germany, Austria, and the Sudetenland on November 9 and 10, and close to one hundred Jews killed, he was more subdued. Watching newsreels of the destruction, he said to his mother, "I do not care for the Jews. But neither do I care for civil disorder in Germany either. Surely there is a better way of dealing with the Jewish problem than this."

Eva merely said, "The longer I am in England, and the longer I live with this family, the less of a Nazi I am becoming and the more I love the things the Nazis hate."

In March 1939, German soldiers marched from the Sudetenland into the remainder of Czechoslovakia and seized it for Nazi Germany. Part of Czechoslovakia became the Protectorate of Bohemia and Moravia, part of it became the Slovak Republic, and the greater part became one with the Third Reich.

"I am betrayed," Chamberlain said to Lord Preston in private. "Hitler has gone back on his word. You will work with the government and myself to prepare our nation and Empire for war. It will not be long before Herr Hitler makes another demand. My sense of it is that it will be Poland. There are already Nazi rumbles about claiming Danzig and a section of Poland so that Germany is no longer divided from its province of East Prussia. I believe we must sign an agreement of some sort guaranteeing Polish sovereignty. You have family in the RAF and the Royal Navy, do you not?"

"Yes, Prime Minister," Lord Preston responded. "And the army."

"You are the very man to have at my side. The Cabinet will take note of your advice since you have so many serving in a military capacity."

"I shall do whatever you ask of me."

"Good, good, very good." Chamberlain's eyes suddenly grew dark. "But what do you think, Lord Preston? Do we have much time? Hitler has played us for the fool so long, I worry we will not be ready should he strike a harder blow at Europe and Great Britain."

"We will do our best, Prime Minister. I'm sure we will be up to the task just as we were twenty years ago."

But to his wife Lord Preston confided, "I don't wish to distress you, my dear, but we are fallen upon hard times. I believe, as the prime minster does, that Herr Hitler will not cease with his demands and that one day those demands will bring us into a state of war."

"Oh, surely not, William." Lady Preston put down her hairbrush. "No one wants nineteen fourteen again, not ourselves and certainly not the Germans. Good will must prevail, good will and calmer heads."

Lord Preston stood looking out the window at the gray sweep of spring rain over Kensington Gate and the city of London. "Good will is unraveling all across Europe, Elizabeth. And as for calmer heads, why, there are none, except those who have, with a steady hand and a steady eye, begun to make preparations for armed conflict. A catastrophe is descending upon us, and I confess it drives me to my knees, my dear. It drives me to my knees and obliterates all thoughts of happiness and joy from my heart."

6

May, 1939
The Hartmann Chalet, Pura, Switzerland

"With the takeover of Czechoslovakia by the Germans and the conquest of Albania by Italy, much has changed, and quickly. You appreciate that, I'm sure, Professor Hartmann." The man tapped a cigarette against his silver cigarette holder.

Albrecht nodded. "Now Greece feels threatened by the so-called Kingdom of Italy, and Poland feels endangered by the Third Reich."

"Exactly." The man tapped his cigarette again. "So you will understand what I am about to tell you."

Albrecht leaned back in his chair in his study. "Go ahead."

"The German ambassador has made it clear that his government does not appreciate your attacks in book form or at the university lectern."

"You mean my attacks against a political entity that murdered scores of Jews last fall and burned their places of worship to the ground?"

The man hesitated a moment and then tapped his cigarette again. "I mean the government of the ambassador to the nation of Germany. He says Herr Hitler has, on a number of occasions, been literally white with fury at things you have said or written." Tap, tap. "I have no doubt Europe will be in flames in a year's time. I do not want to see Switzerland in flames along with it."

"Neither do I."

"So you will cooperate with us when I tell you no more of your books or pamphlets can possibly be published or distributed in our country."

Albrecht sat up straight. "You can't be serious, sir. I have just finished a fourth book addressing the excesses of the Nazi regime, and it's ready to go to print this summer."

"It will not go to print this summer. It will never go to print, Professor Hartmann. Herr Hitler is rattling the saber at his waist entirely too much. Although we can give a good account of ourselves should the German Army attack, we have very little defense against their air force. You saw what happened in Spain. Their bombers would devastate our cities. Yes, we can block the tunnels, yes, we can dynamite the mountain passes and make it difficult for their armor and infantry to advance. But how do we stop the *Luftwaffe*? And suppose they use paratroopers, their *Fallschirmjäger* units? We have reliable intelligence that such military endeavors are well within their grasp. So it would not matter to them if we barricaded the roadways for a few days or weeks. By that time their soldiers would have swarmed over our cities by the thousands by means of parachutes."

"You are exaggerating the danger, sir."

"You are underestimating it. Who is to stop the Germans from invading Switzerland or the rest of Europe? The League of Nations?"

"I will publish my books."

"You will not. Nor will you speak again. The universities are closed to you. So are the pulpits. So are the radio stations—there will be no more broadcasts."

"This is absurd."

The man tapped his cigarette. "These are the precautions one takes when a dangerous man is loose in the neighborhood and you do not wish to provoke him in any way. No one knows what he might do next, what risk he might take. Can you guarantee he will not invade Switzerland?"

"I can guarantee my books will make no difference. Eventually he will invade where and when he wants to. My books have no influence on the strategies of a madman."

The man smiled. "No doubt Herr Hitler has already had his generals draw up a plan for an all-out assault on our nation. You have not caused that. But what you can give Hitler is an excuse. He is always ready to pounce on any excuse. A Nazi diplomat was shot in Paris, and days later synagogues were burned to the ground—some seven thousand of them. We must ask you to stop speaking and stop writing, Professor Hartmann."

"The Swiss government asks me to do this?"

"Yes."

"Switzerland asks me to do this? The bastion of democracy?"

The man's face hardened. "We are not asking. It will be done. As of today. As of this moment."

Albrecht stood up. "Get out of my house."

The man rose. "Being rude to me will not gain you any leverage with the Swiss government."

"I clearly do not have any leverage with the Swiss government. You have muzzled me."

"You are free to remain in our country for as long as you wish. We are not denying you food or drink or a place to live."

"No. You are only denying me a reason to live. Get out."

The man opened the study door. "The ban is in effect immediately. I beg of you not to violate it. You could be imprisoned. Fined. Or sent back to Germany. I do not think you would be welcomed back in Berlin with the same sort of worship and ardor you find among your followers here."

> Dear Mum and Dad,
>
> We must return to England as soon as possible. The Swiss have denied Albrecht the freedom to speak or publish under threat of imprisonment or extradition back to Germany. Their ultimatum has thrown us all into a tizzy. They are afraid of the Germans. The Nazis have complained to them about Albrecht's sermons and books and university lectures, and the Swiss are worried that Hitler will use all of that as an excuse to put Switzerland in its place. They are greatly afraid of bombers over their cities and the use of incendiaries as well as the assault of thousands of soldiers by means of parachutes. It seems fanciful to Albrecht and me, but the ban is already in effect. Once the children have completed their school year we will begin the journey by train from here to the French coast. Pray for us. I will write again once we are on the verge of departing from Pura.
>
> All my love,
>
> Catherine

June, 1939
Kensington Gate, London

"Is this how it is going to be, William?" Lady Preston dropped into her chair in the library with Catherine's letter in her hand. "Must I begin to agonize over my children and grandchildren all over again? I haven't the strength…I swear, I simply do not have the strength."

"We shall help each other, Elizabeth, as we always have. And God shall help us both."

"God? You tell me a match is about to be lit against the dry tinder of Europe and no one will stop it. Certainly God will not stop it, who never stops anything." She pointed with the letter in her hand. "Why have our king and queen been in Canada for over a month? And America? The first time a reigning monarch has traveled to the Dominion of Canada and the first time any British king or queen has visited the United States. Why, William? You know perfectly well why. Our king and queen expect a war, and they want to be sure America and Canada are on our side."

"Calm yourself, my dear. Catherine and Albrecht and the grand-children are in no very great danger."

"No? What about my Robbie in the army? Why, he's not even over the death of his wife—or rather the *murder* of his wife—and I know very well they will come bowing and scraping to him to serve in Europe. What about Edward in the Royal Navy, and Terry, or Kipp and Ben in the Royal Air Force? Do you think they will be in no very great danger in a year's time?"

"We must fast. We must pray. This world is not heaven."

"Most certainly it is not." She waved the letter. "Catherine and Albrecht may have Dover Sky, if they wish, or join Holly and Harrison at Ashton Park. If they would rather be with everyone here in London, the top floor is theirs. Do you agree?"

"I do. Will you allow me to read you some Scripture and to lead in prayer?"

"Oh, yes, yes, yes, but your piety and zeal will have to suffice for the two of us. I am quite at odds with God these days."

"I'm quite sure He is up to the task of Europe as well as your anger against Him, Elizabeth."

Lord Preston walked to the fireplace and opened a large Bible on the mantle.

> God is our refuge and strength, a very present help in trouble. Therefore will not we fear, though the earth be removed, and though the mountains be carried into the midst of the sea. Though the waters thereof roar and be troubled, though the mountains shake with the swelling thereof. There is a river, the streams whereof shall make glad the city of God, the holy place of the tabernacles of the most High. God is in the midst of her; she shall not be moved: God shall help her, and that right early. The heathen raged, the kingdoms were moved: he uttered his voice, the earth melted. The LORD of hosts is with us; the God of Jacob is our refuge. Come, behold the works of the LORD, what desolations he hath made in the earth. He maketh wars to cease unto the end of the earth; he breaketh the bow, and cutteth the spear in sunder; he burneth the chariot in the fire. Be still, and know that I am God: I will be exalted among the heathen, I will be exalted in the earth. The LORD of hosts is with us; the God of Jacob is our refuge.

"He makes the wars cease, Elizabeth," Lord Preston said. "He breaks the bow, cuts the spear in two, and burns the armored chariots in the fire. His timing is not our timing, and our free will must be allowed a space to play itself out. But if war should come upon us, the day will also come when He shall end it, must end it. Blood will be shed because we are granted the right to shed it if we so choose. But bring our wars of terror and folly to an end He will do, my dear, and that is what I am going to pray about."

Lady Preston looked up at him. "And that is something I can say amen to. Go ahead, William. I have my moods, but I will not desert you."

July, 1939
Terry and Libby's residence, HMS Picadilly, Plymouth and Devonport

"So, a toast then." Terry was on his feet. "To Lord Edward Danforth, Commander, Royal Navy, serving aboard His Majesty's Ship *Rodney*. Soon to set sail for destinations unknown."

Edward grunted. "Not that unknown." He sat at the dinner table with his sons, Owen and Colm, on either side of him. "Invergordon. And if we pop the cork with Nazi Germany, Scapa Flow."

"Nevertheless, after Scapa Flow, what and whither?"

Edward half smiled. "Destinations unknown."

"So to that we toast. And to the fine summer we're both enjoying with our ladies and our children."

"Hear, hear," responded Edward.

"We all say 'hear, hear' to that." His wife Charlotte lifted her cup of tea. "It's been a bit of a dream, hasn't it? I wish it could go on forever."

"Don't act as if it's all over." Edward put his arms around his sons. "My understanding is that *Rodney* isn't leaving harbor till the end of the month."

Terry was still on his feet. "And *Hood* is here until mid-August. We shouldn't be leaving at all till we've modernized the whole ship, but mid-August will have to do."

"You'll not find me complaining," said Libby. "I've had you in England since January with the *Hood* being repaired and refit. I thank God for all the time granted us."

"I agree, Mum." Jane smiled and lifted her own cup. "Here's to two of the best naval officers in the world."

"I'll drink to that." Libby quickly poured herself a coffee.

"Is there any sturdier stuff?" asked Owen.

Edward laughed. "You'll make a fine sea dog. Here. Have some port along with me and Terry."

"Thank you, Da."

"I should like some port." Colm's face was round and serious.

Charlotte smiled. "Apple cider shall have to suffice for now, my dear. You're not like your big brother Owen, who grows a foot a year and shall be twenty-one the moment we blink our eyes."

"I'm almost eighteen, Mum," said Owen.

"You're always almost something. Here's your port, my handsome young man."

"Cheers then." Terry downed his glass of port. "God be with us in nineteen thirty-nine."

"And all the years that follow it," added Libby as she sipped her coffee. "Fair winds, smooth seas, and a steady hand at the helm once the winds rise."

"Aye, aye," responded Terry. He took his seat again and looked at the remains of his steak and kidney pie. "I thought I had more of this left."

Jane put a hand on his. "You took several swift bites before you proposed the toast."

"Did I? Or did you?"

"My goodness, no. I'm of Lady Margaret Hall, Father. I shouldn't dream of such a thing."

"Hmm." Terry dug in with his fork, glancing across the table at Owen. "Will it be the navy for you then, Owen, like your father?"

Owen grinned. "Yes, sir. Once I've reached the magic number—"

"Which will be any moment now," his mother interrupted.

"—I shall enlist. I hope to serve aboard a battleship."

"Ah. *Rodney? Hood?* Or another?"

"I should like to be on the *Rodney* or *Hood*. But I'll put my back into it wherever I drop anchor."

"That's the spirit."

Libby drank her coffee. "Are we all ready to head out in the morning? Dad and Mum have spent more than a few pounds on the yard at Kensington Gate to celebrate Catherine and Albrecht's return."

"I'm ready, certainly," said Jane. "I haven't seen Sean or Angelika in ages."

"Sean would be…hmm, sixteen, wouldn't he? And Angelika eight?"

"Nine, Mum."

"Nine. I wonder what she looks like. Catherine hasn't sent photographs in well over a year."

"We'll find out soon enough." Jane glanced around with her empty teacup in her hand. "Fancy not having a servant within ten nautical miles."

"A sacrifice, my dear daughter. I gave them up to help Tavy and Mrs. Longstaff and Norah and the others prepare. It will be quite the lawn party, you know."

Jane gave her mother a full smile. "I look forward to it with relish."

"I think you look forward to Peter and James with relish."

"Well, I haven't seen them all summer what with all that Auxiliary flying they do. I'm starved for a sight of their faces and an afternoon of their wild antics."

"Yes, well, I'm sure they're just as starved for beautiful you. I expect we'll not need to spend a penny on fireworks." Libby looked across the table at Owen. "What about you, Owen? Have any of the girls at school struck your fancy yet?"

Owen dropped his eyes to his empty glass of port and its red and purple residue. "No girl at school, no, Aunt Libby."

"To my mind you'd need one a few years older. You're much too mature for a girl of seventeen." She smiled over the rim of her cup. "Jane's older than her two beaus."

"By half a year at least," Jane piped up.

"What do you think, my handsome nephew? Does the idea of an older woman frighten you away?"

"Honestly, Mum," said Jane, "when you put it like that, anyone would be frightened. I'm sure Owen isn't interested in meeting someone as old as Grandmother."

Owen continued to stare down at his glass. "A woman a few years older wouldn't scare me off, Aunt Libby." He glanced up and grinned, light moving quickly through his sea-blue eyes. "Not if I liked the cut of her jib."

Terry and Edward roared.

"I haven't heard that expression for thirty years," laughed his father. "How'd you come by it?"

"I read it in a book."

Jane smiled at Owen and leaned in to her mother, whispering in her ear. "If I wasn't so caught up in the Evil Twins, I'd snatch Owen away in an instant and run off with him. He's so cute."

"Don't be so sure someone wouldn't fight you for him," Libby whispered back.

"He just said he didn't have anyone."

"If you have a moment to spare tomorrow evening, keep an eye out and watch the set of his sails."

"Oh, for heaven's sake, Mum." Jane burst out laughing, a long-fingered hand clapped to her mouth. "You and all your navy language. You sound so silly."

Twenty-four hours later
Kensington Gate, London

Charles stood apart under a tall oak tree that had no lights on its branches. The rest of the backyard was hung with Chinese paper lanterns that gleamed brighter and brighter as the afternoon turned into dusk. Cousins and uncles and aunts milled around a table laden with food and drink or formed small clusters of talk and laughter. He sipped at his punch and watched.

"It's most extraordinary," Charles heard Lord Preston tell his mother,

Caroline. "Who could have imagined we'd have all the family together this July? Both ships in port for refit, Robbie still at his desk in London, and now Albrecht and Catherine home from Switzerland. I know Albrecht isn't happy about what the Swiss did to him, but Elizabeth and I thank the Lord we have them with us again after so many years. Look around you, my dear. There's not a soul missing."

Eva appeared at Charles's side. "Why aren't you out there chatting with the boys?"

"Oh, why should I be?" responded Charles. "What does a good Nazi have in common with this lot? Royal Navy, Royal Air Force, British Army, Eton, Oxford, House of Commons, all that rubbish, a Chinese woman—"

"Oh, hush, before someone hears you. There's nothing wrong with Jane."

"I thought you were a good Nazi too."

"I don't know. Perhaps I'm a bad Nazi now. But I'm a very good German."

"You've let the English bewitch you."

"No, I don't think that's it. I just feel freer here, that's all."

"Well, of course—your father had you locked up tight as a drum. If you returned to Germany now you'd be just as free as you are here."

"Do you really think so?"

"Of course I do. Keep your head about you, Eva."

"I said I wouldn't go back until there were no more SS. I think there are still plenty of SS, so I'm staying put." She put her arm through his. "Will you escort me while I mingle?"

"No, I think not. You'll have to do without your good little Nazi tonight."

"Come with me, Charles, please. I know you'd enjoy yourself."

"You don't know that at all. Be careful of the Englishmen while you mingle. Aryan beauty seems to dazzle them."

"You sound like one of Goebbels's broadcasts."

"Or my father's?"

Eva walked across the lawn underneath a string of paper lanterns that glowed over her hair and shoulders. Owen was getting a glass of punch and saw her before she saw him. She was smiling at a noisy circle of young men, many of them Owen's own age—Matthew, Kipp and Caroline's other son and Charles's brother; Ramsay, Ben and Victoria's oldest boy;

and Sean, Catherine and Albrecht's son. Nearby, Jane was at the center of attention, ringed by Peter and James, who would both be twenty-two in December, and their brother Billy, who was nineteen. Jane suddenly burst into a laugh and spilled her drink.

"Oh, Peter!" she shrieked. "You're getting worse as you get older!"

A group of children raced past her, shouting and screeching, and Owen thought they were going to knock Eva flat. They were led by Timothy, fourteen, Ramsay's brother. Behind him came Cecilia, nine, Charles and Matthew's sister. Hot on her heels was Colm, ten, Owen's little brother, and Patricia, who would be eleven in September, Robbie's only child. Running to catch up was Angelika, Sean's sister, who had just turned nine. A red balloon sailed over her shoulder, its string held tightly in her fist.

"Good evening." Eva finally spotted Owen and turned toward the punch bowl. "I haven't seen you for weeks. How are you?"

A paper lantern over their heads swayed in a warm breeze. Owen watched the shifting patterns of light and dark move rapidly over her face and didn't reply.

"Hello?" she teased. "Do I look that dreadful?"

He half smiled. "Sorry. I was monitoring the effect of the paper lantern."

"What on earth are you talking about?"

"In plain English, your hair has grown out rather handsomely, your eyes are the most stunning blue, your skin looks like ivory, and everything else about you comes together rather well. You really have recovered from your ordeal."

"On the outside, perhaps."

"I apologize if—"

"Oh, hush, Owen, you're being altogether too polite. Who are you spending your time with here?"

Owen gestured with his glass of punch. "The lads there—Matt and Ramsay and Sean."

"If you can tear yourself away from them I wouldn't mind spending a few minutes with you."

He bowed. "An honor. So long as I don't keep saying the wrong thing."

"You haven't said anything wrong. Thank you for your compliments. I just wish I felt as whole on the inside as I apparently look to you on the outside."

She drifted away to one of the far corners of the yard by the high stone fence, where it was completely dark. He followed her after pouring a second glass of punch. He offered it to her once she turned to face him.

"Oh. *Danke*."

"If I can say your dress looks very nice as well—"

"*Ja, ja*. Go right ahead. It's Bavarian."

"I like it."

"So I'm glad. Somehow it ended up in the baggage Harrison brought with us from Germany." She extended her arm. "Traditionally, it should be short-sleeved."

"It's a warm evening, isn't it? What's chilled you that makes you wear long sleeves?"

"I'm not chilled. When I joined the Nazi Youth, I had tattoos put on my arms. Here on my left shoulder is an eagle with a swastika. On my right is a death's head like the SS use. I'm ashamed of them both, but I can't take them off without ripping the skin off, can I? I'm stuck with them. So I had the long sleeves sewn onto my dress."

"I don't care."

"You should care. Two years ago I was proud of them. Doesn't that make you change your mind about me?"

"I have Jewish blood. So does my brother, Colm. So does my mother. Does that make you change your mind about me?"

Eva's mouth opened halfway. "I....didn't know."

"It's true. My mother told us last year."

Eva let her arms hang down by her side. "So we both have our secrets."

"Not all secrets are the same."

"No. But I will have to think about this."

Owen nodded. "Of course." He drained his glass of punch. "Sorry to have spoiled your evening."

He walked away. Eva remained in the dark, crossing her arms over her chest.

Jane had wandered to another dark spot in the yard with Peter.

"Can anyone see us?" she whispered.

"Not unless they have the eyes of a cat."

"I just want a few minutes of privacy."

"No one's watching. No one cares where we are."

"Except James."

Peter shrugged. "Except James. But he'll get his five minutes later."

"Five minutes? I'm going to give each of you more than five minutes."

"You'll have to choose between us one day, you know. You can't have both of us at the altar."

"I know that."

"No one's getting any younger."

"Oh, heavens, Peter. I'm just twenty-two."

"Yes, you are." Their eyes had adjusted to the darkness and he tugged a small box from his pocket. "Happy birthday."

"Really?" She took the white leather box. "This looks expensive. Please, Peter, don't spoil things by giving me a diamond ring. It's much too soon for anything of that sort."

"It's not a diamond ring."

"Cross your heart?"

"Cross my heart."

"All right then, I'll open it." It was a ring with a dark stone. "Oh, my heavens, what is it?"

"Hold it up to the light."

"There is no light, Peter."

"Hold on."

He brought a lighter from his pocket and flicked it. "My handy Zippo."

"Oh!" The stone turned to a fiery green. "Is it emerald?"

"Yes."

"Where on earth do you get the money for these things? Why emerald?"

"It goes with your eyes."

"My eyes aren't green."

"They don't have to be green for emerald to go with them, do they?"

She slipped it on the ring finger of her right hand. "It's elegant. It's beautiful. I love it."

"Beauty for beauty."

She put her arms around his neck. "I'm in love with you."

"I feel the same way."

"Oh, you have to do better than that if you're going to give a girl an emerald ring."

"I love you, Jane. I've loved you a long time."

"I knew that." She kissed him slowly on the lips. "But there's James too."

"Yes, but you can bring James up when James is the one in your arms. It's my go at the bat this cricket match. Let's just talk about you and me, shall we? No one else interferes. That's the rules, right?"

She smiled. "Right."

And then Peter put his arms around her, and they kissed again.

Libby held Terry's hand as the backyard emptied and led him underneath the long strings of paper lanterns.

"I've loved these since I was a girl," she said.

"It's new for me, but I quite like the effect. I'd like to hang a thousand of these on the *Hood.* It would look majestic."

"Did you see Jane? She must be the happiest girl in England."

"Why? What's happened now? Did one of the boys pop the question?"

"Oh, no, nothing like that. But they both gave her birthday rings tonight. Take a look at her right hand later on. One of the rings has an emerald stone and the other is jade."

"How will this all end? Someone's bound to get hurt."

"Well, I hope it will sort itself out over the next year or two. I don't envy Jane that task. There should be two of her. Then everything would turn out right."

Libby glanced about. The yard was empty, the table with its food and drink removed, the guests indoors. She wrapped her arms around Terry's back.

"I've never been kissed under paper lanterns," she said, smiling up at him.

His hand smoothed back her ginger hair. "You're letting it grow out."

"Glad you noticed."

"If you keep on looking more and more beautiful I really will start kissing you in the most unusual locations—backyards, seashores, on the deck of the *Hood*…"

"On the deck of the *Hood*? Really? Why don't we start with the backyard?"

"You want to kiss right now? Out in the open?"

"No one's here."

"They could take a look out a window."

"Since when do you care about that, Commander Fordyce?"

"I thought you did."

"Not tonight. Maybe not any other night ever again."

Their lips came together. Her grip grew stronger and stronger and she refused to let him break off. The paper lanterns swayed above their heads. The soft light painted them amber and orange.

"Never leave me," she finally whispered.

"I could be ten thousand miles away on the farthest ocean from England and I'd never have left you."

She began to kiss him again. "That's a pleasant thought."

The families had returned to their London homes. Those who were staying at Kensington Gate had turned in, and all the squares and rectangles of windows were dark. A small light glowed on the top floor, where Albrecht and Catherine had chosen to live for the time being. Edward looked up at it from the backyard.

"Do you suppose he's working on a book?" he asked.

Owen shrugged. "If what he says is true, he hasn't had much of a chance to say what he's wanted to say. Now he can."

Edward glanced at his son. "Did something happen tonight?"

"No."

"It's like you have a cloud over you."

Owen shrugged again. "Things didn't work out the way I expected."

"Is this about Eva?"

"A bit."

"I thought you said you were holding off on that for another year?"

"I don't know, Dad. She came up to me. I didn't seek her out."

"What did she want to talk about?"

"I don't know. We didn't get very far."

Father and son moved away from the light of the lanterns and into the darkness against the stone walls.

"Well, son," Edward said, "she is a beautiful woman with a magic all her own. I can't blame you for getting caught up with her. And the age thing doesn't bother your mother or me at all. It's only a few years. What I have a hard time getting around is her commitment to the Nazis."

"That weakens with each month that goes by. Charles is the one clinging on to the whole Nazi thing and marching with the British Union of Fascists."

"Right."

They were silent a few moments. Owen found they could see the stars clearly by the wall and thought about them being strings of paper lanterns high up in the night sky.

"She said she was ashamed of being a Nazi," he told his father.

"Did she?"

"She was wearing a dress with long sleeves. I guess the dress is supposed to be short-sleeved, but she had the long sleeves put on to cover her Nazi tattoos. She hates them."

"I see."

"After she shared that secret, I felt I should share one. I expect I wanted to find out what she thought."

"About what?"

"My Jewish blood."

"You told her?"

"Yes. I just wanted to know."

Edward put his hands in his pockets and looked at his son. "How did she react?"

"Not well. She didn't get upset or anything, but I could see it bothered her."

"All the Nazi isn't out of her yet."

"I don't think it ever will be." He ran his hand over the rough surface of the stone wall. "I want to go to sea, Dad. Get away from all this. Get away from her. Clear out my head. See other parts of the world like you have."

"Run off to sea, eh? Well, many a young man's done that before you. You have your mother's and my permission to enlist once you've turned eighteen and finished school. I would be a very proud father to see you in a naval uniform."

Owen smiled. "Do you think they would ever put me aboard your ship?"

"It might happen. Meantime, finish up your last year. Concentrate on your studies. That will help drive Eva from your head."

"Not so well as a vast ocean will."

"No. But read some sea stories. That will help you out even more. I've put the three C.S. Forester books on your shelf—*The Happy Return, A Ship of the Line,* and *Flying Colors.*"

"When did you do that?"

"Just before we came over here. You could say I had a feeling you might need them. They'll fill your head up with the adventure you crave. Next thing you know you'll be an admiral."

"Thanks, Dad."

Owen took a step toward his father, hesitated, and then put his arms around him.

"I'll miss you," he said.

Edward patted his son's back as they embraced. "Won't be long and I'll be back in port again. We'll catch up on your life then."

The paper lanterns swayed in the night breeze alone for another hour before Tavy and Skitt unplugged them and brought them down, Skitt climbing a ladder while Tavy held it steady.

In bed, Edward lay in his wife Charlotte's arms and told her what he and Owen had talked about, playing with strands of her raven black hair as he spoke.

In the bedroom at their London house, Libby nestled her head on her husband Terry's chest and listened to the strong rhythm of his heart while he smoothed her ginger blonde hair with the palm of his hand.

A few weeks later, at the end of July, Charlotte, Owen, and Colm watched HMS *Rodney* leave Plymouth. In August, Jane and Libby traveled to Portsmouth, where the *Hood* had been undergoing its refit, and stood almost at attention as it slipped its moorings and headed out to sea.

Rodney arrived at Scapa Flow in northern Scotland before any of the other warships. Once the Home Fleet, including *Rodney* and *Hood,* had assembled, it left Scapa Flow on the last day of August. The next day the German Army and Air Force attacked Poland. Britain and France demanded that German forces withdraw, but Berlin didn't respond. Edward was on the bridge of *Rodney* late Sunday morning, September third, the Fleet three hundred miles south of Iceland, when a signal was received from the Admiralty.

TOTAL GERMANY

The bridge was quiet. Edward looked at the faces around him. For months everyone had been expecting it, and now there it was. "Total Germany" was the Royal Navy code word for "Commence hostilities against Germany."

The prime minister's speech was relayed over the Tannoy system to the entire ship's crew.

> I am speaking to you from the Cabinet Room at Ten Downing Street. This morning the British Ambassador in Berlin handed the German government a final note stating that unless we hear from them by eleven o'clock that they were prepared at once to withdraw their troops from Poland, a state of war would exist between us. I have to tell you now that no such undertaking has been received, and that consequently this country is at war with Germany.
>
> Up to the very last it would have been quite possible to have arranged a peaceful and honorable settlement between Germany and Poland, but Hitler would not have it. He had evidently made up his mind to attack Poland, whatever happened, and although he now says he put forward reasonable proposals which were rejected by the Poles, that is not a true statement.
>
> The situation in which no word given by Germany's ruler could be trusted, and no people or country could feel itself safe, has become intolerable. And now that we have resolved to finish it I know that you will play your part with calmness and courage.
>
> Now may God bless you all. May He defend the right. For it is evil things that we shall be fighting against—brute force, bad faith, injustice, oppression, and persecution—and against them I am certain that right will prevail.

The same signal was received aboard the *Hood* and the same speech from the prime minister transmitted to the ship's crew. Terry held the signal in his hand.

"It won't be a short war, will it, sir?" asked one of the young midshipmen. "I wouldn't mind if we were all home for Christmas, but that's a bit of a pipe dream, I'm thinking."

He looked at Terry hopefully, wanting the Commander to refute him. Terry slipped the signal into a pocket of his uniform.

"It won't be a short war, Mr. Midshipman White," Terry replied. "You may count on it being just as long as the last one."

"But we'll win it, sir."

"Aye. We'll carry the day."

Terry's immediate thoughts were of Libby and Jane. *It could be years before I see you.*

Lord Preston listened to Prime Minister Chamberlain's broadcast in the company of his wife and servants in the small library at Kensington Gate. Afterward he prowled the house and grounds, hands behind his back, head down. Now and then others could see his lips moving.

"He is consulting with the Almighty," Lady Preston said to her daughter Catherine and Albrecht. "I hope it does some good."

Albrecht turned away from the window, where he could see Lord Preston pacing the lawn.

"Now more than ever I must finish my book on a Germany that follows its Christian past rather than its Nazi present." Albrecht picked up his cup of tea, finished it, wiped his lips quickly with a napkin, and bowed to Lady Preston. "Excuse me."

"Of course. Each of us must fight the war in his own way. Some with prayers. Some with pens. Others with airplanes and ships." Lady Preston looked at Catherine as Albrecht hurried from the room. "I greatly fear that harm will come to my children. Too many of them are in harm's way. I fear also for my grandchildren. Too many of them are of an age where they may rush to enlist." Her lower lip trembled.

Catherine knelt by her mother's chair and took her hand. "We've got to hold together, Mum. We've been through a lot with the first war and Ireland. We can stick together through this too. Can I pray for you?"

"You can. But don't just pray for me. Pray for the entire family. Edward and Terry are already at sea. I know very well that Kipp and Ben will not wish to remain test pilots now that war is declared."

"Don't fret about Ben and Kipp, Mum. They're too old to fly fighter planes in a war."

"They will find a way around the restrictions—depend on it. And Owen is champing at the bit to serve on board a battleship like his father. To say nothing of Peter and James—they will do anything to win Jane's favor. You can be sure they will jump at the chance to fly with the RAF, what with all the training they've been taking." Lady Preston covered her eyes with her hand and rubbed it back and forth. "God help us."

"We shall pray to that end, Mum."

"Please do. If God hasn't given up on me yet, we may see some light before we reach the end of the tunnel."

Robbie was the first to cause Lady Preston to brace herself with further prayer, Catherine at her side.

A British Expeditionary Force had been set up over the past year with the express purpose of being deployed to Europe if war broke out with Nazi Germany. Now the troops were about to be sent over the Channel. Robbie had been asked to command a regiment even though colonels normally served as staff officers and not as field commanders.

"I was going mad brooding at that desk," he told Lord and Lady Preston as they sat in the parlor at Kensington Gate. "When they made the offer I told them I needed twenty-four hours. It was not a direct order. Since I didn't wish to trouble you I kept it to myself. I only told Jeremy and Emma. They prayed with me. We opened the Bible randomly and were at Psalm 144, even though Jeremy rarely reads that psalm or the ones before or after it. The first verse jumped out at all three of us: "Blessed be the LORD my strength, which teacheth my hands to war, and my fingers to fight." The second verse seemed just as meaningful to us: "My goodness, and my fortress; my high tower, and my deliverer; my shield, and he in whom I trust; who subdueth my people under me." I take it as a sign that I am to do something about defending Britain and defending Europe. I was in Palestine for so many years and Ireland before that. It's time to do something for my home country."

Lady Preston ran her hand along the arm of her chair. "Have you thought about your daughter? Patricia cannot survive the loss of both of her parents at such a tender age."

"She's quite happy here in London with Cecilia and Angelika. If you and Catherine and Albrecht would take her in, I know her tears would dry quickly after my departure."

"But what if you are killed?"

"I won't be killed, Mother. There's no reason I should be killed."

"Yes, you say that, but—"

"I'm a colonel now, Mother. I won't be in the front lines. It's a very different situation from Ireland or even Palestine. Every place is on the front line in Palestine. That is not the case in Europe. Our front line will be along the border between France and Belgium. There will be no car bombs. No assassins in the night. Just our army and the French army against the German army."

"You make it sound like the safest place in the world, my dear. That same region is full of men's bones from the last fight with Germany."

"I brood every day at that desk about Shannon. How I failed her. How I didn't protect her. How my love was not enough to save her. If I don't get out of that office and do something, I shall be a wreck."

Lord Preston put his hand gently on his wife's shoulder. "Of course Patricia is welcome at Kensington Gate, my boy, and I know she will be welcome so far as Catherine and Albrecht and Angelika are concerned. If you must go, I pray you go in peace."

"Thank you, Father."

"I cannot fight the tides of war and fate, can I?" Lady Preston gave her son a lopsided smile. "Come, give me a kiss, and be off on your quest for the grail."

Robbie got up and leaned to kiss his mother on the cheek. "I'll be right as rain."

"It's nice to hear you say so. I hope you are granted the power to bring that promise to pass."

Robbie was gone by the end of September. There were rumblings from the twins, Peter and James, and more rumblings from Owen. These increased after HMS *Courageous* was sunk by a U-boat on September 17, HMS *Royal Oak* was sunk by another U-boat on October 14, and in the middle of it all a bomb from a German aircraft struck the *Hood*. Terry was not hurt.

Jeremy and Emma managed to convince their sons to remain at Oxford for the time being, pointing out they were not navy material anyway, while Edward wrote Owen from the *Rodney* and asked him to stick to his word and not enlist until he had turned eighteen and finished his schooling. To Lady Preston's relief, nothing else happened to the *Hood* or *Rodney*, and nothing happened in Belgium or France either.

November 26

> Dear Mum and Dad,
>
> Your prayers seem to have routed the enemy, at least for the time being. Nothing is happening at all on our front, thanks to you, so now you will have to pray about something else— tommyrot. I swear it is just like what the boys wrote about from the trenches twenty years ago—mud and wet and cold and boredom. However the truth is that spirits are high and morale is good. Give Pat a kiss and hug from me. I have sent her a letter of her own that should arrive the same time as yours or shortly thereafter. All the best.
>
> Much love,
>
> Robbie

Libby and Charlotte got together every week to share whatever letters they might have received from Terry or Edward and to chat, sip tea, and pray. Victoria and Caroline counted themselves blessed that no air war was taking place like what had occurred in Spain, but both were shocked in December when their husbands returned from their base in Suffolk to announce their departure for France in the new year.

"You knew we'd sent aircraft across the Channel," Ben said as Victoria wiped at her eyes with her fingers.

"Bombers. I never read they were sending fighter planes."

"Look, nothing's happening. I'll bet nothing happens in nineteen forty either. The Germans see the buildup of troops and planes, and they've decided to call the whole thing off."

"They've been doing a lot at sea."

"But nothing on land or in the air. Please don't worry."

Victoria flared. "Of course I'm going to worry! We went through all this in nineteen eighteen! You should be flying a desk, not a fighter! What's the matter with you?"

"Kipp and I are fit, and we're still flying like wizards."

"Wizards! Yes, we'll jolly well need a bit of magic if we're to see you home in one piece from this show!"

"Vic, we'll have a treaty with the Third Reich by next summer. All they've really got going for them are the U-boats, and once we pop a few of those they'll pull their troops out of Poland and march back to where they came from."

"You make it sound so easy. Wars with Germany are never that easy."

"What's happened since war was declared in September?"

"The *Royal Oak* went down with eight hundred men. Talk to their Mums and Dads and ask them if anything's happened since September."

Ben tried to take her in his arms, but she pushed him away. He tried again, and she thrust him back. The third time he folded her in his arms, she cried into his chest.

"You barely survived the first one. I feel we're tempting fate cramming you in a cockpit again. It's madness."

"Orders are orders."

"I don't believe it. No one's going to order an old man like you into a Hurricane and drop you off in France. You probably volunteered."

Despite Victoria's tears and anger, her words made Ben laugh. "Old man? You make it sound like I'm ready for a rocking chair."

"I wish you would stay home and sit in a rocking chair. I'd buy you a pipe and slippers and a warm woolen sweater and I'd give you the best hugs and kisses in England every night after work."

"That's an exceptional offer. But I'll have no work to come home from if you'll not let me be a fighter pilot, Vic. You know they took the lot of us test pilots to Boscombe Down in September and gave Martlesham Heath over to Number Eleven Group RAF, Fighter Command, right?"

Victoria was clutching his blue RAF tunic in her fingers, head on his chest, sniffling. "Right."

"But this past week Kipp and I were ordered to report for duty back at Martlesham. We're with Fighter Command now. Same place, different job. If neither of us can be fighter pilots now, we're both out on the street selling pencils in Piccadilly Circus."

"Oh, shut up. You two always get your way when it comes to flying." She struck his chest with her fist. "Go to France then. If it's as dull as you claim it is, I hope you get bored to death."

"That's a hard thing to say to a man just about ready for a rocker and a cup of tea and a casket."

"I'll give you a casket if you try to come home in one. Don't even dream of it. You've never seen anger if you try to get out of the rest of our marriage by dying in France."

"I'll do my best."

"I mean it. I'll break open the coffin and take you by the throat and turn you into another Lazarus. And then I'll really take your head off and hand it to you on a platter."

"Now I'm confused. Are we talking about Lazarus or John the Baptist?"

She hit him again. "It's not funny, Benjamin Whitecross. Stay alive if you know what's good for you."

"I will do." He began to kiss the top of her head. "Your hair smells wizard today."

"You and your wizards. It's fish and chips. Ramsay and Tim wanted some."

"Did you not save any for me then?"

"Do you deserve any?"

"I should think so."

"Why?"

"For surviving twenty odd years of marriage to Victoria Anne Danforth."

She suddenly began to giggle. "Oh, do shut up, Ben."

"Really, when you think of the odds I'm facing with you, why, a Hurricane or Spitfire is a safer place for me than this house."

She laughed harder. "I said shut up." But she did not strike him a third time.

Kipp and Ben left with their Hurricane squadron in January. Their wives, Caroline and Victoria, began to meet with the navy wives, Libby and Charlotte, and soon all four were gathering at St. Andrew's Cross once a week to talk and pray with Emma and Jeremy. To the relief of all, things remained quiet for the pilots and for the troops on the ground, including Robbie. A bomb crashed through the deck of the *Rodney* in April but did not explode, for which they thanked God, and other than that nothing unusual happened to their men in the Royal Navy either.

"I hope the entire war goes on like this," Victoria said, "and then comes to an end this summer."

In his daily broadcasts, Lord Tanner crowed about the sinking of

British ships by U-boats, causing resentment toward him in the Danforth family and making his son, Charles, shrink farther and farther from everyone into the nooks and corners of his house and his room.

"The scoundrel ought to be hung up by his ankles and left to rot," sneered Catherine and Albrecht's son, Sean.

Owen avoided any family event at which Eva was likely to be present, citing school pressures and exams. Several times Lord Preston invited him to come down to Dover for a sail on *Pluck,* but as soon as he learned Eva would be part of the crew he begged off. Once she came by the house and left a letter with his mother. He held on to it for two days, wrestling over whether to open it, and finally placed it in the peat fire when no one else was home.

"Once I imagined having my eighteenth birthday party and inviting her to be present as the guest of honor," he wrote in a journal he kept his poetry in. "But when the great day came I just had the lads over—Ramsay, Sean, and Matt. I found that I didn't miss her and that my heart is now quite closed to all thoughts of her."

Lady Preston was grateful for the silent fall and winter and spring, no longer reluctant to join her husband for morning or evening prayers and happy to attend services at St. Andrew's Cross and listen to her son-in-law's sermons. Seeing the family friend Winston Churchill appointed First Lord of the Admiralty also cheered her up considerably.

"He is out of the dungeon and back beside the throne," she said. "Such a blessed reversal of fortunes. Well, it does not look like his warrior spirit will be much in demand, but I am glad he is back in the government just the same."

"It may not always be like this," her husband warned her. "There were quiet spells in the first war too, but they always came to a rough end."

"Don't be so gloomy, William. It's been almost nine months since the Germans invaded Poland, and all that time they have remained rooted to the spot. Herr Hitler has obviously changed his mind. Nothing more will come of his Polish adventure."

"One thing certain about the man is that he is always scheming. He did nothing about Czechoslovakia after he got his way in the Sudetenland in the fall of thirty-eight. But six months later he swept over the whole country."

Lady Preston glared at her husband. "I don't like being filled with foreboding, William. Things are getting along rather nicely without your prophetic lamentations. You sound too much like Winston in his 'black dog' moods. Try to spread a bit more sunshine and faith around."

"I only urge caution. And no letting up in the matter of prayer. Look at the mess we've fallen into in Norway, letting the Germans march over the border and seize control. Why, we could have prevented the invasion if only we'd put troops there in the fall as Winston wished. Now it's a shambles and everyone is out for Chamberlain's blood. "

"No one is letting up in the matter of prayer, William, I assure you. But we can smile now and again, can't we?"

Lord Preston nodded. "I don't see why not. I simply don't trust Hitler, that's all. What he's done in Czechoslovakia and Norway, he can do in France."

"I intend to ignore him."

"Ah. I wish I could."

"You really must sleep on it, my dear."

"If I sleep on it I shall have a rude awakening."

The rude awakening came on Friday morning, May 10. Tavy's hand shook him awake.

"My lord...my lord."

"Mm? What is it, Tavy?" Lord Preston glanced at the clock in his room. "I see. I've overslept. Thank you for waking me."

"An urgent summons from Prime Minister Chamberlain." He handed Lord Preston two pieces of paper. "These notes were brought to our door."

Lord Preston sat up and unfolded the first.

> The Germans have attacked all along the front. Luxembourg has fallen. The armies of Holland and Belgium are hard pressed and in danger of being overwhelmed. The fighting in France is fierce. Come to Westminster at once. The blow has fallen.
>
> Chamberlain

Lord Preston looked up from the note. "Pray tell Lady Preston we will gather for family prayers in the library. Alert Catherine and Albrecht. I should like all our servants to be present as well. Ten minutes, Tavy. It's a matter of some urgency."

"Very good, my lord."

Once Tavy had left the room, Lord Preston unfolded the second note.

> William,
>
> I must tell you now that I have resigned as prime minister. I made this decision before news of the German assaults in Europe reached us. I no longer have the confidence of the House due to the way the crisis in Norway was handled and felt it was best for the country I step down. It is my belief Winston Churchill will be appointed in my place before the day is out.
>
> Chamberlain

Thursday, May 16, 1940
Ashton Park

"When did all this begin, Liscombe?"

"We fetched the doctor yesterday, my lady. In the evening. Your father seemed to react to the news from the BBC that Holland had capitulated. He cried out something about the Somme and Verdun and collapsed. The doctor tells us it's a stroke, a rather massive one, and that we are to keep him as comfortable as possible. He is not expected to recover."

"I see."

"I'm so sorry, my lady. He was doing very well indeed. Prime Minister Churchill's speech on Monday seemed to stir him up so that he acted like a man half his age. 'I have nothing to offer but blood, toil, tears, and sweat.' He repeated the phrase over and over again."

"Thank you, Liscombe." Lady Preston sat down by her father's bed and took his withered hand. "Please ring up the doctor for me. I should like to speak with him myself about Sir Arthur."

"Yes, my lady."

Liscombe left the bedroom. Holly and Harrison stepped forward.

"He was well up until that broadcast," Holly said, resting a hand on Lady Preston's shoulder. "Always ready for a dispute with Lady Grace."

"Of course." Lady Preston blinked her eyes and gazed at the silent face. "Does she know what has happened?"

"Yes. She knows. She was sitting with him before you came."

There was a thumping, and they turned their heads. Lady Grace had made her way into the room, a cane in each hand.

"Elizabeth." She did not smile. "How are you?"

"I should be much better if Father was recovering."

"Ah." She came in a little closer. "I was consulting with the dukes and duchesses on the other floors. Long gone, of course, so far as their physical presences are concerned. Yet very much with us in spirit."

"I'm glad to hear it."

"They wish us well in this time of crisis. That is to say, both with Sir Arthur's illness and the fall of France."

"France has not fallen yet, Lady Grace."

The older woman met Lady Preston's eyes with a gaze like iron. "How are the children? How are the grandchildren?"

"The grandchildren are fine. All of them are here in England."

"What about Kipp? Edward? Robbie?"

Lady Preston looked down at her father's face. "Edward is on his ship. No harm has come to it. Nor to the ship of our son-in-law, Terrence Fordyce. Robbie's regiment is in full retreat. Kipp's airfield to the north and west of Paris has been bombed, so they have had to move their aircraft as far from the German line of advance as possible. We have not heard from him or Robbie. Or Ben. He is in the same squadron as Kipp."

"Things are taking place in rapid order."

"In too rapid an order for me, Lady Grace."

"'All shall be well, and all shall be well, and all manner of thing shall be well.'"

"I should like to believe that."

"O God, our help in ages past, our hope for years to come, our shelter from the stormy blast, and our eternal home." Lady Grace sang the first verse of the hymn in a steady voice and thumped the end of one cane sharply on the floor. "He saved Ben in the first war. I well remember the day Ben was shot down. He saved Edward twice, didn't He, when first the *Queen Mary* and then the *Tipperary* went down under him?" She thumped her cane again. "We will see the whole brood back safely in England, my dear girl, depend on it."

"Thank you, Lady Grace. But as William is fond of reminding me, this world is not heaven, and if humans will insist on having their wars there will always be sons and daughters who never return to their homes."

Lady Grace set her jaw and her face grew rigid. "Under the shadow of Thy throne still may we dwell secure; sufficient is Thine arm alone, and our defense is sure."

"Ah." Tears slid across Lady Preston's face. "He is not breathing...he is not breathing now."

Harrison went to the other side of the bed and bent over Sir Arthur. Then he straightened.

"He is at rest." Harrison nodded. "He is at peace."

Holly took Lady Preston into her arms. "A good man, Elizabeth, a good and decent man."

Lady Grace continued to sing. "Oh God, our help in ages past, our hope for years to come; be Thou our guide while life shall last, and our eternal home."

Sir Arthur's funeral was on Saturday, May 18. Everyone came up from London. He was buried in the family cemetery near the chapel at Ashton Park. At the brief reception after the service, Owen avoided Eva's eye and stayed close to his cousins Matthew, Ramsay, and Sean. Charles stood stiffly with a plate of cake in his hand in the great hall as people gathered in groups near him and talked about the war.

"If any of you wish to remain overnight or for a few days, you are welcome." Lord Preston smiled. "For those who must return to London, we have several cars available to get you back to Lime Street Station in Liverpool. There will be a train for London in an hour and a half."

Eva remained behind as others climbed into the Rolls Royces. He hated himself for doing it, but Owen glanced back as he climbed in beside Ramsay. She was watching him, and their eyes met. He looked away and slid into the Rolls. Ramsay said something, but Owen didn't reply.

Such blue eyes. Such flaming blue eyes. Did I make a mistake? Should I have read that letter before burning it? What if she apologized? What if she asked me to forgive her?

He almost opened the door and got back out. He grasped the handle. The engine started, and the chauffeur began to guide the car smoothly down the lane and past the old oak trees. Owen sat back and closed his eyes.

"You feeling all right?" asked Ramsay.

"I'm fine," Owen responded.

Saturday, May 25, 1940
The vicarage, St. Andrew's Cross

Jeremy took off his round-rimmed glasses and looked from one woman to the other—Libby, Charlotte, Victoria, and Caroline.

"Look," he said. "There's no use beating around the bush. Yes, we've sent extra troops over there. But the Germans still have the advantage. It's not going well despite the way the papers talk about it and despite the hard fight our lads are putting up. I expect the Nazis will have the ports of Boulogne and Calais in their hands by the end of the day or tomorrow morning. I hate to say that, but I've spoken with Lord Preston about the matter and he's privy to information that isn't being released to the public."

"Has Dad heard anything from Robbie?" asked Libby in a small voice.

"I'm afraid not."

"What about his regiment?"

"We know it hasn't been cut off or forced to surrender. It will undoubtedly be at the coast with the other British troops and the French."

"What do we know about the squadrons?" Victoria's face was an unpleasant yellow and white, like a thick cream. "Is there any news?"

"They are protecting the army. They move their landing fields as often as they must to keep ahead of the German advance."

Caroline knotted her fingers together in her lap. "The *Times* says there are fierce air battles."

"From what I understand they are not exaggerating."

"What...what sort of losses are we taking?"

Jeremy put his glasses back on and glanced at his wife, who sat in a chair by his side. "We're giving as good as we get."

"What does that mean?"

"It means that it isn't all one-sided like it's been with Holland and Belgium and the French, where the Germans destroyed so many of their aircraft on the ground." He paused. "It means Kipp and Ben and the other chaps are brave just like our men at sea are brave and our troops on the ground. It means they aren't getting decimated by the Nazis. It means there's a good chance they're alive and well and flying their Hurricanes."

"How long will it take to find out where they are?" Caroline asked.

Emma leaned forward and curled her hand around Caroline's. "You can imagine how confusing it is over there. Two weeks of fighting and retreating and the Germans surrounding them on every side…it's all a muddle. But eventually things will sort themselves out one way or another."

"The planes can just fly back across the Channel if it comes to that," Jeremy added.

"What about the soldiers then?" asked Libby. "What about Robbie and all the others?"

"They will have to be taken off the coast by our navy. Not all the ports have been captured."

"But when will this happen, Jeremy? When will we hear something?"

"I would say very soon. It must be very soon."

"We should pray," said Emma.

"Yes, please," said Victoria. "I should like that. I'm sure we all would."

Monday, May 27, 1940
Kensington Gate, London

"A phone call for you, my lord."

"I'm about to join my wife and daughter for a time of prayer, Tavy, thank you. Please ask them to leave a message. Our army is trapped on the French coast by the Germans. Only God Almighty can save them."

"I realize the Germans have our lads in a bad way. I agree with you that prayer is sorely needed. But the call is quite urgent, my lord."

"What could be that urgent?"

"It's the small-craft section of the Ministry of Shipping. They wish you to assist in the evacuation of British and French troops from the port of Dunkerque."

"Ha? What?" Lord Preston rushed past his butler to the phone in the parlor. "Hullo? This is Lord Preston."

"My lord. I'm Talbot with the small-craft section of the Ministry of Shipping. You have the sailboat *Pluck,* do you not? It's registered in your name."

"Yes, yes."

"You presently have it at Dover?"

"Yes."

"Now here's the thing. The water is shallow, very shallow indeed, where the destroyers are trying to evacuate our men at the port of Dunkerque. The ships can't get in close enough to hoist the lads on board because the vessels have too great a draft, you see. Some soldiers are standing up to their shoulders or necks in water for hours hoping to get picked up. We need the small boats to get in on those beaches and ferry the men to the big ships. Now, we have a crew who can sail *Pluck* across the Channel and—"

"Out of the question. I have my own crew, handpicked."

"So you would wish to sail the boat yourself?"

"I would. I have a son on that beach."

"My lord, there are almost half a million men hoping to get taken off. You'll not see him."

"Let God and me worry about who I will see and who I will not see. We shall be down to Dover and on our way to France in less than two hours."

"Very good, my lord. Tell the chaps at the docks what you're up to so we'll know you've followed through with the sailing."

"I will follow through with the sailing, Mr. Talbot, you need not lose sleep over that."

Lord Preston hung up and clapped his hands together. "Tavy!"

Tavy rushed into the parlor. "What is it, my lord?"

"Ring up Skitt, there's a good man. And Owen. And Eva. I shan't want too many bodies. We'll need room for as many soldiers as possible."

"What shall I tell them, my lord?"

"We are sailing for France by order of the king. We will be helping evacuate the troops at Dunkerque. My crew must be at Kensington Gate in a quarter of an hour. My chauffeur shall be breaking speed records to Dover, you may be sure of it. Where is he, by the by?"

"Out waxing the Rolls, my lord."

"Let Darrington know what we are about and that we must be on our way in fifteen minutes. Fifteen, mind, not sixteen or twenty. Then ring up the others."

"And if they are not home, my lord?"

"Call whoever pops into your head. I must pack my sea bag in short order."

"Very good, my lord."

Lady Preston came into the parlor as Tavy left it. "I trust I didn't hear what I thought I heard." Lady Preston's hands were on her hips.

"I have no idea what you heard, so I haven't the foggiest idea what you're talking about."

"You're in your seventies, William! Are you mad? You can't go sailing off to France. The Germans are dropping bombs there. Planes are strafing the beaches. There are dogfights over Dunkerque, for heaven's sake, and scores of aircraft are being shot down in flames."

"All the more reason for us to go. We must get our lads off that coast."

"William! For heaven's sake! You're an old man!"

"A state of mind, nothing more. I think forty and therefore I am forty!"

"What? Mad dogs and Englishmen! You're not leaving this house, William Danforth!"

"Of course I am." He grasped his wife gently by the arms. "Our son is on that beach, Elizabeth. He will recognize our boat. I must get him. It's not some other man's job. It's mine."

She bit her lip. "William—"

"'Mad dogs and Englishmen go out in the midday sun.' Isn't that how the song goes? Well, I'm about to go out in the midday sun, my dear, and I'll have my mad dogs with me, and we are going to save a hundred lives, two hundred, and one of them will be my son's."

2:35 p.m.
The English Channel

Owen edged the wheel slightly to port. "You can see the smoke now."

"Yes, we can, by George, we can." Lord Preston had binoculars to his eyes.

"Mind the sailboat to starboard," said Skitt.

"I see it, thanks," responded Owen. "There are another three to port."

"Dozens, actually." Eva was coiling a line.

Owen didn't look at her. "Right."

Lord Preston lowered the binoculars, glanced from Owen to Eva, and returned them to his eyes. "There are several ships burning. There are fires on shore as well. German planes appear to have been bombing the port."

"Are ours up?" asked Skitt.

"They must be but we're still too far away to read plane markings clearly. And they are moving too fast for my eyes. Here." He handed the binoculars to Skitt. "You have a go."

Skitt kept his binoculars on the beaches ahead of them a long time. "Hurricanes are up all right. D'you see that long trail of purple-black smoke there? It's a Nazi plane going down."

"Ah." Lord Preston waved his hand. "We'll be in the thick of it in less than half an hour. Steer clear of the destroyers and troopships, Owen. They're targets for the German aircraft. There are a lot of men on the beaches to port. We shall go in there and collect as many as we can."

"Yes, sir."

Once *Pluck* reached the shallow water, men waded to the craft. Owen and Skitt helped two dozen aboard, told the others they'd be back, and sailed to the nearest destroyer. Cargo nets hung down its sides, and the men got out of the sailboat and began to climb. Four other sailboats were right behind *Pluck*, loaded with soldiers.

"Briskly." Lord Preston clapped his hands. "Briskly."

"Coming about!" called Owen.

The boom swung, Eva and Skitt and Lord Preston ducked their heads, and Eva sprang to sheet the sail home.

"That's nimble of you, my dear." Lord Preston smiled at Eva. "Don't you think so, Owen?"

"Yes, sir."

"We shall carry on through the night, do you all understand that? We must get the men off those beaches. The darkness will be an aid to us. No enemy planes."

"That makes sense." Eva sat on a hatch. "We've plenty of bread and cheese on board. We can share that around to those who have a long wait until they're on a destroyer or troopship."

"Yes, Elizabeth made sure we'd have enough of that to feed the entire army—British and French."

They floated into shore again, and men swarmed on board.

"My, it's nice to see your face, Ginger." One of the soldiers grinned. "I've missed you English girls."

Eva smiled back and patted him on the shoulder but didn't speak. She turned away to help Skitt haul an older soldier over the side. He spat out saltwater and looked at her in surprise.

"The Royal Navy's improved a great deal since last September then," he said.

"Hasn't it just?" responded Skitt.

There was a loud roar, and a plane with black crosses streaked low over the sailboats in the water, wings flashing. Tall geysers burst to port and starboard of *Pluck*. A sailboat near them keeled over sharply in deep water, its hull and sail riddled with bullets, and the soldiers spilled out, yelling as waves swept over their heads.

"Help them!" Lord Preston pointed with his finger.

"Coming about!" shouted Owen. "Duck, lads!"

The boom swung, and a few soldiers practically got their skulls cracked. Eva drew the sheets home, and *Pluck* drove for the struggling men. Skit tossed lines over the side, and several grasped them while the soldiers on *Pluck* tugged.

"Those chaps, those chaps there!" Lord Preston was pointing again, waving his finger wildly. "Get them a line!"

Three soldiers were trying to stay afloat while they kept a fourth man's head out of the water. Blood was on their hands and uniforms from his wounds. None of them were good swimmers, and they were constantly going down and fighting their way back up. The boat was upon them in a moment. An instant later the four men went under and did not reemerge.

"They've gone," said Skitt, leaning over the side with a white life ring in his hand. "Lord help us."

"Take the wheel!" Owen cried to Eva. "I'm going after them."

"I won't!" Eva fired back. "I can swim as well as you!"

"Don't argue with me!"

"I'm not going to argue! I'm going to jump!"

They both hit the water at the same time. Skitt lunged for the wheel as the boat pitched to starboard. Eva came up first, one arm around a young soldier with his helmet still on, hauling him to the side of *Pluck*, stroking with her free hand. The men on board grabbed the youth under the arms and brought him into the sailboat. She immediately dove under again.

"Here! Take him! Quickly!" Owen shot out of the water and lifted a man toward them. "Where's Eva?"

"She's right back under, mate," said a soldier. "Brought us wee Chipper here, better'n new."

Owen was gone beneath the waves.

The men watched, their faces tight. The boat rocked in the swells. There were explosions on the beach and more planes howled over their heads, but they kept their eyes fixed on the sea.

"C'mon, lad, c'mon then," muttered a sergeant.

Owen broke the surface with another soldier.

"Get him on his stomach!" he shouted as they pulled him onto the sailboat. "Get the water out of him! Where's the girl?"

"She's not come back up," the sergeant told him.

Owen dove under the waves. Half a minute passed. Then he exploded out of the sea with Eva and the wounded soldier. Eva gasped and choked as she fought for air, but that didn't stop her from helping Owen swim the wounded and unconscious man to *Pluck*. The men had no sooner dragged him into the boat before another German plane passed over the beaches. This one was met by the *thump thump* of antiaircraft fire from the destroyers and from the shore. The fighter plane sprayed the water and small boats with bullets. Even though she was still rapidly drawing air into her lungs, Owen hauled Eva underwater as shells smacked into the waves near *Pluck*.

"*Nein!*" she cried as he hauled her under.

She struggled against his grip and tried to surface, but he saw the bullets trailing bubbles and streaking toward them and began to stroke for the capsized sailboat, one arm around her waist. One shell stung his foot, but its force was spent. She finally wrestled free and broke into the open on the far side of the sinking boat. He emerged beside her, wiping the saltwater out of his eyes.

"You crazy fool!" Eva spat seawater. "Are you trying to drown me?"

"Didn't you see the plane?" he demanded. "It was right on top of us and its shells were heading straight for you!"

"Why do you exaggerate?"

Owen lifted his foot from the water. It was covered in blood.

"I didn't get that from a barnacle," he said.

She blinked as water ran into her eyes.

"But then you wouldn't let a Jewish boy's hands on you, would you?" he asked.

She slapped him across the face. "Is that what you think?" Her blue eyes were on fire.

"What else am I supposed to think? You're a goose-stepping Nazi!"

She slapped him with the other hand. "You never read my letter did you? You threw it out! You burned it!"

"There was nothing in it."

"There was everything in it. I told you I didn't care if you were Jewish. I said I was sorry. I told you I wanted to talk."

Owen didn't reply. He treaded water and looked at her. "I didn't know," he finally said.

She had one hand on the capsized hull. "Of course you didn't know. You can't burn letters and know what people are saying in them. The Nazis are good at that. Burning letters and burning books."

"I'm sorry."

The blue in her eyes softened a bit. "We had better get back to *Pluck* before your grandfather thinks the worse."

"Eva—"

"We can talk tonight. Something tells me when Lord Preston says we will be ferrying troops through the night he means you and me."

"Don't be so sure. He has a constitution of iron."

"Well, we'll see." A sudden smile went over her lips and eyes. "I missed your eighteenth birthday."

"It's my fault you weren't there."

"I'm not looking to find fault, Owen." She swam the few feet of water that separated them. "*Herzlichen Gluckwunsch zum Geburtstag*—happy birthday." She kissed him on the cheek. "You have grown into quite the man. Your foot is still bleeding. Let's get back to the boat. You were protecting me. *Ich danke Ihnen*—I thank you."

They swam out from behind the hull as Hurricanes showed up over the beach and raced after the German fighters. The soldiers on *Pluck* cheered for the Hurricanes and cheered for Eva and Owen at the same time.

"It's nice to be loved, as you English say," Eva managed to get out as she stroked.

They glanced at each other at the same time. "Yes, it is," he said.

"You are an older soul than eighteen, Owen." She looked straight ahead again. "Will you have the poem for me tonight? I don't suppose you have it on a piece of paper somewhere?"

"I don't need a piece of paper. It's where it always was."

Lord Preston did keep *Pluck* working until long after midnight, though he himself wrapped up in a blanket and slept in the cabin, and so did Skitt. The sailboat moved between ship and shore without stopping. The soldiers built fires on the beach, and the destroyers shone with lights in the dark sea. Owen rigged a lantern high on the mast. He had stripped off his shirt so it wouldn't get snagged, and he left it off after he climbed down.

"What about my poem?" asked Eva as he steered the boat back to get more men.

"All right."

He recited the poem he had written two years before without looking at her, speaking the last stanzas slowly.

> Let me open my wings like the Caspian tern
> Let me burn, let me illumine, like the rays of the sun
>
> I will have the sea and all that it gives
> All that it promises and all that lives
>
> Deep in its soul and I shall be free
> To drink of its years and learn of its hours
>
> To sail on its colors and all of its waters
> With no end in sight
> No ending to light

Then he said, "For Eva."

"Still?" she asked as the darkness slipped past to port and starboard.

"More than ever, I expect."

She slowly put her hand over his as he held the wheel. "Can we stop the boat?"

"Stop it?"

"Or make the half-hour run to shore last twice as long?"

"If we took in more sail. But why would you want to do that?"

"Because I'm tired and I need a few minutes rest."

"You? Tired?"

"It happens sometimes, Englishman. I see German planes over our boat. I see them dropping bombs on ships that are trying to rescue the men. They come in as low as possible and their bullets kick up the sand and water and kill. I remember it is my country doing this. I remember how I used to march and how I betrayed my father because he was hiding Jews and Albrecht. I have tried to pin up the tear in my shirt so the British soldiers don't see my tattoos. I'm exhausted by everything I carry on my heart and in my mind. Please. A few minutes."

"Can you take the mainsail in by yourself? Not all the way. Leave about half the sail up."

"I have the strength, yes."

She braced her legs on the deck and drew the sail down quickly, tying the line off at the cleat.

"Now lash the wheel," she told Owen.

"What do you mean?"

"Let it run parallel to the beach." She placed her hand on his bare chest and over his heart. "It's not so much rest I need as the freedom to speak with you."

"What is there to say?"

"I have a lot to say, Englishman."

He did as she asked.

The lantern light swayed back and forth over his arms and shoulders as the boat moved sluggishly through the swells. They were about five hundred yards offshore. Fires of different sizes flared on the sand, and the destroyers and troopships glimmered behind them, but other than that they sailed on blackness. He turned to face her, and she whispered, "*Sie haben in solch einer schonen jungen Mann herangewachsen.*"

He smiled. "Pardon?"

She smiled back. "I shall have to teach you some German. It might come in handy."

"Because of the war?"

"Because of me. I just told you that you have grown into a beautiful young man."

"Do you mean that?"

"Yes."

"But you—you are such a stunning woman. I feel like I'm not enough for you."

"Anyone who writes poetry like you and sails like you and saves the lives of men like you is more than enough, Owen. You have been part of changing me, renewing me, *ja*? So there is already a special bond between us. Do you have any other poems for me?"

"I did think of some over the past two years. But I thrust them aside. I'm sorry."

"I have seen a little bit of how your mind works, Owen. I think you have not forgotten all of the poetry that has run through your head."

"It's been hard for me to turn into stone."

"If it had been easy I would have known the poetry was just pretty English words with no heart."

He took in a face streaked with grime from the day, the saltwater tangle of her loose hair, the rips on the arms of her shirt, a cut that ran down part of one cheek, the large darkness of her eyes, the light of the lantern that for a moment showed him her features and then slowly took them away again.

"Mate, it's too good to be true." He shook his head.

She smiled. "Say something a bit more profound, please."

"You're so much." He touched her face and hair. "Before I turned my thoughts away from you, I read a poem by T.E. Lawrence. The British call him Lawrence of Arabia. 'I loved you, so I drew these tides of men into my hands and wrote my will across the sky in stars.' I thought of you instantly. And I wrote down in my book something like this. 'All that I wish for comes together in her. Nothing more needs to be placed beyond what has been set in place, nothing must be taken away. The seas, and skies, and constellations are in her, all the nights, and days, and surging breakers. I can only love, if I begin to love her while the dew is still on her heart.'"

She took in her breath. "But that is too beautiful. How can you have written that for me?"

"It wasn't hard. It was just hard to forget I had written them. Just as it was hard to try to forget about you altogether. I never succeeded at either."

"But I was a Nazi."

"I never believed that."

"I was, Owen, you know I was."

He shook his head. "You may have played along. Gone through the motions. Acted the part. Even believed you were what you said you were in front of the Third Reich and SS and Gestapo. But you were never a Nazi, Eva. You fooled Germany and you fooled yourself. But you never fooled me. Even when I was angry and hurt I knew better. I knew you were roses, Eva, not thistles and thorns."

He leaned down and kissed her. Her return kiss was hesitant. It seemed to him she still wanted to argue about who she was or wasn't. But after a few moments she hugged him in closer to herself, her arms crossing his back.

"I care for you very much, Englishman," she said.

"And the Englishman for you."

She patted his back. "*Achtung.* There is a boat moving across our bow. It's about a hundred meters away."

Owen turned quickly to look. "It has so many lights it could be a Christmas tree."

"A good thing."

Owen unlashed the wheel and steered the boat to port. It responded slowly. But the other boat had an engine and was out of their way in half a minute.

"You've never taken the wheel, have you?" Owen asked.

"No."

"Come on. Have a go."

"I don't feel capable of doing that, Owen."

"Here. Take hold. I'll put my hands on yours."

He guided her to the wheel and closed his fingers over hers as she gripped it tightly.

"I can't even see," she said.

"You will in a moment."

Two buildings were burning fiercely to starboard. Even though they were still a quarter mile or more from the beach the tall flames made the whole boat flicker. She moved the wooden wheel cautiously. He took away his hands.

"You see? You're doing fine."

"Not much of a wind. Not many waves. Hardly any sail up."

"It's a good start."

"I miss you."

Cautiously, he put his arms around her from behind and placed his hands on hers again. "How's that?"

"Just right. I could sail all night like this."

"Why don't we?"

"No, Owen." She glanced back at him, firelight rippling over her face and her tangled hair. "We must get as many soldiers off as we can before the planes come back."

"I know that. It was just a wish."

She slipped a hand out from under his and off the wheel and put it to his cheek. "One more kiss."

He bent forward. "I'll never forget this night."

"No one who is here will."

"Even if I close my eyes now it's all darkness and flames and the hands of soldiers reaching for mine. And your face in the middle of it all."

"I hope it stays there." She kissed him again and took her hand back. "Can I steer it to shore?"

"This is as good a spot as any. The soldiers are all along the water's edge."

She edged *Pluck* to starboard. "How is that?"

"Perfect. We'll go right in and get ourselves a couple of dozen."

"Wouldn't it be something to find his son?"

Owen took his arms from around her and stepped back. "Wouldn't it just?"

The sailboat headed toward the rolls of flame from the shattered buildings. In fifteen minutes they were close to the beaches and could see the dark shapes of men wading out to them.

"Here, mate, can you pick us up?" one soldier called out.

"Got room? Got any room on your boat?" called another.

"Are you ferrying us lot back to the ships and England?"

Owen and Eva worked through the rest of the night and early morning, moving *Pluck* as quickly as they could from the beaches and back to the troopships and destroyers. They continued to sail the boat alongside Lord Preston and Skitt well after the sun had cleared the clouds to the east. About noon both fell asleep minutes apart on coils of rope in the cabin. The shriek of German dive-bombers, the crash of Hurricane fighters' machine guns, exploding ships, the boom of antiaircraft fire, and the shouts of men hauling themselves on board *Pluck* didn't disturb them. Before Owen collapsed, Lord Preston asked him if there had been any sign of Robbie or his regiment.

"None, Grandfather. But this is such a long stretch of beach. And we were only evacuating from one small strip of it."

"Quite right. Well, I may catch a glimpse of him today."

"I pray so."

Skitt handed out loaves of bread and wedges of cheese to the soldiers. He kept a duffel bag of food in the cabin for the crew. At sunset a ship's whistle woke Eva. She drank some water, ate some sausage, and went onto the deck.

Lord Preston, great rims of darkness under his eyes, was at the wheel as they sailed toward the beach. "Hullo, my dear."

"I'm sorry I slept, Lord Preston."

"But you must sleep, my girl. How else can you work through the night?"

"Would you like me to take the wheel?"

"I confess I'm quite done in, but let me just get *Pluck* to the shore."

"Where's Skitt?"

"Down a hatch forward. We've got a bit of a leak and once an hour he bails for five minutes."

She looked to where the hatch was open. "I hope it doesn't develop into something serious."

"We'll keep an eye out." He cleared his throat. "No sign of my son."

She put a hand on his arm. "Let's keep on looking. There are so many soldiers."

"Of course."

"You should lie down after this. I will go and wake up Owen, and we'll take over."

"You must have something to eat first. There's a duffel bag in the cabin."

"I saw that. I had a few things, *danke*."

"And there are jugs of fresh water stored in the wooden boxes."

The stars came out, smoke drifted over the beach and the sea from bombed-out houses, and ships' lights winked on. Owen put out more sail while Eva steered toward the ships. Soldiers clambered aboard and chewed on the bread and cheese and sausage as Skitt and Lord Preston slept in the cabin. May 29 became May 30, and May 31 slipped into June. Eva lost track of the days of the week. Her eyes blinked open several evenings in a row to the voice of Lord Preston reading from the same passage in the Bible to the soldiers crowded aboard *Pluck*, a voice that was growing rougher the longer they remained at Dunkerque.

> He that dwelleth in the secret place of the most High shall abide under the shadow of the Almighty. I will say of the LORD, He is my refuge and my fortress: my God; in him will I trust. Surely he shall deliver thee from the snare of the fowler, and from the noisome pestilence. He shall cover thee with his feathers, and under his wings shalt thou trust: his truth shall be thy shield and buckler. Thou shalt not be afraid for the terror by night; nor for the arrow that flieth

by day; nor for the pestilence that walketh in darkness; nor
for the destruction that wasteth at noonday. A thousand
shall fall at thy side, and ten thousand at thy right hand;
but it shall not come nigh thee.

By Sunday, June 2, their water and food were gone. Owen and Eva
had ferried troops during the night but didn't climb down into the cabin
to sleep because Lord Preston was so weak. Skitt had him sit below with
a blanket around his shoulders and helped bring another boatload of soldiers to a destroyer. Eva was at the wheel, Skitt and Owen on the lines.

"I think that's it," said Skitt. "Lord Preston is badly off and we're out of
supplies. We need to head back to Dover."

Eva nodded. "I agree."

"I'll tell him," Owen said.

He went into the cabin and sat next to Lord Preston, who was bent
over and clutching the blanket, almost asleep.

"Grandfather, we have to head back to Dover. We've no more food and
no more water."

"The soldiers…" rasped Lord Preston.

"There are hundreds of other small ships to do the rest of the ferrying.
The shore is not nearly so crowded as it was a week ago. I expect it will be
all over in a couple more days."

"I should like to see Robbie."

"For all we know he's back home already."

"Take another lot back with us to Dover." Lord Preston looked up at
his grandson with watery eyes. "One more lot."

"We have nothing to give them to eat or drink."

"Bring another couple of dozen on board."

"All right." Owen took a pea coat and folded it. "Will you lie back and
use this as a pillow?"

"You'll need me up top."

"No. Skitt's turned into quite the sailor over the past seven days. And
Eva can handle the wheel like a master yachtsman. We'll be fine."

"If you do happen to pick up Robbie—"

"We'll tell you straightaway."

They took on twenty-seven soldiers and headed west for Dover, sitting low in the water. Skitt climbed down through the hatch into the hold

and bailed every half hour till several of the soldiers pitched in and helped. *Pluck* passed burning and sinking ships, took a good wind in her mainsail and the smaller headsail, and fought her way across the Channel despite the weight she had on board. She followed a long line of ships of all kinds back to England, strung out behind one another like a naval parade, passing a similar line of boats sailing from England to Dunkerque. The soldiers cheered as the white chalk cliffs drew closer, and they slapped one another on the back as the boat moored alongside a quay.

"Thanks then, you three," said a corporal. "It's grand to be on good English soil again."

"All the best," said Owen, shaking his hand.

A naval officer came down to look at the boat. "The log says you've been gone since the twenty-seventh of May."

"Yes, sir. We were ferrying men from the beach to the destroyers and troopships."

He nodded. "Well done."

"Thank you, sir."

Skitt had gone up the quay to the street. "The car is where I parked it. Let's get Lord Preston to Dover Sky."

"Right."

Eva was helping Lord Preston out of the cabin. "The rest did him good, but I wish we had some water or tea."

Skitt held up a container. "This thermos was left in the car. Tea."

"Oh, good. Grandfather, how about some tea from this vacuum flask?"

Lord Preston's face was white, but he managed a smile. "That would be the very thing."

Owen moved the boat to its normal mooring on his own, took down the sails, squared everything away, and joined them at the car. Skitt whisked the four of them to Dover Sky. Fairburn, the groundskeeper, doffed his hat as they passed him on the lane to the front door. He called out something none of them could hear. Eva helped Lord Preston out of the car once Skitt had come to a stop.

"Let's get you in and give you a bite to eat." Eva had both her arms around Lord Preston. "Then you could use a bath."

He offered a lopsided smile. "I expect we could all use a bath."

She laughed. "We are a bit untidy, aren't we?"

"A week at sea. Can't be helped."

The front door opened. Robbie was framed there a moment in his soiled and tattered uniform.

"Father!"

He ran down the steps and took the old man in his arms.

"Robbie." Lord Preston's face immediately took on color. "What's this?"

"I've been here less than an hour. A steamer brought my lads and me across—they collected us off the East Pier in Dunkerque. I got a driver to bring me to Dover Sky. I was just talking to Mum. She said you had gone to Dunkerque and been gone a week. She's worried sick."

Lord Preston hugged his son and patted him on the back. "Had to be done. Everyone needed to chip in. We tried to do our part. God be praised...God be praised here you are." Tears hung at the edges of his eyes.

Robbie gave Skitt a quick glance, his eyes hard. "Did you have to take him with you?"

Skitt stood up straight in his torn shirt and pants. "He would not be left behind. You should know your father better than that."

"But to take him to Dunkerque. To take him into harm's way."

"It was I who took them." Lord Preston gripped his son's shoulders. "It was I who ordered them to join me. If they had refused I would have cast *Pluck* off from the pier and sailed to France alone."

"It was foolhardy."

"We got the soldiers onto the warships, didn't we? Got them away from the Germans and safely home? If we'd all held back because of old age or fear, our army would be behind barbed wire by now. Others took the risk. Why shouldn't I?"

Robbie's face remained grim. "I doubt there are any other lords or Members of Parliament out there in the small ships. Mum said Churchill was aghast that you'd crossed the Channel in a sailboat and were hanging about off the Dunkerque beaches."

"Let Winston make the speeches. He's jolly good at that. I'll do the little things."

"Hardly a little thing to be fetching soldiers off a beach that's being bombed and shot to pieces by Stuka dive-bombers, Dad."

Lord Preston put a hand to his son's cheek. "I thank God you're alive. I prayed day and night. And somewhere in another part of England another father is thanking God because the son we hauled aboard *Pluck* is standing alive before him now too. So no more of this. Your return is a cause for celebration, not recrimination. Look at my crew." He extended a hand toward Owen and Skitt and Eva and their grimy faces and clothing. "They have been at Dunkerque with me. They have been saving the lives of the soldiers on the beaches. They have never left my side or let me down. Honor them."

Robbie hesitated. Then he nodded. "You're quite right." He looked at Eva and the two men. "Thank you for bringing my father home alive. And thank you for bringing the boys back to Britain in one piece. God bless you."

Skitt bowed. "Our pleasure, Lord Robert."

Lord Preston rang up his wife while the others scattered to various bathrooms in the large house and scrubbed a week's dirt off their bodies. The cook hustled about in her kitchen preparing a hot meal of roast beef and Yorkshire pudding. Robbie called army headquarters and was granted leave to stay on at Dover Sky with his father for forty-eight hours. Clean clothes were found for everyone, and Robbie dressed in tennis whites while his colonel's uniform was laundered and pressed. After high tea they sat together in the library. Robbie spoke about the fighting that had begun like a lightning flash on May 10 and the mad scramble of retreat that followed the ferocious battles. The others told their stories about sailing *Pluck* to and from the beaches at Dunkerque and the different soldiers they had taken on board. Lord Preston made his way to his bedroom after several hours of talk, but the others fell asleep in their chairs.

Eva and Owen were the last two awake.

"All my lights are going out," whispered Eva, fighting to keep her eyes open.

"Linger with me a bit longer," urged Owen.

"I can't, you know."

"May I come over there and kiss you goodnight?"

"Aren't you too tired to budge? I fear I am."

"No. My motivation is high."

"Well then, pay me a visit, my darling Englishman."

"I will do…shortly." But Owen never pushed himself out of his chair.

Toward dawn, light lanced between two curtains and found its way to Eva's legs, up to her hands loose in her lap, and to her face. Owen woke about the time it had flowed over her fingers to her dress. He watched it move until it finally caught fire in her hair and leaped into the air and was gone. She seemed to feel his gaze and opened her eyes, looking directly at him.

"What are you doing?" she asked in a quiet voice.

"Dreaming."

"With your eyes wide open?"

"Yes."

"You can't do that."

"I just have. Lawrence of Arabia said it made a man that much more dangerous, you know, for him to dream with his eyes open, because he was far more likely to make his dreams come true."

"Yes? And what are your dreams?"

"You."

"Me what?"

"Just you. That's the sum of my dreams. Well, that and going to sea on a great ship."

"*Pluck* was a great ship."

"She was. But I'm thinking of something a bit larger."

She shook her head. "Don't talk to me about the war. I want the war to go away or at least have the good sense to remain on the other side of the Channel." She stretched out her hand. "Come, poet laureate, take me out for some air. I want to hear the robins."

Owen and Eva stepped through the doors and began to wander over the grounds of the summer estate. Fairburn saw them from a distance and lifted his cap. They followed the slope to the swan pond, where several of the majestic birds were drifting about on the water.

"I wish I had breadcrumbs," she said, watching them.

"I can fetch some from the house."

"Don't you dare." She closed her hand over his. "I want you with me every minute." She smiled. "You may have dreamed with your eyes open like Lawrence of Arabia, but mine were shut tight. It was frightening. Faces and red streaks of flame, planes swooping and firing their guns, ships blowing up. No, you stay with me, Sir Owen. The rest of the world will rush upon us soon enough and snatch you away like high tide."

"That's not likely to happen."

"Of course it is. Now it's a war. The German fleet will be scratching and scraping to get out to sea and the British fleet will be only too eager to come to blows with them when they do. And where will you be? Right in the middle of it. So indulge me and walk with me and let's keep the mad rush of a world war at bay for as long as possible."

"Right."

"But before we move off." She glanced about them and put her arms around his neck. "A kiss, my darling man, my hero of Dunkerque."

"I wasn't—"

She brushed his lips with hers. "You were."

As the kiss ended, Eva asked, "Do you ever wonder if other lovers have met here by the pond and done just what we're doing?"

"Oh, I'm sure of it. Dover Sky has been here quite some time."

"So here we are, the latest in a long line."

"Albrecht was here. Before he married Aunt Cathy. So other Germans have preceded you."

"How pleasant." She kissed him again. "The nights in Dunkerque were magic. With all the fear and danger, they were still something out of a legend. Let's add the morning of swans to that."

"I thought you wanted to walk."

"I did. But now I prefer the company of the swans. And you."

He ran his hands through her hair. "Like sunlight."

"I was a mess on *Pluck.*"

"A fine and glorious mess, you were."

"I was dirty and unwashed and my hair was like strands of frayed rope."

He laughed. "How differently girls see things from boys. You were beautiful."

"I don't like hearing about myself in the past tense."

"That's easy enough to rectify. You *are* beautiful."

"*Danke.* Now speak to me properly. The way a poet does."

"'Shall I compare thee to a summer's day? Thou art more lovely and more temperate.'"

"Go on."

Owen continued to recite the sonnet.

> Rough winds do shake the darling buds of May,
> And summer's lease hath all too short a date;
>
> Sometime too hot the eye of heaven shines,
> And often is his gold complexion dimmed;

And every fair from fair sometime declines,
By chance, or nature's changing course untrimmed;

But thy eternal summer shall not fade,
Nor lose possession of that fair thou ow'st;
Nor shall Death brag thou wand'rest in his shade,
When in eternal lines to Time thou grow'st.

"Ah. Finish it, Owen."

"How do you know there's more to the poem?"

"The Nazis weren't in charge of all my education. I know some Shakespeare. He always ends his sonnets with a couplet."

Owen stroked his thumbs slowly and gently underneath her blue eyes. "'So long as men can breathe or eyes can see, so long lives this, and this gives life to thee.'"

"Do you believe that? That a woman can live on and on in a poem?"

"Of course I do. Hasn't she? Won't you?"

"I?"

"Two poems with your name on them are flitting about England. Now that we're through with Dunkerque, I expect there will be a third."

Eva leaned her head against him, and he embraced her tightly.

"I look forward to hearing your next poem about me," she said into his chest.

"I look forward to dreaming it up and writing it."

"Will it take you long, do you think?"

"Oh, no. A few more minutes are all I need."

She laughed softly. "I don't think I can wait that long."

"I could substitute Shakespeare again.

What's in a name? That which we call a rose
By any other name would smell as sweet;
So Eva would, were she not Eva call'd,
Retain that dear perfection which she owes
Without that title. Eva, doff thy name,
And for that name which is no part of thee
Take all myself.

"Ah. Do you not like Eva then?"

"Eva is Eve. It means life. I love your name. The lines from *Romeo and Juliet* were merely to hold you over until I have come up with a better poem."

"You are a Shakespeare who belongs to me. I suppose a girl can wait for her Shakespeare."

A swan suddenly lifted itself up, spread its white wings wide, hung poised on the water a few moments as they watched, and settled itself back on the surface of the green pond.

"I think that will be in the poem," he said, pressing his lips to her hair.

"I like the idea of being compared to a swan."

"I like the idea of a swan being compared to you."

"But how on earth can you do that? I don't have wings."

"Of course you have wings."

"What a crazy Englishman you are. I would love to stay here all day, a thousand days, and listen to you say crazy, beautiful things to me."

"Let's work on a plan, Eva."

"*Ja, ja*, we must certainly have a plan. Nothing goes ahead without a plan."

"You like to make fun, my German girl."

"They're coming across the Channel, aren't they?" she asked him abruptly. "The Nazis and SS and *Luftwaffe* will come across the Channel now, won't they?"

He didn't answer.

"They won't let the Channel stop them, will they," she continued. "What are a few miles of water to a plane? Or a ship?"

He rubbed his hand up and down over her back. "We have some time."

Robbie was still with them, dressed in his clean uniform, when Skitt, Owen, and Eva sat in the library alongside Lord Preston, Fairburn, and the household servants and listened to the prime minister's speech on Tuesday, June 4. The evacuation had been completed—more than three hundred thousand British and French troops had been rescued—and the whole country breathed a surprised sigh of relief and wonder. Churchill rose to the occasion in the House of Commons.

> The British Empire and the French Republic, linked together in their cause and in their need, will defend to the

death their native soil, aiding each other like good comrades to the utmost of their strength. Even though large tracts of Europe and many old and famous States have fallen or may fall into the grip of the Gestapo and all the odious apparatus of Nazi rule, we shall not flag or fail. We shall go on to the end, we shall fight in France, we shall fight on the seas and oceans, we shall fight with growing confidence and growing strength in the air, we shall defend our Island, whatever the cost may be. We shall fight on the beaches, we shall fight on the landing grounds, we shall fight in the fields and in the streets, we shall fight in the hills; we shall never surrender, and even if, which I do not for a moment believe, this Island or a large part of it were subjugated and starving, then our Empire beyond the seas, armed and guarded by the British Fleet, would carry on the struggle, until, in God's good time, the New World, with all its power and might, steps forth to the rescue and the liberation of the old.

7

June, 1940
Camden Lock, London

Paris surrendered on Friday, June 14. Kipp and Ben's squadron left France the following Tuesday, June 18. Their wives were informed that the two pilots were alive and well and had left the battle-torn French Republic. Victoria ran down the street to Caroline's house, crying and out of breath, where she threw herself into the other woman's arms.

"Did they ring you?" Victoria could hardly speak. "Did they tell you?"

"Yes, yes, thank God, Kipp's alive. Is that what they've told you about Ben?"

They hugged and kissed each other on the cheek.

"It's too good to be true, isn't it? After so many weeks of this and that and not knowing the truth?" Victoria hugged Caroline as hard as she could. "I feel like a massive weight has been lifted off my heart."

"Come in, come in," laughed Caroline. "We don't need to make a scene in the street when we can make it perfectly well inside my house. I was just about to listen to the prime minister's speech."

"Another speech?"

"He's trying to lift our spirits again, you know. France will fall any day now, we all expect it, don't we?"

"Nothing he could possibly say would lift my spirits more than the phone call from Captain Harrington at Martlesham Heath." She followed Caroline into the townhouse and saw Matthew, tall and dark, bent over the knobs on a large radio set positioned against a wall. "Hullo, Matt! Such wonderful news!"

He straightened with a grin. "Cheers, Aunt Vic. It's astonishing, it really is." He hugged and kissed her. "I heard you through the door. The RAF gave you good news about Uncle Ben too, didn't they?"

"The best news of all. Our families have good reason to celebrate."

"Where's Ram?"

"Oh, I told him about the telephone call and rushed out the door to come here. Call him up, would you, Matt? Tell him to join us for the broadcast and a bit of a party."

"Will do." He left the room.

Victoria collapsed into a chair. "I'm done in. It's only five minutes and I'm done in." She laughed. "I suppose I should temper my enthusiasm, shouldn't I? It's not as if they're back in England yet. The Channel Islands, the man told me. That's their base for providing air cover for another series of evacuations, did they tell you?"

Caroline was in the kitchen brewing tea and putting biscuits on a plate. "From Brest and Cherbourg and Bordeaux...I can't remember the names of all the ports, but it's almost as many men as they took off the beaches and piers at Dunkerque."

"Good show is all I can say. We certainly could use them here if Hitler thinks of crossing over." She sank her head back on a cushion. "Ben's made it to the Channel Islands. Well, if he's made it that close to home, he has no excuse for making it all the way. I don't care what sort of bombers he has to shoot down or how many of those Messerschmitts he has to cut his way through. He can't escape from that catastrophe in France only to crash into the sea now."

"They're still much closer to France, you know, Aunt Vic," said Matthew, coming back to play with the radio set.

"Who are?" she asked him, head still back, and her eyes closed. "What are?"

"The Channel Islands—Jersey, Guernsey, Alderney, Sark, all the rest."

"I don't care. They're off the continent, so they're practically in England to me." She opened one eye. "Where's Charles today?"

"Don't know. He's a bit miffed that Eva's taken up with Owen."

"Charles is a bit miffed about everything."

Caroline came into the front room with a tray bearing a tea pot, cups, cream and sugar, and the plate of biscuits. "I suppose eventually he'll sort himself out. A mother can only pray and hope for the best."

"Amen to that."

There was a loud knock, and the front door flew open. "Did I miss it, Mum?" asked Ramsay.

Victoria smiled. "Not at all. Come have a cuppa."

"All right."

"Where's your brother?" asked Victoria.

"Drawing some great awful picture. He didn't want to come. Tim, the loner, you know."

"Yes, I know." Victoria lifted her head off the cushion and leaned over to pour herself a cup of tea. Caroline had set the tray on a table between their chairs. "At least he's not mad to dash off and join the RAF like you two."

"Or Peter and James, Mum."

"Peter and James! The Wilde Twins!" Victoria poured cream into her tea. "And they're supposed to be the sons of an Anglican priest. Even Jane with all her charms can't keep those two on the ground. They've already enlisted." She glanced at Ramsay sharply. "Something you won't be doing anytime soon."

Ramsay stood with his tea and a handful of biscuits. "I'll talk to Dad."

"*I'll* talk to Dad, young man. If you want to work in a factory to support the war effort, that's fine, but the RAF is out of the question."

"Work in a factory? Peter and James—"

"Peter and James are in the Auxiliary RAF. It's to be expected that they'd join up, isn't it? Not to mention they have five years on you, Ramsay Whitecross, and hours upon hours of flying experience." She sipped at her tea. "Our family does not need any more pilots."

"Our country does."

"Then our country can provide them. We've done our bit in both wars. They had your father in nineteen eighteen and now they have him again in nineteen forty, and that's enough. Not to mention your Uncle Kipp and James and Peter—they all have their heads in the clouds. No, indeed, the family's RAF quota is quite full."

Ramsay's dark face darkened even more. "You make it sound like the war's won. All we've done is snatch our troops from the jaws of disaster, Mum. We've been beaten in Europe. And they're going to come for us next.

Not with their *Panzers* or their soldiers. With their planes. If we get beaten this time we're done—all Britain is done."

"Britain has enough pilots."

"But it doesn't. We lost hundreds of planes in France. They don't talk about it but I know it. I've heard the Dunkerque soldiers go on about it all. They saw our planes fall from the sky. Not just during the evacuation. From May tenth on. Britain needs more men, Mum. It needs more fliers."

"Britain doesn't need *you*. There are plenty of others to choose from. Now that's enough."

"The war isn't going to go away now that the Germans dominate Europe, Mum. Things are only going to get worse."

"I said, *that's enough*."

Ramsay sat down, his face like a thundercloud. "Just so you know, I'm not going to make boots or uniforms in a factory in the Midlands."

"Fine. You can carry on with your plans for university at King's College."

"Oh, Matt's another one." Caroline took a biscuit from the plate. "'My dad's flying, so I should be flying.' That's his song."

Matthew had his ear to the radio set and the volume turned down low. "A few more minutes," he said. Then he glanced over at his mother. "Well, and so I should. Dad and Uncle Ben can't carry the load forever, can they? It's not as if they're young men anymore."

Caroline lifted her eyebrows. "Oh, really? I suppose that makes me a little old lady too, does it?"

"I'm just saying they need chaps like me and Ram. Even if you and Aunt Vic think they don't."

There was another knock on the door.

"That's Sean," Matthew announced as he crossed the room. "I rang him up." He opened the door. "Cheers."

"Hullo." Sean, tall and dark like Matthew and Ramsay, came into the house. "Aunt Caroline. Aunt Victoria. Cheers, Ram."

"Cheers."

"Hullo, Sean." Caroline got up and gave him a hug and a kiss on the cheek. "How's your Angelika? Your Mum said she had a bad cold."

"She's on the mend, thanks."

Victoria arched an eyebrow. "Have you been recruited by Matt and Ramsay into their Hurricane squadron?"

Sean gave her a smile that instantly lit up his dark features. "You've heard about all that, have you, Aunt Vic?"

"That's all I've heard day and night since the Germans invaded France and Holland and Belgium. Your name never came up though."

"I'm a recent convert."

"Well, I'm terribly sorry to hear it. I thought you had my sister Catherine's no-nonsense approach to life."

"I did, but Da came in on the side of enlistment. He's dead set on overthrowing the Nazis and getting Germany back under a proper democracy. Especially after what we went through over there."

"I know. It was dreadful." Victoria stirred another spoonful of sugar into her tea. "But surely you're not eighteen yet like Ramsay and Matthew?"

"Not quite. But I'm done with my schooling. It's either enlist or on to university to get my doctorate in theology." He laughed. "That's what Da would want. At least you'd think that's what Da would want. But he wants a Germany without the Nazis more than his son lecturing from a university podium. And his attitude is that we shouldn't expect others to do the hard work for us."

"Hear, hear," said Matthew, standing and drinking tea by the radio set.

"What? Your dad is pushing you to enlist?" Ramsay put down his tea. "Just like that?"

"Not just like that. He and Mum have been going over and over the matter. She's no more keen to see me go up in a kite than these two are to see you and Matt up among the clouds."

"You never mentioned it."

"I didn't know how serious Da was about the whole thing. But with the collapse of France he's getting quite professorial."

Ramsay was horrified. "D'you mean to say you could be up flying a Hurricane while I'm sitting like a lump in some lecture hall?"

Sean shrugged. "'God moves in a mysterious way His wonders to perform; He plants His footsteps in the sea and rides upon the storm. Ye fearful saints, fresh courage take; the clouds you so much dread are big with mercy and shall break in blessings on your head.'"

"Oh, shut up." Ramsay looked at his mother. "It's unforgivable."

Victoria gave Sean a sharp look. "I shall have a chat with my sister.

The last thing we need is you up and flying about and driving your cousins mad."

"And their mothers." Caroline indicated a chair. "Do take a seat, sweet nephew. No more of the lecture hall for you. You've given everyone quite enough to think about." She got up. "In fact, let me serve you, if that will keep you quiet."

Sean flopped in the chair beside Caroline's. "Do you have chocolate covered biscuits?"

"Just a moment. There are a few left in the kitchen." She poured him tea. "I'll bring the cream and sugar over."

"No need, Aunt Caroline. I like it without any added petrol."

Victoria tapped her fingers. "Waiting on him hand and foot, are we?"

"Anything to get him away from the podium, Vic."

"It is, perhaps, all greatly exaggerated. Someone needs to give credence to the idea Hitler may well be content with Europe and have no interest in the British Isles whatsoever."

"You don't believe that, Mum," said Ramsay.

"Why not? I do believe it. I want to believe it."

"We've been sinking each other's ships and blowing up each other's planes. There's no going back now."

"Ramsay, my dear, one can always go back."

He shook his head. "Not on wickedness, Mum. Haven't you listened to Uncle Albrecht's story? You know what the Nazis did with the books in the universities. You've seen what they're doing to the Jews." He looked at Sean, who had his cup to his lips. "You've heard Sean tell what it was like to hide in attics and cellars from house to house with the Gestapo hunting them down. You were what, Sean, eleven or twelve years old?"

Victoria tapped her fingers again. "Still. Hitler need not go farther."

"He won't leave us here like a long thorn in Germany's side, Mum. We'll interfere with all his plans, won't we? He's got to pull us out and snap us in two."

"What a cheerful lad you are."

"Here we go. Quiet everyone." Matthew turned up the volume on the radio. "I hope it's a good enough broadcast to settle all the differences of opinion in this room."

"Not likely," responded Victoria, pouring herself another cup of tea.

They all listened to the speech attentively—even Victoria, who was afraid Churchill would fuel her son's ardor to fly and fight. It went on for some time, and as the minutes went by, Victoria felt relieved that Churchill had not come out with any particularly eloquent turns of phrase or fiery expressions that might ignite Ramsay's spirit.

"He's just done," she announced, setting her cup in its small plate with a loud click of china on china.

"Shh, Mum," said Ramsay, annoyed. "The speech isn't over yet."

"There's nothing more to say, is there?"

"Shh! Mum!"

The radio crackled, and Churchill's voice was distorted and indistinct. Matthew jumped up and twisted one of the knobs left and right. Half a minute of this and the sound was restored, much clearer and sharper than before.

> ...the French people. If we are now called upon to endure what they have been suffering, we shall emulate their courage, and if final victory rewards our toils they shall share the gains, aye, and freedom shall be restored to all. We abate nothing of our just demands; not one jot or tittle do we recede. Czechs, Poles, Norwegians, Dutch, Belgians have joined their causes to our own. All these shall be restored.
>
> What General Weygand called the Battle of France is over. I expect that the Battle of Britain is about to begin. Upon this battle depends the survival of Christian civilization. Upon it depends our own British life, and the long continuity of our institutions and our Empire. The whole fury and might of the enemy must very soon be turned on us.
>
> Hitler knows that he will have to break us in this Island or lose the war. If we can stand up to him, all Europe may be free and the life of the world may move forward into broad, sunlit uplands. But if we fail, then the whole world, including the United States, including all that we have known and cared for, will sink into the abyss of a new Dark Age made more sinister, and perhaps more protracted, by the lights of perverted science.

Let us therefore brace ourselves to our duties, and so bear ourselves that, if the British Empire and its Commonwealth last for a thousand years, men will still say, "This was their finest hour."

Ramsay was on his feet.

"You can't deny me this, mother." He wasn't looking at her. "You can't deny me my place."

Victoria had closed her eyes. "We shall talk about it when your father is home."

"I must do something besides take notes in class or sew buttons on greatcoats."

"When your father is home, Ramsay. Which hopefully will be very soon."

"Isn't that right, Matt?" Ramsay looked to his friends. "Isn't it, Sean?"

Matthew nodded, still standing by the radio as the BBC announcer came on. Sean finished a biscuit and wiped the crumbs from his shirt. "I can't stand the thought of those bounders messing up Grandmum's roses at Dover Sky and Ashton Park." Sean looked up. His eyes were dark. "I think of her and how she loves all that and how good she's been to me, and I can't bear the thought of those houses and rose bushes being flattened by bombs and trampled by their rotten jackboots. I won't let them kill her." He got to his feet. "That settles it for me then. I'm off to the recruiting station with my mum and da's blessing. Thanks for the tea, Aunt Caroline." He glanced at Matthew and Ramsay and nodded. "I'll talk to you later and let you know how it goes."

"But you're still seventeen," protested Victoria.

He smiled. "Don't worry about that, Aunt Vic."

France fell four days later, on June 22. Kipp and Ben touched down in the south of England with their squadron on June 23. Within twenty-four hours they were on their way by rail to London after ringing up their wives to announce they were on leave. Kensington Gate became the location for another family gathering, where the two pilots held young men like Peter and James and Ramsay and Matthew spellbound with stories of the air war over France. Sean could not be at the celebration because he was in flight training with the RAF. Robbie was also absent due to his involvement in Home Defense exercises with his regiment.

"Ben." Victoria grasped one of her husband's arms in both of hers and smiled at his audience in the backyard. "I wonder if I might steal you away for a few moments?"

"I was just at Dunkerque."

"My brother can surely speak for both of you."

"Easily done." Kipp lifted his glass of orange squash. "I'll claim some of your victories."

Victoria walked with Ben out of a green and sunny backyard spilling over with people, and into the house.

"What's all this about?" he asked her.

"War isn't a game, Flying Officer Whitecross."

"Did I say it was?"

"When you're out there talking with the boys you act like it is."

She led him to her father's private study and locked the door behind them.

"Now you really have me wondering what's up, Vic."

"Do I? Well, I won't hold you in suspense any longer. Have a seat."

"If I'm going to be shot I'd rather stand."

"Suit yourself."

The blinds were drawn against the sunlight outside, and the room was dark.

Victoria leaned her back against one of her father's tall bookshelves with her hands behind her gripping the edge of a shelf.

"I see what's coming," she said. "It's nineteen fourteen to nineteen eighteen all over again. Only worse. It's bad enough having you up there one day after another. I'm not having Ramsay up there with you."

"Vic, he—"

"I know he feels he needs to be a pilot like his father. That he needs to defend his country and Western civilization—Churchill has him all stirred up. But we've lost one child already, Ben. I'm not prepared to lose two."

"What child?"

"The child who'd be almost twenty years old now. The child I've given a name and whose birthday I honor every year in the privacy of my heart. The child I've always loved and who I'll love forever."

Ben stared as tears stabbed at her cheeks. "It was a miscarriage, Vic," he finally said.

"It was a baby! My baby! A boy! Quentin Paul Whitecross!" She made no attempt to lower her voice or clear the tears from her eyes and face. "All these years I couldn't talk about him, could I? Stiff upper lip and all that. Noble family. Mansions in Lancashire and Kent. Father an MP. Brother an MP. Husband a winner of the Victoria Cross. Show the world what you're made of, Victoria Anne. Show them that the death of your baby doesn't faze you. You're made of sterner stuff."

"I thought—I thought you were over it."

"Over it? In two weeks? Two months? Two years? I've never been over it, Ben Whitecross. I've never been over losing your son and mine."

"You were so happy when Ramsay was born."

"Of course I was happy. I was ecstatic. I gave birth to a son. I adore him. But he wasn't my first son. He was my second. And I still grieve for my first. Yes, I still grieve for him."

She collapsed into his arms, and he held her as close as he ever had. Her body shook with her weeping. He kissed her hair, her cheeks, slick with tears, and her eyes.

"It's all right," he soothed. "I understand now. Forgive me. Of course he's our firstborn. Of course he's our first son. I love the name you've given him. You don't need to have his birthdays in private anymore. I'll celebrate them with you."

"Do you mean it?" She could barely get the words out.

"I mean it. It was a day in April, wasn't it? Early April?"

"April ninth, nineteen twenty-one."

"Right. So he just turned nineteen?"

"Yes."

"Well, bless him, bless his soul. I love you, Vic, and I love him."

She was crying so hard she began to hiccup and struggled for breath.

"Look. I may have missed it first time around, but I'm here for you on the second flypast," he told her. "Don't keep it in anymore. Not with me. When you remember him and it hurts, tell me. Let me hold you. When the fact he isn't out in the yard with Ramsay and Tim breaks your heart, let me know. When the ache won't go away, I'll hold you until it's not so sharp. I'll hold you all day and all night if I have to."

"Ben—"

"Look. I love to fly. It's exciting. And it's exciting to fly in combat—terrifying, but exciting. But I'm no stranger to death, Vic. We lost good men in France. Sure, we all try to brush it off and keep flying. We can't let what happened to our mates paralyze us. Kipp and I and the others were trying to defend hundreds of thousands of people, so we had to put them first, not what we felt. I can tell you this though. No pilot loses another pilot in his squadron without losing a part of himself. Big part, small part—he's never going to be complete again. I want to fly, Vic. And I want to defend the millions of people who live in Britain because before God, and you know this to be true, there is no way on earth they are capable of defending themselves against the Nazi army and air force and navy. I have to do it in my Hurricane or they die. Edward and Terry have to do it in their ships. Robbie has to do it with his regiment. We do it or they die. We do it or the Jews in Britain are done for as well. Charlotte and her sons, Owen and Colm, are finished."

"You don't have to explain yourself, Ben. I understand all that."

He gently tilted her chin upward with his hand. "You don't want to lose Ramsay or Tim the way you lost Quentin. You don't want to lose me. But someone has to defend Charlotte, don't they? And someone has to defend you. The Nazis rained bombs on Spain, Vic. They rained them on Belgium and Poland and Holland and France. They killed without mercy. We can't let them do that here too. And we can't let them enslave us."

"If he doesn't have to go up, Ben, I want Ramsay to stay here with both feet on the ground."

"That's a big if. Who's going to decide?"

"I want to. I need to."

He kissed her forehead. "All right. I'll talk to him. I'll tell him that."

"He won't take it well."

"I'll explain about Quentin. We've never talked about the first baby. That will help him understand."

"He'll resent me, won't he?"

"If he carried a child inside him for nine months he would know why you're afraid." Ben patted her on the back. "Ramsay will grasp more than you think. He's not just a wild eighteen-year-old who wants to fly a fighter plane."

"He seems that way to me most of the time."

"He takes protecting the innocent and defenseless to heart. He really does see himself as a knight of the air."

"I don't want him going up, Ben. Not unless our situation in Britain is desperate."

Ben said nothing, only touching his lips to her auburn hair once again. "I'll be posted to another squadron soon."

"How soon?"

"It's only a matter of weeks."

July 7, 1940

Dear Vic,

I'm writing you from the new air base I've been assigned to in the south—King's Cross. The paint on the huts is still wet. If I had that yacht of your father's and sailed straight across the Channel, the locals tell me I'd wind up in Dieppe.

There is a lovely old church here. Not Methodist, mind you, but it couldn't be, really, since it was built about eight hundred years before John Wesley was born. I gather it has two sister churches and one of them is Jeremy's. The other is St. Simon of Cyrene's Cross in Wiltshire. In any case, I sat in King's Cross church today and prayed about all the young lads in the squadron I'll start leading tomorrow morning. Some of them were probably seventeen only a few months ago. I'd like to pray that I won't lose any, but that's not realistic. I suppose I can pray that I'll only lose a few. But that may not be realistic either depending on what Jerry throws at us.

I think I'll start the briefing tomorrow with a quick prayer and a quick reading from the Bible. Then they'll probably start calling me Ben 'Preacher' Whitecross.

I love you. My love to Ramsay and Tim as well.

Ben

July 11, 1940

Dearest Ben,

Thanks so much for your letter. Way down in West Sussex, are you? Do you know I've never been? But I've heard it's lovely.

I was going to say I'm glad things are fairly quiet for you but I've just had Ramsay rush in and tell me your squadron had a bit of a row yesterday. One Hurricane down and two German bombers down whilst you were protecting a convoy. It isn't you because Ramsay said they mentioned your name as squadron leader. I'm glad you came out all right, obviously, but I'm sorry for the chap who was lost— or did he bale out in time?

We are praying constantly. I expect you know that Kipp is at Pickering Green? That's only a few miles northeast of you. Peter and James are due to be assigned in a few weeks. Jane has joined the WAAF and is already a corporal, which doesn't surprise me at all.

Please write as often as you can. Your letters mean so much to me.

Much love,

Your Vic

July 17, 1940

A quick note. Jerry's really going after our shipping, and we're very busy here. We bagged two Me 109s yesterday, but they shot down three of our Hurricanes. The trouble is, Jerry's got the experience. He's been fighting in Poland and France, and most of our lads have never seen combat before. Of course the longer I can keep our boys alive the sooner they have the experience they need to beat the odds.

Pray for us. I hate seeing the bombers get through and any of our ships sunk or damaged.

Love,

Ben

PS—How are Ramsay and Tim getting on?

July 21, 1940

Dearest Ben,

We're all doing fine here, so please don't worry about us. All the trouble's over the Channel, isn't it? Thank goodness young Owen isn't in the thick of it yet. He hasn't finished his training with the Royal Navy. When it's done he wants to be assigned to a battleship. But there you are protecting the convoys day after day, so that will make his mother glad.

Caroline tells me Kipp is doing pretty much the same thing you are—he's a squadron leader with a lot of young boys to look after. But he's getting along well enough. He has one bomber and one fighter to his credit. Isn't that the same as you?

I saw Sean the other day. Still in training. Tall and dark like our Ramsay and Caroline's Matthew. He seemed to me to be completely at ease with himself. So I've added him to my prayers every morning and evening. Catherine appears to be taking it rather well, and of course Albrecht wanted him to enlist, so he is quite proud of what his son has accomplished.

I hope all the fighting stays over the Channel. Is that what you call an unrealistic prayer?

All our love,

Vic, Ramsay, and Tim

July 31, 1940
Hyde Park, London

"You look smashing in your uniform, Jane, absolutely smashing."

"Why thank you, James. Any further comments, Peter?"

"There are no words. No words in English."

"Hmm. That's very good, very clever."

Jane took her WAAF cap off her head and ran a slender hand over her gleaming black hair. "They're training me to do all sorts of things with radar. It's quite interesting." She put the cap back on. "But that's not why I wanted to meet you two here. I want to talk about us. The pair of you are getting posted August third, aren't you?"

Peter and James were in their blue uniforms just as she was. Both of them nodded.

"So you have to write me no matter where I'm assigned. That's the first thing. Once a week. No less. And if we can arrange our leaves so that we meet in London, that's what we'll do. Even if we have to pair off, so that I take one leave with James and another with Peter. After all, we've paired off before."

"Right," replied Peter.

"I like pairing off," said James.

Peter glanced at him. "That's because you never liked to share, even when we were in the nursery."

"For good reason. You never had enough."

Jane waved her hand. "None of the 'faint heart, fair lady' chatter. I'm serious tonight. Here's something else. Defend the country, defeat the Nazis, but I don't want either of you to become an ace. Do you understand? No aces. The one who becomes an ace is the one I won't marry. Aces take too many risks. Try too many stunts and heroics. They have a higher likelihood of getting themselves killed. So the one who fights well but steers away from being foolhardy is the one who will win the day with me."

Peter made a sour face. "We're twenty-three, and all of this with you is still like a teenager's game."

"Right." James flicked a piece of lint off her uniformed shoulder. "Why can't we be aces? And why can't you marry one of us before we're posted instead of after?"

"I don't like the idea of running away from the Nazis," Peter said.

"Neither do I," James added.

"No one told you to run away from the Nazis."

"'Course you did," Peter said.

"How can we protect you and defend our country if you won't let us go after Jerry tooth and nail?" James asked.

"No one wins a war by being overly cautious."

"Or overly careful."

Jane's dark eyes flickered with light. "No one wins my hand by being overly dead either."

She linked her arms through theirs. "I don't want to argue anymore. It's a lovely summer evening. Let's stroll like proper twenty-three-year-olds instead of squabbling teenagers."

"Righto."

"Right."

"So long as you two remember I'm the one who's twenty-three. You're boys of twenty-two until December."

"She's pulling rank on us," Peter said as they began their walk as a threesome, arms linked.

"She's always pulling something," James replied.

Two hours later
Hyde Park, London

James sat alone with Jane on a park bench, his arm around her shoulders, as they looked at the lights of London filling up the night.

"I know I tease you and we play our games, but I really do care for both of you, James."

"Of course we know that."

"I suppose it is childish. Still like the way we acted when were seventeen and eighteen."

"I expect we'll be doing it in our fifties. It'll keep us young. What's troubling you about all this?"

She faced him. "I can't keep you out of the skies. I can't keep you from fighting German pilots who have been flying missions since they invaded Poland in nineteen thirty-nine. Some since they bombed Spain years before that. But you're the stronger of the two, James. You've got to look out for Peter."

"What? Where did that come from?"

"I recognized it years ago. I would have married you once we were twenty-one but I knew Peter could never handle it. He honestly couldn't. For all the joking and teasing about the best man winning and all that, it would have killed him to watch you marry me."

"Jane, I don't know what to say. I'm sure Peter is stronger than you think he is. He'd be happy for us. He'd be happy for me."

"One part of him would. Another part would break into pieces. I see it, I do, James. I'm so afraid it will be like that once you're posted to your air base. He'll act the role of the cocky young pilot on the ground. He'll fly well when the skies are clear. But once the Germans attack he'll come apart. He won't know whether to dive or climb or bank left. You've got to be right there with him and protect him."

"Jane, Jane." He ran his hand along the side of her face, curling a strand of her night-black hair around his finger. "Do you realize how impossible it is to do what you're asking of me? First of all, they won't assign us to the same squadron. It isn't done. Not with brothers. The second thing is, even if we were in the same fight at the same time by some miracle, to stay glued to him when planes are twisting and turning all over the sky, I'd need seven hands and seven eyes. And the ability to pilot seven planes at the same time wouldn't hurt either."

"I fear for him."

"Perhaps you fear too much. He's strong. He's very strong."

"Not when it comes to me and you."

"Jane, he is."

"I love you. I love you with all I have inside me. I want you to marry me. I don't love Peter that way. I love him, but it's different from the way I feel about you. With Peter it's the deepest of friendships. With you it's… different."

She saw the surprise in his eyes and continued. "Oh, James, I've wanted to say I love you as a woman loves her man for so long, and I was afraid and unsure and I didn't want Peter to be hurt." She pulled him toward her and gripped him as tightly as she could. "What do you feel for me, James? Is it all a contest with your brother or do I really matter to you? Is it games and sport and childhood antics or do you love Jane Fordyce quite a bit?"

He laughed. "The way you go on. But to answer your question, yes, I love Jane Fordyce quite a bit, and this evening is brilliant—the most astonishing turnaround in my life. One moment I'm still vying with my brother for your affections and the next I'm the king of England. It really is remarkable. I must take up prayer as a habit. I beseeched the Almighty on bended knee before Peter and I came out to meet you, but I never expected a waterfall from the heavens."

She ran her fingers back and forth over his lips. "But now I'm worried about Peter again. You mustn't tell him what's happened between us tonight."

"Of course I won't."

"He's a very sensitive man. You both are. I'm certain he will be able to tell something has developed between us if he sees us together."

"He won't see us together. We'll be off to our respective airfields in a couple of days and we certainly won't get leave at the same time—indeed, if we get any leave at all—so he'll not see us together then either."

Jane held his face in both her hands and kissed him. "Still, I worry. I worry about you two flying your airplanes and I worry that you and I will break his heart."

"I say, he really is stronger than you think. Listen. Once we've gone through a few weeks of combat, and you see that he's held up under the strain, wouldn't that be the time to tell Peter what's up and ask him to be my best man?"

She kissed James again. "I don't know. I want us to be married this year. But I don't know."

"If he's strong enough to survive the *Luftwaffe*, don't you think he's strong enough to handle our engagement?"

She kissed him a third time. "I'll have to think it over. I have time for that, don't I?"

"I should say so. Though I hope to see you again in August. Late August, I would expect."

"In late August I'll have an answer for you."

He took her hands in his. "You wear both our rings."

"Yes. And I will keep wearing both your rings until the day you give me a diamond. And maybe beyond that."

He put her hands to his lips. "That doesn't bother me, Jane. So long as you love me and want to be my bride, you can wear a million rings from Peter on your fingers."

"Not a million. Just one. And from you, just two. The jade and the diamond. It doesn't have to be a large diamond. In fact, I'd really rather it wasn't. Just a nice diamond."

"Lady Jane, I won't disappoint. I promise you, I shall never do anything other than what blesses you."

August 9, 1940
The vicarage, St. Andrew's Cross

"Well, then read it out, Em, don't keep us on pins and needles."

"Hush." Emma was reading a letter at the breakfast table, her lips moving as she scanned the page. "In a moment."

"It would be quicker to get in the car and drive down to his air base, Dad," said Billy as he bit into a slice of buttered toast.

"It would indeed. Shall we pop on down to West Sussex after breakfast?"

"I'd love that."

"Oh, be quiet you two." Emma's eyebrows came together. "I'd have Peter's letter done by now if you'd just stop nattering."

Jeremy smiled at his son and poured himself some fresh tea.

"There, I'm done. Is everyone in the Sweet household happy now?" Emma handed the letter to her husband. "I don't know if all he's telling us is the truth because I don't know how much he's permitted to say. But he seems to like the airfield at KC, as he calls King's Cross. He doesn't mind the food, he misses Jane, and he thinks it's an act of God that his squadron leader is his uncle, Ben Whitecross, VC."

"KC. VC. All the crosses." Jeremy breathed on his glasses, wiped them with a white cloth from his pocket, placed them back over his eyes, and began to read the letter his wife had handed him. "Have you ever been to West Sussex?"

"I haven't. Neither has Victoria. Perhaps the two of us ladies should plan an outing."

"They wouldn't let you on the base."

"Of course they would."

"Not in wartime." Jeremy continued to read the letter as he spoke with Emma.

"Then we'd meet Ben and Peter in the village."

He smiled at something he read. "It's lovely, you know. I've been to the Arun Valley. Marvelous."

"We ought to go." Billy spoke up. "Why don't we all dash down for a visit?"

"They frown on that sort of thing," replied Jeremy. "Especially if the enemy is flying about. Your brother says here the Germans have been doing more bombing runs inland, not just on the Channel convoys. It wouldn't really do to take your mother and you into harm's way."

"The people in the village have to deal with it, don't they?'

"Well, I looked into it, and actually quite a few of them aren't there anymore. They've been relocated for the duration of the conflict. The RAF has taken over their houses."

"But some of the village folk must still be around. The RAF can't be green grocers and butchers or hand out beer and chips at the pub."

"No, I expect not."

"It would give me a taste of what the real thing is like."

"You don't need a taste of what the real thing is like." His mother stirred her tea, and the spoon chimed against the sides of the cup. "You have another year to go before we agreed you can enlist. The war might well be over by then."

"Over?"

"Yes. I expect the bombing attacks to dwindle out and Hitler to sit content on his side of the water while we sit content on ours. What does he want with us, really? He has France and Holland and Poland and heaven knows what else. Franco has Spain and Mussolini, Italy. Isn't that enough? What does he want with our dreary weather?"

"It's not bad today, Mum."

"My point is there's no reason to come after us. He can't march his troops or drive his tanks over the Channel."

"He has the planes, Mother. That's why Peter and James are fighting him in Hurricanes."

She shook her head. "Not for long. We really aren't worth the trouble, are we? In another month things will have quieted down."

"Very good." Jeremy passed the letter to Billy. "He sounds like himself. He's been up three or four times, tangled with a few of the *Luftwaffe*'s finest, and come out of his scraps in one piece. I thank God."

"So do I."

A person used the knocker on their front door.

"Who is that?" asked Emma. "No one from the church was supposed to drop by, were they?"

Jeremy wiped his mouth with a napkin and got up from the table. "Not this early."

Emma waited and sipped her tea while Billy read his brother's letter.

"Jane. What a nice surprise."

"Cheers, Uncle Jeremy. I got a few hours off from the Eleven Group Operations Center at Uxbridge so I thought I'd come and see all of you. Have you had any letters from Peter and James?"

"We have. We were just reading Peter's. There was a note from James on Tuesday."

Hearing the voices, Emma smiled and stood up, quickly setting another place at the table. "Here's a welcome visitor."

Billy looked up from the letter and grinned. "Jane. Good-oh."

"She's spoken for."

"Why can't I speak for her too then? I'm twenty."

"She has enough on her hands trying to sort things out between your brothers. It won't help matters to add you to the mix." She bent over and pinched him on the cheek. "Handsome as you are."

"Cut it out, Mum."

Jane walked into the room in her WAAF uniform with Jeremy behind her. "Hullo, Aunt Em. Cheers, Billy. How are you?" She gave her aunt a kiss and mussed Billy's hair. "Ginger just like Peter. Do you grow a foot every day now?"

His face colored the instant she touched him. "Hullo, Jane."

"Sit here." Emma pulled out a chair. "Tell us the news about RAF Hillingdon. Tea?"

"Please." Jane took her cap off. "Well, I've got a flat in Uxbridge now with two other girls so I don't have the long trip to make from Camden Lock every day. They've got me on the plotting table in the operations bunker at Uxbridge, so we handle information from the Observer Corps and the Chain Home Radio Direction Finding—the radar, they call it. I have these little blocks with tags to push about with my pool cue, as I call it. I'm wearing my headset, and they're telling me height, direction, numbers, and squadrons for the enemy planes. I set the blocks up with the proper tags and push them in the direction of their targets. All the bigwigs are staring down at the table from their seats up above. It gives them the big picture at a glance, you see, and all the information they need."

"Is the BBC telling us everything?" asked Billy. "What are the Germans really bombing?"

"Aren't you the inquisitive one? I can't tell you much more than the BBC, Billy. I've signed the Official Secrets Act, and I've sworn I won't keep a diary. You wouldn't want me to be taken out and shot, would you?"

Billy reddened a second time. "No."

Emma set a cup of tea in front of Jane with a plate of crumpets.

"Thanks awfully, Aunt Em, I'm starving." She began to eat a crumpet with one hand and tipped cream into her tea with the other. "If it's a busy day we really are running about. I have to keep my mind absolutely on the numbers they're giving me for my sector." She made a face as she chewed and drank and swallowed. "Not easily done since I have the King's Cross and Pickering Green squadrons to look after—with James at Pickering Green and Peter at the other. I send up a dart of a prayer and make every effort to concentrate on the task at hand. After all, the prayer and the plotting are the best ways I can help them."

Emma smiled, holding her cup in both her hands. "I should think so. Do the boys have much to say in their letters to you?"

Jane laughed. "Oh, much to say! When are either of the twins at a loss for something to say? I so hope they'll both get leave soon. I know it hasn't been long since they've been posted, barely more than a week, but I miss them more than I can tell you."

"I know you do."

Jane winked at Billy while she ate. "When are you going to go up and give your brothers a hand? I'm sure they could use the help."

Billy looked at his mother. "As soon as the recruiting sergeant gives me leave."

"There's plenty of time," his mother replied. "We've been through all that. You're still young."

"How young are you, Billy?" Jane was spreading butter on a crumpet. "Seventeen? Eighteen?"

"I'm twenty."

"Twenty? When did that happen? You still look as young as Matt and Ramsay."

His face went crimson for the third time. "I'm not."

His mother reached over and squeezed his hand. "It's the ginger hair and freckles. Still gives him that boyish look."

Billy's color deepened.

"Oh, in time he'll be a flier like his brothers." Jeremy leaned back in his chair. "Then Jane will see his squadron listed on the Eleven Group wall and be shooting prayers heavenward for him just like she does for his brothers."

Jane dusted her hands off and winked again. "Won't that be a treat,

Billy?" She put her cap back on her head and stood up. "Well, I'm off. I don't want Air Vice Marshal Park sending the Coldstream Guards after me. Ta, Aunt Em, and thanks for tea. All the best, Billy. Your day will come."

Jeremy got to his feet and put his arm around her shoulders. "Thanks for all that you do, Jane."

"All that I do? You mean at Uxbridge or for Peter and James?"

"Both."

"I wish I could do more."

August 12, 1940

> Dear Peter and James,
>
> I am writing this note to both of you—exactly the same note in exactly the same handwriting. God bless you—I love you, I pray for your safety, and I'm so proud of both of you. Your leave can't come soon enough for me. I so look forward to a flick and a meal and a good chat. You're always in my thoughts.
>
> Much love,
>
> Your Jane

August 15, 1940
Operations bunker, RAF Hillingdon, Uxbridge

The headphones crackled in Jane's ears. "Junkers 87s. Twenty plus. Altitude twelve thousand feet, that's angels one twelve. I'll have the bearing in a moment."

"Yes, thank you, I have that," Jane responded into her mouthpiece. "Junkers 87s. Twenty plus. Twelve thousand feet."

"They're after the airfields again. This lot is going after Pickering Green."

Cold came quickly into Jane's hands and chest. "I have that. The Ju 87s have set a course for Pickering Green."

"I have more information. Make that fifty plus. *Luftflotte* Three."

"Fifty plus, thank you, I have it."

"They're being covered by fighter planes at twenty thousand feet."

"Enemy fighters at twenty thousand feet. How many?"

"One moment. Messerschmitt Bf 109s. Twenty plus."

"Bf 109s, twenty plus, twenty thousand feet."

Jane plucked at two blocks and slid pieces of paper into their slots with the correct numbers of the enemy formations. The color on the tags indicated the time the information was relayed to her according to the minute hand of the sector clock on the wall. The clock was marked with red, yellow, and blue triangles, one after the other, each triangle representing a different five-minute segment of time. Glancing at the clock she selected red. In moments she was pushing the wooden blocks with their colored tags over the map with her pool cue, a magnetic rake with a flat tip. She moved them in a northerly direction from the coast of France and over the Channel toward Kent and Pickering Green.

"We have more enemy aircraft, Ju 87s, *Luftflotte* Three, thirty plus, same bearing, fifteen thousand feet."

"Ju 87s, thirty plus, fifteen thousand feet, same bearing."

"They are also covered by Messerschmitt Bf 109s, twenty plus, twenty thousand feet, angels two zero, same bearing."

"Roger, Messerschmitt Bf 109s, twenty plus, twenty thousand feet, same bearing."

She looked up at the sector clock. The minute hand was moving through a five-minute segment with a yellow triangle. She tagged her blocks with yellow. Then she used her rake to push the block indicating the Ju 87 dive-bombers and the block marking the Me 109 fighters into the county of Kent.

So many bombers going after Pickering Green. Get off the ground, James. Don't let them catch you at takeoff. Please, God, get them up.

Rows of lights blinked over her left shoulder.

She turned to look at a huge board that covered one wall. It displayed the name of air bases in 11 Group and the squadrons at each base. The lights made it clear whether the squadrons were in the air, landing, refueling, or fighting.

Both squadrons at Pickering Green were at READINESS, which meant airborne in five minutes.

One was a squadron of Hurricanes, another a squadron of the new Spitfires.

In his last letter James had told her he'd been transferred to Spitfires along with Kipp, who now commanded the Spitfire squadron at Pickering Green while another officer had taken over the Hurricanes.

God, go with him. God, give him wings. Give him eyes as sharp as a hawk's.

A different row of lights winked over the words LEFT GROUND.

Her headphones crackled. "Ju 87s, thirty plus, fifteen thousand feet."

"Roger, I have that, Ju 87s, thirty plus, fifteen thousand feet."

She took a quick look at the sector clock. The minute hand was in a blue triangle. She tagged the wooden block with blue.

The officers looking down would see the red blocks, the yellow blocks, and now the blue blocks, and realize instantly the bombers were descending on Kent and Pickering Green in waves five minutes apart.

A row of lights flashed—ENEMY SIGHTED.

These were the dive-bombers with crooked wings, the Stukas. These were the ones Ben and Kipp had said used sirens to sound more frightening whenever they dived. They had devastated the towns and cities of France and Holland and Belgium and had shattered the Polish Air Force on the ground.

But our boys are up. My James is up. They can fight back. Even if they have to take on the Me 109 fighters at the same time.

Twenty minutes went by as she moved the counters into Sector C, Kent, East Sussex, and West Sussex.

She caught a glimpse of lights going on at King's Cross, where Peter was stationed—ENEMY SIGHTED. All four squadrons were up and engaged, including the Hurricanes commanded by Ben Whitecross. That was the squadron Peter flew with.

The Pickering Green lights came on for both of its squadrons— LANDED AND REFUELING. James was back on the ground with Kipp.

"But how easy is it to land after all those attacks?" she asked under her breath. "How badly off are the runways?"

More bomber formations were moving in on the airfields. More on Pickering Green, Biggin Hill, and Hawkinge in Sector C. More on King's Cross, Tangmere, and Westhampnett in Sector A. She imagined the black ranks of bombers in the blue sky of a fine English summer day. Imagined the Stukas diving with the howl her uncles had told her about. The earth heaving and splitting apart. The Spitfires and Hurricanes pouncing on them. The yellow and red flames and the greasy black smoke Kipp had once described of aircraft burning and tumbling through the air.

"Ju 88s, thirty plus, fifteen thousand feet. Escort of Me 110s, twenty plus, twenty-two thousand feet."

"I have that." Jane glanced at the clock and chose yellow-colored tags. "Junkers 88s, thirty plus, fifteen thousand feet. Me 110s, twenty plus, twenty-two thousand feet." She pushed the wooden counters across the map toward Pickering Green.

This is nothing like the other days. The attacks aren't stopping. It's an onslaught.

Lights. James's squadron at Pickering Green—ORDERED TO STAND BY. They would be scrambling into their airplanes. The row of lights suddenly blinked out as another row of lights came on—AT STANDBY. James and Kipp and the other men were in their cockpits and could be airborne in two minutes. Then, in rapid succession, lights flashed one after another on different headings—ORDERED ON I PATROL, LEFT GROUND, IN POSITION, and DETAILED TO RAID. She had scarcely returned to her board before the four round lights came on at ENEMY SIGHTED. Glancing at King's Cross she saw lights over all its squadrons—AT STANDBY.

"You need to take a break, Jane. You've been on your feet for hours, and there's no sign of the enemy letting up."

Jane shook her head. "I'm fine, Sergeant Turnbull."

The tall woman with short iron-gray hair and dark eyes took the rake from Jane's hand. "I need you sharp. Get a cup of tea and put your feet up. Report back in an hour."

"But I have—"

"That's an order, Corporal. Shirley's here and will take over immediately."

Jane looked at the floor. "Yes, Sergeant."

The woman took her arm. "I know your beaus are up there. Both of them. Now you remember they're fighting for their lives while they're fighting for our lives. They need you at your best if they're going to survive. Understood?"

"Yes, Sergeant."

"Carry on."

Jane went into a small room where two other WAAFs were smoking cigarettes and chatting. They nodded at Jane and carried on. She poured herself a tea and helped herself to a few biscuits, sitting at the far side of the table from the other two women.

"It's building to something, I can tell you that," said the one with red hair. "I heard one of the officers say there have been over five hundred sorties today. Five hundred! And we're nowhere near done."

The blonde flicked the ash from the tip of her cigarette into a small tray. "Does your man think the invasion's bound to be soon?"

"He does. Everything points to that, doesn't it?"

"But we don't have enough soldiers, do we?"

"Us and the Canadians. That's it. They'll put up a fight. But it won't be enough. The Germans have millions of troops. And their planes will be bombing our cities, won't they?"

The blonde drew in on her cigarette while the redhead drank her tea.

"A lot of our boys have gone down," said the redhead. "Poor lads."

"But a lot of Jerry too, surely."

"He can afford it, can't he? He's got thousands more waiting in the wings. We have a few. Just a few."

Jane got up and left the room, cup in hand, and walked the seventy steps to the surface. Armed soldiers nodded at her as she went outside. The sky was a perfect blue and the sun a perfect gold. She walked away from the bunker a few yards, turned her face up into the light, and closed her eyes. The warmth felt good on her skin.

I suppose German girlfriends are praying for their pilots. And here I am praying for mine. Well, it's not as if I'm You and You're my servant and I can force You to do my bidding. I can't bend You to my wishes. It's 'Your will be done,' isn't it, not mine? But is it really Your will for England to be conquered? Is it really Your will for the Nazis to rule Europe? Is it Your will that Peter or James die? Or that any man die today? Yet hundreds are already dead. So what does it mean when we pray that Your will be done? Does that mean everything that happens is Your will? Or do things happen that aren't Your will at all? And if they aren't Your will, whose are they?

She went a little farther and sat down on the grass. The tea was getting cold, so she finished it.

I'm not a theologian like Uncle Albrecht. I read his book on suffering, but it left me with more questions than it answered. You may be an infinite being, but You can't answer all the prayers of the German families and all the prayers of the British families. You already haven't. There will be mothers and wives and girlfriends weeping on both sides of the Channel tonight, isn't that right? I only ask for James and Peter to live. Or if the way war works doesn't make that possible, I ask for one of them to live. I'm not going to say which one. I want James to marry me. But I want Peter to stand with us too. If I were very brave I'd ask You to give me the strength to bear up under whatever happens and not just ask for their lives. But I don't want that sort of strength because I don't want something to happen that requires strength like that. I'm just being honest.

"Jane."

She opened her eyes.

It was Sergeant Turnbull.

She dropped her cup and jumped to her feet. "Yes."

"Jenny's taken ill. I need you to replace her. I'm sorry. You've just had the half hour."

"That's fine. I'm all right." She bent and picked up the cup. "I'll be right there."

"There hasn't been any sort of letup. The bombers are coming in droves."

Jane followed her down the long flight of steps to the underground bunker. She put on a headset, checked that it was working properly, and stood near Shirley, who was pushing bombers and fighter escorts into Sector A and King's Cross.

"Ju 87s. Thirty plus. Fifteen thousand feet."

"Yes," responded Jane. "I have that. Ju 87s. Thirty plus. Fifteen thousand feet."

"I have the bearing."

"Thank you. Relay the bearing, please."

She listened as she was inserting the proper numbers and colors of paper onto the wooden counter. Then she pushed it into Sector C at Biggin Hill and Pickering Green.

ENEMY SIGHTED was lit for both squadrons at Pickering Green and three at King's Cross.

Jane worked until the evening, not standing down until a force of Me 109s and Me 110s prowling London's suburbs was dealt with by the RAF. Messages from Pickering Green and King's Cross were handed to her after she had left the plotting room, one from James and the other from Peter. Both told her they were all right. Peter said he had helped shoot down a Ju 87, a Stuka. Feeling much lighter in her spirits than she had in hours, she walked briskly to her flat. Both her roommates were out. She brought some Colby cheese from the icebox, made some cheese toast, and fell asleep in her bedroom with her uniform on.

"Air Vice Marshal Park will be hosting the prime minister today, Corporal Fordyce," Sergeant Turnbull told her the next morning. "If you glance that way you'll see the pair of them sitting there above us."

"Thank you, Sergeant."

"The RAF flew more than nine hundred sorties yesterday. First reports had more than one hundred and eighty enemy aircraft shot down. Now we are saying it is closer to seventy-five or one hundred."

"What about our losses?"

"The Germans are making extravagant claims. But our sources tell us thirty to forty. Lympne was badly hit and cannot be used as a forward stage for our planes any longer. RAF Manston in Kent took a blow— sixteen men lost, two Spitfires destroyed on the ground. Pickering Green was heavily damaged but they kept filling up the bomb craters and sticking to their missions. RAF Martlesham was knocked about by a flight of Me 109s. It shan't be back in service for two or three days. Ju 87s took out our radar stations at Dover, Rye, and Foreness. I should be grateful if they leave our air bases and radar towers alone today. But I don't think the enemy will be so obliging." The sergeant nodded. "Try your best again today, Jane."

"I shall do."

By midmorning Jane was pushing several wooden counters toward Tangmere and King's Cross once again. She scarcely noticed when the prime minister arrived and was surprised to see him hunched over in a seat above when she took a fifteen-minute break. Things intensified after that, and she never looked at him again. The enemy aircraft went after King's Cross in waves. Lights rippled up and down the large squadron readiness board behind her. She was pushing the wooden counters into Kent as the *Luftwaffe* went after Pickering Green as aggressively as they had the day before.

"Ju 88s. Fifteen plus. Fifteen thousand feet."

"I have that. Junkers 88s. Fifteen plus. Fifteen thousand feet."

"Ju 87s. Same bearing. Ten plus. Twelve thousand feet."

"Fighter escort. Me 110s. Fifteen plus. Twenty thousand feet. Angels two zero. Same bearing."

"Roger. Ju 87s. Ten plus. Twelve thousand feet. Me 110s. Fifteen plus. Twenty thousand feet."

She pushed the wooden blocks into Sector C and toward Pickering Green.

Lights came on and off and on again.

ORDERED TO READINESS. ORDERED TO STAND BY. LEFT GROUND. ORDERED TO RAID. ENEMY SIGHTED.

Finally the voices in her headset went silent.

"You may stand down, Corporal Fordyce."

"Yes, Sergeant."

"Please join me in my private room."

Jane followed Sergeant Turnbull into her office.

"Please shut the door, Corporal, and take a seat."

Jane closed the door. "Thank you, I'll stand."

Sergeant Turnbull did not sit either. "I know the brothers at Pickering Green and King's Cross have been on your mind a great deal."

Jane was at attention. "I don't let it interfere with my work. I concentrate on the information I'm given—"

"I received the following signal an hour ago. 'Peter Sweet was shot down over the Arun Valley in West Sussex in pursuit of enemy fighters. His aircraft's descent was spotted by local farmers, who hurried to the crash site. He was still in the cockpit and was likely dead before he hit the ground. Please convey the condolences of all flight personnel and ground crew at RAF King's Cross to Corporal Jane Fordyce at RAF Hillingdon.'"

The sergeant dropped her hand with the note in it to her side.

Jane stared at her.

"I'm terribly sorry, Jane. So terribly sorry. If it were a different set of circumstances, I should give you leave to travel to King's Cross. But we must have you here. At any rate, you would not be permitted to go to the base. The enemy attacks are far too frequent. But you are relieved for the evening. Is there anything I can do?"

Jane heard her voice. "No. That's quite all right. Thank you for letting me know so promptly."

"I shall see you in the morning then?"

"Of course."

"I'm so sorry, Jane. What a brave lad he was."

Jane made her way up the stairs and along the street, paying no attention to the Friday afternoon traffic or the people on the sidewalks. Her roommates greeted her cheerfully, saw her face, and stopped chattering.

"What is it, Jane?" asked the one with short brown hair.

"What's happened?" The other, a young woman with Chinese blood like Jane, took her hand. "What did you hear?"

"The brothers I told you about, the pilots." Jane felt the heat build in her eyes and her throat tighten. "The one's dead. Shot down."

"Oh, no." The one who was holding her hand embraced her.

The brown-haired one was pale. "He could be wounded."

"They pulled him out of the cockpit, Jenny." The tears burst onto Jane's cheeks. "They were sure he was dead before the crash."

"I'm so sorry, so sorry."

"Best give her the telegram, Jenny," said the young woman holding Jane.

"D'you think that's a good idea, Liz?"

"It can't get worse than it already is, can it?"

Jenny brought the telegram out of her dress pocket.

"I can't read it." Jane gripped Liz's back and sobbed. "I can't see. Tell me what it says, Jenny."

"Are you sure?"

"Please."

Jenny opened it.

> I'M SO SORRY, JANE. NO ONE WAS EVER BRAVER THAN PETER. HE HAD BAGGED ONE ME 109 THAT STRAFED OUR BASE. HE WAS AFTER THE OTHERS. HE OUTDISTANCED ALL OF US. THEY TURNED ON HIM AND IT WAS THREE ON ONE. EVEN THEN THEY HAD A HARD TIME OF IT. HE WILL BE BURIED WITH OUR OTHER PILOTS AT KING'S CROSS CHAPEL. WHEN YOU ARE ABLE TO GET DOWN HERE I WILL TAKE YOU TO HIM. I WISH YOU ALL THE COMFORT GOD CAN GIVE.
>
> MY PRAYERS
>
> BEN

"He's a hero," said Jenny.

"He is that," agreed Liz.

"I'm sorry, I'm sorry." The tears poured across Jane's face. "I should have loved him more. I was sure I'd see him again. I was certain of it."

"Shh…shh…" Liz stroked her back.

"I want to talk about him. I want to talk about Peter all night."

"Then do it. We'll listen, won't we, Jenn? Stay with you right through to morning."

Jenny nodded. "Yes, of course we will. I'll put the kettle on the stove."

"They said he wasn't strong. But they weren't right about that. They weren't, were they? Look how brave he was. Look how he fought the German planes…look how he defended us."

Liz held her more tightly. "He was strong. Very strong. You knew that. That's why you doted on him, Jane. That's why you loved him so much."

After very little sleep, Liz and Jenny walked Jane to the gate at RAF Hillingdon and hugged her before she stepped through. In the bunker she nodded at Sergeant Turnbull and the other WAAFs and put on her headset. The day was slow. During a break, a telegram from RAF Pickering Green was handed to her.

JANE

WE BOTH LOVED YOU. HE LOVED BOTH OF US. THEY WILL BURY HIM TODAY. OUR FIELD WON'T BE OPERATIONAL FOR ANOTHER 24 HOURS BUT I WON'T BE GRANTED LEAVE. BEN WILL SEE THE FUNERAL IS DONE RIGHT. OUR PHONE LINES ARE CUT OR I WOULD HAVE CALLED MUM AND DAD. I WILL TRY AS SOON AS THEY ARE REPAIRED. PETER AND I BOTH SAID IF SOMETHING HAPPENED TO ONE OF US IT WOULD BE UP TO THE OTHER TO LOVE YOU FOR THE REST OF HIS LIFE. THAT IS WHAT I AM GOING TO DO.

JAMES

Rainy weather and poor visibility set in for the week. There were still raids, but nothing like August 15 and 16. Jane remained at the plotting table day after day. On Tuesday, August 20, the WAAFs turned the radio on in their lunchroom to listen to a speech from the prime minister. Jane sat with her fingers around a cup of tea she never drank. She half listened to the broadcast, one part of her mind on Peter lying in the ground, the other on James sitting in his cockpit.

> The great air battle which has been in progress over this Island for the last few weeks has recently attained a high intensity. It is too soon to attempt to assign limits either to its scale or to its duration. We must certainly expect that greater efforts will be made by the enemy than any he has so far put forth. Hostile airfields are still being developed in France and the Low Countries, and the movement of squadrons and material for attacking us is still proceeding...
>
> The gratitude of every home in our Island, in our Empire, and indeed throughout the world, except in the abodes of the guilty, goes out to the British airmen who, undaunted by odds, unwearied in their constant challenge and mortal danger, are turning the tide of the world war by their prowess and by their devotion. Never in the field of human conflict was so much owed by so many to so few.

The young women went back to chatting and laughing after the speech. Jane got to her feet and walked to the operations room, placed a headset on, and stood waiting for directives. Nothing much happened. Eventually she planted herself in a chair set back from the table and map. Across her sectors pilots sat in their cockpits on standby most of the day and the rest of the week. Jane returned home on Friday to find a letter from James, hastily scrawled out on a sheet of paper torn from the back of a book.

> Jane,
>
> I think of you constantly, and I can safely say I pray for you constantly. I'm not exaggerating. Perhaps Peter's death has made a better Christian out of me. I rarely start a day without my tea and my newspaper and my prayers.

The bad weather has given all of us time to take stock. The constant bombing and strafing of our airfields, jumping in and out of the cockpit, sitting in them for what feels like days at a time, twisting and turning after Me 109s, and sticking it to the bombers—the constant go, go, go is beginning to wear on everyone, including the ground crew, who are called upon to work miracles on our planes in the blink of an eye. You really have to wonder how long we can keep this up. We're like cables pulled impossibly tight by a ship too big and too strong for us. The cables are going to break one by one or all at once.

People in the village ask us, "Is it over?" They hope the Germans are done. I shake my head. "They're just waiting for the next stretch of fine weather," I tell them. "The next sunny day they'll pounce on us like a cat on a mouse." I don't say what else is on my mind, but I can tell you. I don't know if we're up for it anymore. We don't have the pilots. There are too few of us. We don't have the strength, really.

Your James, one of the few

Saturday, August 24, 1940
Kensington Gate, London

Lord Preston sat in the backyard and watched a male robin, his chest vividly scarlet, cock his head, listen a moment, and drive his beak into the thick grass. Sunlight striped the yard as the sun continued to rise over the hedges and treetops. Lord Preston leaned his head back and looked at the blue sky over the house.

A beautiful day now. The best weather we've had all week. They will come today. They will most certainly come.

He imagined the dark cross shapes of hundreds of bombers, squadron after squadron, roaring over the Channel and over Kent, just as he had seen them from the porch at Dover Sky two weeks before. He remembered the thumping sound of bombs exploding on the docks at Dover. Saw again the white vapor trails of dogfights between Hurricanes or Spitfires and Messerschmitts high in the air over southern England, for all the world as if dozens of biplanes were trailing smoke to thrill the crowds at an airshow, or as if scores of angels were sketching loops and lines with sticks of chalk.

Not everyone can live forever in wartime. Not everyone can survive. It's like asking that no one on earth die from anything at all, not from accidents or illness or old age. It's like asking that a drowning victim suddenly sport gills so he can breathe underwater, or it's like asking that a man falling from a plane sprout wings so that he will not plunge to his death. We live in a world of trag-edy as well as great beauty, a realm of darkness as well as light.

I know all this, my God. I do not wish to offer You a nonsense prayer and demand that none of my children or grandchildren are injured or killed, that You should choose other people's children for that. I only ask that not all are lost, that not all are sacrificed. In the scheme of things, a scheme I confess I rarely understand, my prayer is that many children return to their parents and grand-parents, in Britain, yes, but in Germany too. I would also pray the war be short.

Yet men have the freedom in this arena of earth to exercise their free will to the blessing or the destruction of others. We are made in Your image, aren't we? Our decisions matter, our choices change whole worlds for good or ill. You are over all, the one true God, yet we have our role to play, and we answer to You for the actions we undertake. We are weighed and measured according to what we do or don't do. So Hitler can prolong the war for years if he so desires. And we can attempt to shorten it if we muster the ability and strength to coun-ter his actions and plans.

Yet You set the ultimate boundaries we cannot cross or exceed. We humans work out our plans within the plans of others and within the greater plans of heaven. Who can comprehend it all? I bow to Your will. Save those we love, so far as it is within Your plans to do so, save them, I ask You, in Christ's name. I pray this well aware there are mysteries of this life and Your ways I shall never penetrate with my thoughts or my worship. The secret things belong unto the Lord our God. But those things which are revealed belong unto us and to our children forever, that we may do all the words of Your law.

"Lord Preston. William."

Lord Preston blinked. "Ah. There you are. Come sit beside me, Albrecht. How is your new book selling, do you know?"

Albrecht took a seat on the bench beside his father-in-law. "Surpris-ingly well for a book on theology. What is most exciting is that my Ger-man edition has been smuggled into the Reich, thousands of them are circulating, and now and then I hear how what I have written blesses someone or lifts them out of the morass of Nazism."

"Praise the Lord exceedingly for that." Lord Preston patted Albrecht's knee. "I wished to tell you something. It must remain a secret between us. I do not want my wife to find out—she frets enough for the family and the grandchildren. Certainly I don't want the wives to hear about this. If it comes to pass there will be time enough to deal with it then. For now I should just like you and me to agree to pray about this matter together."

"Why, certainly, Lord Preston, you may rest assured I will not betray any of your confidences."

"Of course not. I only mention it so you are aware of the gravity of what I am about to tell you." He spotted another robin. "Ah, to be like one of the birds of the air." He fixed his eyes on the green treetops. "I have seen the photographs taken by aerial reconnaissance. The bays across the water are filled with barges and troopships, Albrecht. The Germans are preparing for the invasion. Unquestionably there are gliders as well for airborne assault, in addition to regiments of their *Fallschirmjäger*, who will board aircraft and drop upon England like a hard rain from the southwest."

Albrecht took this in. "I see. But Herr Hitler will not launch these craft if he thinks most of them will be sunk by the RAF."

"This is why there have been so many strikes against our airfields. It has only been quiet due to the inclement weather. I expect to hear from Westminster today that the Germans have renewed their assault." Lord Preston held out his palm. Light dropped into it. "The skies are clear."

"Ramsay and Matthew are both in flight training now."

"Yes. I was somewhat surprised. But once Peter's death was announced and the family saw the grief in Jeremy's and Emma's eyes, Victoria and Caroline no longer felt they could hold back their own sons from defending our nation and our people."

"From defending Christian civilization," Albrecht added quietly. "Just as the prime minister has said."

"You went to the vicarage yesterday, didn't you?"

"I did. Jeremy and Emma are holding up. Catherine accompanied me. We spoke with them, prayed with them, had tea. They have faith they will see him again and that his life made a difference. What more can anyone give them but that peace which God has given them?"

"Quite."

"Jane was there."

"Jane. Was she indeed? I haven't seen her since Peter's death, though Elizabeth and I spoke with her on the phone the day we heard. How is she?"

"She was staying overnight. Not too well, I think. To tell you the truth, a good deal of the strength I saw in Jeremy and Emma was there for Jane, I believe."

"I understand. I will see them tomorrow when we attend services at St. Andrew's Cross. They have heard from James, I expect?"

"By phone and by letter. He was actually hoping to get home on a twenty-four or forty-eight-hour leave this weekend, so perhaps that's still on."

"With the weather like this?"

"Well, we'll see." Albrecht put a hand on Lord Preston's shoulder. "Listen. I wanted to tell you. Catherine and I heard from Sean last night. It was late, so you're the first person I've had a chance to share the news with."

"What's that?"

"Sean is posted to Pickering Green. Not only that, but he's flying Spitfires in your son's squadron. It's a great blessing to Catherine and me that he should be under Kipp's wing."

"Why, this is magnificent, magnificent! I thank God."

"Of course it means he's with James as well. In fact, he told us he had been assigned to A Flight within the squadron, and both Kipp and James are in A Flight along with another fellow. Kipp is keeping his eye on family."

"Just like him. Mind, he doesn't have eyes in the back of his head. God and our prayers will have to lend him a hand."

"*Ja.* As much a hand as possible."

Lord Preston slapped both hands to his knees. "Well, my head was filled with gloomy thoughts due to the photographs of the barges tucked along the French coast, yes, and the acres of army tents spread out under the trees. The loss of my grandchild Peter has not gone down well with me either, of course. Thinking of Sean and James and Kipp in the same squadron, however, puts a bit of life back in my heart. I must tell Elizabeth. She needs a great deal of good cheer to keep going these days. Peter's death was a blow. I shall—"

"My lord."

Tavy had stepped through the open French doors and into the yard.

Lord Preston was on his feet. "Yes? What is it?"

"Westminster rang you up. It was one of the prime minister's secretaries. Mr. Churchill should like to see his inner circle immediately at Ten Downing Street."

"Did they give you any idea what this is about?"

"She said the German bombers were crossing the Channel in droves. In droves, my lord."

Lord Preston gripped the back of the bench. "I see. Thank you, Tavy."

Saturday, August 24, 1940
RAF Pickering Green, Kent

"Squadron scramble! Squadron scramble!"

Kipp broke off his conversation with Sean and jumped from the armchair he'd dragged outside from the Officers' Mess. "Right! Let's go!"

Sean spilled tea over his uniform and leather flight jacket. "I'm with you!"

Pilots were sprinting across the airfield with their parachutes strapped to their backs. Sean ran with his in one hand and the empty teacup in the other.

"Stay glued to me!" Kipp shouted as he jumped onto the wing of his plane. "And to Patrick—you're his wingman!"

"What about vics of three, sir?" Sean shouted back.

"No more vics of three. Jerry's made marmalade out of us in our vics of three. Stick with A Flight and stick with Patrick. I've got the blue nose on my Spit, remember. If you get turned around up there, look for that."

"Yes, sir." Sean clambered up onto the plane next to Kipp, banging his knees and dropping his teacup. "I'll do my best, sir."

"You'll be fine, Sean. But don't fly in a straight line for more than a few seconds. And make sure you swivel your head like a top all the time—you've got to keep an eye out for Jerry. He'll pop out of the sun, the clouds, from above, beneath, you never know."

Kipp started his engine, and the roar obliterated the rest of what he had to say though Sean saw his lips moving.

"Chin up, Cousin." James ran past and gave Sean a thumbs-up. "These scraps never last long. We'll be back down in less than an hour."

"I'm not sure which plane is Patrick's."

James jerked his head to the left. "See him? Has the devil skewering a swastika painted just beneath the canopy."

"The black devil?"

"That's the one."

Sean struggled into his parachute with the help of two of his ground crew and squeezed himself into the cockpit. He wrestled with his seat straps and tried to look over the gauges on the control panel. Engines howled in his ears, and he glanced up. Fighter planes with crosses on their wings were streaking low over the airfield. Flames erupted from their wings and the grass exploded around his aircraft.

He sat frozen.

"Get up, sir, get up!" One of his ground crew was waving his arms. "Those are Me 109s! They'll be back for another pass!"

Sean stared at his controls again.

"Never mind all that, sir. Start the engine and get her in the air. You're a sitting duck."

A hangar suddenly flew apart in a blaze of light. The German fighters shot overhead on a second pass, and their bullets ripped into several of the planes racing down the runway. A Spitfire skewed to the left, purple and black smoke pouring from its riddled fuselage. Other Spitfires swept past on either side of Sean and rose swiftly into the air. For a moment he saw British fighters and German fighters flying together only a few hundred feet from the ground. Then they split apart to the left and the right and their engines screamed as they fought for altitude.

"This is the Squadron Leader." Sean's radio transmitter crackled and buzzed. "Form on me, A Flight. Rendezvous at twenty thousand feet, angels two zero. B Flight and C Flight, form on your commanders."

"This is James."

"Patrick."

"Where are you, Hartmann?" Kipp's voice. "Flying Officer Hartmann?"

Sean had begun to taxi along the runway. "Taking off, sir."

"Taking off?" Kipp was incredulous. "Let's have you up here, Hartmann. Rendezvous twenty thousand feet. Keep up with the formation or Jerry'll have you for tea."

"Yes, sir."

Sean's plane bounced once, twice, three times and fought itself free of RAF Pickering Green. Sean spotted his squadron—ten Spitfires less himself and the one burning on the airstrip—yanked the stick back, and climbed as rapidly as he could. A stream of tracers slipped over the front of his plane. Sean froze for the second time. An Me 109 with a yellow nose and gray paint scheme swooped past underneath. He prayed desperately it would not bank and turn back after him. It disappeared.

Thank You, God. Thank You, God.

"Hartmann?"

"Climbing, sir. Have you in sight, sir. Approaching twelve thousand feet. Speed one hundred and eighty-five miles per hour."

"Cut back on the speed as you climb."

"Yes, sir."

"And make sure you use your oxygen mask, Hartmann."

"It's on, sir." Sean quickly placed it over his mouth and nose.

Steadily he made his way to twenty thousand feet and joined the others, attaching himself to the plane with the black devil. Below and to the south he saw a large bomber formation. Hurricanes were already swooping down on them.

"Squadron leader to A, B, and C Flights. Pickering Green's Hurricanes are going after the Junker 88s. The fighter cover is coming down. We will rise to engage. Follow your flight commanders. Maintain a speed of one hundred and sixty in the climb. Hartmann, stick with Patrick as long as you can. Once the fighting starts, do what you've been trained to do. Short bursts, Hartmann. Keep the eyes in the back of your head open."

Sean stayed just behind Patrick's right wing. At first the enemy planes seemed to Sean to be approaching very slowly, as if they were floating. Suddenly they were on top of the Spitfires and moving like the wind in their dive. Patrick broke right after an Me 109, and Sean quickly followed. He saw tracers from Patrick's wings slice into the Messerschmitt's tail. Suddenly the whole rear section of the enemy fighter snapped off, and the plane went into a spin like a feather. Patrick swung left after another. Sean turned with him, gripping his stick as tightly as he could.

"On your tail, Hartmann! Break left and climb!"

Sean saw tracers streak over his right wing. He shoved the stick to the left and hauled it into the pit of his stomach. Another Me 109 was suddenly right in front of him.

"Cold meat, Hartmann! Give him a squirt!"

Without thinking, Sean thumbed the gun button. The eight Browning machine guns in his wings hurled tracer at the enemy plane. The smell of burnt cordite from the ammunition filled his cockpit.

To his shock, black smoke streamed from the Me 109, and it went into a dive. Its pilot yanked back the canopy and leaped out, tumbling over and over until suddenly a white parachute popped open over his head. Sean shot past the man, glancing back as the German drifted to earth. Tracers snapped over his engine cowling, and he instinctively banked hard to the left and climbed again. An Me 109 tore past off his right wing. He caught a glimpse of a Spitfire burning before he was blinded by the white mist of a summer cloud. In half a minute he was through it and flying upside down. He could see the farmlands of Kent far above his head. After righting his plane and leveling out, he shook his head to clear it and looked to his left and all around for aircraft.

The sky was empty.

The needle on his gas gauge trembled near the bottom. Sean realized he could scarcely think of a single landmark that might help him find his way back to his air base or aerodrome. There was a stone church with a lot of old graves tilting to the right and to the left a few miles from the base. He had noticed it when they'd driven him up to RAF Pickering Green the day before. Banking to the east, he had the Channel off his starboard wing and London off his port wing, its barrage balloons gleaming silver in the sunlight. He found himself praying again. After ten minutes he spotted the church. Keeping it on his right, he saw RAF Pickering Green half a minute later and came in for a landing. He saw nine Spitfires being refueled and rearmed, ground crew crawling over them.

"Hartmann! Well done!"

The pilots crowded around, and Kipp pressed a cup of hot tea into his hand.

"If you make it through your first week you'll live forever," Kipp joked. "You're off to a good start, bagging a Messerschmitt."

Patrick shook Sean's hand, cigarette in his mouth. "There you go. We've told Prescott, the intelligence officer, all about you. But he's got the green form for you to fill out just the same."

"I do indeed." A tall man with dark hair and dark-rimmed eyeglasses pushed his way through the knot of men. "An Me 109, was it then, lad?"

Sean nodded and gulped at his hot tea, wincing as he burned his lips.

"Did you see any special markings on the enemy plane?" asked Prescott.

"I saw a black cross so I fired at it."

The pilots laughed.

Sean looked at Kipp over the rim of his cup. "What happened to the chap whose Spitfire got hit at takeoff?"

"He's all right. Climbed out of it with a few cuts and burns."

"What about the one I saw in flames during the fight?"

"Swansbury? He rang us up from a village pub about fifteen miles away.

He chuted onto an old woman's clothesline." Kipp grinned. "She didn't mind at all. Served him up a tea and some fish and chips."

Prescott was scribbling on some sheets attached to a clipboard. "Your bloke wound up in a pond, Hartmann. Would have drowned but a couple of our farmers fished him out."

A phone rang in a hut nearby. A corporal leaned his head out the open window. "Right! You lot are off again! Squadron scramble!"

The pilots ran for their airplanes. Sean followed, still trying to drink from his teacup. One of his ground crew took the cup while the other helped him get squared away in the narrow cockpit.

"Good luck, sir. Give Jerry what for."

"Thank you. I don't know your name."

"Higgins. And the chap pulling the chocks away from your wheels is Musgrave."

"Very good."

"The Officers' Mess is serving a kipper and chips lunch. Don't be late, and don't get shot down, or you'll miss it."

Sean finally felt like smiling for the first time that morning. "I shall do my best. I think I'm beginning to get the hang of this."

Higgins laughed. "I should say you are. Cheerio."

Sean started the Rolls Royce Merlin engine, and its roar drowned out his words. "I'll be back in half a shake."

Monday, August 26, 1940
A road south of London

"Now, mind, Tavy, no word of this to Lady Preston."

"Not a breath, my lord." Tavy steered the Rolls Royce around a sharp curve.

"She's been down in the mouth since Peter was killed and she wasn't in a very good humor to begin with. The last thing she needs to hear is we were cavorting about the countryside while German bombers were flocking over our heads."

"Yes, m'lord."

"With the Germans bombing London on Saturday night, she'd be frantic if she knew we were out here."

"Mum's the word."

Lord Preston rolled down the window and leaned his head out. "This will do, Tavy. Find some sort of lane and pull off the road. The sky is wide open now."

"Very good, my lord."

Tavy pulled off under some trees. Lord Preston got out and craned his neck at the blue sky. It was criss-crossed with white lines and circled by white swirls.

"They are fighting, Tavy. Fighting for their lives. Fighting for our lives."

His butler stood beside him. "Yes, my lord."

"It's not just my children and grandchildren up there. It's hundreds of other parents' and grandparents' children and grandchildren up there with them."

Tavy nodded.

"Do you have the Bible with you?"

"I do, my lord."

"Please be good enough to read from the verses I selected."

Tavy opened the large Bible under his arm and began to read aloud.

> Have ye not known? Have ye not heard? Hath it not been told you from the beginning? Have ye not understood from the foundations of the earth? It is he that sitteth upon the circle of the earth, and the inhabitants thereof are as grasshoppers; that stretcheth out the heavens as a curtain, and spreadeth them out as a tent to dwell in: that bringeth the princes to nothing; he maketh the judges of the earth as vanity. Yea, they shall not be planted; yea, they shall not be sown: yea, their stock shall not take root in the earth: and he shall also blow upon them, and they shall wither, and the whirlwind shall take them away as stubble. To whom then will ye liken me, or shall I be equal? saith the Holy One. Lift up your eyes on high, and behold who hath created these things, that bringeth out their host by number: he calleth them all by names by the greatness of his might, for that he is strong in power; not one faileth. Why sayest thou, O Jacob, and speakest, O Israel, My way is hid from the LORD, and my judgment is passed over from my God? Hast thou not known? Hast thou not heard, that the everlasting God, the LORD, the Creator of the ends of the

earth, fainteth not, neither is weary? There is no searching of his understanding. He giveth power to the faint; and to them that have no might he increaseth strength. Even the youths shall faint and be weary, and the young men shall utterly fall: but they that wait upon the LORD shall renew their strength; they shall mount up with wings as eagles; they shall run, and not be weary; and they shall walk, and not faint.

"Amen," pronounced Lord Preston, his eyes upon the vapor trails of the aircraft high in the sky.

"Amen," echoed Tavy, closing the Bible carefully and tucking it under his arm once more.

"The Lord God be with them. The Lord God have mercy on them. The Lord God have mercy on our people."

Monday, August 26, 1940
Over Portsmouth

"You can't catch him in a dive, Hartmann! Pull up!"

"On your tail, Patrick! Two Me 110s!"

"Cold meat! Got him! The Heinkel's headed for the drink!"

"Bale out, Swansbury! Hurry, man!"

Sean banked left and then right and came up on an Me 110 from underneath, pressing the gun button for the count of three. The twin-engine German plane kept going. Annoyed, Sean pulled up behind it and fired at point-blank range. Bits came off its tail, but it continued to fly in a straight line. Sean was sure someone had crept in behind him. He gave the Me 110 fighter a final burst and shoved his stick far to the right. Tracers filled the air in front of him, and two Me 109s shrieked over his head. As they passed the Me 110 it exploded, spraying them with bits of wing and fuselage. Shrapnel rattled against Sean's Spitfire too.

"Squadron Leader to all Pickering Green pilots. Check your fuel level. If you can't make it back to base, put down at another airfield."

Sean was chasing an Me 109. For a moment it was directly in his sights, and he thumbed the gun button. Nothing happened. He tried again but his machine guns didn't fire. The Me 109 went into a sharp dive and escaped. Sean hit the control panel with his fist.

"Out of ammo! Or they've jammed! Blast!"

He turned his Spitfire north and east. But he knew he was far from home, and the needle on his fuel gauge had nowhere else to go. Middle Wallop was nearby, but Tangmere was closer and King's Cross closer yet. He spotted the distinctive chapel and the aerodrome right beside it as his engine began to cough.

Cheers, Uncle Ben. I'm dropping in for an unexpected visit. I hope you're at home.

Hurricanes and Spitfires from the King's Cross squadrons were landing and taking off. He circled the field twice and finally picked a moment to touch down.

"What's your complaint, sir?" asked one of the ground crew with a grin.

"Out of petrol."

"We can fix you up. Where's home?"

"Pickering Green."

"That's a fair hike. Who sent you all the way out here?"

"Uxbridge. And I suppose Jerry did too by mounting such a heavy raid over Portsmouth."

"Help yourself to a tea in the Officers' Mess, sir. Anything else you need besides fuel?"

"I have no ammunition. Either that or my guns have jammed."

"I'll not send you on your way without the ability to defend yourself, sir. Pack in some tea and crumpets and we'll have you on your way in half an hour."

Sean climbed down about the same time two more ground crew came over. They joined the one who had been talking with Sean, and all three were examining his wings.

"You don't hold anything back, do you, sir?"

Both wings had been holed by more than half a dozen bullets.

"It was a bit of a scrap," said Sean, standing beside them.

"So it was, sir. We've lost one of our best pilots today and four of our aircraft. But no one's come in with six holes in his wings and climbed from his office cheery as a lark."

"I'm not that cheery. We lost a pilot too as well as three planes. But the long face won't win us the war, will it?"

"No, sir."

"I'll go to the Mess and get my tea. Can you tell me if Squadron Leader Ben Whitecross is on the base?"

"He's only been down five minutes and he's going up again if Jerry's still at Portsmouth."

"Where is he now? Do you know?"

"Giving his report to the intelligence officer. I expect he'll drop in on the Mess for a toast and jam before he climbs back into his Spit."

Sean made his way to the Officers' Mess. He had hardly stepped in the door before Ben Whitecross got up from a nearby table with a slice of heavily buttered toast in his hand.

"I've got to find out what they can tell me about the raid," he was saying. "B Flight all down, Tommy?"

"Yes, sir," replied a lanky red-haired man in his flight jacket and Mae West.

"Everyone all right?"

"Tim's got the burns on his face and hands. But he's not bad. Doc's bandaging him up."

"I'll look in on him."

"Thank you, sir."

Sean remained by the door.

"Excuse me," Ben said and went to go by Sean before he suddenly stopped. "What's this? Sean?"

"Yes, sir."

"Never mind the sir." Ben put an arm around him. "What are you doing here?"

"I was in the mix-up over Portsmouth. Ran out of fuel."

"Splendid. This is my nephew Sean, lads. I haven't seen him in a thousand years. And here he's a pilot and was in the dogfight over Portsmouth today."

Several of the men whistled and clapped.

Ben led him to the bar. "What'll you have?"

"Some tea and toast would be wonderful, Uncle."

"Tea and toast it is. Now don't tell me Uxbridge called you into the raid on Portsmouth?"

"They did. Kipp's my squadron leader."

"Right."

"I expect they're all on their way home now. So was I. But my petrol was low."

"How's Kipp?"

"He made it through the day, sir."

"'Sufficient unto the day is the evil thereof.' What about James?"

"Top notch."

A phone behind the bar rang.

"For you, sir," said a young corporal holding the receiver.

Ben went behind the bar. "Whitecross. Yes, sir. Yes, sir. Very good."

He hung up the phone. All the pilots in the Mess were looking at him.

"Stand down, lads. Stand down and have your bangers and mash. Jerry's gone back to France."

A few men cheered, and the others went back to conversations that immediately became noticeably louder and spiced with more laughter.

"Here's your toast and tea, sir."

"Thank you, Corporal," replied Sean. "What sort of jam is it?"

"Plum, sir. Local people mixed up a batch for us."

Sean took a bite. "Excellent."

"I'll pass that on, sir."

Ben took Sean's arm. "Let's have a sit. You can spare another ten minutes, can't you?"

"I can. Though Kipp might mother hen it."

"I'll ring up Pickering Green once you're airborne."

"Thank you, Uncle."

"How have Jerry been treating your airfield?"

"They hammer us every second or third day. Always more potholes for ground crew to fill. We lose personnel too. It gets a bit wearisome."

Ben had a fresh cup of tea. "If you take a look around you can see what a shambles we're in here."

"You've lost a lot of buildings, that's pretty clear. And I spotted the Spitfire and Hurricane skeletons from the air."

"Jerry's made a hash of the place since July. We'll keep bearing up. We have to, don't we? But I agree. It does get wearisome." He sipped his tea. "Finished your toast? Come on. I want to show you something. A short walk. It'll do us both good to stretch our legs. The Spit's a fine plane but the cockpit isn't designed for comfort, is it?"

"No, sir."

They made their way off the airfield and into the village. Ben took them to the church Sean had seen from the air. It was white and tidy. Only one wall was torn up by machine-gun fire. Next to the church was a graveyard. Set apart from the older headstones were short rows of white crosses with names painted on them in black. Two crosses were set apart from these rows.

"Those two crosses off by themselves are *Luftwaffe* pilots. The rest are lads from the four squadrons we have here at King's Cross." Ben stopped in front of one. "This is your cousin."

Sean came and stood with Ben. "Flying Officer Peter Sweet. 'How are the mighty fallen in the midst of the battle. Second Samuel one twenty-five.'"

"It was the vicar here chose the verse."

"A good choice, Uncle."

"And we still have the battle to finish that he couldn't finish for us."

"Yes, sir."

They lingered another half minute.

Ben clapped a hand on Sean's shoulder. "Let's get you back to mother hen."

As Sean lifted off from King's Cross, the smoke from the bombing raid on Portsmouth covered the western sky behind him. The sun sank into it and turned the color of crimson. Sean headed east for Kent and Pickering Green. Small stars began to light his path like torches on a runway.

Sunday, September 1, 1940
St. Andrew's Cross, London

"Please rise for the singing of the hymn."

Lord Preston stood with Lady Preston at his side. To his right were Albrecht and Catherine and ten-year-old Angelika. Their son, Sean, was at RAF Pickering Green. Next in the pew were Victoria and fifteen-year-old Timothy. Her husband, Ben, was at RAF King's Cross, and her older son, Ramsay, was in flight training with the RAF. Then it was Caroline and ten-year-old Cecilia Printemp. Caroline's younger son, Matthew, was also in flight training, and her husband, Kipp, was at Pickering Green with Sean. Beside Lady Preston sat her daughter Libby all by herself, her husband, Terry, at sea on the *Hood* and her daughter, Jane, in the plotting room at the bunker in Uxbridge. On Libby's right was another navy family, her brother Edward's wife, Charlotte, and her children. Edward was serving on HMS *Rodney*. Sitting with Charlotte was her younger son,

Colm Alexander, eleven, and her older son, Owen, who was in the dark blue uniform of an Able Seaman in the Royal Navy. At his side, grasping his hand as everyone in the pew stood, was Eva von Isenburg, the daughter of Baron von Isenburg in Germany.

Next to her, looking miserable, was Caroline's oldest son, Charles, who stood with a reluctance that was obvious to those sitting beside or behind him. Emma, whose husband entered the pulpit as the singing began, was at Charles's shoulder. With Peter dead and James flying with Kipp and Sean at Pickering Green, only Emma's youngest son, Billy, was at her side, dressed in a morning suit and tie, every inch the noble Cambridge student. The row ended with Robbie, widower and youngest son of Lord and Lady Preston, in the full-dress uniform of a colonel in the British Army, and his daughter, Patricia Claire, twelve and tall for her age, holding the hymnbook for both of them.

In the pew behind were Skitt and his wife, Montgomery, and servants from Kensington Gate, including Tavy, the butler, and Mrs. Longstaff the cook. Montgomery held her two-year-old son, Paul, in her arms. Harrison and his wife Holly remained at Ashton Park along with Lady Grace, Lord Preston's mother.

> Abide with me; fast falls the eventide;
> The darkness deepens; Lord, with me abide.
> When other helpers fail and comforts flee,
> Help of the helpless, O abide with me.
>
> I need Thy presence every passing hour;
> What but Thy grace can foil the tempter's pow'r?
> Who, like Thyself, my guide and stay can be?
> Through cloud and sunshine, Lord, abide with me.
>
> I fear no foe with Thee at hand to bless;
> Ills have no weight and tears no bitterness.
> Where is death's sting? Where, grave, thy victory?
> I triumph still, if Thou abide with me.

Jeremy opened the large Bible that lay before him on the pulpit. "My text is from the book of Judges. It is the story of Gideon's fight against the Midianites. I am certain you are all familiar with the tale. Gideon's army is too large, so God reduces it several times, and it is with this small band that the enemy is defeated. The Lord first tells Gideon he must have fewer soldiers in chapter seven, verse two: 'And the LORD said unto Gideon, The people that are with thee are too many for me to give the Midianites into their hands, lest Israel vaunt themselves against me, saying, Mine own hand hath saved me.' Twenty-two thousand are cut from the ranks. But there are still ten thousand ready to do battle with the Midianites. So God tells Gideon in verse four, 'The people are yet too many.' And the ranks are thinned again. Now there are only three hundred. It is with this three hundred that the Lord defeats the mighty army of the Midianites and Amalekites and all the children of the East who, we are told in verse twelve, 'lay along in the valley like grasshoppers for multitude; and their camels were without number, as the sand by the sea side for multitude.'"

Jeremy removed his round glasses. He looked out from his pulpit high above a congregation that filled every pew. For several moments he didn't speak.

"The Lord works His miracles. But not without us. Not without His church, not without His people. We are the hands and feet, and the Lord Jesus Christ is the head. We need a miracle as big as Gideon's, don't we? Our nation is besieged from the air. The numbers we have to resist the enemy are scarcely more than Gideon had. Our pilots cannot do it alone. Yet they must do what they can. As they do what they can, so God shall intervene and do what only He is able to do."

Jeremy tapped the Bible.

"We must have a Judges chapter seven story going on in these islands. We must pray for it; we must cry out for it. Our pilots and sailors and soldiers are only flesh and blood. Dunkerque was a miracle we sorely needed for our army. Now we must have another in the air. And I tell you this, and I believe it with all my heart—before all is said and done we shall require yet a third miracle from the Almighty on the high seas. But today it is the miracle in the skies we must have in order for Britain to survive, and not only Britain, but Europe, the cradle of Christian civilization." He extended his arm and pointed at the ceiling. "Right now, our pilots are fighting. Right now, our pilots are dying. We sing hymns and their burning aircraft sing their death songs. The airfields are bombed, the convoys are bombed, the ports, the factories, even the streets of Bethnal Green in East London. Where will it end?"

Jeremy lifted the heavy Bible up in both his hands.

"What the Germans do will not decide the fate of nations. It is what the Lord does and it is what we do in accordance with His will. So join me in prayer now for our country, join me in prayer for Gideon and his small band in their winged chariots, join me in crying out for our deliverance from the locusts. Through Jesus Christ our Lord. Amen."

"Amen" rippled through the church and along the pew of Lord and Lady Preston and their family. Only Charles sealed his lips. Only Charles refused to bow his head or close his eyes.

Sunday, September 1, 1940, 12:00 noon
RAF Pickering Green, Kent

The phone in the hut at the side of the runway began to ring. It was picked up immediately by a corporal.

James was in the middle of describing a fight with two Me 109s to Prescott, the intelligence officer.

Kipp was biting into a roast beef sandwich.

Sean was coming from the Mess, carrying a tray with a pot of tea and seven or eight cups.

The corporal thrust his head out of the hut window. "Scramble!"

"You must be joking!" Kipp protested. "That's the third one and it's just noon!"

"They're coming for us, sir. Hundred plus Ju 88s and Messerschmitts going like the devil for Pickering Green and Hornchurch and Biggin Hill."

"A second bombing run against us?"

"They never tell me much, sir, but they did this time. Jerry's on his way."

"Get a kite up!" shouted Kipp, eating his sandwich and running at the same time. "They're hitting our airfield again!"

Swansbury and Evans snatched cups and filled them with tea as Sean stood holding the tray. James scooped up a handful of crumpets and stuffed them in the pockets of his Irvin flying jacket. Patrick took the pot and two cups.

"Fancy having a cuppa with your girl up there, Pat?" shouted Sean as they both sprinted for their planes.

"The other cup's for my angel. I'd never have lived so long but for my angel."

Sean was no sooner in his cockpit and tucking a blue polka-dot scarf inside his uniform collar when dirt and stone flew upward in a huge explosion at the end of the runway. Then another. And another. He saw Swansbury take off. Dirt showered the Spitfires taxiing behind and beside him. A stone cracked the front of his windscreen.

"Chocks away, sir."

Sean waved a hand. "Thanks, Higgins."

He opened the throttle for a short liftoff. Bombs were exploding all around his plane. He saw James make his way through the blasts and into the air, and Kipp and Patrick too. Patrick's Spitfire had four swastikas painted under the picture of the devil and his pitchfork. Sean's ground crew had painted three on his. He got off the ground at the same time as Evans, and they glanced at each other, canopies still open. Evans gave him a thumbs-up.

Tuesday, September 3, 1940, 10:00 a.m.
Kensington Gate, London

"Lord Preston. Sorry to keep you waiting." Albrecht came through the French doors into the backyard.

"Not at all. No time is wasted if you employ it in a manner suited to the occasion. How often do I sit on this bench here? Only when you and I meet. So I look forward to gazing at the trees and hedges and watching the robins and larks." He smiled at Albrecht. "Have you heard from Sean?"

"Pickering Green has been bombed every day. On Sunday they went after it three times altogether. The phone lines have been cut time and time again. We did manage to hear from him last night. He was allowed a sixty-second call from the green grocer's shop in the village. That's where the air base has their communications now."

"He's well then?"

"Yes. Kipp and James too."

"Praise the Lord for that." Lord Preston rubbed his eyes. "We always have much to pray about, you and I, Albrecht. But I would like to begin with a request for a spot of theological insight from you."

"If I can help in any way at all, of course."

"I want to pray for some sort of miracle for the RAF. But just as we prayed for a miracle at Dunkerque and were able to rescue most of the troops, it didn't mean there would be no hardship or difficulties. Indeed, ships were sunk and men killed, and we left behind tanks and trucks and ammunition enough to outfit whole divisions. There were two sides to the coin. Yet I should rather have had Dunkerque, warts and all, than to not have had it and seen the whole British Army captured or destroyed."

"Yes, Lord Preston, I agree."

"Nor did the miracle at Dunkerque end the affair. For now we have the air raids and are praying for a second miracle, despite the rescue God granted us when we retrieved our soldiers from the beaches."

Albrecht nodded. "*Ja.*"

"So my question is this. If I pray fervently for the RAF and their ability to withstand the onslaught of Nazi bombers and fighters, and a sort of Dunkerque is brought about by divine grace where the British pilots and aircraft are saved, where will the burden of the war go next? From the beaches at Dunkerque it went into the air over southern England, principally against our shipping, airfields, and aircraft factories. If the burden of war moves away from the RAF airfields and factories, where will it go? For it has to go somewhere—unless Germany surrenders, which the Third Reich is unlikely to do. Or unless we surrender, which is unthinkable."

Albrecht looked down at the grass between his feet, thinking.

"It is, you see, a matter of some urgency." Lord Preston brought a slip of paper from his coat pocket. "We have been losing too many pilots. It takes two months to train the lads, and we are not replacing them quickly enough. Now there is a move to trim the training even further. If we do that, I fear the youngsters we will be putting into mortal combat will be able to do little more than land and take off."

"I understand."

"There is also the matter of replacing aircraft, both Hurricanes and Spitfires. For a good while we have been able to keep up with the losses. But now the Germans are attacking the factories that build the fighters." Lord Preston squinted at the figures on the piece of paper. "We lost three hundred aircraft in August. We've replaced only a little more than two hundred and fifty of them. So we are falling behind, you see. This week is looking as bad or worse than last week in terms of pilots and airplanes lost. Heaven knows what the figures will be, but we are losing ground, Albrecht. If it keeps up we shall come to the point where we can no longer defend ourselves in the air. Then the invasion will be launched. Then Britain will be conquered."

Albrecht got to his feet and began to pace. "If the Lord sees fit He can certainly rescue the RAF just as He did the British Expeditionary Force. You are quite right that this will be bring blessings but also challenges. Where will the burden of war shift? The sea, I think. Unless…"

"Unless what? Speak up, man."

Albrecht shook his head. "I have never forgotten Spain and Guernica, what the German bombers did to civilian populations. I have not forgotten how they used incendiaries on Warsaw. Or how they flattened Rotterdam in Holland." He sat back down on the bench. "God is no monster. The devil is the monster. If Satan is thwarted at one thing he will try another. If his plans are spoiled at Dunkerque he will go after the British soldiers and the RAF in Britain itself. If he is thwarted there then he will go after something else he can defeat. Our navy, perhaps. Or our cities."

"He has already gone after both."

"He will assault the Royal Navy with a greater viciousness. He will go after the cities with a fury we have not seen in this country. No, we have not seen Rotterdam in this land or Guernica or Warsaw. Not yet."

"That would be a tragedy."

"God will give us the means to resist."

Lord Preston closed his eyes. "This nightmare could be stopped with a surrender. Our surrender."

"That would not end the nightmare."

"No. I expect not. If there were no evil in men's hearts, if there were no immoral inclinations at all, then we should have a better world without having to fight for it."

Albrecht laced his fingers together. "Our world is a strange mix of heaven's will, the will of men and women—which can incline to either the good or the bad—the apparently random acts of volcanoes and earthquakes and hurricanes and asteroids, and the wicked designs of great evil. Ultimately you and I believe in the triumph of the cross and the resurrection. We believe that the righteous will of God shall prevail. But not without a battle."

His eyes grew darker and darker as he spoke. Suddenly he stood up and began to pace again, a short distance back and forth, as if he were behind a lectern at a university.

"At Dunkerque it was the German decision to wait several days," he continued. "During that respite we acted. The weather favored the rescue of British and French and Canadian soldiers. Can you imagine what would have happened if there had been a storm in the Channel? We decided to fight on, so we did what we could to bring our troops home to England and we felt that God was with us. Everything came together to bless us. But every answer to prayer, as I have said, brings fresh challenges as well as fresh blessings. The Germans' will was to pursue us to England. Our will was not to surrender to them. As a result of that clash of wills, the war came to British soil and British skies, and it is still here. Hell would have us defeated. Heaven, we believe, would have us delivered. Fine weather favors the German bombers but it also favors the Spitfires and Hurricanes of the RAF. This mix of wills and weather produces the battle that is being waged above us right now."

"If I pray for the German will to be thwarted, if I pray for the plans of Hitler and Goering and the *Luftwaffe* to come to nothing against the RAF, am I then shifting the war to another part of our country or our armed forces, neither of which may be able to weather it better than our pilots and air crews?"

"You haven't the power to shift it anywhere, Lord Preston. You only have the power to call upon God's will. If the Germans are thwarted in Kent and West Suffolk, we shall thank God, shall we not? But then the Germans will move in another direction, they shall will something else against us, and we shall pray that this new scheme also be stopped, and call upon heaven to defend us. Hell and Hitler shall do their utmost to defeat our will and the will of the Lord. God and England and her allies shall do their utmost to defeat the will of the Nazis and their dark legions. When all is said and done, and we see everything from the perspective of eternity, it shall be obvious how God's will and God's hand were over all things. But for now we fight back against wickedness and cry out for the Lord's help. Sometimes we see things clearly, and other times, when we taste defeat or death, we do not." Albrecht shook his head and laughed. "The lecture makes much better sense in German."

Lord Preston smiled. "It makes sense to me. Many wills are in conflict. We must discern God's will and side with that, no matter what the consequences. I believe He wants the *Luftwaffe* defeated in the south of England, so I shall continue to pray vigorously to that end. Once the *Luftwaffe* is stopped there it will turn somewhere else and start a new attack. When that happens I shall pray with every fiber of my being the new attack be defeated as well. I will never stop praying and resisting until the entire Third Reich and its evil schemes are brought to an end. No matter how long the clash of wills takes place, I will be part of it, and I shall cry out to the living God that His will be done on earth as it is in heaven."

Albrecht put his arm around Lord Preston's shoulders. "I shall cry out with you. I shall cry out for an end to the evil of the Nazi regime. And I shall pray a better Germany, a truer Germany, rises from the embers of the one that was false. *Durch unseren Herrn Jesus Christus*—Through Jesus Christ our Lord."

Tuesday, September 3, 1940, 4:37 p.m.
RAF Pickering Green, Kent

Kipp came into the Officers' Mess with his hands in his pockets and a cold, dark look in his eyes. Men from both of the Pickering Green squadrons glanced his way, and the laughter and loud chatter dropped. James was at a table nearest the door with Patrick and Sean.

"What is it then, sir?" James asked. "What have you heard?"

"Swansbury's bought it. They pulled his body out of the wreck of his Spitfire near Biggin Hill. We lost Evans too. Merchant Marine confirmed a Spitfire with his markings went into the drink after tangling with an Me 109."

"That's rough, sir."

Kipp lingered near the table. "The fellows in the convoy caught a good look at the Messerschmitt. It didn't just have a yellow nose. It had a yellow and black checker pattern over the whole fuselage. I know the pilot from the first war. He should be in mothballs just as I should be. But he stayed fit and lean and now he commands a number of squadrons. He was leading that five hundred plus sweep of Me 109s a few days ago."

"Are you talking about that von Zeltner bloke?" asked Patrick as the talk picked up at the other tables in the Mess.

Kipp looked even more like death than he had when he walked into the room. "Right. Wolfgang von Zeltner."

"Zeltner's quite the ace. Lord Tanner's always crowing about him during his broadcasts. He's the darling of Goering and the Nazis."

"He's not my darling, Patrick. He just killed one of my men. One of your mates."

"Yes, sir."

The phone behind the bar rang. The talking and laughter stopped again. Kipp, hands in his pockets, swung around to look as the corporal picked up the receiver.

"Scramble!" he called out. "Both squadrons!"

Men pushed away from the tables quickly, chairs smacked against the walls, and there was a rush for the door. Kipp waited till the Mess was clear.

"Did they tell you anything else?" he asked the corporal behind the bar.

"Only that it was a big raid headed our way, sir, headed for the airfields in Kent."

"No mention of the *Luftwaffe* squadrons involved?"

"No, sir. They never give us any detailed information. Now and then we might get the sort of numbers that are involved, fifty plus, one hundred plus. But the main thing is they just want us to announce the scramble and get the boys up quickly."

"Right. Well, if they ever bend the rules and tell you any of the German squadrons involved, let me know."

"Yes, sir. Good luck, sir."

"Good luck with what?"

"Up there, sir. You're going to have a go at Jerry."

Kipp half laughed as he went out the door. "I thought you were wishing me luck with something else."

James watched as Sean peeled off to attack the Heinkel 111s, Patrick just ahead of him and already firing. A Flight was after the bombers; B and C Flights were up above tangling with Me 109s and 110s. He waited a moment as Kipp went into a short dive.

You've done well for yourself, Sean, and caught on quickly. Soon you'll be as nimble as Uncle Kipp. I'm not sure where I fit in the scheme of things. Solid, sure, steady, dependable? Not the fastest but the most dogged? A grip on the enemy like a bulldog?

The vast blue shimmered all around him as he dove after a Heinkel and gave it a short burst. He never tired of the beauty of the sky even when it filled with the swift violence of fighter aircraft, even when black smoke and orange flame dominated his windscreen. The Heinkel's starboard engine caught fire, and parachutes suddenly dotted the blue like the white puffs of dandelions. Dark streaks from burning and tumbling bombers interlaced the sky. He moved quickly against another Heinkel, late afternoon sunlight glimmering on its wings, the tracers he fired flowing toward it, red flames wrapping themselves around its body.

Take to the silk, Jerry, take to the silk.

And then a Spitfire fell across his sight and across the sky, one wing gone, the prop spinning wildly, and it was Sean's plane, and there was no chute, there was nothing but an aircraft breaking to pieces over southern England.

Jane waited until the attack was over and done and she'd been ordered to stand down. All the way to her flat she prayed for James. And not only James but his whole squadron, especially the family members who flew with him—her uncle Kipp and cousin Sean. For whatever reason, Sean came to mind again and again, and she prayed a verse Uncle Jeremy had often quoted to her.

"For he shall give his angels charge over thee, to keep thee in all thy ways."

The feeling didn't go away while she chatted with her roommates or after she had laid her head on her pillow. It lingered through the morning even as her work at the plotting table grew more and more intense. It struck her as odd that the moment she began to push counters toward Pickering Green and Biggin Hill, the anxiety about Sean went away, and not only the anxiety but also the fear that usually emerged whenever German attack formations headed toward Pickering Green and James. It didn't make sense to her but she welcomed the peace that went through her and decided it must have been from God.

It seems that You are more real than I think You are.

A fierce assault from hundreds of bombers that afternoon was met by fourteen RAF squadrons, and she was as busy as she had ever been. James's squadron was involved, yet it didn't rob her of the calm that enveloped her. Factories were struck at Brooklands and Rochester, and Canterbury was also hit. She was told during one of her breaks that over six hundred sorties had been flown by the RAF and more than fifty enemy aircraft had been confirmed as shot down, with better than a dozen as probable.

"What about our losses?" she asked.

"Twelve or fifteen so far. Four pilots killed."

Jane poured herself tea, and her hand was steady. "Thank you."

Sitting alone and sipping from her cup, ignoring two WAAFs who went on and on about the likelihood of invasion, she marveled again that warmth had settled inside her instead of coldness and that the peace hadn't been wrenched out of her by the casualty figures. For a few minutes her mind turned to supernatural things, to angels and God and heaven. But soon enough she was back at the plotting table, tagging the wooden blocks, moving them about with her rake, thinking only of airplanes and numbers and sectors. Her walk home was under a soft evening sky that pulsed with copper and blue and added to her feeling of well-being. She watched a large barrage balloon turn slowly on its steel cable, one side of it gold from a sun low in the sky, the other the deep blue of a coming night.

A note was attached to the door of her flat.

> We are out for the evening. If you need anything at all feel
> free to make your request to the man of the house. Ta.
>
> Liz

"Man of the house?" Jane took the slip of paper down. "What rubbish."

The door opened and James was standing there in his blue RAF uniform.

"I thought it was you," he said. "I recognized the light footfall. The same sound I'd hear when you were creeping up on me when we were twelve."

"James!" She threw her arms around him. "What are you doing here? They can't possibly have given you leave in the midst of all this fighting! Are you a ghost?"

"I'll show you how much of a ghost I am."

She was still asking questions when his lips came against hers. Arms around her, he tugged her into the flat, shut the door, and locked it, never breaking the kiss.

"I don't understand," she finally managed to get out. "I don't."

"I love you. I should have thought that part was obvious."

"But how can you be here?"

"They've given me leave. Twenty-four hours, no more, no less. Tomorrow it will be Sean's turn. Then Patrick's. They knew they'd have to do something for us or we'd go mad."

"Sean? Is he all right then?"

"Well, he did get shot down the other day. We finally saw a chute but we thought he'd ended up in the drink. Kipp was fretting it for hours. Sees himself as responsible for all of us from the family, let alone the rest of the squadron." James kissed her slowly on the lips. "Nothing to fear, love. He got picked up by a sailboat after an hour bobbing about in his Mae West. Chilled to the marrow, he told us, but the chaps on the boat filled him with hot tea and wrapped him in wool blankets. Right as rain when last I saw him. He's an ace now, you know. Five Jerry in the bag. So am I, actually. Seven and a half."

"Oh, such good news about Sean." She began to giggle. "How can you have a half? Is there half a German plane floating about out there?"

"There is and I'll get the other half of him soon enough."

She placed a hand on his chest to hold him back a moment. "It's bad, isn't it? It's bad up there."

"Bad enough."

"Shouldn't you have gone to see your mum and dad first?"

"I did. Spent the afternoon with them. Of course they rang everyone up and pretty soon the whole tribe was there. I didn't mind. It was good to see how everyone is getting on."

"You don't have anywhere else to go?"

"Not at all."

"And you chased the girls out?"

"It was their idea. I spent an hour chatting with them. They're quite nice, aren't they?"

"You think they're nice, do you?"

His hands framed her face. "Not as nice as you. Why is your hair pinned up like that?"

She laughed. "What do you think? I should have it down to my shoulders for Vice Marshal Park?"

"You're not at Uxbridge now, are you? So let's do away with the starched shirt military look, shall we?"

"I've just made it in the door, silly boy."

"Can I help?"

"You can unbutton my tunic if you like, and it will just be me in my shirt and skirt. Then I can use my hands to take out those hairpins you find so disagreeable."

"Just the tunic?"

"Just the tunic. If you want to go any further you shall have to marry me."

He smiled as he unbuttoned her blue tunic. "I'm game for that."

"I suppose you'd wed me right now, wouldn't you?"

"I would."

"Well, Mister Fast Flying Fighter Pilot with his shirt unbuttoned at the top, I want something more than a quick run through at the chapel. I want the family there and I should like a nice reception after the ceremony. And a honeymoon. Even if it's only for twenty-four hours, I should like a proper honeymoon."

"I'll see what I can do with the time left to me."

"Oh, no, you don't. This will take some arranging."

"Are you going to use the plotting table at the bunker to set everything up?"

"I might." She shook her dark hair so that it fell loosely about her shoulders. "How's that, ace?"

"Not bad. But there's still this tunic." He peeled it off her back and her arms. "There. That will do nicely. A pretty girl in a white shirt and blue skirt and tie."

"I thought you didn't like starched shirts?"

"Somehow they look better on you than anyone else."

"Oh, do they? That's nice to know."

He took her chin in one hand. "I've missed you. It's been torture, really. I've missed your scent, your eyes, your laugh, everything."

"Well, you don't have to miss them now. Come here."

"I am here."

"Not close enough."

He held her tightly against his chest. "There. Wingtip to wingtip."

She slid her hands over his uniform to his shoulders. "All day I've felt like God's been putting dreams in me. Is this another one? Or a dream come true?"

He kissed her. "Is this what dreams do?"

"It's what dreams come true do." She laced her white-shirted arms about his neck. "How long can you stay?"

"I have to catch the midnight train south. Be ready to fly at first scramble. Until then I'm all yours. And you're all mine."

"It's true. I am." She kissed his cheek. "I'm in love. It's a wonderful feeling. But it doesn't seem quite right to be in such high spirits when there are such frightful things going on around us and so many dying."

"We're fighting so people can be free to be in high spirits, Jane. And our family has paid the price."

Her eyes glimmered. "Do you...do you ever think about him?"

"We were inseparable. I think about him all the time. Especially in the air. It's funny how we both came to love flying when the only reason we kept at it was to impress you."

"You did impress me. Both of you." She traced a line on his face while tears moved slowly down from her eyes. "But you were the one I absolutely fell for. How do you think he feels about that?"

"Right now? From where he sits? He's glad for us, Jane. He couldn't be happier. I was supposed to marry you if anything happened to him, remember? So I'm honoring that. And honoring him. And honoring you."

"So much honor."

His thumb gently rubbed away the teardrops. "Nothing wrong with honor."

"It makes me think of tombs and statues and monuments. I don't want that coldness, James. I don't want that death. They speak it into my headphones every day. 'Heinkels, two hundred plus, angels two zero, twenty thousand feet, bearing on Biggin Hill and Pickering Green and Hornchurch.' I just want love, James. As much love as you can spare me for as long as you can spare it."

"I have lots to spare." He smiled. "I've been saving it up. No one else to give it to. It's always been you. Since we've been kids. You know that. Always been Jane, our beauty from America, our beauty from the Orient. My arms are full of your beauty and my heart is full of love. So naturally I want to give it away."

She began to kiss him again. "Do that, James. Do that and don't stop."

She fell asleep in his arms. He got up slowly, placed a cushion from the sofa under her head, pulled a blanket over her, and walked silently out the door and down the stairs. On the train he found he couldn't sleep and began to read a book a passenger had left behind on a seat.

Hours later, he made his way through the village to the RAF base and saw Kipp climbing into his Spitfire.

"There you are." Kipp grinned. "How was it, James?"

"The best. Your mum and dad and wife say hullo."

"How was Jane?"

"As beautiful as the sunrise."

"Any word on Matthew?"

"I've heard they speeded up his training. They've done that with all the lads."

Kipp jerked his thumb at a nearby Spitfire. "The WAAFs ferried in three new ones yesterday evening. Jump in. Yours was hit by a bomb from an Me 110."

"Rotten. They came for Pickering Green again?"

"They did. We expect more trouble from that lot today. Perfect weather. Vice Marshal Park wants us on standby. He has a hunch they'll go after the Hurricane factory at Brooklands or the Spitfire one in Southampton. And us and Biggin Hill."

James had picked up his flying jacket and gear from his room on the base. He got into the cockpit of the new plane, book still in his hand.

"What's that you have there?" asked Kipp.

James was strapping himself in. "The book? Found it on the train. It's written by an old prof of mine at Oxford. Good man but deucedly hard to understand. His writing is clearer than his lectures."

"What's it about then?"

"It's called *The Hobbit*. A bit of mythology, really. Dwarves and ogres and all that. They have to slay a dragon."

"A dragon?"

"That's what we do, isn't it? I shall get Bobby Scott to paint a dragon on my new plane here. A sort of St. George and the Dragon with a swastika under the dragon's wing and a spear going through his heart."

"Dragonslayer."

"That's it, sir." James glanced over at Patrick sitting in his cockpit and a new pilot he didn't know sitting in another Spitfire nearby. "Sean make it out on leave?"

"He's in London now, yeah."

"The lads look stove in. Even the new bloke looks like he was dragged here behind a lorry."

The dark rings under Kipp's eyes were obvious as the sun rose above the horizon. "We're all knackered, James. But we'll keep going, won't we? No choice."

"Right."

"You look pretty rough yourself. If you'd been smart you'd have spent your twenty-four hour leave sleeping."

"I'm not that smart. Especially when it comes to Jane Fordyce." James craned his neck and looked toward the hangars. "I could use a cuppa to clear out the cobwebs. Do the ground crew have any brewed?"

The radio transmitter, or R/T, suddenly snapped and popped in Kipp's plane. "We have trade for you, Squadron Leader. Bomber force heading straight for Pickering Green. Angels two zero."

"Right. Squadron Leader to A, B, and C Flights. The game's afoot. Rendezvous at twenty thousand feet." Kipp gave James a thumbs up. "Best of luck, Dragonslayer."

"Thank you, sir. Same to you."

The surge James needed forced its way through him the moment he saw the bombers and fighters. For the first time, he imagined Peter tearing past him and tackling the bombers head-on. He chased the ghost and gave a Ju 88 a short burst. Its port engine poured purple-black smoke.

A Spitfire tumbled past underneath him. He caught a glimpse of the pilot slumped forward and the canopy shattered by machine gun fire. It was the new man he had seen in his cockpit on the ground. A moment later another Spitfire raced across in front of him, its wings on fire, an Me 109 peppering it with bullets. In a furious blast of red it exploded. A sudden anger made James turn after the Messerschmitt, close the distance between them rapidly, aim at the cockpit from behind, and press the gun button. Glass and debris flew, and the enemy fighter dropped into a steep dive. James followed it down to where it crashed near a stone barn. He pulled up in time to see Kipp's Spitfire plunge into a grove of trees and shatter, setting them all on fire. A pilot in a parachute was swinging through the sky, but James didn't recognize him. He made it back to the dogfight in time to see Patrick's aircraft split into three pieces. Cold running through him, he tangled with an Me 110 but ran out of ammunition and had to head back to Pickering Green.

"Where are the others in A Flight?" they asked him. "Where are Kipp and Patrick and McGrail?"

James took the mug of tea they thrust into his hands. "Who's McGrail?"

"The new chap."

"He's bought it."

"What about Patrick then? Did you see him?"

"I saw him," James replied.

"Did he take to the silk?"

"No."

Prescott came up with his green forms. "Did you get any?"

"A Junkers 88 and an Me 109. Followed the 109 down to where it crashed by a stone barn."

"Right." Prescott scribbled with his pen. "What about your squadron leader? What about Kipp? Where did he end up?"

"His Spit turned into a fireball when it smacked into some trees. I have no idea where he is. I saw one parachute." James looked into the mug of tea as if he could not figure out what it was. "How are B and C Flights?"

"None of them are back yet." Prescott wrote on a form. "Once we confirm your kills you'll be at nine and a half. I expect they'll make you the new squadron leader, Sweet."

"Kipp will turn up."

"Right. Until then, expect to get the nod."

James glanced at the sky overhead. It was clear and blue and empty.

The next day, the sixth of September, the Germans went after the aircraft factories, particularly the one at Brooklands. Tom Lewis was the new squadron leader for the Hurricanes, and James the new one for the Spitfires since no one had heard from Kipp. Their planes hurtled from one fight to another. More Spitfires and their men were lost; more Hurricanes and their men went down. The squadrons would return to a bombed-out Pickering Green, smoke rising from a smashed and burning hangar, refuel and rearm and return to the air to fight again. James and a new pilot, Brendan Cooke, shared a kill when they both shot down an Me 109. James's tally rose when he pursued a formation of Heinkel 111s, his face like jagged rock, a face unseen by anyone but God and a gunner aboard one of the Heinkels, and very precisely put bullets into the starboard engines of two of the bombers. Both of the Heinkels struggled, turned back toward the Channel and France, and eventually plunged into the water just off the white chalk cliffs of Dover. Three or four chutes floated down after them.

On the ground, Prescott scribbled on his forms. "You're acting like a man who means business."

"There's nothing else to do, is there?"

"Listen. They've found Kipp. His chute only half opened but he made it down alive. Two broken arms. He's at a hospital in London."

"I'm glad to hear it. But that means I'm still stuck with the squadron leader job."

"'Fraid so, laddie. There's no way out of that when you've bagged as many Jerry as you have."

James took tea from a corporal and put it to his lips. "There are ways out of it. I'm just not going to take them."

They both heard the phone ring.

"Scramble!" shouted a private as he threw the window open.

James poured the tea in the dirt and handed the cup to Prescott.

"Best of luck!" called the intelligence officer as James began to run toward his plane.

"It's not a question of luck anymore, is it?" James turned his head as he reached his Spitfire. "It's who's determined to hang on to the bitter end—them or us."

"Perhaps they'll blink, squadron leader."

James got into his cockpit. "They will have to, Prescott, because it won't be me. And it won't be Peter. Neither of us know how to do that anymore. If we ever did."

"You and Peter." Prescott stared at James as he started the engine of his Spitfire. "Quite right, sir."

James imagined Peter at his wingtip. Diving ahead of him into a swarm of enemy fighters and bombers. Giving Heinkels and Dorniers and Junkers and Messerschmitts burst after burst. Peeling away as they erupted in white and blue fire. Hunting more enemy aircraft. Pushing them back from the airfields and factories. Pushing them back from England. Fighting even as other RAF pilots went down. And James fought with him.

"A thousand shall fall at thy side, and ten thousand at thy right hand, but it shall not come nigh thee."

The next day James sat in his plane again and waited. His pilots, many of whom he hardly knew but for Sean, sat in their Spitfires and waited with him. The phone didn't ring. Tea was brought out to the planes. The sun shimmered in a blue sky speckled with high white clouds. James leaned out and drummed his fingers on the painting just beneath his cockpit. It showed a dragon being pierced by the nose and prop of a Spit-fire. The dragon writhed in its death throes. It was black, and the swastika on its side red. Underneath the dragon were thirteen smaller swastikas, also red. Finally Prescott came up to James's plane.

"What's going on?" asked James. "Is the radar knocked out or what is it?"

"The radar's fine, Squadron Leader. It's just that they haven't gone after the usual targets. They've surprised us."

"Where?"

"They've gone after London, Squadron Leader. At least three hundred bombers and six hundred Me 109s. And none of us called up to resist them."

"London. A daylight raid on London."

"Yes. The tonnage they've dropped has been massive. Including incen-diaries." Prescott put a hand on James's aircraft, planting it just on the dragon's head. "The city is in flames. The German press and Lord Tanner are crowing that we couldn't stop the raid because the RAF has ceased to exist as a fighting force. They are telling the world the war is won and that Britain is only days away from capitulation."

9

"Your son seemed in good spirits, my lord." Tavy carefully steered the Rolls around a turn on a narrow London street.

"He did indeed." Lord Preston drummed his fingers restlessly on his knee. "Too good, perhaps. His mother and I don't want him back in the air before he's ready."

"Surely the doctors will keep him at the hospital until he's fully mended."

"Who can say? The fighting is as desperate as ever. The RAF needs pilots badly. Kipp himself would talk himself out of that hospital bed if he could." A smile flashed over his face. "Did you see the card Cecilia made for him? And the jar of flowers she picked?"

"Lovely."

"Lovely indeed."

A bobby, tall helmet strapped firmly to his head, held up his hand in front of them. Tavy brought the car to a halt.

"That's far enough," the police officer said. "No closer to St. Katherine's Dock. We've an unexploded five hundred pounder down there."

Tavy and Lord Preston looked at the shattered buildings and rubble.

"So they're coming after London now, right enough," said Tavy.

"Well, they're still bombing our airfields and factories," Lord Preston replied, "but not on the scale they were in August and the beginning of September. Yes, they appear to be concentrating on London."

Tavy nodded toward a shroud of dark smoke. "They used incendiaries last night."

"It seems to be a favorite weapon of the *Luftwaffe*, the incendiary. Ever since Spain." Lord Preston opened his door. "Well, we can get out and stretch our legs, hm?"

They stood together by the Rolls and continued to survey the bombing damage.

"God's will some would say," Tavy murmured, his eye on a scorched doll with half its long hair burnt away. "The fighting has moved from Kent and West Sussex to us."

Lord Preston's face filled with sharp lines. "Not everything that happens is God's will, Tavy. That's monstrous thinking. It would make our Lord the agent of rape and murder and all manner of evil. That is why we pray, 'Thy will be done on earth as it is in heaven'—because it isn't being done. Yes, of course, ultimately we believe our God is sovereign over all the events and affairs of men. The human race doesn't have the final say. Yet the force of evil on this earth and the will of men to work evil cannot be discounted. Often enough—too often—it is their will that is done. And we must face it with the grace and power of God."

"I understand, my lord. But no doubt there are Christians in Germany praying for their armies and air force to triumph and they are not wicked people. No doubt they believe it is God's will they win this war."

Lord Preston nodded. "They are not wicked people on the whole, most assuredly not. Often we follow our leaders and nations into sheer folly because we are blinded by politics and rhetoric and patriotism. Indeed, I have seen that happen here; I have seen what we did in Ireland. It is for the God of all of us, the God of all Christians, to sort out the misdirection of the human heart and life. Only He knows how to judge rightly. For my part, we didn't attack Germany or wish it ill, though we did wish for a tempering of the harsh Nazi spirit. Now they are bombing our cities and killing our women and children. It's evil, Tavy, and we resist it, praying for God's will to be done—not the devil's, not the Third Reich's, not Hitler's, but God's. And I believe God's will is that we should not be conquered and that the Nazis should not rule over our green and verdant land, regardless of what the German churches pray or think."

Lord Preston slowly went to his knees in the rubble. "Hitler and Goering wished to destroy the RAF by going after the airfields and factories without letup," he continued. "They were thwarted in that endeavor. Now they intend to break us by breaking London and Liverpool and Coventry. They shall not succeed in that enterprise either. For we shall resist them. We shall fight them. We shall pray against them. We will cry out to the Lord our God for our freedom and He shall hear us and blunt the Nazi schemes. And then, Tavy, one day—a day that is not far off—we shall turn our hand to regaining the freedom of our neighbors, the freedom stolen from them because of the wicked will of wicked men."

"I wish that with all my heart. But pardon me, my lord, it often seems it can take a great deal of time and effort before something approaching God's will actually occurs."

"'The Lord is not slack concerning His promise, as some men count slackness; but is longsuffering toward us, not willing that any should perish, but that all should come to repentance.' There is war in heaven, Tavy, just as there is war on earth. You must not think it is over and done because God reigns, for there is rebellion under His divine rule. You must never be persuaded the war is finished because of the cross or because of the resurrection. Christ's work on earth gave us the power and the means and the authority to do battle. Now we must finish the fight. It will be a triumph of good over evil, Tavy. But there will be hardship and sacrifice on the way to that final victory. In the end, each of us will carry on his own cross. I mine, you yours. As you say, it takes time, and indeed it takes much effort. But we do not surrender to the wicked inclination within or without, Tavy, no matter how long it takes or what setbacks occur. When all is said and done, we shall not lose, for our Lord shall not fail us."

Tavy remained standing a moment longer while Lord Preston clasped his hands together. Then he knelt beside him.

"There is no need, Tavy," Lord Preston murmured. "You shall soil your pants."

"Excuse me, my lord, but there is a very great need. Before such a need my pants and my suit matter not at all. Neither do yours."

Lord Preston smiled. "Quite right."

The bobby, hands behind his back, looked them over. "Odd place for a church service, gents."

"I beg to differ, officer," Lord Preston responded. "I cannot think of a better location."

Friday, September 13, 1940
Kensington Gate, London

"I expect I'll turn in now." Lady Preston sat up in her chair in the parlor. "I'm practically falling asleep here."

"Hm." Lord Preston glanced up from his open Bible, reading glasses on his nose. "I shall check in on you in ten or fifteen minutes."

"In ten or fifteen minutes I'll be fast asleep."

"Will you? Then I'll be sure to kiss you goodnight very softly indeed."

A siren began to moan. It was soon followed by the thump of anti-aircraft fire and the bang and crash of explosions.

"What area of the city do you suppose the Germans are bombing this time?" Lady Preston asked.

Lord Preston was listening, cocking his head in the direction of the open window. "I can't tell. At any rate, it's far from here."

But it was not far. At the next second, the windows blew in with a roar, and sharp glass cut apart the wallpaper. Lady Preston shrieked, blood pouring over her face, got up, staggered, and fell. Lord Preston leaped out of his chair to help her, his Bible falling to the floor. Another blast threw him across the room and slammed him against the wall.

"William!"

Lady Preston bent over her husband, grasping his shirt and sweater and arm. "Get up, do you hear me? Get up!"

A third blast seemed to lift the house from its foundation, taking Lady Preston's feet out from under her, and she collapsed by her husband.

Tavy and Norah Cole came running into the room and saw the blood and wreckage and the bent and twisted bodies.

"Oh, my Lord!" Norah's hands flew to her mouth.

Tavy bent over them, blood quickly staining his white shirt. "Lord Preston! Sir William! Elizabeth! Elizabeth!"

Caroline had just pulled the curtains closed when the siren sounded. She glanced at Charles, who was sitting in the corner of the kitchen reading a copy of *Mein Kampf*.

"Do you think we should take Angelika and make our way to the shelter at the end of the street?"

Charles shook his head and turned a page. "They aren't interested in Camden. It's the docks they want. No point in waking Angelika up and spoiling her sleep, is there?"

There was a loud explosion close by. The windows shook.

He lifted his head and saw the fear in his mother's eyes.

"Don't fret," he said. "That was a mistake. The plane missed its target."

All the windows in the kitchen shattered at once, and flying glass cut Caroline's arms and legs open. She cried out Angelika's name and headed toward the staircase, but a second explosion picked her up and hurled her down the hallway. Charles jumped to his feet and went after her, book open in one hand, when two blasts, one on top of the other, twisted him around and tossed him through a window onto the street, banging his head sharply against the pavement.

Victoria was standing in what she often referred to as her Royal Mail backyard since it seemed to her to be hardly larger than a postage stamp. A pair of scissors in her hand, she walked toward the rose bushes that were filling the yard with their rich scent, intending to place half a dozen long-stemmed pinks in a vase. The siren howled just as she bent her nose to take in the perfume of a fully open blossom.

"Mum!" Tim poked his head out of the second-story window. "What should we do?"

She continued to breathe in the fragrance of the pink rose. "Nothing."

A thunderclap. The yard erupting. Mud and grass and rose bushes spinning around her. Her feet off the ground, her body in the air, turning over and over in flashes of light and rushes of fire. Looking at her fingers. Feeling spatters of rain on her face. Whirling. Never knowing when she fell or where.

"Camden. And West London."

Bursts of light. Darkness. More bursts of light. Rumbling finally making its way to their ears.

Emma had her hands around Jeremy's arm as they watched the city's skyline. "Are you sure?"

"I am. I daresay they're aiming for Whitehall and Buckingham Palace."

"Well, I hope you're wrong. That's altogether too close to Mum and Dad's. Not to mention most of our family lives in Camden."

Flak broke open the dark of the sky with white sparks as antiaircraft guns hunted the German bombers.

"It's like fireworks," Emma whispered. "If only we were celebrating."

Billy came through the door to where his parents stood in the street. "Rotten Nazis! Blast them!"

Jeremy and Emma snapped their heads around.

"What is it?" Emma took in the rage on his young face. "You've seen London bombed before."

"You didn't hear the phone ring, did you? Either of you?"

Both his parents' faces went rigid.

"No," replied his father.

"Aunt Victoria's house was hit. Aunt Caroline's house was hit. They've blown Grandfather and Grandmother's home to bits! Blast the Nazis! I hate them! I hate Hitler!"

Saturday, September 14, 1940, 9:00 a.m.
RAF King's Cross, West Sussex

"How on earth did this happen?"

Ben Whitecross stood on the airstrip under gray skies and a light sprinkle of rain. Two young men were facing him in blue RAF uniforms.

One of them shrugged. "I don't know, Dad. I mean, Squadron Leader Whitecross."

"You didn't think to tell them they were posting you to your father's squadron in Eleven Group, Ramsay?"

"I thought I did."

"You thought? Your mother will have me for high tea once she gets wind of this." Ben glanced down at the sheet of paper in his hand. "Wait a minute. What do we have here? Pilot Officer *White*?"

"I didn't tell them that."

"How did they end up with White as your last name? What happened to the rest of it? No wonder you were posted here."

"Sorry, sir."

Ben fixed his eyes on the youth standing at attention next to Ramsay. "Matt."

"Yes, sir."

"Are you another one who lost your voice? Why didn't you tell them I was your uncle?"

"James and Sean are at Pickering Green with Uncle Kipp, sir. Why can't I be posted here with you?"

"Kipp's in a hospital in London."

"Yes, sir, he is now. But he flew with James and Sean for weeks during the thick of the fighting."

"'The thick of the fighting?' Do you think it's let up then?"

"Well, I—"

"We have to stop them from wiping out London, don't we? And they haven't stopped bombing our airfields either." Ben jerked his thumb over his shoulder. "The invasion barges are still queued up in French ports. Hitler has every intention of knocking the RAF out of the game so he can land his troops on our beaches. That's the rosy little picture I want to paint for you today. Seven hundred RAF. Against thousands of the *Luftwaffe's* best pilots. It's desperate. And what do I get for replacements? My son and one of his mates. Both of who finished school a few short weeks ago."

"Dad, you know—"

"Don't call me Dad." Ben glanced back down at the papers they'd given him. "How many hours on Spits, Pilot Officer White?"

"Umm…" Ben could see that Ramsay wanted to count on his fingers. "Five? Five and a half?"

"That's it? That's all?" Ben looked at Matthew. "Please make me happy and tell me you've had ten or twelve or fifteen."

"If you count the Hurricane it's closer to seven or eight, Uncle…Squadron Leader."

"Uncle Squadron Leader? Try not to use that when you're on your R/T. How many hours on Spits? It's a different brew of a fighter than the Hurricane."

"More than four, sir."

"More than four?"

"I keep a log. It's closer to four and a quarter."

Ben put his hands on his hips. "I'm not praying enough. That's it. The Lord looks down and says, 'Whitecross doesn't have enough prayer in his life. Send his son and his nephew as squadron replacements.' I'd better go spend an hour on my knees."

"Yes, sir," responded his son.

"Don't agree with me, Ramsay."

"No, sir."

"I expect you're both squared away. Have your gear in your rooms?"

They nodded.

"Right. Well, I don't have time to ship you back to where you came from today, Pilot Officers White and Danforth. Come with me and I'll show you your kites. The WAAFs ferried them in early this morning."

They and several other raw recruits fell in step behind him. Next to several bombed-out hangars were two new Spitfires. Ben glanced back and saw the excitement in the young men's faces and was unsuccessful in keeping back his own smile.

"Try not to get shot down just when you're up at bat, all right?" Ben rested his hand on the wing of the first Spitfire. "Give those Nazi bowlers some real hardship. Score a hundred runs. Jerry wants to wear us out. Let's prolong the match and grind him down instead."

"Squadron Leader!"

Ben turned around. "What is it, Nesbitt?"

"Urgent call for you, sir. London."

"You mean the lines are working again?"

"For now."

"I'd better get right on it then." Ben started across the runway for his hut. He glanced back. "Did you two have any breakfast?"

"No, sir," replied Ramsay.

"Better hop into the Officers' Mess and get some ham and eggs. If they call us up after Jerry, there's no telling when we'll get the feedbag on you again."

Ben went into his room in a small hut and shut the door.

"Whitecross," he said into the phone.

"Ben, it's Emma. I've been trying to reach you all morning and I keep losing my connection."

"Em. Glad you've got through. How's everything? What's up?"

"The Germans struck Camden and West London last night. Buckingham Palace, Whitehall, Downing Street, Kensington High Street, the lot. Mum and Dad were badly hurt and they're both in hospital."

"What?"

"Your house was bombed too. So was Kipp's. Victoria and Caroline have both been hospitalized."

"Vic!"

"Now listen to me. She's doing well. Holding her own. So is Mum. It's

Dad and Caroline we're worried about. Caroline lost a lot of blood. And Dad hasn't woken up. They're afraid there's been a stroke."

Ice cold swept Ben's body and mind and then a raging heat. "What business do the bombers have going there? They've been hitting the docks. What good are West London and Camden to them?"

"They wanted to go after the king and queen and prime minister, didn't they? Wanted to show us they could strike anyone anywhere."

"What about Tim? Where's Tim?"

"He's fine. He's with us here. Billy's talking to him."

"Not cut up? Not wounded?"

"No."

"How are Catherine and Albrecht? How is Angelika? They were all in your mum and dad's house."

Emma's voice came and went as the phone connection lost power. "The bottom floor is ruined. Completely blown out. But Catherine and the family were in bed on the top floor. They're a bit shell-shocked but they haven't been hurt."

Ben finally sat down in his chair. "Tell me about Caroline."

"Charles was with her. He rescued Cecilia, got her out of her bedroom before the house collapsed. Had them both on the street and made Cecilia lie down next to Caroline so he could cover them both with his body."

"What? Nazi Charles?"

"Another five or six bombs landed on the street. A good number of their neighbors were killed outright. Yes, Nazi Charles kept the flying glass and brick and wood splinters from his mum and little sister. Who would have thought it? He took a lot of wounds."

"Isn't Eva living with them?"

"She's Air Raid Precautions now. She was out on patrol. Her crew was helping out bomb victims a half mile away."

Ben hesitated a moment, forming the unlikely image in his mind of Charles protecting Caroline and Cecilia from a rain of angry debris. "Is Vic awake?"

"Yes. I've been to see her already this morning. They'll not keep her in there long. She—"

The connection was suddenly lost.

"Hullo! Hullo!" Ben slammed the phone down. "Rotten luck!"

He ran his hand over his mouth. *We had rough times at the mission in Kenya, my God. You pulled us through. I need You to do that for us again. All of us. But especially Vic's dad. Especially him. And Caroline. You know Kipp needs her. You know we all do.*

A phone in a nearby hut jangled.

I don't know what to make of Charles. I honestly don't. I got wind that Lord Tanner had whipped him and that the concentration camps had soured him on the Gestapo and SS. But he still seems to think a proper Nazism is not only Germany's future, but Europe's and Britain's. I had it in my mind that he welcomed the bombing, hoping it would bring us to our knees and get a Nazi regime in place well before Guy Fawkes. Lord, I confess to being confused about the young man. I did not think he would risk his life for his mother and sibling. For Eva perhaps, but not for his British family.

"Scramble!"

Ben blinked and jumped to his feet. Ramsay and Matt came tumbling out of the Officers' Mess as Ben was swinging his metal legs into the cockpit.

"Get up!" Ben shouted at them. "Stick with me! And those three blokes with the yellow props on their kites!"

"What?" Ramsay shouted back.

"The two Canucks and the Yank! See them? Ten feet tall?"

Three very tall and very lean men were vaulting into their Spitfires on the far side of the airfield. The yellow props stood out among the white and black ones. Maple leafs for enemy aircraft shot down were on two of the planes. The other had stars.

"Where are we going?" yelled Ramsay.

The thunder of Rolls Royce Merlin engines made it impossible for Ben to reply. Strapping himself into his seat, he could only point at the sky. The Canadian pilots were already moving along the runway. Ben fired off a prayer for Ramsay and Matthew, taxied his aircraft into position behind the Canadians, and was airborne in thirty seconds. He kept his canopy open until he could see that his whole squadron was up. Then he slammed it shut and began the climb to twenty thousand feet along with the others.

Harrison asked three different nurses how to find Caroline's room and finally made his way down a corridor crammed with patients on trolleys. A flash lit up the dark window as he stood in the doorway and saw Caroline motionless on her bed. The flash was followed by a blast that made the glass pane vibrate. Charles was sitting in a chair beside his mother. He looked up.

"Harrison," Charles whispered.

Harrison removed his fedora. "I've been to see the lord and lady and Victoria as well. Lord Preston is still unconscious."

"I've heard Mum talk a bit. There was even a scrap of a laugh once."

"May I join you?"

"Yes. Of course."

Harrison pulled up a chair on the other side of the bed.

"Have you been sitting here by yourself a long time then?" asked Harrison.

"They've all been by at one time or another. Aunt Libby. Uncle Robert. Aunt Emma and Uncle Jeremy. Aunt Char. The lot."

"How's your sister getting along?"

"Cecilia is with Angelika and her parents. She seems to be all right."

"I've been to the others. Lord Preston is not responding. But his wife is up and around and so is your Aunt Victoria. I expect you will see them here tomorrow. The prime minister dropped by briefly to look in on your grandfather."

Charles said nothing.

Harrison cleared his throat. "People tell me you covered your mother and sister with your own body while the bombs were falling."

"Anyone would have done that."

"They say you were wounded."

"Scratches."

"Still. It's unusual behavior for someone who wanted the bombs to drop."

"Not on houses, Harrison. On the docks. On airfields. On factories."

"You know better than that, Charles. The bombs fell on houses and civilians in Guernica and Warsaw and Rotterdam. Why should England be any different?"

Charles looked down. "You must think me an odd Nazi beast. One minute I'm showing you the wounds my father inflicted on me and the next I'm back listening to one of his broadcasts and applauding. I detest the concentration camps and how the Jews have been treated there, yet that doesn't stop me from marching with the British Union of Fascists and shouting anti-Jewish slogans, does it? The truth is that quite often I'm sick of myself and how I swing from one position to the other." His fingers curled around his mother's hand. "They've arrested the BUF leaders."

Harrison nodded. "I'd heard that."

"The police came by and questioned me. I was properly repentant."

"Mm."

"The thing is, I am, you know. At least right now with my mother lying here. One of my mood swings again."

"There's color coming back into her cheeks."

"There is, isn't there?"

"I'm sure she'll pull through. I'll come by again tomorrow with Lady Holly." Harrison stood up.

"Who's taking care of Ashton Park in your absence?"

"The three dogs. And Todd Turpin."

Charles got to his feet and shook Harrison's hand. "I look forward to seeing you and Aunt Holly tomorrow. Thanks for coming by."

"Caroline means a great deal to all of us."

"I appreciate that. Will you…" Charles stopped and then started again. "Will you pray for her, Harrison?"

"I will."

Charles sat back in his chair as Harrison patted the boy on the shoulder and left.

"Now, Mum," Charles asked quietly, "do you think I'll ever get to the point where I'm praying for you for myself?"

Then he closed his eyes for just a moment's rest, but within seconds he was asleep in his chair.

"Charles."

"Mmm?"

"Charles."

Charles's eyes opened. Kipp was standing over him. Both his arms were covered in large casts. Charles scrambled to his feet.

"Kipp…Mr. Danforth."

"Hullo, Charles. I finally made my way here from the other side of the city, Heinkels and five hundred pounders and all. How is she?"

"She…she just lies there without moving. I keep hoping she'll sit up and, well, laugh for me."

"Ah, her wonderful Scarborough laugh." Kipp smiled down at her. "How lovely she is. Always lovely, your mother."

"Yes, sir."

"And you? How are you holding up?"

"I'm all right."

"I was told you took a lot of nasty cuts from flying glass and splinters."

"Not so nasty."

"What about Cecilia?"

"Right as rain. She's with Uncle Albrecht and Aunt Catherine. And Angelika."

"Capital. I'm back home in a couple of days. Not that I'll be able to do much with my arms like this. I hope you'll be there. You'll surely be needed."

"If Mum is better."

"Of course." Kipp carefully lowered himself into the chair Harrison had used.

"And we'll need somewhere else to live."

"I expect we will."

The windows flickered and flashed. A *thump* made them glance out. The far darkness ignited and glowed red.

"Incendiaries fell on our street, just a few of them." Charles's face was lined with crimson and black. "The one body I saw was like melted wax. Just as if a wick had burned right down to the bottom of a candle and guttered there. Do you suppose we'll use…the British will use incendiaries in their bombings?"

"I hope not," Kipp replied. "But wars always go from bad to worse the longer they last. Poison gas in the last war. Fire bombings in this one. Soon you use anything you can get your hands on that will help you win."

"Will the Germans win?"

"They might. But we put six to seven hundred kites up every day against them."

"The bombers still get through."

"When you fill the sky with as many as Jerry does, some are always bound to get through."

Charles looked at the casts on Kipp's arms. "Do you think you'll fly again? Or is that it?"

Kipp shook his head. "I'm not done yet."

Sunday, September 15, 1940
RAF King's Cross, West Sussex

Ramsay sat in his cockpit, "the office" as his father called it, and watched the exhausts on the engine cowlings of the Spitfires blaze a bright blue in the dawn darkness. He was cold and cramped, and the only things that were warm were his hands because they were wrapped around a mug of hot tea. He hardly drank any of it, preferring it remain hot and in the mug where he felt it could do his hands the most good.

Right, Ramsay, are you listening?

I am, Dad.

Don't call me Dad. The Me 109 has a fuel-injected engine. The Spit doesn't. So the Me 109 can go into a steep dive to get away and the fuel continues to feed into the engine. If we go into as steep a dive, the g-force pushes the fuel away from the motor and we stall.

Isn't there anything we can do?

Perform a half roll if you must go after him. That will help keep the petrol feeding into the Rolls Royce engine.

The sun was up. The sky was gold and blue. Ben signaled his squadron to turn their engines off. Several took the opportunity to get out and stretch their legs. Ramsay gave Matthew a thumbs up. Matt grinned and waved his hand. Another hour went by. Ramsay climbed down to the ground when his father approached.

"Take a quick break and get yourself some more tea," Ben said. "Haul Matt along with you."

"Do you think we'll go up today?"

"Oh, we'll go up. It's perfect flying weather. Jerry will be on his way soon."

Ramsay slapped Matt's airplane. "Come on. Let's get some more tea."

"The last thing I need is more tea."

"Well then, use the gent's room, and then get some more tea."

A flare suddenly burst over the runway.

"Scramble!" a corporal shouted from a hut. "All squadrons!"

Ramsay dropped his mug, and it broke in two.

His father was shouting at him. "Never mind all that! Get in and get up!"

"See you in the clouds, Ram!" called Matt.

"I hope so!" Ramsay called back.

In minutes all four King's Cross squadrons were in the air and climbing.

Operations bunker, RAF Hillingdon, Uxbridge

"Heinkel 111s, fifty plus, angels two five, same bearing, straight on for London."

"Yes, I have that," Jane responded. "Heinkel 111s, fifty plus, twenty-five thousand feet, same bearing."

"Fighter escort, Me 109s, sixty plus, angels three zero, same bearing."

"Right, I have that, Me 109s, sixty plus, thirty thousand feet, same bearing."

She began to push wooden counters across the map toward London. All the counters from all the WAAFs were converging on London. Information continued to be relayed to her more and more rapidly, and she placed more and more counters on the map. The destination was always the same.

"The prime minister."

Sergeant Turnbull said it quickly as she walked past, but Jane caught it. She looked up and saw the round figure of Churchill seated beside Air Vice Marshal Park. Her headphones crackled.

"Here's another lot. It looks like they're pulling out all the stops. Junker 88s, sixty plus, angels two five, on the same bearing as the Heinkels. London is the target."

"I have Junker 88s, sixty plus, twenty-five thousand feet."

"Fighter cover at angels three zero, Me 109s, fifty plus."

"Me 109s, fifty plus, thirty thousand feet."

She looked at the sector clock, tagged both counters with yellow, and used her rake to thrust them over the Channel and Kent to London.

Rows of bulbs flashed on and off and on again behind her. The long wall, or tote board, blazed. She glanced quickly at Pickering Green. ENEMY SIGHTED was lit up for both squadrons. Then she saw the same signal blaze across the board for all airfields and all squadrons—ENEMY SIGHTED. Sergeant Turnbull slipped a note into her hand.

11 GROUP, 10 GROUP, AND 12 GROUP ARE ALL
ENGAGED. THIRTY SQUADRONS. NO BREAK IS
POSSIBLE. STAY SHARP.

Jane's headphones crackled to life. "Large formation of Dornier 17s,
forty plus, fifteen thousand feet, fighter cover Me 109s and Me 110s, sixty
plus, twenty thousand feet, bearing on London."

"Thank you," responded Jane, "Dornier 17s, forty plus, fifteen thousand feet, Me 109s and Me 110s, sixty plus, twenty thousand feet, converging on London."

*God, be with our boys. With Sean, with Ben, with Matt, and Ramsay.
And please, please be with James. I don't know how all this works, all this prayer
and faith. But save their lives and save our country.*

Kensington Gate, London

"Get Angelika! Get Cecilia!" Albrecht was stuffing notes into his briefcase. "We must make for the shelter at the end of the street!"

"We'll not make it!" Catherine had ten-year-old Angelika by the hand.
"The siren's been wailing for two minutes!"

"We have to try. I feel like this house is a target. Where's Cecilia?"

"Tavy has her."

"Where is he?"

"Halfway down the block."

"What about Darrington and Mrs. Longstaff and Norah?"

"They're in the cellar. They won't budge."

Albrecht raced out of his room and down the staircase. The bottom
floor was a shambles of broken walls and shattered windows and torn car-
pets. He swung open the door to the basement.

"This place is ready to fall down!" he shouted. "Even a near miss would
do it! You've got to make a run for the shelter with us!"

Only Mrs. Longstaff responded. "Bless you, my legs can't carry me that
fast anymore. And just the other night a shelter took a direct hit, didn't it,
and that put paid to all those poor folk? We'll take our chances here. One
place is as good as another, that's how we all feel."

"You must come with us!"

Catherine was heading out the door. "I'm gone, Albrecht. I can hear the AA fire and the bombs. It's Buckingham Palace again. They're coming this way."

Albrecht slammed the cellar door and ran out into the street after his wife and daughter, briefcase in one hand. The siren continued to howl. He saw dirty black flak bursts in the blue sky and dozens of twin-engine bombers appear over his head with the dark drone of metal insects. Dust and smoke from high explosives spilled over trees and hedges and rose up to form massive pillars of red and black. The ground shook and shook again and it seemed to him his wife and child were running sideways on a slant and that the whole street was about to fall to the right and get pulled under the earth.

"Papa!" Angelika had twisted around to look at him, her mother gripping her hand, to point upward. "A parachute!"

Albrecht spotted a large cylinder floating through the air.

"It's a bomb!" he yelled. "It's a mine! Run away from it! Run to the left and get behind that house!"

A breeze pushed the mine toward Kensington Gate. It swayed back and forth in its harness.

"Get down!" yelled Albrecht.

Catherine and Angelika continued to run straight ahead for the shelter.

There was a huge roar and boiling black smoke. The pavement split under Albrecht's feet, and he heard a sharp cracking as houses burst and toppled. He was on his back and on his stomach and on his back as a wind hurled him down the street. His briefcase was gone, his wife and daughter were gone, Kensington Gate was gone. He went through fire, he went through heat, he went through oil, he put out his hands to try to break the momentum, but a wrist snapped and his cry of pain was just another loud sound among many other loud sounds in the rough whistling shriek of tumbling bombs and falling buildings.

The Fordyce residence, Camden Lock, London

Libby had her arms around Montgomery and two-year-old Paul while Skitt had his arms around all three of them.

Upstairs they could hear glass breaking.

Under their feet, mud and dirt heaved and thick dust filled their mouths and nostrils.

The boy began to wail.

"It'll not last forever, remember that!" Skitt kissed his wife and son. "The planes are passing over. They only have so many bombs. They have other targets."

For a moment it was quiet.

Skitt lifted his head. "That's it then."

An ear-splitting roar. It was as if a beast broke down the cellar door, breathed fire and spit, and dragged all the stone and brick and earth it could tear loose down into the dark on top of them.

RAF King's Cross, West Sussex

"They want you back up as soon as you're refueled and rearmed, sir."

Ben bit into a ham sandwich with one hand and brought a cup of tea to his mouth with the other. "Right, Corporal, as soon as the ground crew have us filled with bullets and petrol we'll give chase." He glanced over the airfield from the doorway of the Officers' Mess. "Ramsay! Matt!"

The two young men broke away from a group of pilots and came across the runway.

"Did you get yourselves something to eat?" asked Ben. "We'll be going up as soon as the kites are ready."

"Not really that hungry, sir," replied Ramsay.

"Neither am I," said Matt.

"Well, force something down. You need to keep your strength up." He gestured with his teacup. "What were you doing hanging about with that mob?"

Ramsay grinned. "They're brilliant."

"Canadians, a Yank, couple of Kiwis, an Aussie, an Afrikaner—we call that lot the League of Nations."

Matt shrugged. "They shook some wool off our backs."

"Glad to hear it." Ben drank his tea. "Look. I waited a bit to get more news. We had family hurt in yesterday's bombing. Ramsay, your mum was wounded, but she's all right."

Ramsay's face tightened up. "How badly wounded?"

"There was a telegram waiting for me when we got down ten minutes ago. She has a broken ankle. Sends her love."

"That's it then? Just her?"

"No. Grandmother and Grandfather got banged up. Both of them are in hospital. Jerry hit West London—the palace, Whitehall, Kensington High Street."

"Are they—are they going to make it?"

"Grandmother's on her feet. Granddad isn't. Not yet." Ben looked at Matthew. "Your mother was hurt. She was unconscious. But the cable says she's pulled through. She's sitting up and taking soup and tea. We can all thank God for that."

Matt's face had gone gray. "Are you sure?"

"I am. It's a lot to take in. But the bombers went after Camden right after they struck Buckingham Palace and Kensington. And our families are packed into Camden like sardines, aren't they?"

"What about Cecilia?" demanded Matt. "And what about Eva?"

"They're fine."

"How do you know that?"

"Because they told me yesterday."

"And you didn't say anything?"

"No. You two had enough on your plates." Ben drank off the rest of his tea, his eyes remaining on Matt. "You still do. You need to keep your wits sharp and your nerves on ice. Your mothers want to see the pair of you again, so fly tight. Two-second bursts. Never fly more than a few moments in a straight line once the fight's on. If hanging about with the yellow props helps, then stick with that mob. But they go for blood, so if you're in their neighborhood you're bound to see a lot of traffic with crosses on the wings."

"You said you were going to send us back to London," Ramsay reminded him.

Ben nodded. "So I did. But you both fly well. I'd never have sent you here with the hours you've had on Spits. But you're here now, aren't you? Goering's got his dander up. We've got to give the *Luftwaffe* blow for blow or we're done. You want to help your families? Shoot down a Heinkel. Shoot down as many as you can. Just a squirt. That's all you need. Get in close from behind or underneath and tag them."

The young men's eyes were dark.

"Rotten luck them hitting Camden," said Ramsay.

"There's nothing there for Hitler," added Matt.

"People are there," replied Ben. "Just as there were in Poland and France. That's what it's about. Killing people and frightening the rest of the country out of its wits. It's worked for Jerry before."

"Not here it won't." Ramsay's face and eyes grew darker. "Not anymore."

A corporal ran up and saluted. "The kites are ready to go for your squadron, sir."

"Right." Ben thrust his head into the Officers' Mess. "My mob. Back up after Jerry. Come on." He faced Ramsay and Matt. "I want you keen. But no heroics. Just blast them out of the sky."

"Yes, sir."

"Yes, Squadron Leader."

"Go." Ben jerked his head in the direction of the aircraft. "Get into your kites."

The Fordyce residence, Camden Lock, London

"Shh."

Eva put a finger to her lips. The two men stopped pulling timbers free of the bricks and dirt.

"Do you hear that?" she whispered. The men shook their heads.

Eva crawled to a corner of what was left of the house. She put her ear up against the earth and rubble.

"There's a baby crying. I'm sure of it." She grabbed a shovel and began to dig dirt away from the spot. "Help me. Quickly."

The men came over.

"We don't want a cave-in," said one.

"We don't want them to suffocate either, do we?" responded Eva. "Work swiftly and carefully but let's get down to them."

A truck inched its way along the battered street. Eva waved to them once she saw the back of the truck was loaded with shovels and picks and ARP volunteers.

"We have a family trapped!" she called. "Help us out, will you?"

The men piled out of the truck and came running toward the ruined house.

"Careful then, careful," said one of the men at Eva's side. "Let's not bring the lot down on their heads."

The group dug slowly and steadily, Eva putting her hand up every few minutes so she could listen for sounds.

Suddenly a man broke into an open space with his spade and shouted, "I see a face!"

Eva scrambled to the hole. "Aunt Libby!"

Libby's face was thick with white dust. The only openings were her eyes and mouth. She lifted Montgomery's son up to Eva.

"Take him! He's choking!"

Eva scooped up the child and ran with him to a patch of grass.

"Get them out!" she called over her shoulder.

"We're doing that," replied one of the men. "Ups a daisy, there you go, ma'am."

Libby was tugged out of the opening.

"Who else is down there with you?" the man asked.

"I can't…I can't…" Libby began to cough.

"Here." He put a canteen in her hands.

Libby gulped at it, spat, and then took in more water.

"A husband and wife," she managed to get out. "They're both unconscious."

"Right. Harry, you're slender as a matchstick. Jump down and push them up to us."

Eva ran her finger in and around the boy's mouth, soaked a cloth from her ARP tunic pocket in water, and wiped his face and hands and nose free of dirt and dust. He looked at her, seemed to hold his breath a moment, then let out a pent-up wail. Eva laughed.

"There, you're fine! Make as much noise as you want!"

She held the boy in her arms and called to the men. "See? He's full of fight!"

The men grinned. "We need plenty of that, right enough," said one.

"Here we go," said another, bending over Montgomery's body. "This one's coming around too."

Eva put one of her arms around Libby as they embraced, holding the boy in the other.

"Thank goodness you came, thank goodness." Libby was striking at tears with her fingers.

Eva kissed her on the cheek. "It's my job to take care of Camden, isn't it? We were in the West End as well, by the palace, and along Kensington High Street." Her face lost its brightness as she told Libby this.

"What's happened?" asked Libby. "What did you see there?"

Eva shook her head. "Albrecht and Catherine and Angelika are alive, heaven knows how. Knocked about, and Albrecht's broken his left hand in two or three places. But alive after a mine exploded at Kensington Gate."

"Mum and Dad's house?"

"They're still at hospital. They weren't at the house."

"But Cecilia was staying there—"

"Tavy got her out and into a shelter at the end of the street. She's fine. And Tavy's her new best friend."

They both smiled.

"That's grand," Libby said. "But there's something else, isn't there?"

Eva held the boy closer and kissed him. His crying had stopped. "The servants wouldn't leave Kensington Gate. They huddled in the cellar during the raid. Only Tavy was out of the house because he took Cecilia to the shelter."

"Why…Mrs. Longstaff…Norah…Darrington…"

Eva kept her eyes on Libby. "Dead. All dead. The house took a direct hit."

Libby put her hand to her mouth. "Oh, no."

"I haven't told anyone yet. Only Tavy."

"Oh, this is terrible, terrible…we've had Mrs. Longstaff with us since I was a girl."

"We've got them both out and awake!" called one of the men. "It's a pretty sight, dust and dirt and all!"

Eva walked quickly toward the ruined house. "That's something, Lib, that's something. We haven't lost Skitt or Montgomery."

"No. I thank God for that." The tears were coming freely now, and she didn't wipe them away. She followed Eva.

Montgomery was flat on her back with a blanket over her, her face washed, and Skitt was sitting up beside his wife, drinking from a canteen.

"Hullo, you two." Libby knelt by Montgomery and smoothed back the young woman's hair. "How are you feeling?"

"Where is Paul?" asked Montgomery.

"Right here." Eva bent down as Montgomery sat up and put the boy in her arms. "His cheeks are red as berries now."

"Oh, bless you, bless you." Montgomery hugged the child. "What would we have done if you hadn't come along, Eva? What would we have done if all of you hadn't come along?"

Skitt nodded, wiping the grime from around his eyes with a cloth. "Thanks, mates."

"Believe me," responded one of the men, "after all we've seen over the past week and more, bringing you up out of that rubble is better than a pint of stout."

"Aye," said another. "And it's the best reason we've had all day to toast you with two or three of them."

Skitt laughed along with the men.

The siren began to moan. Everyone looked up.

"The Spits are on them," growled one man. "Go get 'em, lads, go get 'em."

"Aye," said another. "Bloody their noses and knock 'em out of the sky."

White vapor trails swirled over their heads. As they watched, a Heinkel 111 fell through the air like a bird that had been shot. They couldn't tell where it hit the ground. A huge streak of white flame leaped upward with a tall geyser of water. A Spitfire roared past, banking over Camden and climbing back up into the battle. Everyone cheered, including Eva and Libby and Montgomery.

"That's it!"

"Well done!"

"Send Jerry packing!"

"Give us another!"

Bombs were falling. They heard the whistling screech and the *whump*, *whump* of the high explosives. But no one moved. They continued to watch the fight winding about the blue sky. Skitt pushed himself to his feet.

"I can't stay on the ground anymore, Monty," he said. "I can't."

She rocked Paul in her arms as the white lines went around and around over the London sky. "I know, love."

September 15, 1940
Lord Preston's hospital room, London

Lord Preston's eyes blinked open. "Where am I?"

He came up so swiftly to a sitting position he knocked a glass of water off a table beside him. It shattered, and a nurse ran into the room Lord Preston shared with five other men.

She yanked back the curtains from around his bed.

"Lord Preston!" she exclaimed. "You're up!"

"Of course I'm up!" he snapped. "What's going on?"

"You were wounded, sir. You're in a London hospital."

Lord Preston narrowed his eyes. "Where is my wife?"

"She's in another ward. She's fine, sir, but we have her resting now."

"What about the others? My daughter Catherine? Her husband, Albrecht? Their daughter, Angelika? Where are they?"

"They are well."

"My servants? My home at Kensington Gate?"

"That, I don't know."

The windowpane shook as the sound of distant explosions rumbled into the room.

"Are we under attack?" he asked.

"Yes, my lord. We've been having quite a go these past few days. Our boys are hard pressed. Who would have thought Hitler and the Nazis had so many planes?"

"Is that what it is? Is that what's going on? Waves of bombers coming against London?"

"Yes, sir. And our other cities as well. Please stay in your bed. I must fetch the doctor. And clean up this broken glass."

"You must fetch me a Bible first."

"A Bible?"

"Yes, yes, a Bible, do you not have one of those lying about?"

"Why, of course. But I must get the doctor."

He wagged his finger at her. "By all means get Doctor Fiddlesticks, but the Bible first, if you please."

She left and returned in a moment with an old, black, dog-eared Bible. "It's seen better times," she said.

"We've all seen better times, my dear. It's the Bible that brings those times to us if we take its wisdom to heart, hm?"

"Yes, sir. I shall just get the doctor now. And a broom."

"Very good. I shall be awaiting the arrival of both."

Lord Preston thumbed through the well-worn Bible as more explosions sounded outside his window.

"Ah," he said and stopped.

He looked about for his reading glasses. Finally he had to settle for holding the Bible a yard from his face.

"Lord, hear my prayer," he said.

The lights blinked on and off, and his room seemed to move. A far off grumbling grew louder and louder as he began reading out loud.

> He that dwelleth in the secret place of the most High shall abide under the shadow of the Almighty. I will say of the LORD, He is my refuge and my fortress: my God; in him will I trust…

Over the skies of West Sussex and the English Channel, Ben and Ramsay drove their aircraft at the thick formations of bombers, Matt twisting and turning with them, any fear or anxiety at flying and fighting gone from the young men's minds and spirits. Ramsay and Matt stayed as close to the yellow props and to the League of Nations as they dared, their windscreens filling with tracers and streams of smoke, and did their best to get under and over and behind aircraft streaking past at nearly four hundred miles per hour.

> …Surely he shall deliver thee from the snare of the fowler, and from the noisome pestilence. He shall cover thee with his feathers, and under his wings shalt thou trust: his truth shall be thy shield and buckler. Thou shalt not be afraid for the terror by night; nor for the arrow that flieth by day; nor for the pestilence that walketh in darkness; nor for the destruction that wasteth at noonday…

The Hurricanes and Spitfires at Pickering Green rose from the long green fields of Kent and roared into the bombers and their fighter escorts. Sean flew as if he had been flying from birth—James admired his cousin's natural touch and the way he could make his airplane flow like water in between the Heinkels and Dorniers and Me 109s.

"Just the bulldog me," he muttered under his breath. "That will have to jolly well be good enough. What say, Peter?"

He imagined his brother's Spitfire doing a half roll and diving after an Me 109 that was trailing orange and purple sparks. James thrust his stick forward.

"Right, I'm with you, mate," he said.

...A thousand shall fall at thy side, and ten thousand at
thy right hand; but it shall not come nigh thee. Only
with thine eyes shalt thou behold and see the reward of
the wicked. Because thou hast made the LORD, which is
my refuge, even the most High, thy habitation; there shall
no evil befall thee, neither shall any plague come nigh thy
dwelling...

Charlotte could hear the bombs and the antiaircraft fire as she sat in an
Anderson shelter with eleven-year-old Colm. Edward had made sure one
was buried in the backyard on his last leave. It was four feet underground
with curved sides of corrugated iron and a wooden door. She had banked
two feet of soil on top, transplanted rose bushes, and made a flowerbed.

"Where's everyone else in our family?" asked Colm.

"I honestly don't know, dear." Charlotte had her arm around him in the
dark. "We never really got a chance to discuss it at a family gathering, did
we? No one thought the Germans were going to attack London like this."

"How long will we have to sit here?"

"We'll hear the all clear. It won't be too long."

"This morning it was two hours. I thought I was going to suffocate."

"Well, you didn't, did you?"

"When is the Royal Navy going to do something?"

"It's not the navy's job to deal with the German Air Force, Colm. Your
uncles and cousins in the RAF must tend to that."

"All those chalk marks in the heavens?"

Charlotte smiled in the dark. "Yes, all those."

"I hope everyone else has a shelter as good as ours."

"I'm not sure what everyone has. Some people like to use their cellars. Grandmother and Grandfather have a cellar. So do Uncle Terry and
Aunt Libby."

"Didn't Aunt Caroline and Aunt Victoria have cellars or shelters?"

"I don't know. I thought one of them had a shelter in the back just like
us."

"Then why didn't they use it? Why are they in hospital? And why didn't
Grandpa and Grandmother use theirs?"

"Shh. The attack came very fast. Most people were still in their houses.
We happened to be playing tag in the backyard."

The shelter shook, and there was a muffled blast.

Colm's eyes widened. "It could cave in on us."

Her arm around his shoulders drew him in closer. "There's not enough to bury you and me. You're well over five feet tall, and there's only four feet of dirt."

"What if we can't breathe?"

"Your father put in a special pipe so we would have plenty of fresh air. It sticks out far above ground."

"What if they use poison gas?"

"Shh. Now you're letting your imagination run away with you."

He was silent a moment. "I wish we could have one big shelter," he finally said. "And all my cousins in it with me. And plenty of sausages and cake. And Owen here too with all sorts of navy stories."

She smiled. "Perhaps there will be a shelter like that one day if the war goes on long enough."

> ...For he shall give his angels charge over thee, to keep thee in all thy ways. They shall bear thee up in their hands, lest thou dash thy foot against a stone. Thou shalt tread upon the lion and adder: the young lion and the dragon shalt thou trample under feet...

Matt watched Ramsay's plane slice across the sky in front of him like a knife, the sunlight sparking along the edges of its wings. For an instant he saw the guns flash, and a Dornier rolled over on its back—it was like a photographic image and it hung suspended before his eyes two or three seconds. Then his Spitfire shuddered and slewed to the left. An Me 109 roared over him. Flames spurted along his engine cowling. He went into a downward spiral.

"Take to the silk, Matt!" Ramsay shouted over the R/T.

Matt loosened the straps on his seat. There were no thoughts in his mind as he yanked open the canopy. The Spitfire spun upside down, and he fell out of the cockpit. The air was like raw ice on his face. Planes with black crosses and blue, white, and red roundels blurred as he dropped past them. He pulled on the cord and the chute opened with a *whump*, giving his shoulders and chest a hard jerk. Suddenly he could see the barrage balloons bobbing over London, dark flak puffs, white vapor trails, swirling patterns of aircraft that looked like rolling balls of gnats and midges, bright winks of flame as planes exploded and burned, a line of gulls swinging to the west like a scythe, the green under him so green, the blue around him and over him so blue. He floated onto the roof of a barn, just missing the large haystacks he was hoping he'd land on. The parachute dragged him across the rough shingles and tangled in his arms and legs. For a moment he simply lay there on his side looking down at three or four cows and a black and white dog that began to bark furiously.

"You one of us, mate?" a tall man called up to him.

"I hope so!" Matt called back.

The man and his companions laughed. "That's a good Lancashire accent, that is," said one. "Jerry'd have a hard time getting his tongue around that."

"What did he say?"

"I'm not sure. But he's our lad, all right." The tall man cupped his hands around his mouth. "Hang on! We'll get a ladder up to you!"

"Thanks. I'm not in any great rush."

"What did he say?" The men looked at one another.

"It doesn't matter, does it?" asked the tall man. "He's British as mushy peas. Where'd the big ladder wind up? Where'd we stow it?"

"I think it's by the hayrick there."

"Right. Timmy, Tad, go fetch it will you?" The tall man called to Matt again. "We'll have you down quick as you can say Bob's your uncle. Then we'll brew you up a nice tea."

"Bless you," Matt responded. "Tea would make all the difference in the world to me right now."

"What's that he says?"

"Never mind. Just ask Nancy to brew up a pot, all right? A big one. The lad's had quite the day, hasn't he?"

> ...Because he hath set his love upon me, therefore will I deliver him: I will set him on high, because he hath known my name. He shall call upon me, and I will answer him: I will be with him in trouble; I will deliver him, and honor him. With long life will I satisfy him, and show him my salvation.

"Dad."

"Hm?"

"Dad. It's Robbie."

Lord Preston opened his eyes, the Bible still open in his lap. "My boy." He smiled. "How wonderful to see you."

Robbie bent over and kissed him on the cheek. "It's more wonderful to see you. You gave us all quite a fright."

"The doctor gave me a look over. No evidence of a stroke. He said I was top-notch."

"I'm so pleased to hear that."

"I confess I don't recall much except being thrown across the room by a bomb."

"You and Mum were both hurt. But she's fine. She's napping now, and so are Caroline and Victoria. Otherwise I'd have them with me. "

"Caroline and Victoria? What?"

"They were hurt in the same bombing raid. But they're doing well. They shall all walk out of here tomorrow."

"I must see them."

Robbie gently put a hand to his father's chest. "Steady on, Dad. Let them have their rest. We can get together later tonight."

"You're sure they're all right?"

"The docs wouldn't be discharging them if they weren't."

"What time is it?" asked Lord Preston.

"About nine thirty," his son replied.

"Then I've missed the BBC news. I wanted to hear about the fighting today. I was praying about it quite a bit."

Robbie sat on the edge of the bed. "It was a good day, Dad, possibly the very best. Almost two hundred German aircraft shot down, they say, with only a fraction of ours lost."

"Two hundred! My word!"

"That was what the announcer told us. One hundred and eighty-five or eighty-seven or something like that. But you know how it is. Two or three pilots claim the same bomber, and in the end we wind up with half that number shot down. I expect we'll have destroyed fifty or sixty, not two hundred."

"Nevertheless. That will set the *Luftwaffe* back on their heels a bit."

Robbie nodded. "I expect it will. But the show's not over yet. If they have any luck at all with the weather they'll be back again in full force."

"Less two hundred airplanes."

"Right. Less fifty or sixty or two hundred airplanes."

Lord Preston half laughed. "My word, that is extraordinary. Praise God."

"Yes, Dad, we ought to do that. But listen, I must tell you something else."

"What is it? More good news, I hope?"

"It isn't really." Robbie took his father's hand. "Dad, bombs hit Camden and West London again today. A mine exploded on top of Kensington Gate. It's gone. Nothing left but rubble."

"Gone completely?"

"Yes. But that's not the worst of it. Some of the servants chose to hide in the cellar rather than make their way to the shelter at the end of the street."

"Who?"

"Mrs. Longstaff. Darrington. Norah Cole."

"Are they here in hospital?" Lord Preston started to get up. "I must look in on them."

"Dad." Robbie's hand was still on his shoulder. "They're not here. They're dead. All three were killed in the blast."

Lord Preston sank back. "All? Where was Tavy?"

"In the shelter with young Cecilia."

"What about Albrecht and Catherine? What about Angelika?"

"They're safe. They were out of the house."

Lord Preston closed his eyes. "I feel you have more to tell me."

"Libby's house came down from the bombs. She was in the cellar with Skitt and Monty and the toddler. Eva helped dig them out. They're more than fine."

"Don't spare me."

"Honestly, they are. I saw them myself. Shaken up but making out all right."

Lord Preston puffed his cheek and let out a stream of air. "Well."

Robbie was silent.

Lord Preston stared at him. "What else? What is it?"

"James is missing."

"James!"

"His Spitfire went into the Channel. No one saw a chute."

Lord Preston put a hand over his eyes. "There is a possibility he may have made it out of the cockpit. Been picked up by us or the Germans."

jkl.

"Of course."

"Have Emma and Jeremy been informed?"

"Yes, but someone will need to tell Jane," Robbie said. "If she can be reached. It seems she's always on duty in that bunker, tracking the enemy."

"Such a mix of news, Robbie. Such a mix of dark and light. So many blows have rained upon us."

The windowpane flickered red, and they both heard a muffled roar. Then another. And another.

"I shall tell Jane," Lord Preston suddenly said. "The duty should fall to me. It must fall to me."

"Dad, you're not well."

"I'm well enough. I don't need to be in this bed a minute longer. Not with Hitler doing his best to break our will. Not with that monster doing his best to break our family."

Robbie didn't reply.

His father reached out a hand. "Perhaps you will pray with me, Robert."

Robbie gripped his father's hand. "Of course."

"And everyone else?" Lord Preston asked, his face the color of ashes. "Patricia? Charlotte and Colm? The other pilots in the family?"

"Everyone else is all right so far as we know."

Wednesday, September 18, 1940
RAF King's Cross, West Sussex

Ben put down the phone and walked from his office, hands in his pockets. His pilots were sitting about by the runway in various chairs. Matt had the nicest, a large overstuffed armchair the farmers had brought in the truck when they returned him to the base. Ben positioned himself in front of them, head still down.

"What's happened?" asked Ramsay.

Matt sat up in his armchair. "What news, sir?"

"That was from your cousin Sean at Pickering Green. James's body washed ashore last night. Some fishermen found him."

No one spoke.

"Sean is squadron leader now," Ben went on. "Evidently Lord Tanner made some sort of mocking broadcast about Wolfgang von Zeltner shooting down the twins of Lord Preston's family."

"What?" Ramsay bristled. "You don't believe that rubbish."

"Von Zeltner is claiming both as his kills."

"Wasn't this Zeltner a stunt flier at the Olympics?" asked Matt.

"Yes, him and Udet," replied Ben.

"And now he's some sort of grand German ace?"

"Right."

"You're not going to go along with the idea that he shot Peter down in August and that now he's tagged James too, are you, sir? That's just Lord Tanner trying to get under the skin of the Danforth family, isn't it?"

"I wouldn't put it past Tanner to lie about the whole thing. But I wouldn't put it past von Zeltner to have done the shooting either. Especially if he thinks it'll get Kipp or myself up in the air for solo combat."

"Solo combat, sir?" Ramsay's face and body tightened. "Isn't that a bit old? Something you'd have done in the Great War?"

"I am a bit old, Ram. And a bit odd. So is Kipp. So is von Zeltner. I expect if I don't do it, Kipp will the moment his arms have mended. He will be livid, absolutely livid."

"I'm sorry, sir. It's rotten luck for Uncle Jeremy and Aunt Emma. But I'd rather you didn't do the Albert Ball and von Richthofen thing from nineteen seventeen. Albert Ball lost that matchup, didn't he?"

Ben glanced at his son. "Sometimes, the way things roll out in your life, you're not left with any choice."

A phone rang. Everyone in the squadron was looking at Ben when a corporal shouted, "Scramble!"

For the longest moment no one moved.

"Right," Ben finally said. "Let's get back at it and throw Jerry out the back door for good."

Jane Fordyce's flat, London

"Grandfather!"

Jane threw her arms around Lord Preston after she opened the door to his knock.

"Hullo, my dear." Lord Preston hugged her. "I feared you might not be in. I tried calling."

"Oh, I've only just come back from the bunker. It seems I'm hardly ever here. I'm sorry. I must look a sight."

"You look splendid."

She laughed. "That's just what James would say. He must get it from you." She patted him on the back. "I have a twenty-four hour leave. I was actually going to pop over and see you in the morning. It's too difficult to get around at night during the raids. I'm so glad you're out of the hospital and doing well."

"I'm not quite at the top of my form, but a few more days will see me there."

She released him, smoothed down her WAAF uniform, and smiled. "Well. Fancy you having no trouble crossing London with Jerry overhead. Will you have some tea?"

"My dear…" Lord Preston could not finish his sentence. "My dear…" Again he stopped.

"Grandfather, it won't be any trouble. Let me just put the kettle on."

Lord Preston reached out for her arm and held it gently. "My dear…" he tried a third time.

"Whatever is the matter?" Jane placed her hand over his. "Is everything all right at home? Is Grandmother well? Mum told me she was getting along beautifully."

Lord Preston nodded. "She is—she's capital, I thank God." He did not let go of her arm. "My girl, there is something else."

Jane's smile left her face. "What is it? What's happened?"

"James…" It was all he could get out. "James…"

Jane's eyes went black as night. "He's wounded. He's hurt."

Lord Preston did not respond.

She pulled away. "I'll get my coat. I'll go to him. I don't care where he is. The RAF will get me a lorry."

Lord Preston finally forced the words out of his mouth and throat. "He's been killed. Shot down over the Channel. They've recovered his body. He's to be buried with his brother Peter. I'm so sorry, my girl, so very sorry."

Jane did not move. The blood left her face. "Are they sure?"

Lord Preston took off his hat and held it in his hands. "There is no doubt."

"But we were to be married, Grandfather. Before Christmas. I was to be his bride." Tears shot across her cheeks. "We'd talked about it. Made plans. If Peter died, James had sworn to marry me. On oath."

"I know, my girl."

"On oath. You can't break an oath. You *can't*."

"And he hasn't. Even in death he loves you. Even at the side of Christ he adores you. Both of the brothers do."

Jane covered her face with her hands. "I don't want James at the side of Christ. I don't want either of them at the side of Christ. I want them here, Grandfather, I want the two of them right here by my side."

"I know."

"I can't live anymore. I can't. God cannot take both of them away and expect me to survive. He's asking too much." She collapsed into Lord Preston's arms and buried her face in the shoulder of his thick coat, her tears soaking into the dark blue cloth. "I feel dead inside. Absolutely dead."

"I'm sorry, my girl. I can't begin…I can't begin…"

But Lord Preston broke down before he could finish his sentence. They held each other tightly as light flashed behind the drawn shades of the windows and the sound of exploding bombs reached their ears through the glass.

September–October, 1940

German raids on London and other British cities intensified during September. On September 24, a night bombing by more than two hundred and fifty aircraft set London ablaze. People began to flock to the underground tube stations for shelter, bringing food and bedding with them and camping out on the platforms. Even though bombs hit the Marble Arch tube station in September, killing twenty people, and the Balham tube station in October, killing sixty-eight men, women, and children, Londoners continued to seek refuge in the underground.

Washroom facilities and first-aid stations were set up, along with canteens that distributed food and drink. Thousands of bunks were put in place at almost eighty stations, and shelter marshals began to patrol the nightly gatherings.

"We must decide what we're going to do and where we're going to live," advised Lord Preston at a family meeting at the vicarage of St. Andrew's Cross. "Perhaps most of us ought to remove ourselves to Ashton Park and get well away from the bombing attacks on London."

Victoria glowered, on her feet and using a crutch as her ankle mended. "We are not going to run from the Nazis with our tails between our legs, Father."

In the end, it was decided to send the children to Ashton Park and have them under the care of Harrison and Holly. Montgomery also went there with two-year-old Paul, while Skitt, refused by the RAF, enlisted in the army. Victoria ordered a grumbling Tim to Ashton Park, and with her house a rubble, she moved in with her brother Robbie, who likewise had seen his daughter, Patricia, off to the family estate in Lancashire. Caroline packed Cecilia off to Ashton Park as well and, her own house also in ruins, joined Victoria and Robbie, though Robbie was at the townhouse very little due to his military duties.

Eva kept a room there, and so did Charles, who joined the ARP in early October. Libby, her townhouse gone, was welcomed in by Charlotte so that both navy wives now lived together under the same roof and used the same Anderson shelter in the backyard, while Colm was sent by train to Liverpool and Ashton Park along with the other children. Catherine and Albrecht had a tearful goodbye with Angelika, who traveled with Colm and Tavy to the estate, and were offered a set of rooms at the vicarage. Lord Preston was also at the vicarage, at Jeremy and Emma's invitation, continuing to sit as an MP in the House of Commons and to work as one of Churchill's advisors. Lady Preston relocated to Ashton Park to be with the children.

"The service you held for Mrs. Longstaff and Darrington and Norah was lovely," remarked Lord Preston the day after the funeral.

Jeremy took off his glasses and cleaned them with a small cloth. "Thank you. It was the very least I could do."

"And not only lovely but spiritually significant."

Lord Preston stood by the fireplace in the parlor. Photographs of Peter and James in their RAF uniforms were arranged on either side of the mantle with a vase of flowers in between. Emma watched the two men from her chair, her eyes dark. She had replaced the fresh cut flowers twice since James's death.

"I expect you should have liked to have said something at your son's funeral," said Lord Preston, taking down James's picture so he could examine it more closely.

"I'm not sure I could have borne up under the strain, to tell you the truth." Jeremy continued to rub at his glasses. "Full military honors. Ben and members of his squadron, especially Matthew and Ramsay, bearing the casket from the lorry to the gravesite at King's Cross. James resting alongside his brother Peter. The vicar at the church and the RAF chaplain conducting the service together. Ben delivering the eulogy. There is nothing more that I could wish for." He put his glasses back on. "Except a resurrection of the dead."

"Quite."

"Baron von Zeltner sent a note via the American embassy," said Emma from her chair. "And a handsome wreath."

"Von Zeltner!" reacted Lord Preston.

"We have hung the wreath in the library next to a picture of the twins at Oxford. The baron claims to have had nothing to do with shooting down Peter or James, though he admits the pilots were under his command."

"That's not what Lord Tanner broadcast."

"Von Zeltner says that was a propaganda stunt. And, he feels, a deliberate attack on the Danforth family approved by Goebbels."

Lord Preston put his hands behind his back. "I have wished a thousand times I had hired anyone but Lord Tanner to manage the hunting lodge in Scotland."

"The wheels of God and the wheels of human destiny are never motionless." Jeremy gazed at his sons' photographs. "We could have held Billy back until he turned twenty-one next year. But what would have been the point? He left Cambridge the day after James was reported missing and enlisted in the RAF. Evidently he had been talking with them above half a year. His physical examination found him flawless. They will rush him through the training as fast as they can."

"I'm not happy with that plan. Ben tells me the new recruits can rarely do more than take off and land in a Hurricane or Spitfire."

Jeremy shook his head, still looking at the pictures. "Billy would not be restrained."

Lord Preston turned to look at Emma. "How is Jane?"

"She is not at all well. She blames herself for the fact they took up flying in the first place. I wish you would go and see her again, Father. The poor girl is quite devastated."

He nodded, the lines on his face deepening. "Then I shall. Let me see the week out first." He coughed. "Kipp didn't move into Robbie's townhouse with Caroline and Victoria."

"No," Emma responded. "He has gone back to his rooms at Pickering Green. I'm sure he must be driving poor Sean around the bend. All Kipp wants is to get up and go after the bombers. And shoot down von Zeltner. But his arms are still weeks away from permitting that."

"But von Zeltner denied having anything to do with the twins' deaths."

"Kipp doesn't believe that."

RAF Pickering Green, Kent

At Pickering Green, Sean was drinking from a cup of tea and standing with a cluster of new recruits. Kipp, arms still in casts, was a few feet away.

"For those of you who have forgotten who I am, I'm Squadron Leader Sean Hartmann. This gentleman, Flying Officer Kipp Danforth, is recovering from his injuries and will soon be back at the helm. Until then, I'm Mother Goose. What do you think of our new pilots, sir?"

"I wish I was going up there with you," Kipp said. "Best of luck and God's blessing. It's all fast and furious once you engage the enemy. But should any of you notice an Me 109 with a black and yellow checker pattern, let me know as soon as you land, all right? If you shoot him down I'll be brassed off because that's something I very much want to do myself."

The recruits stared at him.

Sean read from a sheet of paper in his hand. "So we've got Flight Sergeants Packer and Peterson and Miller and Wilkie." Sean looked up at their faces. "Which is which?"

No one said a thing.

"Let's go down the row then. Who are you?"

"Packer, sir."

"Tall and thin." Sean looked at the next person. "And you?"

"Miller, sir."

"Short and thin. You look like a Quaker neighbor I had once. Next?"

"Peterson. Sir."

"Viking."

"Swedish background, yes, sir."

"And finally we have Wilkie."

"Yes, sir. No Swedish background at all, sir."

"No? That's a relief. I think one per squadron is enough. Where from?"

"Hampstead Heath, sir."

"Really? Ever read Bram Stoker?"

"No, sir."

"Well, Lucy the vampire was terrorizing people on Hampstead Heath. Your skin is fairly white, isn't it? Get out in the sun much?"

"Don't care for the summer heat, sir."

"No? What about mirrors?"

"Pardon me?"

Sean smiled. "Never mind, Wilkie the Vampire. Mirrors it is. Now listen up, all of you. When we go up, stick as close to me as you can. Once you're in combat, twist and turn like the devil was on your tail. Never fly straight and level for more than a few seconds at a time. Don't challenge the Me 109 in a dive—it has a fuel injected engine and you don't. The g-force will push the fuel out of your motor and you'll stall. On the other hand, if you want to get away, pull a tight turn because the 109 won't be able to follow you through that."

Wilkie and Miller nodded at the same time.

"Bear in mind that the tighter the turn, the stronger the g's. You'll black out. Don't be alarmed if that happens. You won't be gone long, and the stick will still be in your hand a few seconds later when you wake up."

Only Wilkie nodded.

"Everything will be happening at four hundred miles an hour," Sean continued. "I know you haven't had a lot of hours on Spits. Do your best. Get in close. Underneath and behind. Just a squirt. That's enough bullets to do the damage."

"A squirt?" Packer squinted at Sean. "Could you be more precise?"

"Count one and two," Sean replied. "You remind me of a Puritan."

"A quick count or a slow count?" asked Peterson.

"The Viking." Sean stared at him over the rim of his cup as he sipped his tea. "Take all the time you like. So long as it's no more than two seconds."

A ringing phone. A shout. "Fighters! Angels one five! Large formation!"

"That's more news than we usually get before we're in the clouds." Sean dropped his cup in the grass. "Jump in your kites. Climb to twenty thousand feet and we'll gain height on the enemy. Keep me in sight."

"How will we know it's you?" asked Wilkie, beginning to run.

"Everyone looks the same up there," added Miller, trying to run ahead of Wilkie.

"I have a dragon painted on my Spit now, do you see it, Mirrors? Do you see it, Quaker?" Sean vaulted into his cockpit. "There's a great spear going through its swastika heart. That's me. You can't miss that dragon, even in a fight."

Caroline and Victoria's townhouse, Camden Lock, London

Two weeks later, close to the end of September, Eva was sleeping in her room at Robbie's townhouse, where Caroline and Victoria had gone to live along with Charles and herself. Charles was asleep across the hall. It was one in the afternoon, but Eva and Charles had been dealing with the latest bombing attack on London till well past midnight.

"Beauty. Hey." It was Owen in his dark naval uniform and cap.

Eva wrinkled her nose. "Mm?"

"*Ich liebe dich.*"

She put her pillow over her head. "Who are you?"

"The man in the moon."

She began to laugh under the pillow. "Not in the middle of the day."

He sat on the edge of her bed. "Sometimes you can see the moon setting in the west in the daytime."

"Well, moon, you're disturbing my beauty sleep."

"I don't think that's true. You look spectacular."

"How would you know? You can't see my face."

"I can see the top of your shoulder and the gold of your hair. Takes my breath away."

"Oh, really, sailor?" Eva threw off her pillow and smiled up at him. "So if you have no breath, how are you going to be able to talk to me?"

"I don't want to talk."

He slipped his arms under her and lifted her off the bed, blankets and all, and began to kiss her on the lips. Finally she pushed him back with a gasp.

"Are you trying to kill me?" she asked, catching her breath.

"The last time you accused me of that I was trying to save you from a German fighter at Dunkerque."

"*Ja*, well, what are you trying to save me from now?"

"Too much sleep. I only have a day's leave. Instead of wasting it dreaming of me, why not spend it looking at me?"

She put her arms about his neck. "What makes you think I'm dreaming of you?"

"You would never waste your time dreaming of someone else, would you?"

"What a bold sea dog." She kissed the side of his face. "Who let you in the door?"

"Aunt Victoria."

"You couldn't have known which room was mine. All the doors look the same."

"Charles doesn't use perfume. You do."

She slapped his arm playfully. "You can't tell."

"I can."

She returned to kissing him. "Twice I've been woken up by air raids during the day. You're a pleasant surprise. Why'd they give you leave?"

Owen hesitated a moment as they kissed. Then he said, "I'm shipping out."

She immediately pulled away. "You're not."

"They're sending a bunch of us up to Scapa Flow in a fortnight. They haven't told me which ship yet."

"A fortnight. Thank goodness. At least we have some time. Will they give you another leave?"

"I hope so."

"You must get over to your mum's and see her."

"I will." Owen took off his dark blue cap. "What time do you go on duty?"

"Eight or nine."

"Make it nine."

"There might be an early raid."

He lifted long strands of her blond hair in his hand and put his lips to it. "I'll pray the Germans are late."

"Does God listen to your prayers?"

"Sometimes. You're alive, aren't you? Despite the fact that every night the Nazis are doing their best to kill you."

"Me and thousands of others."

"So far the bounders have missed. And I'll continue to pray that they miss."

She touched her forehead against his. "What shall I pray for you?"

"That if the *Bismarck* tries to break out into the Atlantic we'll be able to stop her."

"She's a big ship, isn't she?"

"Very big. I've seen some photographs from the German press. You can't see a lot of detail, of course, but she's a Goliath."

"So are you David?" She kissed his forehead. "What shall I pray for David?"

"That I have a great big slingshot in my hand the day *Bismarck* makes her run for blue water."

"Are you going to be on the *Rodney* or the *Hood*?"

"Either will do."

"All right. And another prayer for you to come back safely to port."

"I'm in port now."

"Oh, how glad I am for that." She reached up and kissed him again.

Parliament buildings, London

The next afternoon Lord Preston was standing in the street outside Church House, a large building where the House of Commons and House of Lords now met. Like many others, he was staring up at white vapor trails high in the sky. A siren had sounded and been followed by the all clear five minutes later.

"I'm sure the fight's over," he heard another MP say. "Otherwise they'd be herding us into the shelter."

"What are we looking at then?" asked a small man at the MP's elbow.

"A clash that occurred ten or fifteen minutes ago. The vapor trails are dispersing."

Lord Preston felt a hand on his arm. "Lord Preston." A woman's voice.

He turned. "Ah. How may I help you?"

A woman in a fine dress with glittering dark eyes smiled. "Please excuse my intrusion. I don't expect you to remember me, but I am Lady Kate Hall."

"Lady Kate Hall! Yes, yes, of course I remember you. What a delightful surprise."

"You must wonder what I am doing here since you have always seen me in the company of Lord Tanner Buchanan."

"Well, you will most certainly not have come from Germany and Lord Tanner today, hm?"

"No, not at all. My ship from America docked last night."

"Flying the American flag?"

"Yes. The vessel is registered in the United States."

"Any trouble with the U-boats?"

"None. As I say, the flag was prominently displayed."

"That didn't stop them in the last war. Well, well, how nice to see you, Lady Kate. Is there anything I can do for you?"

"I'm sailing for Spain in the morning on another American vessel. I should very much like to speak with you, if I may."

"Naturally. There is a lovely tearoom just down the way. Would that do?"

"So long as we have a quiet corner, my lord."

"Most certainly we will. I shall request it."

Once in the tearoom, they were seated at a table far from the others. Lady Kate tugged off burgundy gloves that matched her burgundy dress and hat as the waiter set a tray with teacups, cream, sugar, and scones before them.

"Shall I pour, my dear?" asked Lord Preston.

"I don't mind my tea a bit stronger, my lord."

"Very good. I'm of the same inclination when it comes to tea. Will you take a scone and some butter in the meantime?"

"Thank you very much." Lady Kate slit open her scone with one knife and buttered it with another. "You must wonder what all this is about."

"I expect—"

"I won't beat around the bush. I cannot abide…simply cannot abide Lord Tanner's behavior of late. I always knew he had his rough spots, of course, and there was that incident with the Scarborough woman, Lady Caroline—they practically got married!—yet such things were smoothed out and softened by his many kindnesses toward me. But since this silly war started in May, he's been impossible. I don't know what I shall do."

"I see. We have, of course, known the rough side of his hand on more than one occasion."

Her face drooped. She reached across the tabletop and took Lord Preston's hand.

"I have forced myself to listen to his broadcasts. Not all of them, but enough. I heard his talk about your grandson James. Talk is not the right word. That he should revel in death and killing…war is bad enough, but that he should glory in it?" Lady Kate picked up the teapot and poured into her cup and Lord Preston's. It was a dark stream. "I was in America at the time. I fired off a cable. 'No more of this,' I told him. 'Let Goebbels get another barking dog.' Do you know what he wrote back?"

"I don't."

"'Shut up,' he said. 'Keep your trap shut, go where I tell you to go, and do what I tell you to do. Return to Germany at once.'"

"That's unpleasant."

Lady Kate drained her teacup and refilled it. "More than unpleasant. I was going to break off our relationship then and there. But no, I thought. I won't do this from ten thousand miles away. That's not what an American woman does. I will give him a piece of my mind face-to-face, not from behind a telegraph key. So I am on my way to Berlin by way of Spain. But it was imperative I see you first."

"Why is that?"

"He will never apologize. Nor will Goebbels or Herr Hitler. So I must do it on their behalf. Someone must act civilized in an uncivilized time. That's the sole reason I'm here. To apologize for my fiancé's behavior. And Germany's. There was no call for him to broadcast what he did about the deaths of your two grandsons. It was despicable…utterly despicable. I shall tell him that to his face. And I shall add a slap to that face while I'm at it."

"Lady Kate." Lord Preston set down his cup. "I'm grateful for your sympathy, indeed, even your anger. But it was not you who committed the sin. Therefore I do not want the responsibility of atoning for it resting upon your young shoulders. God will deal with Nazi Germany and Lord Tanner in His own good time. We can fight the Heinkels and Messerschmitts in our skies, but we cannot lay a hand on the Buchanans and Hitlers. Not yet."

"I can."

"What do you mean?"

"I will be in Berlin in a few weeks."

"Yes, I understand that."

"I will add to the slap perhaps…something stronger."

"Lady Kate, you will be in Nazi Germany, not New York City. American or not, your neutrality will only protect you so far. I pray you will not do anything rash."

For the first time Lady Kate put cream in her tea. After she stirred it, she put the small spoon in her mouth and drew it out slowly.

"What you consider rash and what I consider rash may be entirely different, Lord Preston," she said.

A week after his first leave, Owen popped up again. This time he made his way to where Eva and Charles and their group were helping evacuate families from a row of houses beginning to catch fire from incendiaries. By the time the air raid was over and many of the fires had been put out,

Owen's uniform was scorched and reeked of smoke and oil and tar and burned rubber.

"Thanks awfully." Charles shook Owen's hand, dying flames throwing light on their bodies and faces. "It was grand to have your help."

"I didn't want to waste my leave waiting for you and Eva to show up back at the house. As it is, I gained back five hours of it."

A smile moved over Charles's lips and left. "Best of luck with the other nineteen."

A truck dropped them off at Robbie's townhouse. Victoria and Caroline fussed over them and set out tea and jam.

"Did any bombs fall near here, Mum?" Charles asked Caroline.

"No, we were all right. How did it go with you?"

"The same mess."

"Your uniform's ruined," Victoria told Owen. "I shall do my best to clean and press it for you, but I'm afraid you'll catch it when you get back to your naval base tomorrow."

"Once I tell them I was doing my bit during an air raid they won't say a thing, Aunt Vic."

"Have you spoken with your mother?"

"I dropped in on her in the afternoon, about teatime. We spent a couple of hours together and it was great fun. She had all sorts of news about Dad and the *Rodney*."

"Wonderful. Now get out of that uniform. And do a quick sponge bath. All three of you need that."

"I won't have anything to wear," protested Owen.

"I bought a robe for your Uncle Kipp," said Caroline. "Not that he's ever here to wear it. You can borrow that for now. In the morning you'll have a brand-new uniform."

"Don't get carried away, Caroline Danforth," snipped Victoria.

Owen changed out of his uniform in a water closet that had a sink and a toilet. He used a cloth to wash himself down. There was a rap on the door, and Aunt Victoria's hand came through a crack holding a navy-blue robe.

"Thanks, Aunt Vic," he said, taking it. "It's the right color, isn't it?"

"Just don't go racing off to save London in it or you shall have to buy Caroline and Kipp a new one."

"Right."

"Are you done in there?"

"I am. Be out in half a moment."

"Leave your uniform hanging up and I shall collect it in a bit. Eva needs to use the closet now."

"Eva? What's she been doing up till now then?"

"Letting the gentlemen go first."

"Charles has the other water closet? If I'd have known that I'd never have gone in here first."

"Well, she'll be glad you did. You were easily the worst of the lot. Did you scrub down your hair?"

"I did. It's still soaking."

"Come along to the kitchen once you're out. We have a pot of fresh tea brewing."

Owen slipped on the robe, knotted the belt at the waist, glanced at himself in the small mirror while he ran his hand through his wet hair, and stepped out of the closet. Eva was leaning against the wall opposite the door holding pajamas and a robe of her own.

"Hullo, that's the same color as my robe," he said.

"Fancy that."

"You talk more like an English girl all the time."

"Do I? Well, there's a reason for that, isn't there?"

"Listen, if I'd have known you'd be the odd man out I'd never have gone into the closet first."

"I don't mind at all—I really don't. Now I can take all the time I like without feeling guilty."

Owen looked up and down the hall and gripped her gently on her arms just below her shoulders. "Don't waste your time in there."

"What?"

"I like you fine just the way you are. In fact, I find it exciting."

"Are you daft? I smell like a sewer and my hair and face are as greasy as motorcar oil."

He kissed the side of her neck. "I don't mind."

"You're mad." She tried to push him away. "You'll soil your uncle's new robe to begin with."

"I'll buy him another. One kiss is worth twenty pounds."

"You really are mad. Stop it, Owen."

"When I came upon you tonight the fires had started, and the sweat and heat and grime were shining on your face, and there you were saving people's lives, and I thought, *My God, You have given me such a beautiful woman.* You were so attractive right at that moment I swore I wouldn't lay my head on my pillow before I'd kissed you looking the same way you looked then. And that's the way you look now, isn't it?"

Her mouth was half open. "I shouldn't have let you talk. You always bewitch me when you talk."

"It's true. I'll never forget that moment with the bombs falling and the houses bursting into flames and your face there, so sweet and so full of strength. I don't want a clean face to kiss. I don't want all that beauty scrubbed off. I want this." His large hands cupped her face and streaks of grease came off on his fingers. His kiss was strong and full.

"Crazy English boy with the blue eyes and curly dark hair," she said, returning his kisses. "What are you doing to me?"

"Nothing that the crazy German girl hasn't done to me already."

"Is that right?"

"It is." He pulled her in against his chest. "Heaven knows when I'll see you again. There won't be another leave. We're up to the Orkneys the day after tomorrow. I'm going to the *Rodney.*"

"Do you mean it? Are they truly sending you north this time?"

"They are."

"And to your father's ship?"

"Astonishing, isn't it? You'd have thought a clerk would have caught that."

"I don't know what to say. Now that it's actually happening it all seems rather sudden."

"Well, I know what to say, Eva. Don't spend your time washing your face in the sink. Spend it with me. I'll take your grime off with my own hands and lips if you must have it gone."

She hugged him with a fierce burst of strength. "My love, I do have to clean myself up. I couldn't possibly go to bed the way I am. A man could, but a woman couldn't. But since you say you'll remove my grime with your own hands then let's see you do it."

"I...I don't have a cloth or water or—"

"Of course you do." She tugged him into the water closet, shut the door, and locked it. "This is the perfect place. And here's the water."

She turned on the tap and began to spray him. He shouted for her to stop, but she kept her hand at an angle to the flow so that it squirted all over him. Finally he got an arm around her, pushed her back from the sink, soaked a cloth in the water with his free hand, and began to wipe at the skin around her eyes.

"Look at that," he said as she laughed and wrestled with his arm. "I didn't know you had blue eyes."

"No? After all this time?"

"I thought they were brown. I guess it was the dirt."

Eva laughed again, still wrestling. "Perhaps you're right."

"What else will I discover?"

She suddenly kissed him as hard as she could on the lips. "Keep at it and you'll find out, won't you?"

She was asleep at three in the afternoon when Owen left the house. His aunts had done wonders with his uniform, and it had never fit him better. But Eva didn't see how it looked on him. He kissed her cheek and hair and lips, and she murmured in her dreams. Then he was out the door and headed for the train station.

"You watch out now," his Aunt Victoria said. "That girl dotes on you. Your mother does. We all do. You must come back hale and hearty."

"I shall if you pray aright."

"Oh, we'll pray aright. You just do your part."

"Aye, aye, sir." Owen saluted. "I'll just pop in on Mum on my way to the station. All the best, you two."

Caroline lifted her hand in farewell. "So long, sailor."

"God bless," said Victoria, hugging her arms around her in a sudden October gust.

The vicarage, St. Andrew's Cross, London

That afternoon Lord Preston secluded himself in the library at the vicarage and listened to Lord Tanner give his daily broadcast. Lord Preston used the five minutes to pray for his former groundskeeper at the Scottish hunting lodge. He was aware the broadcast would offend Jeremy and Emma, so he kept the volume as low as possible.

"Ah, my poor friends, allies of Berlin and Marshal Blücher at Waterloo as we fought side by side against the perfidious French, what has possessed you to carry on with this useless struggle? Why not join the Greater

German Empire and save the lives of your women and children? Four hundred dead one night. Five hundred another. Handsome architecture ruined. Treasures of the past lost forever. Why? So Churchill can remain in power? Come, come. You cannot stop our bombers. No matter what the RAF does, they get through day after day and night after night. London is in ruins. Liverpool. Coventry. Stop this madness. Link arms with the Third Reich. Think what a wonderful day you could wake up to to-morrow—no bombs, no fires, no death. It's time to turn the page. You have fought bravely—foolishly, but bravely. Yet you must face the fact that your best pilots are dead. Men like Flying Officers Peter and James Sweet are in their graves, cold and hard and silent as rock while the *Luftwaffe* is ripe with a victorious spirit and a triumphant will. Why should we kill any more of your pilots? Why should we kill any more of your civilians? Choose today whom you will serve—the rotting old Empire of Churchill or the strong new Empire of Nazi Germany."

Lord Preston turned the radio off. There might have been more, but he didn't have the stomach to listen to it.

I confess I don't know how to pray, Lord God. I cannot say I do not wish him taken out of the picture and away from that microphone of his altogether. At the same time I pray for his soul; I pray it may be redeemed. I doubt he wants to be redeemed or even feels that he in any way needs redemption. Yet I pray for him just the same. Silence him and spare him. That is how I shall put it.

RAF Pickering Green, Kent

The next day Squadron Leader Sean Hartmann stood in an on-again, off-again drizzle at Pickering Green, tea in one hand and biscuit in the other, and spoke with his squadron.

"You've all done well…very well indeed. With Jerry's switch in tactics—coming in as high as thirty thousand feet over the Channel, just using Me 109s and Me 110s to attack by day so that every battle is a fighter-to-fighter combat—you've had to reach down and come up with your best and you've done it. Goering can't keep this up forever. The weather's getting more and more miserable. Stick to it a few more weeks and I promise you we'll have seen an end to the threat of invasion."

He sipped his tea before he carried on.

"So now we're going up to wait for those sinners at angels two five. That way we can get at them quickly whether they're flying at thirty thousand feet or twenty thousand. It takes too long for us to scramble after them and climb to high altitude. Once they've crossed the Channel they only need seventeen to twenty minutes to reach London. Heaven knows the city takes enough of a beating by night. Let's see what we can do to make it more bearable for them by day. Mirrors, Quaker, bag us some Hun, will you?"

"Yes, sir," Wilkie and Miller said at the same time.

"Puritan, Viking, you've each got two Me 110s. See if you can double that today. Every Jerry out of the air saves a life down below."

"I have the synchronization of the flying and the shooting down pat now, I think," replied Packer, squinting as raindrops spattered against his eyes.

"Not flying the same old way every time," added Peterson. "Trying new tricks, new angles of attack, coming in at Jerry with a new slant every time. That seems to help."

Sean smiled. "Right. Let's jump in our kites and get to twenty-five thousand feet quick as we can. We'll pounce on those Nazi mice like proper British alley cats."

As they broke up and moved away to their planes, several of them glanced back at the Officers' Mess. Kipp was framed in the doorway, one arm free of its cast.

Seeing him, Sean said to the others, "And keep one eye out for Moby Dick."

The vicarage, St. Andrew's Cross, London

The next afternoon Lord Preston was again home early from Church House. Emma was out for a visit with Jane. Jeremy was working in his office in the church building. Even though the vicarage was empty, Lord Preston shut the door to the library firmly and kept the volume on the radio as low as he could. Lord Tanner's words were still clear.

"I have with me in the studio today my American fiancée. I have asked her to add her voice to mine in an effort to persuade you to end this war against the German people."

"I wish my British friends well." It was Lady Kate Hall's voice.

Lord Preston had been leaning forward to listen to the broadcast. Now he leaned back in surprise, staring at the tall radio set as if he could see her face in it.

"I appeal to you once again in the spirit of Marshal Blücher of Waterloo, the German commander—we must be allies. My fiancée Katarina appeals to you in the spirit of your great friends in America."

"It is pointless to keep on fighting," said Lady Kate. "The cost is too high."

"Look at your casualties for October," Lord Tanner added. "It's horrendous. By our calculations, over six thousand civilians killed and over eight thousand badly injured. Many of them will never walk or talk again. For what? What sort of country will you have left to you in a few more weeks? How many people will want to live among ash heaps and blackened timbers? Death is in the air, death is on the ground, death is under your feet, and more death is yet to come. You wretched, miserable English, what has all your stubbornness bought you? Better the swastika than the Union Jack, better Hitler than Churchill, better the *Luftwaffe* to guard your skies than the RAF."

"And better death than dishonor," said Lady Kate.

Suddenly there was a shot. And another shot.

It sounded to Lord Preston as if chairs fell over and doors slammed. The radio began to give off a high-pitched squeal.

"Fight, England! Fight and you will win! Hold on now and you will win! Believe me! There will be no invasion! *Morgenstund' hat Gold im Mund*!"

The broadcast went dead. Then, suddenly, Nazi marching music blared from the radio set.

A moment later it was a speech by Hitler with the chant "Hitler, Hitler, Hitler" rising from the audience whenever he paused. Lord Preston immediately recognized it as a speech from the month before, delivered in early September. While his mind whirled, trying to understand what had happened to Lord Tanner and Lady Kate, thinking Gestapo had come into the studio and shot her, a narrator came on and translated Hitler's speech into English.

"If the British Air Force drops two, three, or four thousand kilos of bombs, we will drop a hundred thousand, two hundred thousand, four hundred thousand kilos or more in one night. If they declare that they will attack our cities on a large scale, we will wipe theirs out! We will put a stop to the game of these night-pirates, so help us God!"

Deafening screams of support forced Hitler to pause.

"The hour will come when one or the other of us will break, and that one will not be National Socialist Germany!"

A roar that made the speaker in the radio set buzz.

"In England they're filled with curiosity and keep asking, 'Why doesn't he come?'"

Laughter.

"Be calm. He's coming, he's coming!"

More laughter. Cries of "*Heil* Hitler" and "*Sieg Heil, Sieg Heil, Sieg Heil.*"

"Hail victory!" the translator said in a loud voice.

Lord Preston snapped the radio set off with the sharp twist of a dial.

October 29, 1940
The skies over Kent

"A tight left, Mirrors! A tight left! He's on your tail!"

Wilkie saw the tracers from the Me 109 zip over his starboard wing as he banked hard to the left. Within seconds his vision began to blur as he made the turn tighter and tighter and faster and faster. Suddenly everything was gray and he couldn't feel his hand on the stick. Then he blacked out. Five seconds later he blinked open his eyes and saw the German fighter that had been behind him was now off his port wing. He rammed the stick over to the left again and came at the enemy plane side-on. The pilot was a pink face with an oxygen mask. Wilkie pressed the fire button. The smell of burnt cordite filled the cockpit. The Me 109 slewed to the left, smoke pouring out of its engine.

"Well done, Mirrors!" Sean watched the Messerschmitt drop into a dive and its pilot parachute out. "Heads up, Quaker! Dropping out of what sun we've got! Shake him!"

Hurtling at another Me 109, Sean lost sight of Miller's Spitfire that had gone into a short, stiff climb and a loop. His own target flashed over with fire as he thumbed the gun button. Pulling away he saw it explode in a blur of orange. He caught a quick glimpse of Packer and Peterson turning and tumbling with almost acrobatic precision, German fighters diving after them, overshooting the Spitfires and falling into the range of the eight machine guns in their wings, large holes opening in the German fuselages and tail fins.

At the last moment, before he was swallowed up by a dark cloud, Sean spotted Miller finishing his loop on the tail of the Messerschmitt chasing him, and jagged chunks of metal flying from the Me 109 and spinning through the air as Miller peppered the Messerschmitt. A minute later, once he had emerged from the cloud, Sean saw the fight was miles behind him to the east and banked his Spitfire in that direction. By the time he reached the dogfight again it was over, the Germans fleeing south across the Channel, some of his squadron racing after them, the others heading for Pickering Green.

"Squadron Leader to all pilots," he said into his R/T. "Check your fuel levels and make your way back to base. Prescott will have a lot of green forms for you to fill out. Congratulations."

"We got them this time, sir," Wilkie radioed. "I'm sure we knocked eight or nine out of the sky."

"Eight or nine bombs that won't drop on Camden or the West End or any part of London. I say again, well done, Mirrors, Viking, Quaker, Puritan…well done, all of you."

"This calls for a spot of tea, Squadron Leader."

Sean relaxed radio discipline for a moment and laughed over the R/T. "Enough tea to float the British Isles, I think, Flight Sergeant Wilkie. I trust you'll join me in a cup?"

"As many cups as possible, sir."

"That is a lot of cups, Flight Sergeant."

"Yes, sir."

October 30, 1940
The prime minister's residence, 10 Downing Street

"Come in, Lord Preston. Shut the door." Churchill lit a cigar and settled in his chair.

Lord Preston took the first seat he saw in the small room.

"Never been in here before, eh?" asked Churchill.

"Not in this room, no, Mister Prime Minister."

"Hardly anyone knows about it. Scarcely bigger than a wardrobe. One of my favorite rooms. No one ever finds me here. They think it's a broom closet."

Smoke from his cigar quickly filled the space. Lord Preston put his hand over his mouth and nose. Churchill didn't notice.

"I have something rather singular to relate to you, William. That Lord Tanner fellow who used to be a servant of yours years ago—Goebbels' barking dog with his propaganda broadcasts. He was shot and killed during his broadcast the other day. And it was his fiancée who shot him. An American woman, Lady Kate Hall. She had a small pistol in her stocking or some such thing, or so MI-Six tells me. I understand she was supposed to make her own pitch for our surrender. After she shot him she shouted into the microphone for England to fight on. '*Morgenstund' hat Gold im Mund!*—The early morning hour has gold in its mouth!' A German proverb. I expect she was addressing that to our fighter pilots. It is the most extraordinary thing. Did you know her at all?"

Lord Preston was stunned by the news, and it took him a long moment to answer. He sat looking at the prime minister.

"I did, Winston. Or I thought I did. She had a great deal of pluck. But I confess I did not see this coming."

Churchill grunted. "Neither did Lord Tanner or the Gestapo, apparently." Churchill drew on his large cigar. "We knew the invasion barges were dispersed in mid-September. Though part of the reasoning behind that was to prevent the RAF and Royal Navy from destroying them. Now we have evidence that just in the past few days several military units earmarked for the invasion have been deployed elsewhere." A gleam came into Churchill's eye through the haze of smoke. "He's calling it off, William. Herr Hitler has decided he doesn't have all the cards he needs for a successful assault on Britain's shores. Even though the tides would have remained favorable till the fourth of November, he's pulling out troops. We must remain vigilant, of course, but the weather is turning in our favor as well. A heavy chop in the Channel, strong winds, heavy rain…the bleakest and, for our purposes, the best sort of English weather. The same sort of brew that scuttled the Spanish Armada's plans. Thank God for the miserable weather He's given Britain from time immemorial, eh?"

Lord Preston was still taking it all in. "Yes, thank Him." He stared at a portrait of William Pitt the Younger on the wall behind Churchill. "Do we know what happened to Lady Kate Hall?"

"The Nazis won't say. She is an American, after all. They don't want to ruffle Roosevelt's feathers."

Lord Preston continued to stare at the portrait. "Silenced but not spared. That was the judgment on Lord Tanner."

Churchill narrowed his eyes and puffed on his cigar. "What in heaven's name do you mean by that?"

All Hallow's Eve, October 31, 1940
RAF King's Cross, West Sussex

"Are we going up, Squadron Leader?" asked Ramsay over his R/T.

"Are we going up, sir?" pressed Matt, right after Ramsay.

The pilots had been sitting in their cockpits for more than an hour, canopies pulled to, drizzle from low gray clouds coming and going.

"Jerry's launched his attacks in rotten weather before," Ben snapped. "Clouds and wet didn't stop him through August and September. Count your blessings and stay in your offices."

But a few minutes later Ben radioed Operations in their hut a hundred yards away. "Do you have any trade for us?"

"Nothing on the radar yet, Squadron Leader. No orders from Uxbridge. Please maintain your positions."

There was a cloudburst, and the rain pelted the wings and windscreens of the Spitfires. The pilots and planes sat on the runway another ten minutes watching gray raindrops bounce off gray wingtips. Ben radioed Operations a second time.

"I ask again, do you have any trade for us?"

"We have nothing, Squadron Leader."

"It's raining cats and dogs. Permission to stand down."

"Permission granted. Stand down, Squadron Leader. There's nothing happening in any of the sectors."

"Right, you all heard that," Ben said over the R/T. "I'll meet you lot in the Officers' Mess."

"The Germans aren't coming, are they, sir?" asked Matt.

"It looks not. We have, I thank God, a change in the weather."

The bombers did not come the next day. Or the day after. Or the day after that. During the daylight hours they never came again.

11

December 24, 1940
Ashton Park

My dearest Terry,

There you are on the *Mighty Hood* bobbing about, and here I am rooted to the spot. Well, not actually rooted, I do move around a bit. We have all gone up to Ashton Park for Christmas to be with Lady Grace and Mum and the children. I have squirreled myself away in the Nelson Room because it makes me feel closer to you. The rest of the household is asleep after a rather rambunctious evening— you remember how lively our Christmas Eves can be.

The air war that was filling our skies all summer and fall appears to be gone forever. The Blitz is still on—it was a very blitzy few days before Christmas—but all the dog-fights and attacks on the airfields and the daylight raids on London are nothing but memories. Of course the night bombing is bad enough, but thank goodness we've weathered the storm the *Luftwaffe* sent our way for so many months.

I had hoped to see Jane here, but she is just finishing up her flight training and couldn't get away. She expects to start ferrying aircraft in January. The last time we got together I thought she was doing rather well, but she admits to having her midnight days, as she calls them. Poor thing, she has lost a great deal of weight, far too much really. Please pray for her.

Robbie is posted to Africa immediately after Christmas, and so is Skitt, who is now a corporal in Robbie's regiment. Patricia will stay here at Ashton Park with Mum. Skitt's little boy, Paul, is already here with Montgomery, so that's taken care of. But tears all around as more of our lads head off to fight this awful war that was forced upon us.

Owen was supposed to join his father on *Rodney*, but once they realized his father was an officer on the ship they transferred him to HMS *Prince of Wales*—a ship that hasn't even been finished up yet and that is sitting in the docks at Birkenhead. He's still sulking but bearing up well and writes Charlotte that he is a Leading Seaman now, a nice little promotion for him.

As for Edward, his letters are few and far between to Charlotte, but she reports he is getting along though chafing at the bit for some action. He's hoping the *Bismarck* and *Prinz Eugen* will try to break out to the Atlantic and that he'll be the one to bar their passage. I suppose you and everyone else on the *Hood* feel the same way.

I should tell you Kipp's other cast is due to come off in the new year and no one is looking forward to that, least of all Mum and Dad and Caroline. You know he has this thing about hunting down Wolfgang von Zeltner. He holds him responsible for the deaths of the twins. Of course he'll have to get the strength in his arms up to snuff, and he'll need to take a refresher on the new Spitfires, but you and I both know none of that will hold Kipp back for long. The whole thing is rather a cause for concern. When Sean was on leave earlier in the month he said Kipp reminded him of Captain Ahab after the great whale.

I'm getting sleepy, so I'll put my pen down for now and get this in the post first thing after the holidays. All our boys in the squadrons are fine, including Sean at Pickering Green and Ben, Ramsay, and Matt at King's Cross. If I've got it right, Billy is posted to the new RAF base at Hunters Down, which is an odd coincidence because I'm sure Jane told me that her first task would be to help get a lot of Spits to the base in January and February. I gather it's not quite operational yet. Well, it will do her good to see a familiar face.

I'm positively knackered. I love you with all my heart.

Your Libby

December 27, 1940
HMS Hood, *the North Atlantic*

Dear Lib,

I haven't heard from you since Henry VIII was on the throne. That's how it feels. Mail takes so long to reach us. And I hardly know what to write if I don't have anything from you or Jane to write back to. The censors chop up every letter that mentions our whereabouts or what we're doing, so what is there to say? Mind you, I don't think they care if the Germans know we had a splendid Christmas dinner, so I can tell you about that. I expect it wasn't as lavish as what you had in London or Ashton Park, but it certainly cheered up the crew. A little bit of action in forty-one would go a long way to putting some zest back in the lads.

Hope and pray all is well. Miss you terribly. I so wish I could take you in my arms again and disappear to that little beachside cottage you ferreted me away to years ago. Plenty of time once there's peace and Hitler's in the grave.

All my love,

Terry

January 2, 1941
Camden Lock, London

My Terry,

I expect you will have heard about the firebombing on the night of December 29. I'm so sorry I couldn't get a letter off to you sooner than this, but we are as well as can be expected. You needn't fret any longer. Jane was far from London and out of harm's way, so please don't lose any more sleep over her or me.

Oh, but it was horrid—it was diabolical. The city was a great Guy Fawkes bonfire from one end to the other. Heaven knows how many people were killed. And the tide of the Thames was at its lowest, so it was harder for the fire crews to pump water onto the blazes. Of course the Nazis would have planned for that.

St. Andrew's Cross is gone. Completely gutted. It was a Sunday, and we had all gathered at the vicarage for a family meal and prayers and then a service at the church. The incendiaries began to fall, and we simply could not put them all out. Jeremy got badly burned in the attempt, and he's laid up now. Dad told me sixteen or seventeen churches or more were burned to the ground. St. Paul's Cathedral would have been one of them, but they managed to beat back the flames. You must have seen the photograph the Daily Mail reporter took of St. Paul's dome surrounded by fire and smoke.

The entire neighborhood was devastated. What a shocking night. Like some sort of visit to hell, a visit no one wanted to make. The only thing we were able to do was keep the fire from spreading to the vicarage. But now there is no church for the vicarage to be part of. I am not sure what Jeremy and the Church of England will do about all this. It's a proper mess.

I can relate one bright spot to you, and then I must get this in the mail. Eva is with the ARP, as you know, and so is Charles. They helped fight a fire and evacuate an entire neighborhood the flames were threatening. Indeed the whole area went up like a torch for blocks and blocks. Some of the firefighters working alongside the ARP were killed. How Eva and Charles came through with only a few cuts and burns is beyond me. I can only use the word miracle—what other word would suit? They helped get about three hundred people out, and here's the thing. Long after other ARP volunteers and fire crews had retired, the pair of them remained in the area, saving as many as they could at great danger to themselves. It's quite marvelous really. Dad tells me they are going to get some sort of special medal for what they did. The other astonishing bit is Kipp went looking for Charles and Eva, he was frantic, and he helped them with the last row of houses. Then he hurried them out to safety along with the rest of the evacuees. Eva says Charles embraced Kipp, and there were tears on Charles's face. Who would have thought it possible after all Charles's antagonism and the dark mood he was in since Lord Tanner was shot and killed? But Caroline has been praying like a nun for all her children, Matt and Charles in particular. That such a grace should emerge from such a hell can only be the touch of God.

Must post this note so you know all is well.

My love and prayers,

Your Libby

February 4, 1941
HMS Hood, *the North Atlantic*

Dearest Libby,

I thanked God when I got your letter—literally dropped to my knees in my cabin. We had read all about the firestorm the German bombers unleashed, but none of us with London family knew how things stood with wives and children and sweethearts. So on the one hand, I slept like a baby after I heard from you. On the other hand, I woke with a burning anger to put paid to Adolf Hitler and all his Nazi war machines. If we come to blows with *Bismarck* five minutes after I sign this note, it couldn't be soon enough for me or any of us on board the ship.

I love you.

Terry

Friday, February 14, 1941
RAF Hunters Down, Hampshire

"Hullo. I think you've brought me my very own plane."

Jane had been pulling off her leather flight helmet and gloves as she walked across the grass airstrip. She turned at the sound of the voice. "What's that?"

"I say, you've finally brought my Spit to me and it looks marvelous. Bless you, Flight Sergeant." Billy Sweet bowed. "It's always an occasion when the Women's Auxiliary Air Force drops in from the heavens."

Jane laughed and then bit her lip. "Oh, Billy, you're such a card. It's so nice to see you. I had no idea you were at Hunters Down." She hugged him briefly and patted him on the back. "You look so much like Peter with your ginger hair and sound so much like James when you talk. It's bitter-sweet, isn't it?"

"I'm sorry, Jane."

"What do you have to be sorry about? It's marvelous that you look like your brothers. It just gives me a bit of a sting, that's all."

He didn't reply.

Awkwardly, feeling out of place with Billy at the airfield, she tried to be playful. "When did you lose your freckles?"

"Flight training. My first solo chased them right off my face."

She laughed again.

He noticed the rings on her fingers. She followed his eyes.

"I'll never take them off," she said. "Not for anyone."

"I didn't know you'd been given a proper diamond."

"It was from James. I'd agreed to marry him."

"Did Peter know?"

"He was to be best man. But no, he never knew."

Billy put his hands in his pockets and looked over his shoulder at the windsock. "How are you getting back then?"

"There will be a vehicle in the morning."

"Look here. Why don't you drop your gear in the room they've assigned you and let me take you out for a plate of fish and chips in the village? The pub food is very good."

"I'm all in, actually. I was up at the crack of dawn."

"You have to eat, Jane. Or at least the Jane I knew had to eat."

"I'll eat something after I wake up in the morning. Promise."

"Come on, Jane. I haven't seen you in months. Let me treat you. Isn't that what the Sweet brothers are supposed to do?"

"Two of them were."

"Well, now here's the third. You don't have to marry him but you jolly well can't turn your back on him."

"I can, you know."

"Let me get you a nice cup of tea and a hot plate of fish and chips. While you eat I can tell you what a spectacular pilot Billy Sweet is and how he far outshines anyone living today."

She put her hand to her mouth. "I shouldn't be laughing. Why am I laughing?"

"That's the Sweet way."

"It is, isn't it? Next you'll be telling me you have some note from your brothers that you're to take care of me if something happens to both of them."

"I do have that note."

"I'd like to see it." She pinched him on the cheek. "No more Sweets in my life. You're much too young, it's far too soon for me, and in any case, I'd much prefer it if we remained second or third cousins, or whatever we are, and good friends. All right?"

"I'm almost twenty-one."

"And I'm almost twenty-four. I'll have fish and chips with you in the village if you agree to my terms. Otherwise it's time for my nap."

Billy made a face. "I really am supposed to take care of you."

"Well, you can by feeding me. That's all I need, that's all I want. And I won't take anything more than that from you. I mean it, Billy. You're the brother that stays the friend, charming as you are and dashing as you look. Four other WAAFs flew in with me. Chat them up. Think of me as your big sister."

"But you're not. And it's Valentine's Day."

"As far as you and I are concerned, there's no such thing as Valentine's Day. Now, will you walk me into the village on those terms or do I find a pillow where I can lay my head?"

"I won't walk you there," he replied.

"You won't?"

"The squadron has bicycles. Come on then, Sister Jane."

"Sister Jane. You make me sound like a nun."

"That's about the measure of my relationship to you, isn't it?"

She patted his face. "Don't pout. Let me get out of my gear and I'll be right with you."

He flashed a sudden smile that made his face as bright as his ginger hair. "I'll fetch the bikes."

Jane found the room she was sharing with two other WAAFs and peeled off her heavy flight jacket.

"Who was that you were talking with?" asked one of the WAAFs as she brushed out her hair. "You don't waste any time, do you?"

"Oh, don't talk rot." Jane sat on the edge of her bed and tugged off her leather and fleece flight pants. "He's a cousin. He's been posted here. There's nothing more to it than that."

"If that's the case, you don't mind if I strike up a friendship, do you? He's on the good side of gorgeous."

"I don't mind at all, Alice." Jane smiled and took the brush from her friend's hand and began to use it on her own hair. "But first, he's promised me fish and chips. After that you can do whatever you want with him."

Alice laughed. "That sounds fair."

A week later Jane and Alice and another WAAF ferried in three more Spitfires for the new air base. Alice lost no time in getting out of her flight gear and into a fresh WAAF uniform and heading off with Billy in a motorcar for a larger town twenty miles away.

"Do you feel all right about that?" asked the other WAAF as she and Jane took turns in the shower after Alice disappeared with Billy.

"Of course I feel all right, Margaret," Jane replied. "Why shouldn't I feel all right? He's a handsome boy and Alice is a pretty girl. They look splendid together."

Margaret toweled down her red hair. "Think how splendid you'd look on his arm."

"For heaven's sake. Why is everybody going on about Billy and me? He's too young—"

"He isn't, you know," interjected Margaret.

"—and it's too soon."

"You told me your fiancé died almost six months ago. That's half a year."

"It's not long enough. And Billy is the brother of my fiancé…both of my fiancés."

"So?"

"So I don't want any more brothers. Ever."

"Are you sure, Jane?"

"I'm jolly well sure. I don't want to hear anything more about him. I shall request that I not ferry aircraft to this base after this assignment. You and Alice can handle that. I'll take care of Middle Wallop."

"Suit yourself."

"I intend to, thank you."

Jane's request was denied, and she found herself back at Hunters Down in the middle of March. She and Alice were flying in replacements for aircraft that had been damaged in combat. The RAF had been conducting what it called Circus operations since the middle of January, with British fighters and bombers attacking German targets in Europe at the same time. A number of RAF aircrew had already been lost over France or in the cold waters of the Channel. As Jane yanked back her canopy and spotted a cluster of pilots standing by one of the hangars, she immediately experienced a rush of bad feelings.

"What's up, do you suppose?" she asked Alice as they walked across the runway.

"I hate to ask, but I suppose we must."

The men avoided their eyes when Alice and Jane came up.

"Cheers, mates," Alice greeted them. "Storm brewing?"

No one responded. One of the men offered them a package of cigarettes. Alice took two and stuffed the extra in her jacket pocket.

"Right," she said. "I've got a smoke out of you. Now maybe you could tell me what's going on? We've brought two new Spits in for your squadron."

"We'll be needing a lot more than that." The man who had offered her the cigarettes nodded his head south toward the Channel. "A bit of bad luck. Two of our lads have bought it, and another two are missing."

The familiar feeling of ice in Jane's stomach and along her back and arms went right through her.

Alice accepted a light from one of the men. "Who's gone?"

"Burton and Chambers."

"Who's missing then?"

"Addison. And your chum, Billy Sweet."

Alice continued to smoke without flinching. "I see."

"No one saw either of them go down. If they parachuted into France, they're prisoners of war and that's that. But if they went into the drink and there's no one to pick them up, they've had it."

"They've got their Mae Wests, don't they?"

"The water's like the North Pole."

Jane went to her room and sat on the edge of her bed. She didn't want to cry, but she couldn't stop herself. Alice came in and put an arm around her.

"You'll be all right," said Alice.

"No, I don't think I will."

"Feelings for your cousin?"

"Yes...of course I have feelings. He's family."

"If he made it back in and I offered him up to you for a date, what would you say?"

"What?"

"If I went out with Flying Officer Cigarette there—he's not half bad—and let you have my Billy for the evening, would you take me up on it?"

"Of course not. This isn't a game. If he comes back in I shall give him a hug and thank God and then go on about my business."

"I ought to say that was my final offer, but I'll give you until he lands safely. That will help you know what you feel or don't feel about him."

Jane snapped up her head, her cheeks wet. "Are you deaf? I don't feel anything other than what a cousin feels for a cousin."

"I see it otherwise."

"You do? How's that?"

"I've watched you watching us. Not much of the cousin thing about your eyes then, is there?"

"You're mistaken."

"Women fool men. Women even fool themselves. But they don't fool other women."

There was a fast knocking on the door.

"What is it?" asked Alice sharply.

"Flying Officer Sweet's coming in! He's trailing smoke, but he's coming in."

The two women rushed out. The Spitfire swooped straight down, one wing dipping, bounced three or four times, slewed in a circle, and came to a violent stop, its tail rising as its nose plowed into the grass and dirt. Flames began to ripple along the fuselage.

"Get him out!" Alice and Jane heard a man shout. "You've got less than half a minute!"

A rescue truck was already roaring across the runway, but Jane couldn't stand still.

"Where are you going?" Alice grabbed Jane by the arm. "You can't do anything."

Jane shook Alice loose and began to run. "Eva pulls men from burning buildings. Why can't I pull Billy from a burning plane?"

"Get back!" one of the rescue crew shouted at her as they pumped water over the plane.

Jane jumped onto the wing and pulled at the canopy with all her strength. One of the rescue crew leaped up to help her. With a crack the canopy opened and slid back. Jane took Billy's head and shoulders in her arms while the man beside her tore off the seat straps. Billy's eyes were closed, and blood had dried at the corner of his mouth.

"I'll get his legs!" the man barked. "Have you got his head?"

"Yes."

"Let's go. Smartly now. One, two, three—heave!"

They half dragged, half carried him out of the cockpit and moved him as far away from the plane as they could. The others in the rescue crew continued to hose down the wings and fuselage. Smoke rolled over the airfield.

"Are you hit, sir?" asked the man, bending over Billy after they had laid him on the grass.

Billy's eyelids barely moved. "Don't know," he managed to get out.

Jane continued to cradle his head with her hands. "There's blood at the side of your mouth."

"Bit my tongue." He tried to look up at her. "Fancy having you hold my head in your lap, cousin."

"Shut up."

The man from the rescue crew looked at her in surprise.

Tears were cutting down her cheeks. "It wouldn't surprise me if you arranged this whole affair with the *Luftwaffe* just so you could snag my feelings and give them a go."

"Arrange getting shot down?"

"I wouldn't put it past you, Billy Sweet. You're cut from the same cloth as your brothers."

"Clerical cloth?"

"Sweet, gorgeous, and clever. And impossible for me not to care about no matter how hard I try."

"So you do have feelings for me?"

"I said I did, didn't I?"

"Does this mean—?"

"It doesn't mean anything at all. Here comes the ambulance. We'll talk later—once they've given you a clean bill of health. *If* they give you a clean bill of health."

"Nothing will keep me from having a clean bill of health right now. You're better than a shot of morphine."

"Shut up." Jane still had tears on her cheeks.

Billy Sweet walked out of the infirmary in his flight gear a half hour later.

"That's it?" demanded Jane. "That's all?"

"It is."

"What about the blood?"

"I told you. I bit my tongue."

"I think you did that on purpose too."

"Think what you like. You always have." He shoved his hands in his pockets. "There are problems that have to be dealt with, though they are not of a medical nature."

"What problems?" asked Jane.

"I promised the night to Alice weeks ago."

"Is that what you think? I've made my own arrangements. Or she has. Alice said we could have the evening together if we wanted it. Just this once."

"She did?"

"She did."

"Why would she do that?"

"Ask her."

Billy shook his head. "No, I think not. She might change her mind." He gestured with his thumb. "I have to talk with the intelligence officer and fill out some forms. Will you wait?"

"Of course I'll wait." Jane folded her arms over her chest. "I'm sorry about your men."

"Thanks. The war didn't end with the fight over Britain. That was just the opening bell." He began to walk away, stopped, and looked back. "You look absolute in an Irvin flight jacket."

"I have it on because of the wind. It's sharp."

"I don't care why you have it on, Jane. You look absolute."

"Absolute what? What you're saying doesn't make sense."

"It does to me."

An hour later, as they ate and chatted in the village pub, Jane reached across the table and put her hand over his.

"I can't have you die, Billy Sweet," she said, cutting him off in mid-sentence. "It was too hard with your brothers. I can't go through that again. You must live forever."

Billy splashed more malt vinegar onto his chips. "Then I shall."

"Thank you, but I just said it to say it. You can't guarantee immortality. I wish you could. I suppose that and your age are the things that have held me back from even dreaming of dreaming about you."

"I like older women."

"You don't even know any older women except me."

"Well, you're the only woman I like."

"Right. What about Alice?"

"Alice was an interlude," Billy said, popping a chip into his mouth. "Until you came to your senses."

"Really?"

He shrugged. "She's very cute. But I hoped going out with her might make you look at matters differently."

Jane tapped her fingers on the side of her teacup. "Alice swears it did."

"Did it or didn't it?"

"Billy, all this is happening faster than the new Spitfire Mark Fives doing an attack run. I fly them now, so I know how fast they can go. I can't go that fast, Billy. I care about you more than I want to admit. I have feelings I don't want to own up to. You're too beautiful, you're too fun, you're too much like your brothers, and on top of that, you have your own little twists I used to think were cute but which now I find far too attractive. So I want you to take me back to my room and we'll talk again when I ferry more aircraft down here. I'm getting trained on the Hurricane II and your other squadron here is slated to get those in short order. I'll be back in two weeks."

"What? That's tonight's date? That's it?"

Jane got up. "That's our date."

"It was no different than buying you fish and chips when you were my cousin."

"I still am your cousin. After a fashion."

"This is quite a disappointment."

"Is it? Well, Billy, I need some time to sort myself out when it comes to you, and my reaction to your crash landing is not the most useful way to do that." She made her way to the doors of the pub. "Will you cycle back with me?"

"Of course I will."

"It's actually a clear evening, so the ride need not be as disappointing as the date."

Billy put a few shillings on the table. "It won't be. It's pleasant enough just to be around you."

"Do you mean that?"

He smiled and opened the door for her. "I do mean it. Come on. Let's have a bit of a race."

"Oh, I can't pedal fast in a skirt."

"No excuses from the Women's Auxiliary Air Force."

Back at her room, Jane washed up, pulled on her pajamas, and climbed into bed but did not find sleep. When Alice came in at midnight she was still awake.

"How was it?" Jane asked.

"It was an adventure, I'll say that." Alice sat on Jane's bed. "How about you?"

"Fish and chips, a chat, and home."

"That's it?"

"That's all I wanted."

"Well, you don't look like a person who's satisfied."

"I'm confused."

"Sure sign of love."

Jane made a face. "I want him to be close to me, but then I don't want him to be close to me. I want to chat with him, but then I don't want to chat with him. I'm only certain about one thing—I have no wish for him to die like his brothers."

"I expect that's the biggest barrier, isn't it? Flying Officer Cigarette—Albert—told me he thinks they'll be doing this 'leaning into France' stuff for months to come." Alice gripped one of Jane's hands. "To my mind, you have one of two choices, my dear. Take him in your arms—"

"I don't want to take him in my arms."

"—or shun him completely. Nothing else will do. You're either in for a penny, in for a pound, or you're not in at all."

"Then I'm not in at all."

"Fine, love. I'll back your request to be assigned to other bases when it comes to ferrying aircraft. Any other air bases but this one."

Jane exhaled slowly. "Suits me."

For more than a month Jane flew aircraft to other airfields that were "leaning into France" and carrying out Circuses. As she met and spent time with different pilots and touched down at different airstrips, she was confident Billy Sweet would eventually be dislodged from her thoughts and feelings. But a day came when Margaret and Alice were both so ill from the flu they couldn't climb into their Spitfire Mark Vs, let alone ferry them to Hunters Down. Jane and another WAAF, Shirley Thomas, were ordered to take the Spitfires to Hampshire and Hunters Down. As Jane flew, she rehearsed what she would do when she reached Billy's air base.

I shall land the plane and go immediately to my room and to bed. I shall not see anyone and shall leave orders that I'm not to be disturbed. In the morning I'll be up and gone, and that will be that.

As she circled Hunters Down and began to descend, she saw Billy getting into his Spitfire. He hadn't put his leather flight helmet on yet, and his shock of bright hair was obvious. She looked away but not soon enough. A warmth went through her from head to foot, and for a brief moment she imagined what it would be like if he wrapped his arms about her and held her with so much strength she could barely get her breath. She pushed the warmth and the daydream out of her.

No. Absolutely not.

Shortly after she landed, Billy took off with three other Spitfires.

It was four in the afternoon. Shirley wanted to nap, so Jane took a bicycle, pedaled to the village on her own, ordered fish and chips at the pub, and lingered over her tea, trying to empty her mind of intrusive images of Billy. When a couple kissed briefly at a table nearby, the sensation of what Billy's lips might be like on hers flashed across her mind. The force of it made her bow her head, close her eyes, and take a deep breath.

This is ridiculous. He's just a boy.

She cycled around the village a half hour and headed to the base in a silvery glow of spring light. She saw immediately that the four Spitfires hadn't returned. She glanced at her watch. It was after six.

"Come on then," she murmured as she leaned her bike by her door. "What's keeping you?"

The silver vanished from the sky, and the light dimmed. Three white gulls called to each other and swung over the base. She folded her arms over her chest and uniform tunic and waited. After five minutes she decided to go inside and lie down. But she never budged from where she was standing.

"Here they come," a man's voice called out. "All four. Jolly good."

The pitch of their engines was solid. Jane watched the first of them come in, lower its wheels, and do the Spitfire bounce.

That's it then. I shall go and have a lie down.

But she remained where she was, arms folded across her chest.

Billy was the last one out of his plane. He stood talking with two members of his ground crew a few minutes. They examined the tail of his Spitfire. She could see two bullet holes in it.

This is precisely why we can't have a relationship. Death is always knocking at the door.

But a moment later she had other thoughts. *Oh, hurry up, will you? I'm chilled. I just want to say hello and do the polite thing. Then I'd like a good long sleep.*

She saw him laugh and run his hand through his hair and clap a fellow pilot on the shoulder. The smile instantly made heat go through her. It felt as if someone had started a Rolls Royce Merlin V12 in her chest and rammed the throttle forward.

Almost fifteen hundred horsepower. Dear Lord, I really can't take this anymore. If he dies, he dies. If he lives, he lives. But I want him. It's madness...it honestly is madness, but I want him very much.

The intelligence officer spoke with Billy. Other pilots from the squadron crowded around and chatted while he filled out a green form. Jane remained rooted by her door. Finally Billy and the others started heading for the Officers' Mess. In half a minute he was almost out of sight. Jane bit her lip and made her decision. She stepped out into the open.

"Hullo! Billy Sweet!"

Billy stopped and looked. "Jane? Did you ferry aircraft in this afternoon?"

"I did!"

"I'm just going to have a sit down with the lads. Can we go to the pub for fish and chips in an hour? It's good to see you. I thought you were never coming back."

Billy Sweet! Are you doing this to annoy me or are you really that daft? "Actually, Billy, if I could see you for half a minute...I have news from London."

"News from London? Is something up?" He started toward Jane and glanced back at his companions. "Meet you in the Mess." He made his way to her side, all smiles gone. "Is something wrong then? Bad news from Terry or Owen or one of the boys at King's Cross?"

"Oh, there's something wrong all right. There's a lot wrong. But nothing that can't be fixed by the right person with the right amount of time on his hands."

"What?"

She pulled him out of sight behind the building. Her first kiss was short but strong, and she drew back after a minute, listening to her breath, listening to his breath, measuring the pace of her heart and how she felt from top to bottom.

His face was flushed. "What's going on?"

"Is it so difficult to figure out, Flying Officer Sweet?" She put both arms around him. "I've made up my mind."

Her grip on him strengthened, and then he took the initiative, gathered her face and night-black hair into both hands, and leaned in to kiss her. Jane didn't know how to respond. Peter or James, even in their most passionate moments, had never been this volcanic. She clung to his back as if she were going to fall from a great height.

12

May 1, 1941
RAF Hunters Down

Dear Eva,

I'm dashing this off before bed. I haven't told anyone else, but I wanted to tell you. It's Billy—yes, Billy Sweet. I know, it's mad, absolutely mad, and I have no idea how his mum and dad are going to take this. First the eldest two sons. And now the last of the lot, their pride and joy. I fought it—believe me, I fought it tooth and nail, and if it hadn't been for ferrying aircraft down to his base, all might have been well. But he so much wants to take care of me, to take over where the twins left off, to do for me what they weren't able to do. And he is so tender, so manly and boyish and rugged and all kinds of sweetness rolled into one. Yes, I know he could get killed. But I would rather have his love now and lose it, if that has to happen, than never to be loved by him at all. I always thought he was just a child—you know how it is, the kid brother. Now he's almost more than I can handle, and I'm supposed to be the older and more mature partner. I'm really quite dizzy about it all.

Have to get up early for my ride back from the base, so must say goodbye for now. Please tell me how things are with Owen. It was a kind of explosion when it happened with him, wasn't it? And you're the older of the pair of you, aren't you? How is all that working out? You must miss him terribly. At least Billy and I are only miles apart, not oceans apart. I pray for you. Please write because I don't know who else to talk to about all this. I really don't know if my mum will approve of this at all.

Love,

Jane

May 7, 1941
Camden Lock, London

Dear Jane,

Can you imagine? I just got back from the worst night to find a letter from you and another from Owen. Love is in the air despite all that war tries to do! I'm so happy for you, Jane—you've had such a rough go, and Billy really is a darling. I'll pray for the two of you. Things will work out, I know it, just as they have with Owen and me. Who says the woman must always be the younger one? That's what Grandfather told me once while we were out sailing. I'm sure Billy's parents will get over any discomfort they feel once they see how happy he is. After all, you had nothing to do with what happened to the twins. You loved them both to the end. You can bring nothing but good back into Aunt Emma and Uncle Jeremy's lives. And do write your mum. I'm sure Aunt Libby will be thrilled.

As for Owen and me, oceans apart or not, we get along famously. For a long time he was hanging about Birkenhead, and I actually got to see him once or twice when he was on leave, sirens wailing and bombs dropping all around us here. But his ship was finished at the end of March, and now he's up north at Scapa Flow. But never mind, Owen writes quite a lot, and his letters are full of beautiful poetry.

He's adorable. I'm always hoping the *Prince of Wales* will show up in Portsmouth one day and he'll have another seventy-two hour leave. But I know that's not going to happen while *Bismarck* is at Gotenhafen and hoping to slip out past Sweden and Norway into the Atlantic. So until that's settled, up north my beloved sits, while I am down here with the German bombers and the ruined buildings and the rubble. But the Nazis will not have their way forever. And one day Owen shall be in my arms again and Billy in yours, and nothing and no one shall separate any of us. What do you say to a double wedding ceremony later this year?

Write again. And write your mum.

Love,

Eva

May 22, 1941
Caroline and Victoria's townhouse, Camden Lock, London

"Aunt Libby? Hullo?"

"Hullo. This is Libby Fordyce."

"Oh. Aunt Libby. I'm glad I've got you on the phone. I've been writing Jane quite a bit. Have you heard from her?"

"Is that you, Eva? Yes, yes, I have."

"Has she said anything?"

Libby laughed. "She's said an awful lot if you mean Billy Sweet."

"Oh. How do you feel about that?"

"I feel fine, Eva. So do Em and Jeremy. Really, Jane's one of the finest girls in the world. You needn't hold the secret close to your heart any longer."

"I'm so glad to hear this," Eva said into the phone.

"It's something on the order of wonderful, isn't it? I must thank you for being such a good friend to Jane."

"I so look forward to seeing her again, Aunt Libby. And having the four of us—Owen and me and Jane and Billy—embark on some sort of grand outing together."

"Do you think you'll have time for that with this big war going on, Jane?"

"A three-day leave is all we need to do something spectacular."

Sirens began to howl.

"Oh, Aunt Lib, I have to run and grab my helmet and rush out the door. There's our night raid. Leave a message for Aunt Char, will you? I've had a letter from Owen and he's doing very well up in the Orkneys, though he does complain about the wind. He's seen his father on two occasions in port, and Lord Edward is at the top of his game, he says. So please tell her the Danforth men are getting along very well while they wait patiently upon the German Navy to move its queen and bishop."

"I shall tell her."

"Aunt Lib, he's seen your husband too; they even had a meal together, all three of them, Terry, Edward, and Owen. Uncle Terry called it the Orkney Family Reunion. He was quite the card, Owen says. Had them all in stitches—yes, even oh-so-serious Uncle Edward! Such stories they'll have to tell us."

"They shall indeed."

"Our ARP lorry is here and Charles is shouting for me. Uncle Terry was in the best of health. You ought to get into that shelter in the back-yard now, Aunt Lib."

"I shall do. God bless you, Eva."

"He was in the very best of health. God go with you too."

At noon the next day, Eva turned over in bed, opened her eyes momentarily, closed them again, settled under her blankets, then suddenly lifted her head and sat up.

"Grandfather."

Lord Preston sat in a chair beside her. He smiled. "Hullo, my dear."

She leaned over and hugged him. "What are you doing here?"

"I wasn't sure when you might wake up. I know you had a very late night just as you always do when there's a raid."

She looked at his eyes. "What is it? What's wrong?"

"I came to bring you news. It will be in the papers tonight or tomorrow. But I wished for you to hear it before that."

She waited, hands still on his arms.

"*Bismarck* and *Prinz Eugen* have left port. They've been out for days. The Swedes have spotted them, and the RAF has photographed them."

"Where are they now?"

"I expect they're preparing to make a dash through the Denmark Strait and into the open Atlantic."

Her face lost its color. "There will be a fight, won't there? And my Owen will be in it."

"Certainly there must be a fight. The *Bismarck* is a monster on the loose and would blast our convoys and their escorts out of existence. Without the convoys bringing supplies from Canada and Newfoundland we are finished. And certainly our Owen will be in it. HMS *Prince of Wales* and six destroyers have been dispatched from Scapa Flow to deal with *Bismarck*. Your Uncle Terry will be in it as well. The *Hood* has been dispatched to the Denmark Strait in addition to the *Prince of Wales*."

"Are they enough?"

"I don't know. *Bismarck* hasn't been out of the shipbuilders' yard a year. She's brand-new. *Hood* is a strong ship but she's an old ship, my dear. Your Uncle Terry often said it needed an overhaul from stem to stern—its armor plating, its guns, its engines."

"What about *Rodney*? She's quite new, isn't she? Owen says she has sixteen-inch guns."

"*Rodney* is more than ten years old, but I agree with you. She should be in the Denmark Strait."

"Why isn't she?"

"She's on convoy duty. On her way to Halifax." Lord Preston patted Eva on the hand. "Let us remember your Owen's ship is quite the newest of them all. Not even been at sea two months. She has fourteen-inch guns like *King George the Fifth*. Ten of them. Not the fifteen-inch guns of *Bismarck* or *Hood*, but well capable of inflicting serious damage on anything afloat. And well out-powering the eight-inch guns of the *Prinz Eugen*. You have nothing to fret about on that score."

He saw the fear working its way around her eyes like a drop of water.

"My dear, the fight has been a clash of wills in the air for so many months, hasn't it? Yes, it has been on the land too when it comes to Egypt, Crete, and Greece. But here on our island home it has been a 'tumult in the clouds,' as the poet puts it. Now it shall be a battle of wills on the high seas. And that's only fitting. At sea our navy has saved Britain again and again. It must do so once more by the grace of God."

The fear continued to roam her face and eyes, looking for a way out. He clasped both her hands in his.

"Forgive me for prattling on like the old man that I am. Our family has stood on prayer for generations, through storm and shadow as well as marvelous seasons of abundant light. It must do so again. And you are part of that family now."

Eva hung her head. "I wish I had never marched. Never taken the oath of allegiance to Adolf Hitler. I wish the Nazis had never been allowed to come to power in my country and that the *Bismarck* had never been built."

"I know, my dear. Believe me, the same thing might have happened here if Mosley had had his way. But I don't for a minute believe Germany will remain under Herr Hitler's rule, not for a minute. Brave men like your father will never yield to despotism."

"I don't even know if he's dead or alive."

"My sources assure me he is alive and has not been discovered by Himmler and the SS."

"I felt he treated me harshly. Therefore I have treated him harshly. I wish I could sit down and have a long talk with him. I'm not the woman I was in Nazi Germany."

"He reaches out to you."

"What do you mean?"

"Letters have come by means of diplomatic pouch from the American embassy in Berlin to their embassy here in London."

"Why didn't you tell me?"

"Harrison actually informed you twice. He thought you were going to scratch his eyes out."

She put both hands over her face. "*Mein Gott es tut mir leid.*" Her voice was muffled by her hands. "I'm so sorry." She looked up at Lord Preston. "I should like to read the letters now. Is that possible?"

He nodded. "It is indeed possible. As God would have it I placed those letters in my rooms at Ashton Park. They were not destroyed when Kensington Gate and the entire neighborhood was blown up by the mine."

"Thank God."

"Yes, thank Him. And now we must pray to Him. We must go in our hearts and minds to the Denmark Strait where your young Horatio faces a more formidable foe than the French and Spanish fleet off Trafalgar."

She clutched his hands and twisted her fingers around his. "I can't lose Owen, Grandfather. I can't bear to lose him."

"Nor can I."

"Remember how young he was at Dunkerque? Remember how handsome and brave? Remember his poems? God must save him."

"Him and Terry and Edward and England." He bowed his head, their hands remaining wound together. "Let me begin."

She bowed her head as well. "Yes, Grandfather. His will be done on earth as it is in heaven—*Sein Wille geschehe auf Erden wie im Himmel ist.*"

"His will be done on earth as it is in heaven," repeated Lord Preston. "Not evil's will. Not the will of wicked men. His will."

There was silence in the room. Lord Preston began to hum softly. Soon words came with the humming.

> Eternal Father, strong to save,
> Whose arm doth bind the restless wave,
> Who bidst the mighty ocean deep
> Its own appointed limits keep:
> O hear us when we cry to Thee
> For those in peril on the sea.

Silence again.

"The Navy Hymn," whispered Lord Preston. "God, You are on those waters with them right now. You hear prayers from German and Englishman alike. But Christ, our Christ, be with Owen, be with Terry, and if it should come to that, be with my son Edward as well. God, have mercy. Christ, have mercy. A price will be paid. A price is always paid. Only let the right prevail. Only let Your good will prevail."

Saturday, May 24, 1941
Denmark Strait Between Greenland and Iceland

Spray burst over the bow of HMS *Prince of Wales.*

Leading Seaman Owen Danforth stood ready on the bridge to run messages to any part of the ship should communications be disabled. Captain John Leach glanced back at him.

"I trust you know the lay of the ship?"

"Aye, aye, captain," Owen responded.

Leach turned back to his officers. "Gun turrets will have to rely on the range finders in the control tower. The spray over the bow will not permit use of the turret range finders. Make sure that's understood."

"Yes, captain," said an officer at his side.

"Do we still have *Bismarck* in sight, Kenley?"

"Aye, aye, sir. Just over eleven miles. Twenty thousand yards."

"All turrets come to bear. Prepare to open fire."

"Prepare to open fire, aye, aye, sir."

"Can we get a broadside on the *Bismarck*?" asked Captain Leach.

"No, sir," Kenley replied. "Our angle of approach doesn't permit it. The aft turrets won't be able to engage."

"Very well."

Owen could see the *Hood* four cables ahead of them—half a mile—seas breaking over her bow and deck. The long fifteen-inch guns began to elevate. He imagined his uncle, Commander Terry Fordyce, standing on the bridge by Vice Admiral Lancelot Holland, taking and giving orders in his easy way as their guns sighted in on *Bismarck* and *Prinz Eugen*.

There was a sudden roar, and dark smoke boiled over the forward turrets of the *Hood*.

"Mark the time," said Captain Leach in a calm voice.

"Oh five fifty-two, sir," Kenley said crisply.

"Fire."

Kenley adjusted his headphones. "Aye, aye, sir. All turrets sighted on the enemy, open fire."

The *Prince of Wales* shuddered, flame belched from the fourteen-inch guns, and smoke poured over the ship and was pushed away by the wind. Ten seconds later there was another three-gun salvo.

"Mark the time," ordered Leach.

"Oh five fifty-three, sir," Kenley responded.

"We appear to have overshot Bismarck by a thousand yards, sir," another officer with bright blond hair piped up.

"Ensure the control tower makes the necessary adjustments. Resume firing."

"Resume firing, aye, aye, captain," replied the blond officer. "We have a jam at A turret."

"Carry on with the guns that are sighted in and working."

The battleship shook again as the *Prince of Wales* fired.

"We've straddled *Bismarck*, sir," said Kenley. "And we appear to have some hits."

"Continue firing. Begin port turn."

"Begin port turn, aye, aye, captain."

"We are taking fire from *Prinz Eugen,* sir," warned the blond officer.

"Keep our guns on *Bismarck.*"

"Aye, aye, sir."

Owen watched as their guns and the *Hood*'s spat fire. Suddenly tall geysers of white water sprang up around the *Hood.*

"*Bismarck* has straddled *Hood,* sir," said Kenley.

Half a minute later tall columns of white and gray water surrounded the *Hood* again.

"They have her range," muttered Leach. "Continue rapid fire at *Bismarck.* Let's hit her a second time."

"Aye, aye, sir."

Flames and smoke shot up as high as the *Hood*'s masts. Owen thought a gun turret had malfunctioned on the great battleship and exploded. A huge rush of orange fire and smoke tore the ship from his sight. A moment later he glimpsed the bow and the stern both rising out of the water and *Hood* rapidly disappearing into the sea.

What's happened? She's blown apart!

"She's sunk!" one officer exclaimed. "*Hood*'s sunk!"

"Hard starboard!" snapped Leach. "We don't want to hit the debris!"

The turn brought *Prince of Wales* closer to *Bismarck* and *Prinz Eugen.* Massive towers of water burst around her.

"We are taking fire from both enemy ships now, sir. All their guns are ranging in on us."

Owen watched in a daze as they sliced over the spot where the *Hood* had been steaming half a minute before. He looked for heads, hundreds of heads of swimming men, but he saw only large chunks of jagged steel swirling in a kind of whirlpool as *Hood* continued to sink swiftly to the sea floor.

Uncle Terry! Swim up! Get out and swim up!

A blow threw Owen sideways, and he braced his hands against the bulkhead to keep from falling down.

"We're hit!" shouted one of the officers.

"I need a damage report," commanded Leach. "An accurate one. As soon as possible." He fixed his eyes on Owen. "See what you can find out and report back to me."

Owen stood up straight and saluted. "Aye, aye, captain."

He turned. The bridge exploded behind him and hurled him into the air. The force of the blast slammed his head into a wall of steel.

May 24, 1941
HMS Rodney, *the North Atlantic*

"Commander Danforth." A sailor saluted Edward at the door to his quarters. Edward returned the salute.

"Commodore Dalrymple-Hamilton requests your presence on the bridge."

Edward made his way over the deck, through waves of sea spray, and climbed up to the bridge, gripping the handrails tightly. Dalrymple-Hamilton swiveled in his chair to look at him. All the officers did. Edward saluted.

"We've received a signal concerning a naval action in the Denmark Strait early this morning. *Hood* and the *Prince of Wales* engaged *Bismarck* and *Prinz Eugen*." The commodore paused. "*Hood* was sunk. *Prince of Wales* took a number of hits including one on the bridge that killed most of the officers. She was forced to withdraw under a smokescreen."

Edward felt as if the commodore had struck him across the face with the flat of his hand. "What sort of survivors are we talking about on the *Hood*, sir?"

"None. Though one report says three."

"None? Three? How's that, sir?"

"She blew up, Commander. Sank immediately."

"Do we have the names of the three survivors, sir?"

"No. I'm aware you have family on board the *Hood*."

"My sister's husband, sir."

"I'm very sorry, Commander. I'll let you know the moment we receive the names of any who were rescued."

"Thank you, sir." He kept his eyes on the commodore. "Do we know who the casualties on the *Prince of Wales* were?"

"Not yet. It's your son, isn't it?"

"Yes, sir."

"A rotten morning, Commander. All I can offer you is this direct signal from the prime minister."

He extended his hand toward Edward.

"The prime minister?" Edward took the piece of paper from the commodore's fingers.

"By way of the Admiralty. But it's his words. In this case, short and to the point."

Edward unfolded the note.

SINK THE BISMARCK

Edward looked up.

"We are five hundred miles northwest of Ireland," related the commodore. "At this point we part company with the troopship of civilians we were escorting to Canada and leave it in the capable hands of HMS *Eskimo*. We are taking the destroyers *Somali*, *Mashona*, and *Tartar* with us in pursuit of the *Bismarck*."

"Yes, sir," responded Edward.

"Do you recall the firebombing of London on December twenty-ninth? The prime minister saw that St. Paul's Cathedral was about to be destroyed and declared it must be saved at all costs. He knew it was a symbol not only of London but of the British people. The same is true of the *Hood*. It was a symbol of our nation. We cannot save her, so we must avenge her. The *Bismarck* represents the German Empire, and we must do our part to remove that symbol from Hitler and the Third Reich. At all costs. We cannot let them keep that symbol. Do you take my meaning, Commander?"

"Yes, sir."

"It is the belief of all on this bridge that according to information we have received, *Bismarck* is headed to Brest, not out to sea to prey on British shipping. This can only mean she sustained a certain amount of damage during her brief engagement with *Hood* and the *Prince of Wales*. Accordingly, we are about to make a turn to port and head south and east to cut her off. We shall need an all-out effort from the crew in the engine room if we are to have any hope of catching *Bismarck*. And more than a bit of luck or some sort of miracle since *Bismarck* can steam faster than any of our ships. Do you believe in luck, Commander?"

"I expect I do, sir."

"Do you believe in miracles?"

"I expect I do, sir."

"When you get a few minutes you may go to the ship's chapel and offer a prayer up for us all. Meantime, not being able to make our own luck or our own miracles, we do what we can do and make steam. Even that needs a touch from Lady Luck or the Almighty. You know how worn out our boilers are. We are due for a complete refit. The men are doing their best with what we have. Work with them, Commander. Assist them in any way you can. Let me know immediately if they need anything. We must make speed and we cannot do it without a Herculean effort from the engine room and her crew."

"Aye, aye, sir." Edward saluted. "I shall get right on it."

Commodore Dalrymple-Hamilton returned the salute. "I shall let you know the moment I have news regarding the crews of *Prince of Wales* and *Hood.*"

"Thank you, sir."

"Carry on."

Sunday, May 25, 1941
London

"The Lord sustain us in this continuing battle. The Lord comfort all those who grieve the loss of their loved ones on the *Hood.*" Jeremy's voice broke. "The Lord comfort my sister in the loss of her husband, Commander Terrence Fordyce, RN. No finer man graced the uniform of the Royal Navy. Christ be with us all, and Christ be with our sailors and our nation. Amen."

Several amens sounded in the hall used for the St. Andrew's Cross congregation since the church building's destruction.

Lord Preston, tears on his face, put his daughter Libby's hands to his lips. "I shall pray for you without ceasing. I shall do whatever I can do. We all shall, the whole family."

"Of course you will, Father." Libby's face was streaming. "I know I will not be alone."

Lord Preston turned to Jane. "This is no less true for you, my dear. You have lost a father. We love you with all our hearts."

Jane bowed her head under a dark veil. "Thank you, Grandfather."

Both Jane and her mother were dressed in black.

People crowded around the two women and the Danforth family to express their condolences. Lord Preston eventually broke away, one arm around his wife, and walked outside. They stood there a moment, watching the traffic, watching the people. At one end of the street a newsboy shouted, "The *Mighty Hood* sunk. Nation in a state of shock. *Bismarck* free to attack our convoys. Prime minister orders the pursuit of the German battleship by all available vessels."

Lady Preston's eyes filled. "Is it just my imagination, William, or is everyone walking more slowly, are all the cars and lorries moving so much more slowly up and down our avenues and streets?"

"I don't think it's an exaggeration to say a shroud has descended upon our city and the entire island. The air war has been vicious but we have endured, so the Blitz has felt to all of us like a victory. But the loss of the *Hood* is a defeat. It makes it feel as if no matter what we do, eventually the Nazis shall overwhelm us and conquer our nation."

"Surely now the Americans will come in."

"They will not come in, Elizabeth. President Roosevelt will be sympathetic, but it's not their ship that was lost. Not their *Arizona* or *California* or *Oklahoma*. The day someone sinks their ships is the day they will enter the war. It was the same way in nineteen seventeen."

She wiped at her eyes with a handkerchief. "Where is Charlotte? We must speak with Charlotte. And Eva, poor Eva. Is there any more news about the casualties aboard the *Prince of Wales*? Any news at all about Owen?"

"I'm afraid not."

"Surely Edward is in it now?"

"Yes, of course. *Rodney* is in pursuit. I don't see how they will catch *Bismarck* to tell you the truth. But let us keep that to ourselves."

"We cannot have lost Owen too, we simply cannot. Would God be so cruel, William? Is He that sort of God?"

"He is not that sort of God. But we live in a world where people die and cannot all be saved. This is not Eden; it is not paradise. We must bear up. Faith is our anchor. Not having an anchor, not having faith, only makes matters worse and improves nothing."

"There is Charlotte coming out of the hall. Eva is with her." Lady Preston began to walk toward them. "I didn't see them come in. I have no idea where they sat."

"I saw them." Lord Preston joined her. "They were at the back. Far at the back. I couldn't spot them when we left."

"The poor children. Our poor country. Fourteen hundred drowned."

"God have mercy," Lord Preston said softly as Eva's tear-worn face turned toward him. "Christ have mercy."

Monday, May 26, 1941
HMS Rodney, *the North Atlantic*

"You wanted to see me, sir?"

The commodore opened the door to his quarters wider. "I did. Step in, Commander."

Edward stepped into the room and shut the door to spray and wind and shrieking gulls.

Dalrymple-Hamilton smiled. "I wish to congratulate you. I don't know how you and the engine room crew are doing it. Several times during this chase we've gone two knots beyond our designed speed."

"The men are marvels, sir."

"How are you keeping the boilers from bursting?"

"We're plugging leaks constantly, sir. And pumping seawater on top of the engine parts that are overheating." Edward cleared his throat. "Sir, the lads are passing out from the heat in the engine room."

"I see by the look of your uniform it must be something of an inferno down there, yes."

"Their effort really must not go unsung, sir."

"With you and me and the other officers it shan't. Whether the rest of the world ever finds out depends upon what happens over the next day or two. A Catalina flying boat spotted *Bismarck* at ten thirty hours. It was one hundred ten miles southeast of us. So we are holding our present course. Nevertheless it's bound to reach safety before we or any of the ships can attack her. Have you been down to the ship's chapel, Commander?"

"I haven't, sir."

"Spare a moment and see what you can offer up. I can tell you this—the *Ark Royal* aircraft carrier is set to launch a torpedo attack on *Bismarck*. I'll be using the Tannoy to tell the men. The *Victorious* wasn't successful with her air strike on the twenty-fourth. But who knows? Perhaps *Ark Royal* and her Fairey Swordfish biplanes will be lucky—or blessed." He handed a sheet of paper to Edward. "The casualty list from HMS *Prince of Wales.*"

Edward's stomach tightened as his eyes ran over the names. Then he relaxed. "Thank goodness, sir. My son's name is not here."

The commodore nodded. "It isn't. But I regret to say the list is not complete. I've been informed some have died of their injuries. They promised to send a more complete list soon."

The fear returned to Edward's stomach and chest with a harsh grip. "Excuse me, sir—can't they just tell me if Leading Seaman Owen Danforth is alive or dead?"

"I asked them that twice. But I have received no reply."

Edward handed the sheet back to him. "Thank you, sir."

"Dreadfully sorry, Commander."

Edward saluted and left the commodore's quarters. He returned to the sting of the wind and waves that hurled saltwater over *Rodney* like gunfire. For a moment he stared at the bow of the battleship and its rough rhythm of plunging into the heavy seas and lifting out of the boil again and again, water seething over the deck and the hull. He removed his officer's cap and bared his head.

You gave the soldiers salvation at Dunkerque, didn't You? You gave the RAF their victory last summer and fall. You've given Londoners the strength to endure the Blitz. Now You must give the navy something. You must. Over a hundred years have gone by since Trafalgar, but You are the great God who forgets nothing. You remember Lord Nelson's prayer, I know You do, and I offer it up again on this windswept sea. "May the great God, whom I worship, grant to my country and for the benefit of Europe in general, a great and glorious victory. And may no misconduct, in anyone, tarnish it. And may humanity after victory be the predominant feature in the British fleet. For myself individually, I commit my life to Him who made me, and may His blessing alight upon my endeavors for serving my country faithfully. To Him I resign myself and the just cause which is entrusted to me to defend. Amen. Amen. Amen."

Edward lifted his head to the sky and let the wind and water lash his face. "And please, God, I ask You for my son."

Before midnight Commodore Dalrymple-Hamilton told the ship's crew there had been torpedo attacks on the *Bismarck* from biplanes on the aircraft carrier *Ark Royal.* However, he cautioned them that no damage to the German battleship appeared to have resulted and that, despite the best efforts of the *Rodney's* crew, he did not believe they could catch *Bismarck* before she reached safe harbor in France. Edward felt the dejection on board the ship as he made his way to his room and collapsed exhausted on his bunk.

I see you lying and looking at the ceiling, Charlotte, my love, and I feel the fright in you for Owen and for me. My boy Colm is worried for his brother and father as he lies in the dark of Ashton Park. Eva—there you are rescuing people from burning buildings, but you couldn't rescue the man you love from a burning ship; you couldn't rescue Owen—is that what you're thinking? Is that what I'm feeling from you as Rodney *pounds desperately through the waves to try to avenge my son and the man you love? And what good is revenge? What difference will it make?*

Edward turned on his side, put out his hand, and touched the cold metal of the bulkhead.

My sister is a widow for the second time in her life. She cries and does not sleep. Her daughter, Jane, has lost a father, and she lies on her bed tonight and cannot dream. Terry was kind to her from the beginning, gentle and kind and playful. He rests on the seabed with over a thousand men, but none of those who loved him or loved his shipmates can rest. Not this night. Perhaps not any night.

Edward was once more on his back, staring up into the dark.

If we sink the Bismarck *she will no longer be a widow maker. No longer the maker of orphans or the fatherless. If we sink the* Bismarck *she can no longer wreak havoc and kill. That is more justice than it is revenge.*

Sleep began to overwhelm him.

A sailor knocked on his door. "A message from the commodore, sir."

Edward took the note and switched on his light while the able seaman waited for a response.

NEW REPORTS INDICATE THE BISMARCK IS GOING IN CIRCLES AND NO LONGER MAKING HEADWAY. EITHER HER STEERING MECHANISM OR HER RUDDER APPEARS TO BE DAMAGED. THIS MAY HAVE HAPPENED DURING THE TORPEDO ATTACK. THE POSSIBILITY OF CATCHING HER IS NO LONGER REMOTE. DID YOU OFFER UP A PRAYER TO THE LORD OF THE SEA?

Edward scribbled out a message on the back of the note. "I offered up Nelson's prayer before Trafalgar." He handed the note to the sailor. "Take this to the commodore."

He sat on the edge of his bunk. Thoughts and images were swirling in his head.

Did You answer my prayer, my God? Did You answer the prayers of ten thousand Englishmen and ignore the prayers of the German fleet and nation?

An alarm suddenly blared over the Tannoy. "Action stations! Action stations!"

Edward vaulted off his bunk toward his action station at the bridge.

As he ran, he watched the gunnery crew climb to the armored control tower above the bridge. These were the sailors who used the range finder and fired the sixteen-inch guns. Edward watched them take their stations.

"Shoot true," he murmured under his breath.

When he entered the bridge the commodore turned to him. "Admiral Tovey is near us on the *King George the Fifth*. He believes there will be night action. Stand by."

"Aye, aye, sir."

But they stood through the dark of the night and only watched the bow cut into the waves and rear its head again, smothered in white foam against the blackness of sea and sky.

Eventually there was a gray dawn, a pale sun, and an ocean restless with waves. Edward checked his watch—seven twenty-two, Wednesday, May 27. The cruiser *Norfolk* steamed up from the south and joined them. Edward kept his eyes focused on the line between sky and sea. In a short time the cruiser *Dorsetshire* was also there.

"*Bismarck* sighted from the tower," said one of the officers suddenly.

"Where away?" asked the commodore.

"Five degrees off the starboard bow. Twenty-five thousand yards."

"Just over fourteen miles." Dalrymple-Hamilton leaned forward in his seat. "Is Lieutenant Commander Crawford in the tower with the gunnery crew?"

"Yes, sir. He confirms *Bismarck* is in sight."

Edward glanced at his watch again. Eight forty-four.

"Tell him to prepare to fire."

"Aye, aye, sir." The officer spoke into the microphone. "Prepare to fire."

A minute went by. Two minutes.

"Range?" asked Dalrymple-Hamilton.

"Twenty-three thousand, four hundred yards, sir."

"Open fire."

"Aye, aye, sir." The officer spoke calmly into the microphone again. "Fire."

A heartbeat. The ting-ting of the warning fire bells.

The ship shook, and the sixteen-inch guns of A and B turret thundered. Smoke and flame burst over the front of *Rodney*.

"Crawford reports *Bismarck* has returned fire, sir."

"Very well."

Edward and the others on the bridge clearly heard the screech of the shells passing overhead.

A half minute later there was another shriek from tons of flying metal. Massive columns of white water shot up to port and starboard.

"She's straddled us." Dalrymple-Hamilton kept his eyes forward. "Close the distance and continue firing."

"Aye, aye, sir. Close the distance and continue firing."

Again the howl of flying steel. Again the huge spouts of water and the crash of high explosives.

"Crawford reports we have straddled *Bismarck* on our third salvo."

"Very good."

"Crawford reports we have two hits from our fourth salvo."

"Very good. Carry on."

"Fires in *Bismarck*'s forecastle. Their A and B turrets appear to have been hit."

Rodney's guns poured more fire and rattled the bridge with their blasts.

"We have a hit on the *Bismarck*'s upper deck."

The scream of *Bismarck*'s shells. More geysers. No longer close to *Rodney*.

"We've straddled the enemy again, sir. The bridge has been destroyed. So has their conning tower."

Edward's watch read nine thirteen.

The lads in the engine room told me they had family killed in Coventry and Liverpool and Nottingham by the German bombers. Others had family killed and maimed in London and Dover and Portsmouth. The men have not forgotten or forgiven. I expect the sailors loading shells into our sixteen-inch guns are no different. Nor the men directing the fire from the tower.

"We've straddled her again, sir. Spotters report a hit behind the funnel."

Nine twenty-seven.

"Spotters report we've knocked out D turret, sir."

Nine thirty-one.

The distance between *Rodney* and *Bismarck* gradually closed to less than three thousand yards—less than two miles.

Edward and the commodore and the others could see *Bismarck* plainly from the bridge.

"It's completely on fire from bow to stern," whispered Edward.

Rodney's guns blasted *Bismarck* again and again. Edward watched a shell travel from their guns straight into the *Bismarck*'s B turret and blow it apart.

"Their Bruno turret is hit, sir," an officer informed Dalrymple-Hamilton.

"I see that. Are the six-inch guns engaging as rapidly as possible?"

"Yes, sir. The range is perfect for them. Almost four hundred six-inch shells have been fired. And over two hundred sixteen-inch shells. *Bismarck*'s return fire has been erratic. Her last salvo was observed at nine thirty-one."

"We shall follow the standard rules of engagement and continue to fire until the *Bismarck* strikes her colors and surrenders or she is sunk. We shall fire so long as Sir Admiral Tovey on *King George the Fifth* orders the battleships and the cruisers to keep inflicting damage on the enemy."

"Aye, aye, sir."

Bismarck seemed to vanish in high white shell splashes and black smoke—red flame spitting and roiling and stabbing—reemerging bright with a fierce burning, and disappearing again as more near misses threw up tall columns of spray or hits that struck the German battleship with more flame and more explosions.

Edward finally closed his eyes.

> LORD, *make me to know mine end, and the measure of my days, what it is; that I may know how frail I am. Behold, thou hast made my days as an handbreadth; and mine age is as nothing before thee: verily every man in his best state is altogether vanity. Surely every man walketh in a vain show: surely they are disquieted in vain: he heapeth up riches, and knoweth not who shall gather them.*

Sunday, May 27, House of Commons, Church House, London

At eleven a.m. Winston Churchill rose to address the House of Commons at Church House.

"This morning, shortly after daybreak, the *Bismarck*, virtually immobilized, without help, was attacked by British battleships that pursued her. I don't know the result of this action. It seems however, that *Bismarck* was not sunk by gunfire, and now will be sunk by torpedoes. It is believed that this is happening right now. Great as is our loss in the *Hood*, the *Bismarck* must be regarded as the most powerful enemy battleship, as she is the newest enemy battleship, and the striking of her from the German Navy is a very definite simplification of the task of maintaining effective mastery of the northern sea and maintenance of the northern blockade."

He sat back down. A note was handed to him. He stood a second time.

"I have just received news that the *Bismarck* is sunk."

The hall erupted in cheers and cries and applause. Lord Preston rose to his feet along with the others but made no sound and did not clap his hands. The cheering continued for several minutes. He made his way through the press of MPs and out into the street where he hailed a cab. Alighting at a house in Camden, he knocked on the door. Charlotte answered.

"Father," she said. "I thought you were in the House of Commons today."

"I have just come from there. Where is Libby?"

"We were both having tea in the parlor."

He took her hand. "Let us go there."

Libby saw her father and got to her feet.

"What is it?" she asked.

"*Bismarck* is sunk. The prime minister has just announced it." He cleared his throat and repeated the words. "*Bismarck* is sunk."

At first Libby didn't respond.

"I suppose I feel differently from many in England," she said after several moments. "I cannot be happy about more death even if it is the death of the enemy. I wish *Bismarck* had surrendered."

"So do I."

"I pray Edward is well. When will we find out?"

"Very soon, I should think."

"And what about Owen? Poor Char has been going about with a tre-
mendous burden on her shoulders."

"I expect we shall know about Owen too before the day is out."

Libby walked across the room and hugged Charlotte. Then she put
her arms around her father.

"People say they are surprised I'm not bitter at God, Papa. But I have
led a blessed life. Michael was a wonderful husband, and so was Terry. I
should not have missed it for the world. If I had been told at twenty whom
I was to marry and that I would lose them both, I suppose I would not
have gone ahead. But now that I look back I can only thank God for how
He has cared for me. I loved both the men He gave me with all my heart,
and they loved me back in the same way."

Sunday, May 27, aboard HMS Rodney *in the North Atlantic*

At the same moment, hundreds of miles away on the North Atlantic,
Rodney was making her way through wind-ragged seas toward Scotland.
She would put up in Greenock on the River Clyde for fuel and oil before
departing for the South Boston Navy Yard in America for repair and a refit
of her engines and boilers. Edward returned to the bridge after a visit to
the engine room and saluted.

"The lads are in fine spirits, sir," he reported. "They were glad to hear
my account of the battle."

"If it hadn't been for their efforts with those boilers and engines,"
responded the commodore, "there wouldn't have been a battle, certainly
not a successful one. I hope you conveyed my hearty thanks to them all."

"I did, sir. One of them replied with Nelson's admonition at Trafalgar.
"England expects that every man will do his duty."

Dalrymple-Hamilton laughed. "Did he? God bless him. And God
bless you." He handed Edward a note. "We've just received this signal."

> LEADING SEAMAN OWEN DANFORTH WAS
> INJURED IN HMS PRINCE OF WALE'S BAT-
> TLE WITH THE BISMARCK. HE HAS BEEN LAID
> UP IN SICK BAY. INJURIES ARE MINOR AND
> A FULL RECOVERY IS EXPECTED. HE SENDS

CONGRATULATIONS TO HIS FATHER ON HMS
RODNEY'S SINKING OF THE BISMARCK. PSALM
18:37.

"Oh, sir." Edward read the note a second time. His throat tightened. "This is very good news indeed. Thank God."

"I'll add a heartfelt Church of England amen to that, Commander."

"We use the verse for Royal Navy shorthand, but I don't recall it off the top of my head."

The commodore smiled. "It has been a turbulent three or four days, and the Protestant chaplain informs me there are more than thirty-one thousand verses in the Bible. You can't be expected to remember them all."

"Still, I should like to know what the verse said he sent to me."

"'I have pursued mine enemies, and overtaken them: neither did I turn again till they were consumed.' Victory at sea, Commander. And, in your case, the greater victory of a son brought back from the dead."

13

November 30, 1941
Ashton Park

"It is that rarest of things," Lord Preston murmured. "A blue sky in November."

He stood on the sea cliff and closed his eyes to the cut of the wind and the knifing brilliance of the sun on the waters. Behind him he heard the laughter of the children and the good-natured shouts of Todd Turpin and Harrison as they took them on a walk through the woods.

We have come through a hurricane, my Lord. I thank You for the lives of the very young.

He opened his eyes, took in the light, and saw again Eva as she had hurled herself into Owen's arms, almost knocking him off his crutches and off his feet as he returned home on leave. Another image emerged, out of the swirl of blue water and sparkling light, of Billy embracing Jane on their wedding day at Dover Sky, his hands lifting her white veil and cupping her face while placing a gentle kiss on her lips. Matt was there in RAF blue to applaud, and Ramsay, and Ben from King's Cross, as well as Sean and Kipp along with their Pickering Green squadron, including Wilkie, Miller, Peterson, and Packer. Jeremy performed the wedding ceremony for his son, Billy, and his bride under a bright September sky by the swan pond.

"My lord."

Lord Preston heard the jingle of a harness and the stamp of hooves behind him. He turned to see Tavy holding the traces of a black gelding that was pulling a small buggy.

"Horse and cart, Tavy?"

"You wished to be at the airfield for Lord Kipp's arrival. We don't have a car that can negotiate this track. And he is due to land in less than ten minutes."

"Ah."

Tavy helped Lord Preston up to the seat beside him.

"I shouldn't mind handling the reins a bit," Lord Preston said.

"By all means, my lord."

Lord Preston took up the traces and urged the gelding into a tight circle and back the way he had come. Most of the ash trees were bare, so sunlight was free to streak down through the branches and set on fire everything in its path. It gleamed along the two men's shoulders.

"A splendid day, Tavy."

"Lovely, my lord."

"We prayed our way through the storm."

"We did indeed, my lord."

"Not to say there isn't more to pray about. The fighting between Rommel and our Eighth Army in North Africa is fierce. Robbie and Skitt are in it up to their necks."

"War in heaven, war on earth, as you have emphasized on several occasions."

"Yes, Tavy, the clash of wills. I pray for Robbie and Skitt's well-being. And I pray for the defeat of the Nazi and Italian armies. Just as we prayed during the air war over Britain, that the wicked would perish and their schemes along with them."

"Amen."

"This continues to be my prayers—our prayers—for Edward on *Rodney,* though the ship rests in Iceland for the time being. And for Owen, reassigned to *King George the Fifth*—I believe I have that right—fighting in the waters off Norway and escorting convoys to Russia. Russia, hmm, how odd to say that, but Herr Hitler has attacked the Slavic people as well as everybody else."

"He has."

"The brightest news is Jeremy may well be tapped on the shoulder for bishop. I know his name has come before the prime minister and all the proper church officials. It was his leadership during the Blitz, you see, the spirit and backbone he put into people."

"I have found his services to be inspiring. Still, m'lord, a rough go for him and his wife."

"Of course. Two sons gone. The price paid. A terrible price paid. My first grandchildren. How I miss them. But even in my grief I am not left without the grace of God. Billy's marriage to Jane was beautiful and memorable."

"It was indeed."

The sound of an airplane came to their ears. They glanced at each other. Tavy smiled.

"To speak of grace, my lord. There is a sound we used to hear every day. And every time we heard it we knew it to be a blessing, for it meant someone was coming to stand between you and me and the schoolyard bully."

Lord Preston nodded. "It meant our liberty."

"Have you heard that song the American chap wrote?"

"Hm?"

"The one about the white cliffs of Dover."

"'Bluebirds over the cliffs'? Is that the one?"

"Yes, m'lord."

"There are no bluebirds here, Tavy."

"Still, m'lord, you have the lyrics. 'There'll be love and laughter and peace ever after, tomorrow, when the world is free.' That must tug at your heartstrings."

"There are no bluebirds, Tavy."

"'I'll never forget, the people I met braving those angry skies.'"

"Does it say that?"

"Yes, my lord. 'I remember well as the shadows fell, the light of hope in their eyes.'"

"Hm. The Yanks would do well to get in the fight rather than write sentimental songs about it."

"I believe we will see them come in soon, Lord Preston."

"You do? What makes you think that?"

"I sense it."

"Well, 'tis news to me and likely news to them. We shall see if history proves you a prophet, Tavy."

"Oh, no, my lord, I'm just a simple butler."

"Ha. You are much more than that to our family. Much, much more. I do not forget how you saved young Cecilia's life."

"Oh, my lord, anyone would have done that."

"Indeed? Run down a street with bombs falling to get a girl to a shelter when you could have run faster on your own?"

"My lord. I could never have abandoned her."

"As I say, you are much more than our butler." Lord Preston began to hum the tune to "The White Cliffs of Dover" as he flicked the reins. "Elizabeth likes the song, and anything that cheers her heart after the loss of so many in the family I thank God for."

They emerged from the ash grove and drove by the manor. The children were on the far side of a wide meadow and pointing at the sky. A Spitfire was circling Ashton Park. Finally it began to descend. Todd Turpin and Harrison made sure the boys and girls in their charge stayed well back. The Spitfire bounced once and rolled over the grass, prop spinning.

"A safe flight, my lord."

"Thank you. I have no doubt it will be."

Lord Preston strode across the runway to the plane. It was at a standstill with both the prop and the Rolls Royce engine still turning over. Kipp reached down from the front cockpit and shook his father's hand.

"Hullo, Dad. Do you need help getting into the rear cockpit then?"

"I do not."

"All the gear you need is under your seat—jacket and pants and helmet."

"Capital."

"We rigged this kite up at Pickering Green so we could train the recruits better. They were coming to us so raw. A few hours with a good instructor and their survival rate tripled."

"Excellent." Lord Preston clambered on top of the wing, slipped into the cockpit, and began pulling on the pants and Irvin flight jacket. "Your mother made a great deal of fuss about this flight. Thank goodness she is with Emma and Jeremy in London today."

Kipp waved at the children. "How's she getting along?"

"How are we all getting along with a war rumbling about the world? One day at a time and by the grace of God."

"Right."

"I've got everything on now."

"The R/T switch is just there by your hand so we can talk."

"There's a gun button!"

"Only for practice. The real one's up here with me."

"Is this plane loaded with ammunition?"

"Of course it's loaded, Dad. Suppose a mob of Me 109s came over the Channel?"

"They don't do that anymore."

"My goodness, Dad, we can't take the chance."

"Your mother would be tossing me out of the plane on my ear if she heard you say that. A combat pilot in my seventies! I trust the affair between you and von Zeltner is no longer ongoing."

"You know the prime minster stopped the fighter sweeps into France just the other day? We lost over two hundred pilots this summer."

"I do know Winston was concerned about that, yes."

Kipp was quiet a few moments. There was only the sound of the engine and the swish of the prop swirling.

"Von Zeltner was shot down last week, Dad. Not by me. A chap in Ben's squadron at King's Cross. He crashed near the base. Ben and Matt and a few others pulled him free and got him to the infirmary. But he only lived another hour."

"I see."

"He was able to talk. Ben spent some time with him. Von Zeltner repeated what he has maintained all along, that he didn't shoot down the twins. Ben believed him. It tied in with what he'd heard from other German POWs. And I have to admit, it ties in with what I've heard but didn't want to hear, especially about the lies Lord Tanner liked to work with. Ben prayed with von Zeltner just before he died. They buried him with full military honors in the graveyard at King's Cross chapel."

Kipp was leaning his head out of the cockpit to talk with his father. Lord Preston studied his son's face and eyes and listened to his words.

"And do you believe von Zeltner?" Lord Preston asked.

"I do. That part of my war is over."

Kipp faced forward. The Spitfire began to taxi out and turn into the wind. Kipp slammed his canopy shut, and Lord Preston followed suit. The howl of the engine increased, and the plane sped down the runway and lifted into the air. Lord Preston glanced at Ashton Park and could see his grandchildren waving their arms as wildly as they could. He doubted they could see what he was doing but he raised one of his hands and saluted them.

"What is the great surprise you have in store for me?" Lord Preston asked over the R/T. "It's not my birthday, and Christmas is a month away."

"Didn't you name me Kipp Andrew Danforth?"

"So we did."

"Today is November thirtieth."

"Jog my memory."

"St. Andrew's Day. My day, you always used to say when I was a boy."

"Ha ha. So I did. Is that what this is all about?"

"To a point. You'll understand once we've reached Kent. Do you mind if I push it a bit?"

"Go ahead, my boy."

Lord Preston felt the sudden thrust force him back against his seat. Wisps of cloud streamed past. Soon enough London was on their port wing, and then the green farmlands of southern England.

"There's Dover Sky, Father."

Lord Preston glanced down at the white manor glistening in the sharp November light. "I see it. She looks splendid."

A few minutes later the R/T crackled again. "Pickering Green."

Lord Preston saw the airfield and its hangars and huts spread out below him. "The famous base. But where are the aircraft?"

Kipp didn't reply right away. "There's a chap flying with the Royal Canadian Air Force, a Yank who was keen to get in the fight even though America wasn't in it. Four-twelve Squadron. Pilot Officer Gillespie Magee. He wrote a bit of a poem. A friend of his is a friend of mine, and a copy of it wound up in my hands. I quite like it. Indeed all the lads like it, including Sean here at Pickering Green; Ben, Matt, and Ramsay at King's Cross; and Billy at Hunters Down. Would you like to hear some of it?"

"Of course, but where are we going now?"

"West Sussex. Hampshire."

"Whatever for?"

But Kipp had begun to recite the poem.

> Oh! I have slipped the surly bonds of Earth
> And danced the skies on laughter-silvered wings;
> Sunward I've climbed, and joined the tumbling mirth
> Of sun-split clouds—and done a hundred things
> You have not dreamed of—wheeled and soared and swung

High in the sunlit silence. Hov'ring there,
I've chased the shouting wind along, and flung
My eager craft through footless halls of air.

Planes began to appear to the left and right, Hurricanes and Spitfires. "What's this?" asked Lord Preston, startled. "There are dozens of fighters."

"Scores actually. Since the prime minister cancelled the fighter sweeps, some of the airfields decided to get the squadrons up in a big wing at least once a week to keep the boys' skills sharp. You remember we used a big wing a few times in nineteen-forty? I thought you'd like to see one."

Lord Preston's eyes widened. "It's extraordinary. Who do we have here?"

"Billy and his squadron are up. D'you see him there? He just waggled his wings at us. Ben's up with his squadron. Sean's just tucked in behind us. We're surrounded by laughter-silvered wings."

Lord Preston laughed. "What a blessing. But I don't understand why you took the trouble of flying me here to see it."

"You prayed for us, didn't you, Dad? You and Mom and the rest of the family? Prayed for our soldiers and our sailors and our airmen? Backed Mr. Churchill when others had no use for him? Well, here's some of the few and a few others to say thanks. I couldn't stuff everyone in my two-seater. But you'll do handsomely."

"Thank you, my boy, it's a marvel."

The blue sky seemed filled to the heights with British fighter planes.

"'There be three things which are too wonderful for me, yea, four which I know not,'" murmured Lord Preston as they flew wingtip to wingtip with the other aircraft. "'The way of an eagle in the air; the way of a serpent upon a rock; the way of a ship in the midst of the sea; and the way of a man with a maid.' An eagle in the air. 'The words of Agur the son of Jakeh, even the prophecy... Who hath ascended up into heaven, or descended? Who hath gathered the wind in his fists? Who hath bound the waters in a garment? Who hath established all the ends of the earth? What is his name, and what is his son's name, if thou canst tell?'"

Their Spitfire banked when the wing commander and the squadron leaders banked, and fifty aircraft followed suit. There was the Channel blazing like a bonfire. There was the shore. There were the green fields over which the planes of one nation had fought the planes of another nation until freedom had been wrested from the smoke-torn skies.

"Ah, Elizabeth, Elizabeth, I wish you were with me. You would never come, but I wish you were in the cockpit at my side. A price was paid for freedom by our family. Just as God paid a price, just as His Son paid a price, for a greater freedom. Lives were not lost, no, they were not lost forever. Not lost forever and not in vain, never in vain, my dear. The Lord grant you peace in your deepest heart. The Lord grant us peace and an incomprehensible joy in the midst of the titanic struggle of these years, indeed, the struggle of our lives."

The R/T hummed. "You all right back there, Dad?"

"Never better. Thank you again for bringing me up here to see all the squadrons together. It truly is astonishing." Lord Preston gazed out at the mixture of blue sky, flashing wings, and dazzling light. "You were going to recite the rest of the poem."

"What's that?"

"The poem you started. You were going to finish it."

"Finish it for yourself, Father. You'll find it in your jacket pocket."

Lord Preston dug around and came up with a small piece of paper. "This isn't your handwriting, Kipp."

"Caroline's actually. Apparently mine wasn't quite up to snuff."

Lord Preston held the note as steadily as he could and read it. He closed his eyes and let his head fall back against the seat.

"Praise You," he whispered.

"What say, Dad?"

"I say, let's fly, my boy. Fly. Go higher and go farther and don't stop, never stop, never dream of stopping."

> Up, up the long, delirious, burning blue,
> I've topped the windswept heights with easy grace.
> Where never lark, or even eagle flew—
> And, while with silent, lifting mind I've trod
> The high untresspassed sanctity of space,
> —Put out my hand, and touched the face of God.

About Murray Pura

Murray Pura earned his Master of Divinity degree from Acadia University in Wolfville, Nova Scotia, and his ThM degree in theology and interdisciplinary studies from Regent College in Vancouver, British Columbia. For more than twenty-five years, in addition to writing, he has pastored churches in Nova Scotia, British Columbia, and Alberta. Murray's writings have been short-listed for the Dartmouth Book Award, the John Spencer Hill Literary Award, the Paraclete Fiction Award, and Toronto's Kobzar Literary Award. In 2012 he won the Word Award of Toronto for Best Historial Novel. Murray pastors and writes in southern Alberta near the Rocky Mountains. He and his wife, Linda, have a son and a daughter.

Visit Murray's website at **www.murraypura.com**.

ALSO BY MURRAY PURA...

The Snapshots in History series

The Wings of Morning

This exciting historical romance is set in 1917 during World War I. Jude Whetstone and Lyyndaya Kurtz, whose families are converts to the Amish faith, are slowly falling in love. Jude has also fallen in love with that new-fangled invention, the aeroplane. The Amish communities have rejected the telephone and have forbidden motorcar ownership but not yet electricity or aeroplanes.

Though exempt from military service on religious grounds, Jude is manipulated by unscrupulous army officers into enlisting in order to protect several Amish men. No one in the community understands Jude's sudden enlistment, so he is shunned. Lyyndaya's despair deepens at the reports that Jude has been shot down in France. In her grief, she turns to nursing Spanish flu victims in Philadelphia. After many months of caring for stricken soldiers, Lyyndaya is stunned when an emaciated Jude turns up in her ward.

Lyyndaya's joy at receiving Jude back from the dead is quickly diminished when the Amish leadership insist the shunning remain in force. How then can they marry without the blessing of their families? Will happiness elude them forever?

The Face of Heaven

In April 1861, Lyndel Keim discovers two runaway slaves in her family's barn. When the men are captured, Lyndel and her young Amish beau, Nathaniel King, find themselves at odds with their pacifist Amish colony.

Nathaniel enlists in what will become the famous Iron Brigade of the Union Army. Lyndel enters the fray as a Brigade nurse on the battlefield, sticking close to Nathaniel as they both witness the horrors of war—including the battles at Chancellorsville, Fredericksburg, and Antietam. Despite the pair's heroic sacrifices, the Amish only see that Lyndel and Nathaniel have become part of the war effort, and both are banished. A severe battle wound at Gettysburg threatens Nathaniel's life. Lyndel must call upon her faith in God to endure the savage conflict and to face its painful aftermath, not knowing if Nathaniel is alive or dead. Will the momentous battle change her life forever, just as it will change the course of the war and the history of her country?